Mac Rutherford is 52, un   ....a..
village near Cambridge. Educated at Huntingdon Grammar
School, he eschewed the chances offered him to play
professional soccer and cricket, and was not interested in
attending university. He began travelling extensively and
has to date travelled around the world nine times. He has
enjoyed a vast number of different occupations, including
working as a stuntman, furniture designer, property
developer, landlord and insurance broker.

For some years he has worked in antiques and currently he
designs interiors for pubs and hotels. A self-confessed
hedonist he is an avid socialiser with a great sense of
humour and many varied interests. He enjoys eating and
drinking and is an accomplished cook and raconteur.

Mac has lived in Cambridge since the 1960's, apart from
an enjoyable two year sojourn working in the South of
France, and shorter periods spent in the USA and other
parts of Europe.

CAMBRIDGE
CIRCUS

Mac Rutherford

Cambridge Circus

Vanguard Press

A CIP catalogue record for this title is
available from the British Library
ISBN 1 903489 32 6

*Vanguard Press is an imprint of
Pegasus Elliot MacKenzie Publishers*
www.pegasuspublishers.com

First Published in 2001

**Vanguard Press
Sheraton House Castle Park
Cambridge England**

Printed & Bound in Great Britain

Dedication

To all the great people that I have so enjoyed meeting during my time in Cambridge, and the many friends that I have made, I dedicate this book.

INTRODUCTION

This story is set in the historic university City of Cambridge and concerns four young men from varied backgrounds who meet up with each other in the mid-1960s and begin sharing a house together, soon becoming inseparable friends.

These four young men are all fairly normal, active, fun-loving, intelligent males but, as is usual with many males in their early twenties, they are packed full of testosterone and raging hormones. Carried along by the numerous sweeping changes taking place in Britain during this period, they became heavily influenced by the free and easy attitudes prevalent at the time, which helped to develop their sometimes irreverent attitude to life in general, with a particularly irresponsible attitude to relationships, due to the new sexual revolution taking place, which soon became the order of the day for many young people in the 'sixties.

Cambridge at this time was still a relatively small city, with a population of around 100,000 people, including the annual influx of thousands of foreign students. Unlike today, where the university has taken over most of the central homes for student accommodation, much of the central housing stock was occupied by local townspeople. With the world-renowned university dominating the centre of Cambridge and its assortment of beautiful college buildings and gardens attracting hordes of tourists each year, together with the mass of foreign students who invaded the city to study English, there was an enormous vibrancy and vitality about the city. The students were much more evident, still wearing their traditional black gowns; they also tended to use the city's facilities more than today, when each college now boasts its own subsidised bar, disco and sports club.

Aided by the city's easy accessibility to London, the relaxed and easy-going environment of the university city attracted many young people from home and abroad in search of work and the good life. As the phenomena known as the 'swinging sixties' began spreading across Britain, the vivid cosmopolitan atmosphere in Cambridge, already exuding an atmosphere of vibrancy and vitality, ensured that Cambridge was probably second only to London as the most 'swinging' English city at this time.

There were many causes for this unprecedented change in people's lives. There was the new sexual revolution in full swing in Britain, with drugs also becoming freely available and widely experimented with. Alcohol consumption amongst the young soared during this period. There were few drink/driving laws, though the breathalyser was introduced in 1966 but had little impact initially. Parking meters and yellow lines had not been introduced and most towns and cities were easily accessible to traffic. It was freedoms like these that appeared to make life in general more unencumbered compared to the countless rules and regulations that abound today in modern Britain. There appeared to be a lack of seriousness and stress in people's lives which made for a more light-hearted, self-indulgent approach to life in general; again a trait particularly noticeable amongst the younger generation.

The 'sixties revolution' brought other important issues to the fore with the many changing attitudes to life in general being encouraged by this new permissive society which made young people at the time feel that at last they could change the world for the better. A breakdown in the old class values began with the successful emergence of the working classes into many of the new 'in' professions, such as modelling, hairdressing, photography, pop-music, fashion design and television. Some of the individual successes in these industries, such as Twiggy, The Beatles and David Bailey, became the celebrity icons of the sixties generation, breaking down many of the barriers of the establishment's way of life.

With the increasing use of drugs (particularly cannabis and amphetamines) and the greater use of alcohol amongst the young, together with the increasing cultural importance of pop-music, the revolution spawned the new hippie movement, giving many young people an excuse to opt out of conventional society into an alternative free lifestyle. Indeed, in 1967 the flower power movement (which was basically hippie orientated), declared the *'Summer of Love'* - a sexual adventure for all those who wished to join - proclaiming free love, psychedelic clothing and recreational drug taking. Their idols were the American 'high priests' of the hippie movement - Allen Ginsberg and Timothy Leary, who promoted drug taking and free love.

Another major impact was in 1961 with the arrival of the long awaited contraceptive pill. This, for the first time, gave women liberation from the many time-honoured and unreliable methods of contraception previously available to them. They now had the ability to cease worrying about the fear of pregnancy and to actually start to enjoy sex. The pill meant that women were given the capacity to decide for themselves how they were going to conduct their sexual lives. With the easy access to the pill from most general practitioners, a more relaxed and casual attitude to sex developed at this time and women, especially the young and unmarried, began to realise that they too could enjoy sex in the same way that men had always enjoyed it, in a free and easy manner without any worries.

But, these new, freer attitudes to life had their downsides too. There was sometimes a conflict of conscience as most young women were expected by men to be on the pill, putting enormous expectations and great pressures on them especially when the more outgoing women appeared to flaunt their new-found sexuality. The change in woman's attitudes continued with the advent of the sexy mini-skirt in the early '60s and the invention of the much maligned tights for women in 1966 which gave birth to the term 'Dolly Bird' to the wearers of these garments.

Unfortunately, the inevitable happened and, in 1966, for example, 20,000 illegitimate children were born; many were given away for adoption or taken away from their mothers. There were huge increases in various types of venereal diseases, including gonorrhoea and syphilis. Indeed, so large were the numbers attending the VD clinics at some hospitals, that the clinics became nicknamed the 'Social Club'. For those women of the catholic religion who had become used to relying on it, the Pope suddenly denounced the 'pill'. The freedom that these women had enjoyed with their partners was destroyed, although many continued to use the pill in secret.

For many young people, the so-called revolution, the casual attitude to sex and the breakdown of old values led to enormous conflicts of ideas and emotions. Britain was being heavily influenced by the USA at this time, with the Vietnam War raging and the Negro Civil Rights marches in full swing, which coupled with a massive influx of fashion and pop-music from across the Atlantic, all helped to confuse young people's thinking at the time.

The socialist government in Britain led by Harold Wilson came increasingly under pressure as religious values, morality and the methods of governing society came into question. There were incessant strikes, the pound had been devalued and the 'couldn't care less, can't be bothered' culture commenced as people's attitudes changed drastically. Family life was beginning to break up and decline, whilst inner cities were being demolished, leading to waste lands and devastation, and the breakdown of the old working class communities that were the core of city life.

There is little doubt that the 'sixties revolution, especially for the young people who were swept up in the fun and the changes taking place, was a unique period in history with many of the younger generation believing that they had the power to change the world for the better. So, these were just some of the attitudes and influences that prevailed on these young men when they met in Cambridge during this time of great change.

Chapter One

Chris Moore stepped smartly off the crowded 11:00 train from Liverpool Street onto the railway station at Cambridge one gloomy, grey, cold morning in November 1965. He was wearing his favourite old blue *Levis,* red tag button fly, a battered leather jacket and carried an equally battered leather holdall in one hand, whilst under his opposite arm he bore an assortment of very large stuffed animals bulging out of several torn and tattered American brown bags. He'd won these toys at a shooting gallery at a fair in New York City where he'd been amazed to be given such fine gifts for his skill in hitting the moving targets. In England he would have been lucky to receive a toilet roll wrapped in cat fur masquerading as a teddy bear. He'd recently celebrated his twenty-fourth birthday by taking off for the U.S.A. after a broken romance. He had spent five months travelling around the vast county, marvelling at all the sights that he had heard so much about, and generally enjoying himself whilst trying to erase the memory of the misdemeanour that had caused the break-up of his ten-month relationship with his former girlfriend. Unfortunately, his money had run out and, unable to obtain a work permit, he had been forced to return to England.

The collection of stuffed toys were intended by Chris as a present for Louise, the five-year-old daughter of his ex-girlfriend Jane. Chris still hungered after Jane; he'd thought of little else whilst he had been away. She had, after all, been the best lay he'd ever had and he secretly hoped that these presents, brought partly as gifts and partly as a peace-offering for her young daughter, might ingratiate himself with Jane again.

How he regretted that party where he had allowed himself to become so outrageously drunk and had then foolishly become involved with Mary, who was also one of Jane's best and closest friends, and how senselessly he had ended up leaving the party with Mary and spending the night with her at her small flat nearby. Jane had been informed of Chris and Mary's indiscretion by another friend at the same party and the next day, Jane had tearfully, but forcefully, ended their relationship. Chris had returned the next morning to find his belongings thrown out into the front garden of her home. Despite his prolonged pleadings to be forgiven, Jane had remained adamant. He was forced, embarrassingly, to retrieve his possessions which were strewn all over the garden and tearfully left to stay the night at a local bed and breakfast establishment.

Soon afterwards he had set off the for the USA, partly to try and forget Jane and partly to fulfil a childhood dream. For years he had dreamed of the chance to see for himself the images and stereotypes of that country as portrayed in the countless movies, comics, TV footage and pop-music that had assaulted his senses throughout his adolescence. But during his travels, his thoughts were constantly invaded with images of Jane and even of her small daughter, Louise, whom he had become very fond of. He tried desperately to rekindle their relationship through several long-distance 'phone calls and numerous letters and postcards dispatched from the various states he visited. After five or six calls he thought he perceived a change in her manner to him on the 'phone. There seemed to be a softness in her voice, and a gentleness in her tone while she seemed to receive his calls with far more warmth than before. After some months she had even told him that she had forgiven him for cheating on her and, from that moment, he had started to regain his confidence with the hope that there might possibly be a chance that their relationship could be resurrected when he returned home.

Now, back in England, he had immediately returned to Cambridge, the city where he and Jane had shared her home before his act of unfaithfulness. As he emerged from the down-at-heel station, his hopes were high that he would be able to rekindle his relationship with Jane and, hopefully, move back into her comfortable central home and find the job that he now so badly needed.

As he turned into the familiar tree-lined road where she lived, he could feel his heart pounding hard beneath his jacket. His mouth tasted dry and his gloveless hands felt very cold in

14

the early March wind.

He arrived at Jane's house and tried to dredge some saliva into his mouth to alleviate the dryness; he walked hesitantly up to her front door and took a deep breath as he rang the bell, wondering how she would react to finding him standing unannounced on her front step. Would she forgive him and welcome him with open arms and ask him to stay? Would it be like old times he asked himself briefly as he felt a slight sexual stirring mix in with his sense of anticipation?

The door opened and there stood Jane, her mouth dropped slightly in astonishment at seeing him standing there. She quickly gathered her composure and gave him a warm hug and a soft kiss on the cheek before ushering him into the kitchen. Chris said a silent prayer to himself asking whoever was up there to make sure that everything would turn out well; an odd habit of his as he was an atheist.

He didn't want to rush matters or overwhelm Jane; he intended to apologise to her for his mistake and ask for her forgiveness, but he wanted to wait for the right opportunity. As he handed over the assortment of stuffed animals for Louise who was attending her primary school, the old longings for Jane swelled up inside him. She had a new, short haircut, he noted, which greatly enhanced her pretty chiselled features. Her skin looked so clear and firm and she was wearing his favourite sweater. It was the present he had given her for her last birthday, the tightness of which greatly emphasised her soft bosom.

'Chris, you really shouldn't have,' said Jane. 'Louise will be thrilled to bits with these. Where did you get them from? And how was your trip to America?'

'I actually won them on a shooting game at a fair in New York City,' he explained. 'I knew Louise would like them so I brought them back for her. But I also wanted to see you again, Jane.' Chris was immediately conscious that he'd blurted out this last sentence too quickly and gazed at Jane earnestly for any sign of acceptance. But she turned away to continue fixing a cup of coffee for him and he suddenly felt uneasy, something in her manner told him something was wrong, very wrong.

'I know,' he heard her saying as she turned and handed him the coffee. She averted her gaze and contemplated the floor for a second or two. She raised her head and he thought he caught a glimpse of sadness as she stared at him, looking directly into his eyes. Was it compassion he saw there?

'Look, Chris, there is something you need to know. I don't know what you expected coming here like this, and I did mean what I said to you on the phone, that I do forgive you but I've recently met someone else and he's living with me here now, so I'm really sorry but we won't be able to resurrect our relationship if that's what you'd hoped for. I hope we can still be friends, but that's all.'

Chris felt himself falter slightly, lost for words. He wanted to plead with her, to hold her, to make her see sense, to tell her how much he'd missed her and how he would make it up to her - surely this wasn't happening? The anguish he felt inside was not how the reunion with Jane was meant to be. A sick, ugly sensation of nausea took hold of his body. He felt drops of sweat beading on his brow and a sudden tightness gripped his stomach. He suppressed the feeling to retch and tried to regain his composure. He licked his dry lips and fought back the tears he could feel welling up in the corner of his eyes. He felt shocked and humiliated as he realised that his dream that Jane would take him back was being shattered before him. He sensed Jane feeling sorry for him as she stood watching him helplessly from across the kitchen, knowing that she had crushed his hopes to pieces.

'If only I hadn't shagged that bloody Mary,' he thought bitterly to himself for the hundredth time; wishing he could now just vanish into thin air so acute was his embarrassment. He felt that he wanted to cry so the tears could carry the pain away, but he couldn't lose face in front of Jane even though she had hurt him so much.

Just at that moment, the door flew open and a tall, muscular man entered the kitchen. With a cursory glance at Chris, he walked over to Jane and gave her a rough embrace. Chris noticed the heavy seven o'clock shadow bristling on his face as he kissed Jane.

'Who's this then?' the man demanded rudely, nodding towards Chris whilst accepting the mug of coffee that Jane proffered him.

'Gary, this is Chris. He's an old friend. I told you about him,

16

he's just got back from America and brought some lovely presents for Louise. Aren't they lovely?' She smiled gently and picked up one of the stuffed animals, a large, cuddly brown teddy bear and showed it to Gary. Chris, even in his despair, thought it was a kind touch of Jane's to call him an old friend for he could sense the obvious aggression in Gary who stood glaring across at him, making him feel extremely nervous.

'Oh, so this is the bloke that's been sending you all those lovey-dovey letters and postcards from American, is it?' Gary demanded brusquely.

'Yes, that's right. But he now knows about us, so we've decided we're going to be just good friends,' Jane replied quickly. Sensing Gary's animosity towards Chris she calmly and tightly held him about the waist. There was a moments' ugly silence; Chris could feel the tears welling up again. The aggressive attitude displayed by Gary had made him even more depressed. His favourite old motto, 'I'm a lover, not a fighter,' flashed through his mind and he quickly decided it would be prudent to leave. He gulped his coffee down and picked up his holdall.

'Well, it's been lovely to see you again, Jane,' he heard himself saying. 'Say hello to Louise and tell her I hope she likes the toys. Nice to meet you, Gary,' he said, hesitantly glancing over at the other man still held in Jane's embrace. Chris looked again at Jane, at her new short hair and trim figure and tried to suppress the emptiness and longing that was now surging up unbearably inside his body.

'Bye, Jane,' Chris said opening the door and stepping outside, striving to appear calm and relaxed. He was determined not to turn around as he walked away down the path, but then heard Gary's voice bellowing after him.

'Don't you ever fucking come round her again,' Gary shouted vehemently at Chris's departing back. Chris half-turned at the gate to see Jane pulling Gary back into the kitchen. With a last anxious wide-eyed glance at him, she closed the door firmly.

'Christ,' he thought to himself, 'she's ended up with a fucking moron. That's all I wanted. I've lost any chance of getting back with Jane, I've got nowhere to live and I could have ended up with that bloody gorilla flipping and beating the crap out of me.

Welcome back home. Life can only get better, can't it?' he asked himself, feeling crushed and dispirited from the battering of his emotions during the preceding few minutes. At that moment, a light shower of rain started falling. Chris, feeling more depressed by the second, pulled the collar of his jacket further up round his neck as he felt the cold rain drops sting his face gently. Several large tears fell noiselessly from his eyes and mingled with the rain running down his cheeks.

'Christ,' he mumbled to himself, 'I really did care for that woman more than I thought I did, but I've only got myself to blame for being such a shit and losing her.' He brushed the salty teardrops from his cheeks and set off down the road, taking a furtive glance behind to ensure that Gary wasn't pursuing him. 'What am I going to do now?' he wondered morosely as he trudged aimlessly away, feeling more dejected than he could ever remember.

The sour taste of the confrontation with Gary, coupled with the abject humiliation that he felt at having been rejected by Jane, particularly when he'd journeyed back from the States convinced that the feelings that she had conveyed to him on the 'phone would lead to a reunion, led Chris into a deep depression that was not aided by the rain falling more heavily as he walked along Mill Road towards the city centre.

This was the first time that Chris could remember a woman having hurt him; normally, the women in his life came and went for short periods only, but Jane had been very different. She had aroused strong feelings of unbridled passion in him when he had first met her. He'd lusted for her then, but there had been something else, something quite strange. He had felt a great desire to be with her, to do things together. He'd missed her when she wasn't there. No other woman had aroused feelings in him like she had. But he'd fucked it all up for a quick screw with her best friend. That was the trouble, women had always been attracted to him and made themselves available. He had sensed his attraction from an early age; even during his early teens when female classmates had sent him suggestive love letters and had waited to be kissed behind the bike-sheds at school, sometimes even fondled, he recalled nostalgically.

He found a small cafe and wandered in for a cup of tea. The

18

steamed-up windows and the smell of wet clothes and stale grease in the crowded room did little to reduce the forlornness that he felt. He drank his mug of hot, sweet tea and lit a Pall Mall which made him feel somewhat better. But even the attention of the waitress, an attractive dark-haired Spanish girl, who tried to engage him in conversation and, at one point, put her arm on the back of his chair and bent down to talk to him over the hubbub so that the muskiness of her perfume overcame the wet clothes smell; even she could not alter his mood. He felt so deflated that he could not even summon the will to ask for her 'phone number to enter into the little black address book that he carried everywhere.

He stubbed out his cigarette and finished his tea. Feeling warmer now, he decided that he had to pull himself together, there was no point in sitting around feeling sorry for himself. His first priority was to find somewhere to live so that he had a base from which to search for a job. He vaguely remembered an accommodation agency, the St. Andrew's Bureau, tucked away on the upper floor of an old office building in St. Andrew's Street in the centre of the city, so he left the cafe and made his way across Parker's Piece into the town centre. He soon found the old building which had a brass plate on the wall advertising the bureau and ascended the rickety stairs up to the top floor where the office was located. He found himself in an untidy, book-lined, musty smelling room, explaining to the kindly lady in charge how desperate he was to find accommodation immediately. He realised that he must appear very dishevelled to her, with his wet hair and damp clothes but, by using his natural charm, he soon had a list of half-a-dozen bedsitters to view that very afternoon. The lady even telephoned some of the landlords to make appointments for him, 'which I certainly don't do for most people,' she told him sweetly.

Later that afternoon the weather had cleared, but after several hours of pounding the streets, Chris had acquired several painful blisters and felt hot, sweaty, tired and desolate. He had viewed several rooms - most of which had been dingy and filthy. This had rather shocked him as he previously had no inkling that such places could exist in a civilised city like Cambridge. He had been quite disgusted by the state of some of the bedsitters and almost suicidal when looking around one of the worst places he'd been shown.

'It's got such a lovely view,' the scrawny middle-aged woman with a hairy chin and stained apron had told him as she showed him the vacant front room in her lodging house.

It's also fucking filthy, stinks of rancid cooking oil, must and dirt, it's freezing cold, and the mattress on the bed is stained and so bloody old the springs are almost coming through the material. The room hasn't seen a lick of paint for twenty years and the meter is probably fixed so you hardly receive any gas for your money. Not only that, the bathroom is down the hall and is shared with several other people; it smells of shit and damp, the taps are dripping into the filthy basin and the obscene crusty bath has black lines round it where no-one has bothered to clean it; no-one has flushed the turds down the toilet, and where's the pissing toilet seat? That's what he wanted to scream at her - just to see the old bat's face - but, unbelievably, he heard himself quietly telling her, 'Thanks for showing me the room, I've got another one to see so I'll ring you later if I'm interested.'

Out in the street again, he breathed deeply and exhaled loudly, forcing the ennui and staleness out of his lungs. He felt distinctly annoyed with himself that he hadn't told the woman the truth. He would have liked to have seen her reaction. Would she have stuttered and spluttered, shamefacedly, or would she have torn him off a strip for being impudent?

'Oh God, please let me find something soon,' he muttered to himself as he wearily hurried to the next house on his list. There was a hint of desperation in his stride now, but as he knocked on the door of No. 11 Norwich Street, he was somewhat amazed to see the door open and to find a face that he immediately recognised peering surprisedly back at him. The spectacles had changed, the old round NHS shape transformed into a larger brown frame, but the pale face was the same, topped with the familiar mass of longish blonde hair. Before him stood an old school acquaintance, Mike Bowes, who appeared equally stunned at coming face-to-face with Chris. It emerged, after a brief and frantic conversation between them that Mike was also on the same quest for accommodation. He explained to Chris that he was training as an accountant with a local firm in

Cambridge whilst studying part-time for his articles. He had a temporary room in a rather unruly lodging house nearby but was looking for another room because his house was occupied by a number of constantly noisy foreign students, whereas he needed periods of peace and quiet to study for his exams.

At twenty-four, Chris was a year older than Mike and at their grammar school in Huntingdon had been in the sixth form whilst Mike had been in the fifth form. Chris, a natural sportsman, had excelled at sports and had been a stalwart of the soccer, rugger and cricket XI's but his written work had been ill-disciplined and his attitude, according to his school reports, had often been disruptive to the rest of the class. He had eventually emerged from school with a less than satisfactory academic record, much to the chagrin of his devoted parents. Mike, in contrast, was much quieter and more reserved, slightly introverted in fact, and though not terribly keen on sports he had achieved excellent results in his examinations.

Mike particularly remembered Chris as being somewhat of a tearaway and a member of a clique at the school renowned for their prowess at sporting activities; but also prone to unruly and disruptive behaviour. This extended to the bullying of younger boys and hanging around with some of the more unsavoury town girls, smoking, drinking heavily and being generally obnoxious. This behaviour had, of course, made them revered by some of the younger pupils. Mike had distanced himself from this group altogether, not having had much in common with them anyway.

An incident came into Mike's mind where he remembered Chris and his cronies had been involved in tying up a classmate's ankles, probably for some minor indiscretion, and had left him hanging upside down naked from a tree in a wood adjacent to the school. They had completely covered the hapless victim's naked body with a mixture of shaving foam and strawberry jam which had encouraged a large number of wasps to begin crawling over his body to eat the jam, subsequently stinging the poor boy several times. His frantic cries for help had only been heard some sixty-minutes later by another pupil who had ventured into the wood for an illicit cigarette in his break. The traumatised victim was immediately cut down by a member of staff. The group responsible, including Chris Moore (who was the suspected ringleader), were severely castigated by the Headmaster in front of the entire school and were extremely lucky to escape expulsion.

This misdemeanour had immediately elevated Chris and his cronies to an even higher status amongst the younger members of the school and the incident was passed down into the unwritten folklore of the school to be recalled for many years by pupils present at the time.

Despite the fact that the two young men had not been close friends at school, they knew each other well enough to reminisce about their old school and various mutual friends, recalling tales of escapades and the horrors inflicted on selected miscreants by some of the most hated and reviled teachers.

As so often happens in life, pure acquaintances who have only known each other modestly in the past may meet up again to discover a compatibility in each other that was never revealed or discovered in the earlier years. Circumstances had deemed that Mike and Chris had never had cause to converse together at length and, therefore, had not been able to acquaint themselves of their mutual likes and dislikes. The mere fact that Chris had been in a form above Mike's had helped to distance them both at school.

Although Chris was feeling completely ravaged by the events of the day, he declined to mention Jane to Mike, besides he hardly knew Mike and it certainly wasn't right to burden him with the misery of his own personal affairs.

In their excitement, the pair had quite forgotten the agent who had just shown Mike the room. He stood in the hallway impatiently rattling his bunch of keys. 'Are you going to look at the room?' he asked Chris in a slightly irritated manner. 'I've got to leave shortly.'

'Well, yes of course I will,' Chris replied, turning to follow the agent upstairs. 'What did you think of the room Mike?' he asked with interest.

'Well, it's OK, but it's got bunk beds, so I wasn't sure about it,' Mike replied.

'Come up again and have a look at it with me,' said Chris thoughtfully; the mention of bunk beds having sent an idea running through Chris's brain.

'OK,' said Mike heartily, 'see what you think.'

Chris was shown into a tired room about twelve by ten feet, desperately needing a coat of paint. Partitioned off from the main room by a flimsy wooden structure was a little kitchenette with a small two-hob gas cooker and a sink with a minute fridge underneath. Despite the shabby character of the room, it was far cleaner than any of the other rooms that Chris had visited that day. What was intriguing were the bunk beds, set against a wall, that Mike had mentioned. The agent ushered them down the hall and showed them the toilet and bathroom which were both relatively clean, he explained that they were shared with another bedsit on the same floor. Chris noticed that the other occupant kept his or her toilet requisites neatly stacked in the bathroom cabinet, so it appeared that they were fairly tidy which went down well with Chris, who was a very meticulous person.

Chris gently took Mike's arm and steered him out onto the landing.

'Mike,' he said earnestly, 'this isn't much, but it's got those bunk beds and its central and warm. I know it's sort of short notice, but would you consider sharing with me, even if it is just for a few months to see how we get on?'

Mike gazed myopically at Chris, remembering how in awe of him he used to be at school, yet thinking how easily they had conversed with each other during the previous ten minutes. 'This unexpected meeting could be the catalyst I need to get me out of my shell,' he thought briefly, feeling somewhat excited at the prospect.

'Do you seriously think that we'd get on OK Chris? I mean if we are serious about it, we're probably two completely different people. If my school memories are correct, you were the sporty one with all the girls, always in trouble. I was the studious one, with specs, who did well at exams but would do anything to get out of any activity to do with sport. We never really knew each other for those very reasons,' said Mike realistically. Yet, he was still excited about suddenly being asked to share with Chris, who was still something of a hero to him.

'Yes, I agree. But, we can give it a try,' Chris replied. I mean, I know it's quite small and it's not the bloody Ritz, but I'm really desperate for a place. I've got nowhere to live at all at the moment. Besides, it would kill two birds with one stone and give us both a place to live, certainly you would find it more peaceful.

Mike stepped inside the room once more and glanced around again. After a moments consideration, he turned and smiled at Chris. 'Right, let's go for it,' he said warmly.

'Great!' yelled Chris and extended his hand to Mike who shook it vigorously.

'Yes, we'd like to take it between us,' Chris called to the agent who was waiting in the hall downstairs, obviously very anxious to leave for his next appointment.

'OK boys, then the best thing to do is to return to the agency and complete the necessary forms and paperwork as soon as you can.'

Outside, walking back to the Bureau, Chris, although still attempting to erase the earlier events with Jane from his thoughts, sensed a new vigour in his stride and was pleased that Mike appeared to feel very happy with the arrangement that had been agreed so suddenly between them both.

'If you've got nowhere to stay tonight Chris, you can kip on the floor of my room,' Mike said considerately.

'Yeah, that would be great Mike, if it's no trouble,' replied Chris. 'It will only be for a couple of days if we can wangle a really early move into the new place.'

For the second time that day, Chris trudged up the creaky stairs to the little book-lined room of the St. Andrew's Bureau on the second floor where he and Mike sat down before the agency lady who quickly completed the necessary forms, including taking the names of people they both knew who would give them references.

'Is there any way we can move in almost straightaway?' Chris asked, giving the lady what he hoped was his forlorn, but needing sympathy look.

'Well, these forms have to be processed and the landlady has to be informed. It takes a little time,' she replied.

'But I've got nowhere to live at all. Is there any chance that you could complete it really, really quickly for us?' Chris pleaded, adding a slight quaver to his voice which he hoped would add a certain pathos to their situation. He sensed that she had a soft spot for him and he wanted to make sure that she would put all her efforts into attending to their situation.

'We'd be eternally grateful to you,' added Mike gently, 'for whatever you can do.'

'I'll do my best. Why don't you give me a ring tomorrow afternoon,' she smiled, her blue eyes twinkling behind her glasses. 'I'll ring for your references first thing in the morning for you both.'

'Oh, thanks,' they cried simultaneously. 'Thank you very much.' They were almost bowing and scraping as they backed out of the room.

When they emerged onto the street below, Chris turned to Mike who was laughing at the way they had tried to flatter the woman. 'We did almost everything but kiss her arse, but she's a good sort. I think she'll arrange it quickly for us,' he said.

Later that evening, after a cheap, but filling Greek meal and a couple of even cheaper bottles of Retsina, they sat in Mike's room talking and smoking late into the night. Acquaintances from school were remembered and reviewed; some were vividly and cruelly dissected, whilst their own particular hopes and aspirations for the future were discussed avidly.

During their earlier meal, Chris had taken the opportunity to fully explain to Mike the traumatic experience he'd suffered earlier in the day and how depressed he felt about the situation. Mike listened intently to his anguished outpourings, understanding the need for Chris to be able to talk to someone who would understand.

'I just felt so completely and utterly dejected when I left her house and then having to trudge around the city in the pouring rain looking for a bloody room. When I suddenly came across you like that, the surprise took my mind off everything for a while,' Chris explained, grateful for Mike's interest.

Mike decided that Chris must have been very much in love with Jane to have such strong feelings and to want to share them like this. He had only vaguely known Chris at school where he had been the great athlete, the rebel, the leader of his little gang who was looked up to by the rest of the pupils and possibly even feared by some. Any sign of weakness, such as a confession like this, would have been unthinkable and would have been denounced by his peers immediately. Chris had always seemed to have the pick of the most attractive girls at school and Mike remembered how in awe of Chris he had been, watching him performing so well on the sports field and, even after school, when he'd often seen him walking in the town with the older girls, kissing and cuddling them.

Now, lying flat on the floor, taking long drags of his much loved Pall Mall's, Chris unburdened his feelings and Mike felt a sense of strength within himself as he sat and listened intently, adding the odd word of agreement or sympathy. Chris needed his support at this moment and he was only too happy to be a good listener. Many years later Mike would look back and realise that these few hours, where he simply sat quietly listening to Chris pour his heart out, was the time when their great friendship and loyalty to each other was born and when he realised that Chris was just an ordinary mortal rather than the schoolboy memories that he had retained of him, those recollections being of a person totally aloof and arrogant.

Later, when Chris had almost exhausted himself, Mike took the opportunity to gain Chris's interest by providing him with a rundown on life in the city. He told Chris about the hordes of foreign students sent to the city to study English by their rich, upper-class parents who believed, quite rightly, that the Cambridge name on their child's diploma would give it a certain cachet back home.

Chris, having been heavily involved with Jane and her daughter during his affair with her, had taken little interest in the goings-on in the city and, although he had certainly noted the preponderance of pretty young girls, he had been too wrapped up in his own affairs to contemplate such matters at that time.

Mike told Chris about the multitude of language schools, some good, some bad, providing for an intake of several thousand foreign students a year. The majority of these students were female, many of them very desirable having attended the best finishing schools and coming from very well-heeled parents. Some of these families were so rich that the parents provided enormous monthly allowances to their sons or daughters, whilst the students who were not so lucky often worked as au-pairs or took part-time employment in the numerous bars and restaurants throughout the city to help pay for their studies.

'Let me tell you Chris,' added Mike, 'there's a small group of guys who exist like gigolos here. They search out the rich birds and live off their parents allowances. These guys have a philosophy; they give the girls lots of affection, a really good fucking and then they're hooked. The girls will do anything to keep these blokes so that they don't lose face with their friends. One guy I know, he's got a car and whole wardrobe of clothes from one bird, her father's an ambassador and sends her any amount of money she wants. At the moment, there are masses of Swedish girls around because the standard of living is so high there, and you know what they say about Sweden, anything goes there, the women screw around all the time.'

'Phew,' said Chris somewhat fascinated by Mike's revelations. 'That's amazing. I can hardly wait to get stuck into Cambridge life - in more ways than one! I reckon there's a whole new life around the corner after hearing all this about the city from you tonight.'

'I'm sure you'll get over Jane in no time, believe me Chris,' assured Mike. 'It really is bloody good fun here and there's so much totty around, you just can't go wrong. It's almost like being on holiday every day in this town. I like to think of it as a "girlie bank", when you want one you can go out and pick one, like a withdrawal, and when you want another, you just pick another one. They're all out there, they're all available, they're absolutely free and they nearly all fuck! It's just wonderful!'

The rigours of the day, followed by the meal and wine, combined with the jet-lag from his recent flight from New York, suddenly caused Chris to feel terribly tired. He could hardly keep his eyes open, they felt so heavy that he just wanted to fall asleep where he was sitting. With a great effort he forced himself to smile at Mike's enthusiasm. He felt so much better now that he'd unburdened himself to someone. He felt very grateful indeed to Mike for just listening to him and then making him feel better with all his stories.

'Thanks Mike, you've made it all sound so fantastic that it's really cheered me up. Now we've got a flat I need to find a job and then I'll be able to enjoy it all. Thanks for taking time to listen to my troubles, Mike. I'm sure we're really going to have fun together in this town.'

Mike smiled back warmly and watched Chris's fluttering eyes, the lids obviously feeling heavy as he made desperate attempts to keep them open. Suddenly, Chris's head fell to one side on the large cushion that he reclined on. He almost immediately fell asleep where he lay.

Mike, still feeling utterly amazed by the events of the day, stared down at Chris and decided to leave him sleeping soundly on the floor. He fetched a heavy blanket and lay it over Chris to keep off the cold and the sly draught that sometimes blew under the door. He sat back quietly with a fresh mug of coffee, lit another cigarette and briefly took stock of his chance meeting with Chris and their new partnership. Chris, his new friend who he had once held so much in awe, now lay sleeping like a baby, exhausted, snoring lightly. He drained his coffee, feeling his own eyes drooping with tiredness. He removed his glasses and gently rubbed his eyelids, feeling the soreness ease as he did so. He rose slowly, glanced down once more at Chris before staggering off to bed himself, still pondering about how uncertain life was and how quickly circumstances could change one's destiny.

Late the following morning, Chris woke from his deep sleep. Immediately the events of the previous day flooded into his brain. He tried to cast them aside, eager to start his new life and still vaguely excited about his meeting with Mike and the new flat they were going to share together. He rang the Bureau to check how matters were progressing and was overjoyed when the lady informed him that the flat was now theirs and that he could collect the key. She had apparently taken a liking to both young men and, sensing Chris's predicament, had pushed the landlady to speed up the transaction. Chris promptly rang Mike at his office with the good news. Mike received Chris's called with an excited yell of pleasure which astonished those working around him who thought of Mike as a quiet, rather placid person, certainly not noted for such public displays of emotion.

Chris collected the keys from the Bureau that afternoon, planting a kiss on the lady's cheek in gratitude and presenting her with a small bouquet of flowers that he had surreptitiously picked from the garden of the house Mike lived in. Though slightly embarrassed by Chris's gesture, she decided that she had been right about these two young men and felt happy that she had pushed their application through so quickly. Later that evening, Chris helped load Mike's few possessions and his own solitary battered case into Mike's rusty old Ford Consul and they drove to their new flat in Norwich Street. Once ensconced in their new abode, they celebrated by breaking open a bottle of 'Olde English' medium port, a leftover Christmas present of Mike's, followed by a slightly drunken game of 'spoof' played so that the winner could have the privilege of choosing the top or bottom bunk.

Mike eventually won and chose the top bunk but Chris was not displeased as he had decided to choose the bottom one if he had won. He did not let on to Mike as he decided to allow him to feel 'top dog', he was just grateful to have found their accommodation so quickly and pleased to have Mike's new-found friendship as well.

'Now that we've confirmed bunk priorities, I think we need to clarify a couple of points Mike - you don't fart in your sleep do you?' asked Chris seriously.

'It depends how bad the curry's been that night! But, as I sleep on my stomach, you'll be happy to know they won't be forcing their way through the mattress, though they might float up and swirl about the ceiling, but they shouldn't bother you,' Mike laughed. 'Also I don't have smelly feet either, so you won't get asphyxiated.'

'What if we're out and pull a couple of birds, what the hell are we going to do then?' Chris asked. 'There's hardly room to swing a cat, let alone a bird.'

'That would bring a whole new meaning to the phrase "bunk-up", wouldn't it?' Mike replied. 'We'll just have to get over that problem when we come to it. But I know one thing, I wouldn't want to do too much shagging in these beds, the whole structure might just fall apart.'

Chapter Two

They soon settled down to life in Norwich Street. Mike continued working for his accountancy firm whilst studying two or three evenings a week for his exams. Chris made himself enough to pay the rent from a variety of part-time jobs, mainly working in pubs and sometimes taking the odd office cleaning contract. However, Chris soon became very conscious of the fact that Mike was ensconced in a job that would eventually lead to what would become a profitable and enjoyable career, whilst he was simply drifting along with little regard to his future. But then, he surmised, this is the 'sixties' where free love and the easy life is most important. Many of the people that he came into contact with had few worries, their attitude was to have fun and to hell with tomorrow. 'Today is where it's at man,' was the hippie's favourite saying and there were plenty of these long-haired, flower-bedecked, cannabis smoking young people in Cambridge. Chris soon got to know several very well, but he didn't really want to go so far as join them although he, like so many of the younger generation, shared many of their beliefs. He also came to realise that Mike was a far more serious person than himself and that had probably been one of the reasons that they had never been friends at school; but now he was getting to know Mike, he was certain that they could have a great time together in Cambridge. He did however need to do something other than a string of odd jobs for the rest of his life and he resolved to look around for something more permanent in the way of employment.

Chris had, at twenty-four, much going for him. He was a little over six feet tall, dark haired and good looking. He had a good grammar school education behind him. If he had not allowed himself to become side-tracked by the sports which he so loved and by his insatiable appetite for pursuing girls, he could have amassed more than the mere handful of 'O' and 'A' levels which he had attained at school. He had tentatively toyed with the idea of applying for University, desperately urged on by his parents, but without the necessary qualifications and inclination, the plan had been shelved. He had told his parents that he would not know what to study at university anyway. He had wandered through a succession of minor office positions and various manual jobs, interspersed with a little travelling in Europe and his recent lengthy visit to the U.S.A. He had actually enjoyed the freedom of not being tied to either a job or a woman until the day he had met Jane at a party in London. After that initial meeting, they had spent a great deal of time together and he had been so smitten with her that when she had invited him to share her home in Cambridge, he had moved in within two days. But now he needed desperately to find himself a more permanent job to pay the rent and to enable him to enjoy the life that Mike had told him was there waiting for him in Cambridge. He sat one morning in the 'Kenco' coffee bar, smoking and deliberating. He was, he decided, extremely lucky. He was fit, intelligent, attractive and, although he wasn't exactly sure of where he was heading at this stage in his life, he had plenty on the plus side. But his meagre funds were running low and finding a good job was now a priority for him.

Chris ran his fingers down the list of job vacancies in the local *Cambridge Evening News*, occasionally sipping his coffee, trying not to drink it too quickly, keeping it at a reasonable level in the cup so the waitress would not clear it away. He felt hungry but could not afford to spend his limited cash on anything on the menu, so every now and then he surreptitiously resorted to squeezing blobs of ketchup from the plastic tomato container at his table onto his coffee spoon and slurping it up to quell his hunger.

He was surprised to find an acquaintance of Mike's taking a seat at the next table. Mike had introduced Frank Noble to Chris a couple of evenings before at a local pub. Frank lived near Mike's old lodging house and was a chef with a local catering company called 'Drones'. He was a big man, six feet tall, weighing about eighteen stone with ginger hair and blue eyes. Frank was using Drones as a stepping-stone to achieve his ambition to work in a top London restaurant.

Noting Chris perusing the vacancies column, Frank suggested that he might be interested in considering a job at Drones as they were constantly seeking staff due to the high turnover and unsociable hours. 'What's the company like?' Chris asked with some interest.

'It's a small family-run outside catering company,' explained Frank, ' based just off East Road. They cater for outside weddings, parties and receptions. They often attend some quite sizeable functions, such as Lord Mayor's Banquets and important society weddings at stately homes. I've worked there for two years and I'm very happy. I'm on a good salary but most people are waiting staff or kitchen helpers and they just get cash-in-hand on a casual basis.

'So, most vacancies are for waiting staff?' asked Chris.

'Yes, but I'm sure you'd be able to start immediately, so at least you'd have some cash right away. They will train you and supply your uniform. Another point is that there are plenty of birds on the job.'

Already interested, Chris's ears pricked up at the mention of birds on the job and decided that he'd like to inquire into whether there was a vacancy available. Frank suggested that they meet later that day at the start of his shift and he would introduce Chris to the manager.

Just before 4:30 that afternoon, Chris met Frank and they walked over to Drones' business premises where Frank introduced Chris to Bill Tripp, the manager. He was a very large, almost obese, man with an abrupt manner. Chris instantly decided that this was a man who would not take shit from anyone, probably because he was used to dealing with so many temporary staff and their noted unreliability.

After probing Chris with a few preliminary questions, Mr. Tripp appeared satisfied and asked Chris if he would like to start the next day at 6 o'clock in the evening. Chris accepted gladly. He was to be employed as a waiter and, although inexperienced, Mr. Tripp assured him that he would learn very quickly. Most of the catering was on a set menu basis which meant that it was basically a matter of serving the food and collecting the plates without the problems caused by customers ordering their own selection.

Bill Tripp took Chris on a quick tour of the premises which

were housed in two small terraced houses with a long, wooden, single-storey extension to the rear of the buildings. Chris was astonished at the unexpected level of noise from the clatter of pots and pans being loaded and unloaded into vans, the continual shouting and yelling of people scattered throughout the premises - some were engaged in washing-up huge stacks of dirty plates and cutlery in two large stone sinks, whilst further into the kitchen he could see vast cakes being transferred into one of the massive stainless steel ovens. He smelt cabbage and carrots being cooked in several large portable vats as steam hissed from their lids. The manager informed Chris that these vegetables were often half-cooked on the premises and then finished off at the venue later. People rushed around, fetching and carrying various bags of vegetables and assorted cooking equipment. To Chris it seemed like complete chaos. In one section of the building he noticed huge piles of clean plates nestling next to stacks of white linen arranged on shelves. There were boxes of cutlery adjacent to vast aluminium food containers and quantities of sauce boats and coffee cups. Piles of greying tea-towels were sandwiched between large catering tins of peas and tomatoes, nothing appeared to be arranged in any particular order. Chris was startled to notice a rat run across the floor between the stacked aisles, but Bill Tripp appeared not to notice it. Small birds were flying about the roof, escaping in and out of holes under the eaves of the decrepit wooden buildings. There was a constant chattering of bird song in the background. Chris's feet kept sticking to the dirty floor as he breathed in the odious smell of stale grease and dirt - a smell that would pervade his nostrils endlessly for the next few weeks.

Reporting for work the next evening, Chris soon found himself in the thick of things. His first task was to help load the two old ex-furniture vans used by the company to convey the complete catering requirements for the next day's outside function. There were huge electric boilers on wheels for cooking vegetables, large trays of cutlery, silver candelabra, table clothes and napkins, sets of silver condiments, ladles, cooking knives, catering jars of mustard and mayonnaise, frying pans and mobile refrigerators crammed with meat and fish. These were piled into the old vans with some semblance of order overseen by none other than the boss, Mr. Drones himself. A tall self-effacing man of military bearing with slicked back black hair, he would distance himself in the background, pacing slowly up and down whilst casting occasional worried glances at the staff who were loading up. If anything was not carried out correctly and according to plan, he would whisper into the ear of the foreman, an ebullient Irishman called Paddy O'Shea, who doubled up as the Head Waiter. Paddy would stride over and berate anyone not doing their job properly and was not averse to cuffing them around the ear. Frank told Chris to be sure that he did not upset Paddy as he was known to be a good fighting man who could bear a grudge if anyone upset him badly.

Chris soon found himself working sixteen to eighteen hours a day and quickly discovered why most of the staff did not stay for long. He had never worked so physically hard in his life and was often completely shattered at the end of his shift, sometimes being too tired even to remove his clothes when he returned to the flat, merely flopping into his bunk for a few hours sleep before rising at some unreasonable hour, trying not to wake Mike before another long stint. He was nevertheless grateful for the chance to work and save some money, which was always paid in cash in small brown envelopes. As he was usually so tired at the end of each working day, he found himself with little opportunity to spend his wages.

He soon found himself working at some sizeable and important functions which he thoroughly enjoyed. He found it more exhilarating to attend the Lord Mayor's Banquet at Great Yarmouth or the Apprentice's Prize Winning dinner at Daventry, than to work at the average wedding in someone's garden marquee or a function at the local village hall.

One other reason that Chris enjoyed working at Drones was the number of ribald females that worked there, just as Frank Noble had promised. Whatever type of work one did at Drones, either in the kitchen, the laundry, cooking or waiting - it was all hard menial work and everyone was expected to help one another. Much of the daily grind was offset by coarse jokes or lewd gossip pertaining to other staff members, while most of the conversation was accompanied by uncouth sexual innuendo, regardless of gender. A 'laugh' was what made the long hours bearable, but the relentless mickey taking amongst the staff could be extremely callous and ruthless. On several occasions, Chris saw people reduced to tears during his time there.

Chris occasionally dated one or two of the girls working at the premises, returning to their place if they had one after entertaining them with a few drinks, spending his few precious hours off sleeping and screwing before jumping up and returning to work for his next shift. He soon spotted a very attractive young cook who was one of the more permanent members of the staff. Her name was Ann Stokes and, despite her reputation as a dreadful gossip, Chris was very attracted to her. Unfortunately she already had a steady boyfriend, so Chris was left merely admiring her from afar.

One Saturday he sat next to her as they were being driven to work at a large wedding in Saffron Walden, a pretty, mediaeval town near Cambridge. She seemed morose and quiet, far from her usual talkative self. It turned out that her boyfriend had left her for another woman and Chris asked her out for a drink to make her feel better. They met up three days later when they both had a free evening and went to the ABC Cinema to see Sean Connery in the new James Bond movie, *Thunderball*. Chris who was particularly exhausted, having worked four long shifts on the trot, fell asleep several times in the cinema. However, later that evening, after several drinks in the 'Castle' pub where Chris had listened intently as Ann told him about the break-up of her relationship and after a little canoodling on the way home, they had ended up in Ann's bedsitter and eventually in her bed. Unfortunately, Chris was so tired that he was unable to achieve an erection. Whatever Ann did to him, and he had to admit to himself later that she really tried, Chris just could not get it up. Exhausted and humiliated he just fell asleep hoping that matters would be better in the morning.

He woke late the next morning, luckily he was on the afternoon shift, and saw a note lying on the pillow next to him. He reach out and picked it up, unfolding it carefully.

'Try two lolly-pop sticks and a rubber band next time,' he read. The writing was scrawled in red lipstick.

'Oh, shit,' he said out loud, a sinking sensation coming over him. He felt a sense of shame intrude upon his feelings and anger that she had left such a tawdry note; but then dismissed the thought deciding that she would have left it in fun. 'She must have realised how tired I was. Christ, I was so bloody knackered it was impossible to think straight, let alone make love.'

Chris knew that because of his fatigue, it had affected his desire. He very rarely had any problems with erections and last night's failure had certainly not been caused because he did not fancy Ann. On the contrary, he had really wanted her, fancying her from afar for some time as he had done. He was sure that he would take her out again and make up for it. Surely this little note was just a bit of a joke on her part? As he showered in Ann's bathroom, he thought about the note again, 'No, surely she wouldn't have written it maliciously?' Oh well, he would see her later that day at work and ask her out again. 'Christ, she won't know what's hit her the next time I get her into bed,' he smiled as he rinsed the soap from his body. As he did so, thinking about her fine lithe body brought on an erection. Chris looked down in disbelief. 'If only she was here now,' he muttered to himself, 'and if only you'd stood up for me last night,' he muttered down at his proud member.

Returning to Drones that afternoon to start his shift, he immediately sensed something was wrong. There was an unfamiliar atmosphere, much different to the buzz of conversation and the general kitchen noises that he had become familiar with. He noticed a couple of the washer-uppers nudging each other and sniggering, casting odd glances in his direction. As he walked into the kitchen where Ann worked, several heads turned in his direction only to avert their gaze when he turned to acknowledge them. Ann stared intently at him as he walked towards her. She was encased in her white uniform with a big apron wrapped around her waist, and stood at a stove stirring a large aluminium pot of gravy. 'Oh hello lover boy,' she said in a somewhat derisory voice rather louder than he would have liked. 'And what do you want?' she demanded, her voice rising even louder, as she stirred the gravy slowly, her eyes staring at him menacingly. 'Can we have a quiet word please Ann?' said Chris quietly, trying to ignore the other girls in the kitchen, who appeared to be openly smirking at him. He realised, with a horrible sinking feeling in the pit of his stomach, that she must have cruelly disclosed last night's shortcomings to the other staff. He felt himself flushing with humiliation and, unused to the heat in the kitchen, he began to feel that he might be physically sick.

'Listen, I've got nothing to say to you,' she exclaimed. 'You're a waste of time. I reckon that you're a bloody queer!'

The watching girls convulsed with shrieks and howls of derisive laughter as Chris stared in disbelief at Ann, wishing the walls would fall in and cover him.

'Look, I was absolutely knackered last night. I've just come to say that I enjoyed the evening, it was really nice, and if we could go out again, I could make it up to you,' he said, edging nearer to her and talking almost in a whisper so that none of the others could hear him. The trouble was, he knew by the way she had already reacted, that she was not about to be placated. She was, he concluded, a rather nasty piece of work. What justification could she have for making him suffer in front of her captive audience. Was she possibly making him pay because her boyfriend had left her?

'Nice evening,' he heard her yelling. 'My idea of a nice evening is with a bloke who fancies me, giving me several inches of hard cock, not pissing about making excuses for not getting it up like you did last night.'

The girls cheered and yelled abuse at Chris, standing around him clapping and chanting obscenely. He felt completely shattered and demoralised. 'Was this why men became homosexual?' he wondered. 'What if I go through the rest of my life and never get another erection after this?'

Overwhelmed with embarrassment, he turned away from Ann and walked quickly out of the kitchen and down the corridor. He heard the abusive chanting and clapping turn to waves of coarse laughter. He felt angry now. The bitch was making him a scapegoat and there was only one way out. He stopped outside Bill Tripp's office and knocked on the door. A voice told him to enter. There was Mr. Tripp, sitting at a large desk working on a ledger.

'What can I do for you son?' he asked, smiling up at Chris.

'I'm afraid because of a personal matter, I've got to leave,' said Chris, feeling a sense of sadness engulf him. He did not

37

want to leave but he felt there was no alternative for him now. He gazed down at Bill, looking for a reaction. He was upset for him too. He probably did not have many people stay too long because of the nature of the business, but he liked Bill and knew that Bill felt the same about him.

Bill Tripp had certainly grown to like Chris who had worked for the company for some weeks now. He had hoped to offer Chris some management training. 'I'm sure I can help you sort it out lad, if you'll let me,' assured Mr. Tripp, rising to his feet and seeming concerned for Chris.

'It's not that easy, Mr. Tripp,' said Chris. 'I just won't be able to stay here, much as I'd like to. I've really enjoyed working here, but it's something that I can't discuss.' He knew that he couldn't compete with Ann Stokes. She had been ensconced at Drones for ages, knew everyone and with all her cronies around her and her malicious tongue, she would always have the upper hand. The embarrassing scene in the kitchen just now would be relayed around the rest of the staff in no time, if not already.

'OK, Chris,' replied Mr. Tripp, extending his hand to Chris. They shook hands and the older man smiled sympathetically. 'I won't press you lad, but if you do want to return at any time, you'll be most welcome. I'll have your money ready tomorrow. Will you collect it or shall we post it to you by recorded delivery?'

'Post it please,' replied Chris, 'and thank you again Mr. Tripp for all your help.'

'Goodbye,' said Bill Tripp, easing himself slowly down into his chair again.

Chris turned and walked out of the office, closing the door quietly behind him. He walked briskly down the corridor and out of the premises, his eyes glued to the floor not daring to even sneak a glance at the couple of people he passed for fear of being taunted. He felt himself shaking now and an anger began welling up inside him that something so trivial had become such a powerful weapon in the hands of that bitch. She had used his temporary impotence as a tool to humiliate and persecute him, using him as a scapegoat for her ignorance, helped by her friends who had vilified and abused him in the kitchen. Because of her, he'd had to leave his job which he had really enjoyed. He could have stayed, but at what cost? Everyone would have known what had happened and he knew that he would continually have been the subject of abuse and verbal gamesmanship. His time at work would have degenerated into a living nightmare. No, he had made the right decision, as sudden as it was. But it had left a sad, sour taste in his mouth. He had not even been able to say goodbye to Frank Noble either.

He stepped into a pub and ordered a pint of beer. Sitting at a quiet table, he lit a cigarette and pondered his position. He had saved quite a bit of money from his few weeks at Drones but he needed to get another job soon. He had got used to working hard and the rent still needed to be paid. He had to buy a local paper next and see what was available. The cigarette and the beer made him feel slightly calmer and, as he rose and left the pub, he determined that the nasty and perverse actions of Ann Stokes would not stop him enjoying his life and attaining his goals.

Later that evening, he recounted to Mike the events of the previous twenty-four hours, sparing no details, even down to his erectile dysfunctions, whilst Mike listened in sheer amazement, angry that a woman behaving so cruelly had affected Chris so much that he had given in his notice. 'What a bitch,' Mike said angrily, not surprised that Chris had suffered such a problem. He realised how hard Chris had been working lately and knowing himself the problems that fatigue and alcohol could cause a man in moments of passion; usually it was only a temporary thing, but it was a real bummer when it happened. 'At least there's loads more ladies waiting out there for you who are going to prove her wrong,' continued Mike, helping to alter Chris's dejected mood. 'The best thing you can do is get out there and pick yourself another one as soon as possible.'

Chris yawned heavily and lumbered slowly to his feet. 'I think the best thing I can do is to get a bloody good night's sleep, which I haven't had for ages, and then start looking for another job tomorrow. Thanks for listening to my troubles once again, Mike.'

'Well, I'll hit the bunk too. It'll be the first time we've gone to bed together for weeks,' laughed Mike.

Chapter Three

Sadly, it only took a few months of living together before both Chris and Mike decided the flat was too cramped and lacking in privacy for their combined lifestyles.

With Chris once again entertaining several jobs that demanded working unsociable hours, he was often returning home, or even rising for work, in the early hours of the morning and he sometimes woke Mike who was a light sleeper. It was either the rustling of his clothes being put on or taken off or the creaking of the tiered beds when Chris crept into his bunk; anything could easily interrupt Mike's light rest and Chris disliked the incessant creeping about the flat.

There was also, to Chris's joy and amazement, the female problem. They were both meeting and gaining many new friends in the city. Mike, buoyed up by Chris's natural effervescence and high spirits, was becoming far more outgoing. He soon found that Chris's presence rubbed off on him and boosted his new-found confidence. They became members of most of the local clubs, such as *'Les Jeux Interdit'* and the murky *'Taboo Club'*. They were often to be found at the *'International Centre'*, a club where foreign students could meet each other. Mike and Chris had soon discovered that this was the ideal pick-up place, giving them a choice of around a hundred girls during any night of the week. Chris coined the phrase, 'Sitting Fucks', much to Mike's amusement. 'Just walk in and they're sitting around just waiting to be picked-up,' said Chris who had found it hard to believe when they first went there. Before long they were being invited to parties several nights a week in the swinging city and meeting and sleeping with a vast array of lovely girls who made themselves very available.

The limitations of their accommodation had become only too obvious the first time that they had met a couple of local girls who were on a night out together and the boys had invited them back to their flat for drinks. They had sat down together one evening and discussed just such a situation as they both knew that it would inevitably occur at some point. They had both decided that neither of them would wish to make love to two girls in the same room for, although they were both randy and eager to have sex with as many girls as possible, they both felt that screwing was a personal thing. There were occasional orgies in some quarters and, with the flower power and hippie movement, they were apparently quite popular. However, they both agreed that communal sex was not for them. They also felt that they would lose respect for any girl who was happy to see sex other than as a personal act in private, although Chris had once asked Mike, 'In all seriousness, do we really respect most of these girls anyway?'

So later this particular evening, the two girls were encased comfortably on the bottom bunk, in the tiny flat. Chris had opened a bottle of red wine and Elvis Presley's love songs were playing softly in the background. The boys had adjourned to the bathroom down the landing to discuss their tactics. 'Look Mike, this one's really hot for me. She's already cleaning my ear out with her tongue,' declared Chris hoarsely, wringing his hands with excitement. 'We agreed when we discussed this before that one of us would have to leave with his girl so that the other can get a shag here.'

'My girl's pretty randy too,' Mike replied. 'We'll have to toss a coin for who goes and who stays. Do you think if one of them goes the other might want to leave as well?' he asked Chris with concern in his eyes.

'Fuck me, then we're up shit creek without a paddle,' said Chris. 'No, these girls both live in different parts of Cambridge but, if the loser doesn't have a flat or lives with her parents, then whichever one of us loses the toss, can drive up to Lime Kiln Hill in your car, that's pretty quiet and romantic.'

Lime Kiln Hill was a small rise above the flatness of the city where there was a parking area. It was a well-known spot for lovers to park at night when the lights of the city made the view more dramatic.

Mike produced a coin from his pocket, expertly flicking it in the air and catching it in his hand. He then turned to Chris, a grin on his face. 'Heads or tails?' he asked.

'Tails,' replied Chris confidently.

Mike open his hand and they both gazed down at the coin.

'Oh shit,' cried Mike. 'I'm out in the cold.'

'Sorry pal,' said Chris, patting Mike's shoulder compassionately. He was secretly relieved that he was the lucky one but still felt sorry for Mike who now had to explain to his girl what was going on and hope that she would be willing to leave her friend and go off in the car with him.

They both returned to the room where Mike asked his girl, Elaine, to step outside for a moment. He closed the door and turned to face her in the small hallway. 'Look Elaine, you can see the situation we're in,' he said softly, holding her face gently between his hands and kissing her softly on the lips several times. 'Chris is horny as hell and so is Jo, but we're a little tight on space in our room. Do you understand? We need to be on our own as well, don't we?'

Without reply, Elaine leaned back against the wall and pulled Mike against her, her hands clasped around his neck. She kissed him hard, her tongue forcing his mouth open. They became locked in a passionate embrace. Mike broke free, gasping for air. 'Look, let's take my car and go somewhere and leave them together here,' he suggested breathlessly, pleased that she understood the situation and hoping that she would agree.

'Yes, I want to be on my own with you, I think you're cute. We were a bit worried about those bunk beds. When you went to the toilet, we told each other that no way were we going to screw in those at the same time,' she revealed. 'We're not the type of girls that go in for that sort of thing.'

'Well, we wouldn't have done that anyway,' Mike replied truthfully, pleased that she thought him cute.

When Mike opened the door, Chris and Jo immediately sprang apart in surprise. Mike grabbed his car keys and the half bottle of red wine as they all said goodbye to each other. Minutes later Mike was driving Elaine as fast as he could go in his battered old Ford Consul up to Lime Kiln Hill.

Within seconds of their departure, Chris and Jo had stripped each other naked, pulling and tearing each other's clothes off, almost collapsing with laughter and lust as they did so. They were soon engaged in a furious bout of lovemaking, not in the bunk beds but on the small area of rough carpet in the room.

'Oh God, I've got you all to myself now,' Jo explained, tightening her legs around his back, trying to ignore the burning sensation as the abrasive carpet tore into her shoulders as Chris pounded into her, the skin on his knees and elbows reddening and bleeding as they scraped on the carpet.

Later, as they lay sweating and breathless, they surveyed each other's abrasions.

'Bloody hell, Jo, are you a masochist? Look at your skin, it's just torn away,' Chris said. 'I'll put some cream on your shoulders - and anywhere else it hurts!'

'Do you think the bunk bed would stand up to it?' laughed Jo with a shy smile, 'just in case we fancy another round.'

Chapter Four

At seven o'clock the next morning, Mike tapped on the flat door in case Chris was still engaged with Jo. When Chris opened the door, Mike, peering over his shoulder, saw that the room was empty.

Chris was wearing his dressing gown and although he smiled, his eyes were bloodshot and his face was pale and stubbled. He looked as though he had enjoyed a hectic night.

'Hi Mike, I've just taken Jo home and I've only just got back. How did you get on?' Chris asked as he filled the kettle with water to make some tea.

Mike's eyes blinked wearily behind his spectacles. His hair was tousled and his clothes badly creased. 'It was really weird,' he explained. 'She was a real nut. We drove up to the hill and started kissing and petting and then we got stripped off ready to fuck when I had a sudden urgent desire to have a piss. Luckily there were no other cars around, so I got out, stark bollock naked to have a quick pee against a tree. Bit of poetry there! When I went to get back into the car, the bitch had locked the doors. There was quite a chilly wind blowing up the hill and I was fucking frozen. I didn't even have my glasses on. But the unbelievable thing was, she pushed her tits, and she's got huge knockers, right against the inside of the window so they splayed out like huge fried eggs, flaunting them at me and laughing like a clown. So, I'm stuck outside the car, freezing my bollocks off, desperately but pointlessly trying to get hold of her tits behind the glass and she thinks it's a bloody scream. Eventually she saw I was getting annoyed and let me back in. But it took ages for me to warm up again and by that time I felt so tired, I almost gave up on her and took her home. Luckily she became very attentive to me and got me back in the mood again. She certainly knew a trick or two and eventually we ended up having a really good screw. Afterwards I drove her back to her parent's house and she cooked me a fried breakfast whilst her parents were still asleep upstairs.'

'You lucky bugger,' cried Chris. 'Anyway, I'm glad that it all turned out OK. I felt a bit guilty about winning the toss,' he added as he poured the tea and handed a steaming mug to Mike.

'Don't,' replied Mike, shaking his head, 'one of us had to lose and it worked out very well for me. But, how was your girl?'

'Bloody exhausting and pretty rough,' replied Chris pulling up the sleeves of his gown to reveal plasters on each elbow. He then parted the front of his dressing gown to reveal plasters on each knee. 'That's what happens when you shag on a hard carpet. 'Jo's covered in plasters too, but it was well worth it.'

'Crikey, that looks pretty nasty. All I've got in the way of war wounds will probably be a cold after Elaine locked me out of the bloody car,' said Mike ruefully.

This is the first time we've had a problem though. Most of the girls we've shagged have had their own flats, but I really do feel that we're going to need a bigger place eventually,' said Chris. 'Don't you agree, Mike?'

'Yeah, I do,' nodded Mike, 'it really is far too cramped in here, more than I thought it would be.'

'I feel guilty and selfish because I may have pushed you into taking this place and sharing with me because I needed somewhere so badly,' said Chris.

'No way, I've enjoyed every minute - well, almost!' laughed Mike. 'But you're right Chris, we do need a bigger place. It must still be central but I really do need my own space for studying, possibly a two-bedroom flat or even a house. That would be ideal for us.'

'OK. We can take our time though. Maybe on Saturday we could look around some of the agencies for something more suitable,' said Chris.

'Sounds good to me,' said Mike, suddenly visualising himself studying at a large desk in a large room whilst a pneumatic blonde lay naked on the bed impatiently waiting for him to finish his studies and attend to her. He smiled at the thought and then dismissed it from his mind and poured another cup of tea, checking the time on the clock on the windowsill. He didn't relish the thought of going to work, feeling so tired after his night of exertion. Chris interrupted his thoughts again.

'We're going to be late for work if we don't hurry. Toss you for who gets the bathroom first.'

Mike groaned gently and tried to tell himself that it didn't matter as his call for tails lost once again. As Chris triumphantly shot off down the hallway to shower and shave, Mike's thoughts turned again to a place with his own quiet room where they wouldn't always be on top of each other.

Although no suitable accommodation surfaced the next Saturday, their search gave them the opportunity to inform all the estate agents and accommodation bureau of their requirements. All their friends and acquaintances were told of the possibility of a move whilst they spent long hours devouring the 'To Let' columns of the local newspaper. As the weeks passed they were offered several flats only to decline them all as unsuitable, either because they were too far from the centre of the city or because they were just too expensive.

As Chris sat smoking one morning, drinking coffee and opening the post, he could tell from the envelopes and postmarks that the letters were mainly from the letting agents, so most he glanced at briefly before being consigned to the bin as being unsuitable, but one item greatly aroused his curiosity. The pamphlet gave details of a flat in Mawson Road, a popular road in a sought-after area half a mile from the city centre. It was rather larger than the flats that they had been looking at. In fact, this flat comprised four double bedrooms with a huge lounge measuring thirty by eighteen feet. The flat was on the first and second floors of an extended Victorian semi-detached villa and was in an unmodernised state, particularly the kitchen and bathroom. The property was fully furnished too. But what interested Chris was the rent, at £25 a month it seemed incredibly low, especially for such a large flat. What did they care if it needed modernising? He was so excited that he wrapped a towel around his naked body and ran downstairs to the pay 'phone situated in the front hallway. He rang the agent and made an appointment to view the flat at five o'clock that afternoon. He rang Mike immediately who, though rather bemused, said he would try to arrange to leave the office early

46

and meet him at the property. Chris's enthusiasm, as he read the details of the flat over the 'phone to him, was so infectious that Mike managed to make a deal with John Grey the office manager to leave early by promising to work late the next day. Mr. Grey, who liked Mike, felt that he had a promising career ahead of him and wanted him to stay with the company.

At five o'clock Mike met Chris outside the house. The door was partly open and the hall light on, so the agent was obviously on time. As they rang the bell, they could see two doorways, one was supposedly a downstairs flat, the other led upstairs to the top flat.

'Looks fine so far,' said Mike eagerly, 'but what are we going to do with four bedrooms?'

'Install hot and cold running women, maybe,' said Chris. 'Seriously though, I've been thinking about that all afternoon. If we could find two more guys to fit in, we could let the other two rooms and then the rent would be even cheaper, everyone would have their own bedroom and we'd have the bloody great lounge to share communally.'

'Let's see the flat first,' said Mike as they heard a voice call down to them. Mike pushed the door open and led the way up the creaky stairs which were covered by threadbare carpet.

'Bill Johnson, Cutters Estate Agents,' barked the large bespectacled man standing at the top of the stairs as he extended his hand. He smiled warmly as he shook hands with both of the boys. 'Please have a good look round. It's been somewhat neglected over the years. I believe a little old lady lived here until she died a couple of months ago and the executors just want to rent the flat but don't want to do anything to it. That's why the rent is so low. It could actually be made to look quite nice. You've certainly got the space here,' he concluded.

Chris and Mike wandered inquisitively from room to room. There was a musty smell of dust and neglect. They marvelled at the large bedrooms, one of which was located up a separate stairway to the second floor, with sloping ceilings and a dormer window.

In the kitchen sat an old gas stove that dated from before the war. There was a battered old porcelain sink and a large range of cupboards and shelves around the walls. An old pine table and four chairs sat in the middle of the room. 'Ideal for Sunday

47

breakfast with the birds,' said Chris, his sense of romanticism coming to the fore.

The bathroom was cold and foreboding. The large bath was battered and chipped with a dark tide-mark running around the inside. The toilet bowl was badly stained and the brown and beige lino that bubbled and cracked across the floor had certainly seen better days.

It was the size of the lounge that was the clincher. It was huge. Chris, who had become so excited by the initial details, now revelled in the true size of the room. His mind ran riot as he gazed around, enraptured by the high walls, the ornate coving and the huge windows at one end overlooking the garden. 'Christ Mike, think of the parties we could have here - music, dancing, hoards of gorgeous women running around the place. It would be fantastic,' he enthused wildly, almost breaking out into a dance himself.

Mike's enthusiasm was less immediate and for good reason. He now enjoyed Chris's company enormously. He had been right in his observations when he had met Chris that eventful day and they had decided to share the Norwich Street flat. Chris had certainly brought him out of his shell and he had needed that, someone to push and cajole him into having more fun with his life, letting his hair down more often. Chris's enthusiasm was infectious. But, he worried, what if they couldn't let the rooms, how would they afford it? He was still studying for his articles and his trainee salary was so low that he was still dependent on his parents to supplement his income even though he was loathe to do so. His parents were not rich, but it was sometimes a necessity to ask them for money when funds were low.

The pair found Mr. Johnson and told him they would be in touch the following day when they had talked the accommodation over.

Chris suggested a drink, so they wandered round to the Salisbury Arms a hundred yards away. The pub had just opened for the evening and there were only a few regulars in, so they sat together at the bar munching through a couple of packets of crisps whilst enjoying two warm pints of Guinness. Chris was finding it difficult to contain his enthusiasm for the flat. 'It's absolutely fucking brilliant, don't you agree Mike, it's a fabulous pad?' he enthused, his eyes blazing in delight.

'Yes, I do. But I'm slightly concerned about whether we can fill the rooms and find the right guys to share with us - who like to have fun and like shagging women and getting pissed now and again. Also, can we afford the rent?' said Mike pessimistically. 'I really do like the flat though, Chris. I think we could make it look great,' he added, visualising the walls freshly painted.

Chris nodded. He had anticipated Mike's concerns and had given the matter some consideration that afternoon. 'I think I've got someone who might be interested in sharing with us, especially when he realises what a great pad this is. This guy is mad as a fucking hatter, but he loves all the things that we enjoy, I'm sure you'll get on with him.'

'Who's that?' asked Mike trying to imagine who this someone could possibly be.

'He's the Indian chap, Raz. You must know him, he's always down at the Déjà Vu Club, spending his time pulling birds and laughing all the time. He's really great fun. He's a bit of an intellectual piss artist, he's been to University here at Cambridge.'

'Oh, I know the guy you mean,' cried Mike immediately recognising the character Chris was talking about. 'He drives an old MG sports car and always wears bow ties, he's a big guy, rather a flamboyant character!'

'Yes, that's the chap,' said Chris. 'He works for a publisher in Bridge Street. His family left their business in Uganda shortly before Idi Amin took over. They came over to London but Raz moved to Cambridge to take his degree. He liked Cambridge so much that he decided to stay. His family still live in London, but he's made loads of friends here. He lives in some poxy room in the Romsey Town area, which is pretty rough. He mentioned to me a couple of weeks ago that he'd like to move nearer the centre and share with some like-minded people. Well, that could be us in our new flat.'

'OK, let's have a chat with him and see what he feels about it and we can decide whether he'd fit in with us. But isn't he a Sikh? He won't have any religious hang-ups will he?' asked Mike. 'I don't think temples, shrines and Buddhas are our scene,' he added, knowing little about what Sikh's actually believed in.

'No, Raz is great. He calls a spade a spade and religion is definitely not a problem for him. He drinks like a fucking fish, smokes a lot and goes after the ladies. He's got a great sense of humour, but he can also be serious when he needs to be. I really do think he'd be a great guy for us to share with.'

Mike, who was more serious and far less impulsive than Chris, decided that Raz sharing with them could be a good idea, but he wanted to be sure, to have a chat with the Indian and then to decide. If they were going to take the flat he was determined to make sure that their flatmates would be truly compatible and to make sure that Chris understood that. Mike knew from the short time that they had shared their flat together that Chris, who was always so overly impulsive and enthusiastic, could charge ahead and possibly make some wrong decisions, content to face the consequences later. Even Chris's relationship with Jane had ended because of his reckless behaviour with another woman. Mike actually admired his approach in some ways, but felt that his 'bull at a gate' approach needed to be reined in sometimes. He was happy to do that for his friend if only to allow him to take a little more time to ponder over some decisions which affected them both.

Chris ran through his worn black address book, sure that he'd collected Raz's number somewhere. He kept the numbers of many of the people that he met, 'just in case' he would say to Mike with a wry smile. He found Raz's number and dialled it from the call box in the rear of the pub. Luckily he caught Raz just about to leave the publishing house and quickly explained the reason for his call.

Raz seemed pleasantly surprised that Chris had remembered their somewhat drunken conversation in the club a couple of weeks previously. 'I'm sharing with a load of cockroaches and an army of mice and they don't pay any bloody rent at all,' he had moaned to Chris, trying to lean closer to Chris's ear and whisper so that the slightly drunk but very pretty Australian backpacker that he was trying to pull couldn't hear him. He wanted her in his bed that night and was certain she would not be terribly keen if she knew that there were vermin running around his room. 'I would like to be closer to the city centre, so if you do hear of any accommodation going please let me know,' Raz had asked. Chris had taken down his number and Raz had returned to chat up the Aussie girl. Chris had stored their conversation in the back of his mind as he did with countless fragments of idle chat, many of them surfacing fruitfully at later dates.

Chris and Mike knew Raz had arrived fifteen minutes later when they heard the soft throaty rumble of the exhaust of his MG as he parked outside the pub. He came through the door, a big dark handsome man with fluid movements. He glanced around and immediately spotted them at the bar. His face lit up with the huge beaming smile that they would get to know so well and extended a huge hand towards Chris. 'Hi Chris. Thank you so much for your call.'

'Hi Raz. Let me introduce you to my flatmate Mike.'

'Yeah, I believe I've seen you around,' said Raz shaking hands with Mike.

Mike noticed that Raz seemed to exude an aura of happiness and well-being, it almost seemed to flow out of his whole body. He took an instant liking to the big man. Raz was wearing a bow tie with his tweed jacket, an affectation that Mike decided had been influenced by the university where it was quite fashionable for some students and dons to wear them.

Chris ordered a beer for Raz, who took a long draught and sat back in his chair, heaving a deep sigh of satisfaction. He grinned at them both, his face becoming a picture of anticipation as he waited for Chris to speak. 'We've been to see a flat in Mawson Road, just around the corner. It's a fantastic pad, four bedrooms. It needs a little cleaning and decorating, but we've got to let the agent know tomorrow otherwise they'll show it to someone else and we'll lose it. Mike and I need to move into a bigger place, but we need to let the other two bedrooms, preferably to like-minded lunatics like yourself, Raz. What do you think?'

'How much is the rent?' asked Raz.

'It's £25 monthly, which is just over six quid each, plus a share of the bills.'

'What about the bedrooms, what size are they?' Raz asked again.

'They are all a good size, all double rooms, perfect for randy bachelor boys like us,' replied Chris.

'Sounds perfect,' Raz smiled. 'I'm paying £7 for my cruddy shit-hole at the moment and I do like a little privacy when I take the odd lady home, so a bedroom each sounds great. If you guys say it's OK, then I'm happy,' he grinned. 'As long as you're happy with me,' he added, shrugging his large shoulders.

'It's not the Hilton Hotel, that's for sure. But it's a really good location and with a clean up and with each of us having our own bedroom, it will be fantastic. If you're agreeable Raz, we can inform the agent tomorrow. It will take about a week to go through, to give our notices in on our present accommodation and advertise for a fourth nutcase to share with,' said Chris. 'OK with you Mike?' he asked.

Mike winked and nodded at Chris then reached out and shook Raz's hand. 'Welcome to the fold, Raz,' he smiled, feeling happy and satisfied that even with such a brief meeting, Raz came across as a genuine, trustworthy person with a great sense of humour. He sensed that Raz would get on well with Chris and himself, he seemed so positive and happy. He reflected that this was the second time that he'd accepted a flatmate within minutes. After all, Raz could be a bloody psychopath or an axe murderer for all they knew, but his charisma had cast aside any doubts that he might have had before meeting him. Mike felt very satisfied with their mutual decision.

The next morning Chris rang the agent to confirm that they would like the flat. They were told to obtain their references and the deposit which they managed to hand over within two days. Several days later Chris collected the keys and they all moved into Mawson Road. Raz, taking his first look around, pronounced it 'bloody marvellous'. They agreed to draw straws for the choice of bedrooms; Chris suggesting that was the fairest way. Surprisingly, each of them somehow selected the bedroom that they each wanted the most, so a better start to their new venture together could not have been imagined. It was the start of an era. It was just as well that none of them could have foreseen the madness and mayhem of their time together as none of them would have believed it.

Chapter Five

Almost a month after taking possession of their flat, they had still not found a suitable candidate to take the fourth bedroom. Already many attractive women were beginning to pass through the place as the young men revelled in their new abode, particularly enjoying the freedom of being able to entertain girls in their own bedrooms. Someone suggested that it might be fun to have a 'flat warming' party but Mike, always the practical one, put forward the idea of a painting party as they had not got around to decorating the place.

So, late one Saturday afternoon, they invited some girls around from a flat they lived in just around the corner. Chris had engaged one of these girls in conversation after she had smiled at him when she passed by while he was idly standing outside the front door. Encouraged by the fact that she lived with five other girls, mostly nurses and teachers, the boys had invited them round for the painting party. They were told to wear their oldest clothes while the boys would provide the paint, the brushes and a plentiful supply of booze. Mike's idea was that everyone participated in wielding a paintbrush and was given a wall to paint. His theory was that the flat would be decorated in next to no time. Unfortunately, it did not quite work out like that. As the party progressed, everyone became very drunk indeed. There appeared to be more paint covering people's clothes and dripping over the floor, than had actually been painted on the walls.

Whilst engaged in an early kiss with Chris, one of the girls had clumsily stepped into a large tin of red emulsion, spilling it all over the lounge carpet. Whilst frantic efforts were made to clear it up with basins of cold water and old towels, the girl concerned stood on an old newspaper to take off her paint-sodden jeans so that she wouldn't stamp paint everywhere and make matters worse. She then went off in the direction of the bathroom to wash her foot which she had encased in a plastic bag. Chris, who instantly noticed that she had really shapely legs, immediately followed her to offer his help and neatly side-tracked her into his bedroom; the pair of them were not seen again that day.

Somehow, due to the drunken state that they had all descended into, several of the party had begun jousting with their paintbrushes and even more of the red paint had managed to appear on the carpet, the skirting boards, the curtains and many other areas where it was not intended causing the original idea of painting the flat to get completely out of hand.

The calamitous evening ended up with two of the other girls pairing off with Raz and Mike who welcomed their paint-splattered bodies into their beds with relish.

Mike, who had earlier shown great consternation as the paint began to be flung recklessly around, had become so drunk himself as the evening progressed that his only concern at this late stage was for the nurse underneath him, with her paint encrusted hair and red and green streaked arms. As she gripped her legs tightly around his body, sweating and moaning beneath him and covering his sheets with a melange of colour, he had completely forgotten all about the painting party, as indeed had Chris albeit much earlier in the proceedings.

When the flatmates sat together half-awake and bleary-eyed the next morning, having rid themselves of the girls who had stayed with them, nursing fearsome hangovers and drinking gallons of tea to clear their heads, the devastation throughout the flat became strikingly obvious to each of them. Paint was daubed everywhere, even the walls that had been completed looked dreadful, stark evidence of how quickly everyone had become hopelessly drunk. There were streaks and runs down every wall, the whole episode had turned into a complete disaster.

'It will take us more time to clean up the mess than it did to paint the fucking place,' Chris exclaimed angrily to Mike who had thought up the idea of the painting party.

'Yeah, unfortunately everyone's painting skills have left a great deal to be desired. I'm only sorry that drink and sex both reared their ugly heads and we ended up with this bloody mess,' said Mike dryly. In his eyes, though, hopefully, it would not take long to put everything right and looking on the bright side, they had all enjoyed a terrific party, which had ended up with a lovely girl in each of their beds.

Mike suggested that the next two weekends should be allocated to cleaning the paint from all the unwanted surfaces and to complete the painting of the walls to everyone's satisfaction. So that was what they did. Mike instigated the final stages of decoration, telling the others it was a necessary step to create their own special atmosphere, even though they were all pissed off at having to clean up the extensive mess after the painting party fiasco.

Inspecting the flat two weeks later when they had finally finished the cleaning and painting, Raz remarked that the flat had made a transformation from 'severely pissed' to 'surrealist', which the others had to agree was a pretty damned clever remark taking into account all that had happened.

The hallway had been painted in a horrendous dark red colour which Mike had bought at a half-price sale in the local D.I.Y. shop. Although he was a little reticent when he arrived home with it, Mike was overruled by Raz and Chris who returned to the shop and purchased several more tins of the red paint. They proceeded to paint the entire lounge and the ceiling in red too. They had used the rickety dining table, moving it across the room bit by bit as they balanced precariously and drunkenly on the table top, slapping the red paint onto the dusty, cob-webbed ceiling. They had listened to their favourite Buddy Holly and Elvis Presley records playing non-stop as they worked, sustained by several cases of beer over both of the week-ends it had taken to finish the flat. Once the job was completed, they together wandered around the rooms, inspecting their efforts. The lounge aroused mixed feelings. 'It looks remarkably like a whore's boudoir,' remarked Chris appreciatively.

'How many have you been in then?' inquired Mike, who had decided that the lounge looked rather better than he had thought it would.

'It certainly reminds me of the brothels in India,' interrupted Raz. 'They always seem to paint them red. In India red is a sexy colour.'

'Then, as long as we treat it as a sexy colour, we should find all our efforts have been worthwhile,' said Chris who was already contemplating the idea of another party now that the decorating had been completed.

Mike liked the way the tatty carpet and the battered furniture combined with the red decor. He suggested to the others that it was very reminiscent of the threadbare county house look that seemed to be so popular. 'You know that in *Country Life* and some of the design mags, you see that well-used sort of worn look to things.'

'Oh, so you fancy yourself as an interior designer now we've painted the flat, just because you bought the first tin of bloody paint,' Chris teased. 'Perhaps we should have let you do all the painting, Mike.'

'Piss off,' said Mike. 'I'm just saying that I think the flat looks really good now and, yes, I'm glad that I suggested that we decorate and I do think the red looks great, but I'm also bloody glad that its now finished.'

Two weeks later Mike came in for some stick from the other two. He had been to his optician to have his eyes tested for some new lenses for his spectacles. During the test it emerged that he was colour-blind. 'I just can't believe it!' he exclaimed in amazement.

'Well, it's true I'm afraid Sir,' the optician replied. 'Red will appear to be green and yellow will appear to be blue in your case.'

'You bought that red paint and didn't even know what fucking colour it was,' cried Chris later when Mike had told him. 'It's absolutely unbelievable.'

Almost a month later, after a discussion with Raz, Chris suggested that it might be fun and, indeed, would be expected by many of their close friends, to organise a flat warming party. The distinct smell of new paint and turpentine still hung heavily in the air, despite their leaving all the windows wide-open for at least two weeks.

'The main criteria must be that we invite twice as many women as men,' Chris informed the others. 'That gives each of us a lot more choice, being the greedy, horny bastards that we are.'

'But the birds will start complaining that there are so few

blokes, won't they?' muttered Raz who was ironing his office shirts as the others lounged around the kitchen smoking and listening to the new Kinks L.P.

'No, women don't seem to mind so much. It's the men who get really pissed off when there's no talent available at a party. The women just sit around and gossip, then they all get up and dance together. They just handle it better,' explained Chris authoritatively.

Chris and Mike veered off the subject and began discussing the respective merits of Cassius Clay over Henry Cooper but Raz gradually steered them back on course and engaged the other two in some serious discussion about the forthcoming house warming party. He was particularly keen to finalise the plans because he was, as the others would soon discover, the complete party animal, a relentless ball of energy. He wanted to be at every party and every disco that he could get to whilst hoping to screw almost every girl that he set eyes on.

'What can we do to make our party just a little bit different?' asked Mike.

'Make it virgins only,' suggested Chris. 'Or, what about a 'come naked' party? Or, a C.U.M. party for short!'

'That's disgusting Chris,' retorted Mike thinking that sometimes Chris went too far. 'You'll get your come-uppance one day for remarks like that.'

Raz sat half-listening to their banter, toying with an idea at the back of his mind. He had recently met a Swedish blonde at the Déjà Vu Club and after a few drinks and some rather horny clinches on the dance floor, he had invited her back to the then partly decorated flat where she had stayed the night with him. After making love and trying to sleep, he had found the blonde's presence very disconcerting as he was constantly being woken every quarter of an hour or so when she jumped from the bed, pulled the top bed sheet around herself and then ran down the corridor to the bathroom. After the sixth time this had occurred, Raz finally had to ask her what the problem was. Rather self-consciously she had told him that their love-making had brought on a painful bout of cystitis which had caused her to make these hurried rushes to the toilet. Whilst she stood there confessing to him, with a sheet wrapped around her, the only illumination coming from the moonlight streaming through a gap in the curtains, looking both sexy and uncomfortable at the same time, her image reminded Raz of several old movies, notably *The Robe* and *Ben Hur* where Jean Simmons and Gina Lollabrigida had been sexily dressed in togas, the simple dress of the Roman period. 'Why don't we have a Roman party?' he suggested snapping out of his daydream. 'Not only is it a great idea, but it's so simple. It costs nothing to wrap yourself in a bloody sheet, you only need a belt of some kind and some sandals, or maybe an olive branch wrapped around your head.'

'And all rather easy to remove at the appropriate time. Good thinking, Raz,' said Chris his mind running riot as he visualised the flat full of girls wearing nothing but a sheet, ready to jump into bed with him as soon as he demanded it - then, with just one strong tug of their 'toga', they lay naked before him. The Roman's had certainly had the right idea he decided with a smile.

'Yes, I think that's a really great idea,' agreed Mike. 'A Roman toga party sounds terrific!

'Do we agree then?' asked Raz triumphantly, pleased that his idea had found favour with the others. 'What do we all say? Shall we set a date sometime soon?'

'Bloody right,' cried Chris excitedly.

'The sooner, the better,' added Mike. 'Let's warm the flat up with wall-to-wall women.

'If we'd had wall-to-wall women in the first place, we would never have needed to paint the place at all,' laughed Chris.

Chapter Six

With the communal areas of the flat decorated, the forthcoming party found the boys competing to complete the decorating of their individual rooms. They spent a reasonable amount of time and effort in finishing each room to their own particular tastes. Raz's current job in publishing had been preceded by a stint with an electronic engineering company and he had still retained a love of messing about with anything mechanical or electrical. He had already fitted his own room with electric curtains, dimmer switches operating the lights and a home-made device which, at the touch of a button, could change his lighting from bright white light to dark tones of red and green. He had completely enclosed his bed with reams of muslin that he had hung from the ceiling; the general effect was reminiscent of a huge mosquito net enclosing the bed. Sitting on a table by his bed sat his Grundig tape recorder and on one special long-playing tape he had recorded three hours of thunderstorms, rain and lightening effects, copied from a tape a friend had sent him from the USA. Raz had read about these effects in a movie magazine. They were apparently used by several of Hollywood's most eligible bachelors for seduction purposes in their boudoirs. They had also become the rage in the hippie communities of San Francisco and Los Angeles.

Raz related to the others how the girls he entertained enjoyed the tapes. He explained that it was like making love in a tent in the wilds with a violent thunderstorm raging outside. When used in conjunction with his lighting effects, the whole scenario seemed even more surrealistic. Raz was secretly delighted with himself for setting his bed up in this way, especially when he realised so many girls were both amused and intrigued by his unusual set-up. He found himself quietly perusing the idea one day; there was indeed something quite weird about lying in his bed, enclosed by the swathes of cloth, encased in an orange glow, with the realistic sounds of thunder and tropical rain falling outside 'his tent', particularly when he was entertaining a girl that he especially fancied as these effects seemed to enthral and excite them so much.

Mike's bedroom, in comparison, was completely different to the others. It was sparsely furnished and stacked full of books on accountancy and economics as he was trying to study at home as much as he could for his endless examinations. His room was dominated by a heavy oak pedestal desk that he had purloined from the lounge when they had first moved in. Apart from his bed, the only other furniture was a large over-stuffed Victorian armchair that he loved to settle into to read. His room was generally a complete mess with books and clothes scattered untidily over the floor and furniture. He had paid much less attention to the decoration of his room than the other two, and was leagues behind them in the art of seductive or alluring decor. Mike was certainly as interested as his friends in the pursuit of females and pleasure, but he was too involved in his studies to pay overdue attention to what he considered extreme frivolity, although when the occasion demanded it, he was as keen as the others were to entice the girls back to his room.

But it was Chris who had the most interesting room, and also the most unusual decor. He had an adventurous streak when it came to decorating and was not averse to raiding the local shops for 'anything that he could do something with'. His room was packed with lamps made out of old tins, a table made from boxes, cheap antiques, old pictures and mirrors. He had concealed the cracks in his ceiling by completely covering it with egg trays, which he had then sprayed with metallic silver paint. He had found some old wooden beams and fashioned them into a four poster bed with curtains at each corner hanging from hooks he had positioned on the top of the posts. He was the proud owner of a mighty stereo system bought from a hi-fi enthusiast who had been forced to sell it quickly as he had badly needed the money to pay a debt. It had come complete with two huge Pye speakers that the enthusiast had commissioned directly from the factory in Cambridge. There were no chairs in the room, just some oversized cushions lying around the floor, with a pair of chrome-legged cabinets sitting on each side of the bed. Chris often enjoyed himself by attending the weekly auction sales at Hammonds, a small auctioneers just down the road from their flat. The sales would comprise a variety of goods, including antique furniture, household goods, bric-a-brac and junk. Chris loved the friendly atmosphere and he was soon on good terms with the two knowledgeable porters, Alf and Ernie, a likeable pair of jovial men both in their sixties who performed a double act full of snappy repartée whenever there was a sale on. Chris made sure he got to know Mr. Hammond, the auctioneer, and soon found out that the better acquainted you were on the 'inside', the better the information and service you received. He was soon able to recognise most of the dealers and to understand their particular traits when bidding for goods; the way some scratched their nose or gave a quick wink to show the auctioneer they were bidding, almost imperceptible to the average punter.

Occasionally Chris would invite his latest foreign lady of the moment to accompany him to the auction. They were usually both bemused and enthralled at the proceedings and he was confident that he would be scoring brownie points by introducing these young girls to such an interesting piece of English life, certainly most of them had never seen or experienced anything like it before.

On one particular preview day (the day before the sale), he was casually foraging around the lots trying to find a bargain to bid for when he came across what appeared to be a dirty, dusty, heavily chromed chair stacked beneath some broken tables and woodworm infested chairs. As furniture was sparse in his room, he was desperately on the look-out for something unusual, but trendy. Chrome, vinyl and plastic were very popular and he could see the possibilities in this chair. He pulled as much of the rubbish aside as he could. On closer inspection he realised that the red vinyl covered chair was in fact a discarded dentist's chair. He could make out the heavy round chrome base and various levers on the side. He noted that the chrome appeared to be in excellent condition underneath the dust and grime and likewise the vinyl covering. He was immediately excited by the prospect of owning the chair and visualised it sitting in the middle of his room, the chrome gleaming brightly. Because it was so unusual it seemed perfect to enhance his interior.

The next day, full of excitement and anticipation, Chris arrived at the auction. He was accompanied by his latest conquest, an intelligent, attractive, auburn-haired, French girl named Françoise who had taken the morning off from her English language course at the Bell School of Languages. Urged on by Chris, she had rung the school to excuse her absence by informing them that she had a bad cold. Chris had met Françoise the evening before in the Anchor pub where he had impressed her with his silly sense of humour and some rather lewd jokes. They had consumed quite a large amount of alcohol and found themselves nicely inebriated by closing time. He had invited her home for coffee and then bedded her. Unfortunately he had been unable to perform very well due to the excessive amount of alcohol he had drunk, but in the morning he had felt rejuvenated and they had enjoyed a leisurely and very satisfying early morning screw. They had then walked down to The Whim for breakfast. The café-cum-restaurant was a Cambridge institution run by two lovely old ladies. Chris and Françoise had eaten eggs and bacon with thick toast and home-made marmalade, washed down with lashings of 'Jacksons' breakfast tea. It was here, his arm tightly round her shoulders as he kissed her with his marmalade sweet lips, that he had persuaded her to telephone the school. They had then walked happily over to the auction house where Chris had informed Françoise that she would learn more about the English in a couple of hours at Hammonds than she would from two weeks at the Bell School. Although she had agreed to go with him, she was still uncertain as to what an auction was and found herself even more astonished when they arrived to be presented with a bewildering array of goods stacked throughout the building. Much of this appeared to her to be complete rubbish. Chris tried patiently to explain to her how the auction worked, but when he pointed out the barely discernible dentist's chair, still lying covered by the mound of rotting furniture, she was completely dumbfounded, especially when he told her that he was hoping to buy it.

'Why do you want to 'ave 'zis dirty old chair?' Françoise asked incredulously, beginning to wonder about Chris a little.

'Because it's so different, it's such an unusual piece of

62

furniture to have in your home. No-one else will have one like it,' explained Chris excitedly.

As the auction proceeded Françoise was intrigued by the rapid bidding and the general good humour and banter. Gradually she began to comprehend a little of what was going on. Lot 132 was announced by the auctioneer as 'a dentist's chrome chair, about 1950/55; with a good clean-up and the purchase of a pair of pliers, you'll be pulling those molars out in no time!' the auctioneer joked. He commenced the bidding, asking for bids of £20, then £10 and, finally receiving no response, he came down to £5. Eventually someone called out with a bid for £3. Chris nodded at the auctioneer to raise the bid to £4. A person standing behind Chris raised the bidding to £5, so Chris nodded again, excitement building up inside him. '£6,' said the auctioneer, do I hear seven?' His experienced eye roamed the room for what seemed to Chris to be ages but was in fact only three seconds. Then the auctioneer's gavel banged down. 'Sold for £6 to Mr. Chris Moore, and so on to Lot 133.'

The auction continued as Chris stood there absolutely delighted, his face split into a huge smile. He hugged Françoise happily and kissed her cheek with delight. 'That's brilliant,' he told her. 'It's a real bargain!'

Françoise, still unsure as to why Chris was so enamoured with the odd chair, was nevertheless very pleased to see his excitement and squeezed his arm with pleasure. 'I am veree happy for you,' she said. 'Now you 'ave your chair.'

Chris stepped into the musty office and paid for his purchase. Two hours later, having cajoled a van from a friend he'd spotted at the auction, the chair was delivered to the flat where they managed to manhandle it up the stairs into Chris's bedroom. It sat majestically on several old sheets of newspaper, looking even dirtier and grubbier than it had in the dingy auction room.

Françoise decided to take the opportunity to do a little shopping and to buy some wine. When she had left, Chris immediately started to clean the chair. He filled a large plastic bowl with hot water and poured in some washing-up liquid. Using a stiff brush and some old cloths, he scrubbed and wiped, delving vigorously into each nook and cranny he could find. Within half-an-hour the chrome was gleaming and the red vinyl seat and upholstered arms were shining brightly. Chris sat looking at the chair approvingly, it was like a piece of modern art he decided. He felt very pleased with himself for seeing its potential. He had discovered during the cleaning process that the chair had a small vacuum pump attached to it and, by pulling an adjacent lever, the chair hissed up and down two or three feet. By pulling another lever, the backrest inclined backwards and the whole chair tilted downwards. By pulling the lever back, the footwell was lowered and the whole chair tilted forwards. The mechanisms were very squeaky so Chris got out his trusty 3-in-1 oil can and oiled them thoroughly. Satisfied, that the cleaning job was completed, he pulled the old newspapers out from the base of the chair and threw them into the wastebasket. He sat in the chair and began experimenting with the levers; up and down, tilt to the back, tilt to the front, straight out and he was flat on his back. 'It's bloody brilliant,' he yelled loudly in delight, suddenly realising that his chair might have some unusual possibilities. 'Christ,' he said to himself disbelievingly, 'this chair could actually be the ultimate fucking machine. I've not even thought about it before, but it could be a great experience to have it away in this chair.' As he sat there thinking about this prospect, he was interrupted by Françoise returning, bearing some food for their supper and a cold bottle of white wine.

He opened the bottle, found two glasses and poured them both some wine. He had become very stimulated at the prospect of copulating on his new chair and became somewhat agitated now that Françoise was pacing admiringly around the chair. 'The chair looks great now,' she exclaimed in obvious surprise, running her hand along the chrome frame. 'I really did not believe that it would look so beautiful.'

'Well, I'm glad that you like it now,' Chris replied. 'Do you understand why I wanted it so badly?'

'Yes, yes, I do. It's very pretty,' she assured him. 'May I sit in it,' she asked, not realising he was desperately willing her to do so.

'Please, go ahead Françoise,' breathed Chris not believing his luck.

Françoise stepped carefully onto the chrome footplate and sat back in the chair, her hands clasped the ends of the armrests as she smiled across at Chris, a smile of childish delight, almost a seal of approval. Chris stepped onto the footplate facing Françoise, he bent down and kissed her lips gently, then more firmly, his tongue exploring her mouth, feeling her tongue seeking his, softly, gently, but suddenly becoming probing and more urgent, more demanding. He kissed her harder, with added vigour and became conscious of their laboured breathing becoming harsher and louder in the quiet room. As his right hand gently cupped her breast over her blouse, her breathing became quicker and he could feel her face becoming hotter as she pressed against him. He expertly moved his arm gently round her waist and under the back of her blouse and, as he pulled her body slightly towards him, she deftly arched her back to help him as he bent his forefinger under the hook of her brassiere, pulling it slightly until he felt the tension ease as her bra came loose.

They were kissing more urgently now. She gasped as his hand slid slowly around her naked breast, his finger tracing the outline of her erect nipple. He pulled her blouse over her head, taking her bra with it. He lowered his face into her soft breasts and gently sucked her nipples. She strained beneath him, hot and frenzied, as she found his belt buckle, rapidly undoing it. She fiercely tugged his zip down and pulled his erect cock from out of his jeans, revelling in the hardness and heat of it. She rubbed his cock, gently cupping his balls with her other hand, as Chris groaned with pleasure, desperate to make love to her. He pulled her skirt up and pulled her knickers roughly down her legs. Pulling them free, he threw them to the ground. Françoise raised her legs as Chris eased himself towards her opened thighs and expertly guided his cock into her. Clasping him tightly, her buttocks clenched, she began moving in time with Chris's forcing rhythm. The red vinyl covering began squeaking violently as he pounded into her, while she let out little squeals of delight. Her arms desperately grasped his body to her, her legs wrapped around his waist as she tried to clasp her feet together behind his back to pull him further into her. The chair was rocking slightly on its base, and began emitting an assortment of metallic clanking sounds as the pair rocked to and fro in their frenzy of sexual passion.

With such intensity, Chris had almost forgotten the levers on his chair, but the constant metallic knocking sound abruptly reminded him. He leaned over Françoise's body with his right arm and sought desperately to find the front lever, whilst continuing to concentrate on fucking Françoise. His hand found a lever and pulling it hard there was a loud hissing sound as the chair started rising. Françoise opened her eyes, beads of sweat gathering on her forehead as she laughed up at Chris. 'You're crazy,' she cried as the chair hissed upwards.

'Wait 'til you see this one,' he smiled, leaning over her again to the left, finding the other lever and pulling it hard down. Françoise's eyes opened wide, slightly alarmed, as the chair immediately tilted backwards with a sharp crack and then they started inclining downwards as the vacuum hissed away. Their heads were now tilted down at a lower level than their feet. Chris had to fight to stop himself sliding down head-first over Françoise. He felt a strange sensation in his genitals. It seemed as though the sudden change in elevation had somehow sucked his cock even deeper into Françoise. It felt as though his balls were becoming enveloped as well. Françoise was squealing breathlessly underneath him, both with fright and with pleasure, but also because his weight was pressing down on her. It had seemed much easier, thought Chris, when he had simply sat in the chair earlier on and experimented with the levers; it had seemed fairly tame then. Now, it was a sheer physical test just to try and stay on the bloody thing. The vinyl seat squealed violently beneath Françoise as her bum sweated and strained, sliding backwards and forwards faster and more vigorously as Chris thrust in and out, in and out, sweat pouring from their semi-clothed bodies; the chair continually emitting a multitude of metallic grunts and thumps.

'Merde, merde,' cried Françoise loudly as she came suddenly and violently, her back arching, her body tightening as her eyes rolled wide in her scarlet face, sweat running in rivulets down her face and neck. She squeezed Chris tighter and tighter, her legs tightening like a vice around him, her nails digging through his shirt as, gasping and fighting for breath, Chris came seconds later. He let out a brief scream as he flooded into her, his body taut and hard at that moment. Sweat poured down his face and onto Françoise's breasts as he finished climaxing and collapsed, uncoiling like a spring on top of her. They lay hot and heaving, trying to gulp some air into their starved lungs, unable to move as the chair groaned slightly beneath them, a faint hissing sound still discernible from below the seat.

Chris could hear Françoise's heart beating loudly as he lay exhausted against her sweat soaked breasts. Suddenly he became conscious of how squashed he felt and how uncomfortable Françoise must feel, with both of them jammed together in the chair, his weight bearing down on her so heavily. 'Shall we move over to the comfort of the bed?' he asked her, wondering if he had the energy to get up immediately.

'I think I like zis chair,' said Françoise happily ignoring his question. 'I am veree glad that you buy it.'

'Thank you,' he replied. 'I think I'm going to like it too.' He smiled with self contentment, his mind already drifting, visualising crowds of gorgeous girls standing around him, clamouring to be fucked in the gleaming chair that they had heard so much about.

Chapter Seven

Chris found himself quite taken with Françoise and, unusually for him, he made arrangements to see her again. He invited her to see the movie *Girl on a Motorcycle* starring Marianne Faithful, who was the girlfriend of Mick Jagger of the *Rolling Stones*. Chris had 'a thing' about Marianne Faithful and the reviews of the movie had been full of the sexual vibrancy that she gave off on screen, either naked or clad in tight black leather.

The next evening Chris and Françoise found themselves in the back row of the Regal Cinema. During the trailers, Chris had kissed Françoise several times, sensing the unbridled passion within her that he had experienced the day before. It was exciting for him to be with a woman who wanted sex as much as a man and who was not afraid to communicate her desires. Too much of his time seemed to be spent pussy-footing around with so many girls who seemed to drop their knickers because it was expected of them, but doing so without giving off any real feelings or passion. Sometimes it all seemed rather pointless to Chris, though the chase was what made it all worthwhile. The seduction was like a game but often the ending, the actual fucking, was a real let down; but then maybe it was for the girls as well. He had often heard girls talking amongst themselves about the short-comings of men and their failure to realise most women needed plenty of time spent on foreplay before sex. It was not just a case of 'wham, bam, thank you Ma'am' as so many men seemed to think; to Chris making love was really an art form, something to be savoured and enjoyed by both parties.

As they sat watching the film, Françoise disengaged her hand from his and began to gently and slowly rub her fingers up and down his inner thigh, her fingers curving round softly under his testicles. He felt what seemed like electric shocks passing through his jeans. Some of the images on the screen had already titillated his senses, so he quickly found himself becoming aroused at her attentions. He glanced sideways at Françoise, who seemed to be deliberately keeping her attention fixed firmly on the screen as she slowly caressed him. He began to feel more excited as he clenched his thighs and squirmed slightly in his seat trying not to bring attention to himself. Fortunately, there was no-one sitting within three seats of him, for she had now moved her hand further up and had begun massaging his cock through his jeans, rubbing her fingertips up and down the shaft. He moved uneasily in his seat as the excitement coursed through his body. His breathing became faster as he felt her fingers pulling at his brass fly buttons. He turned again to look at her, willing her to turn, but still she sat looking straight ahead seemingly intent on watching the movie. He realised that she was teasing him, deliberately staying aloof, pretending not to notice him writhing about whilst trying not to utter a sound. She had expertly opened his fly and her searching fingers pulled his underpants down to expose the head of his cock. She slowly extracted his penis from his open fly and began rubbing her hand very slowly up and down his erection, gently but firmly. He glanced desperately at the next person three seats away, hoping they would not glance in his direction, but the cinema was dark, an erotic sex scene had just started with a mélange of blurred images which made him feel even hornier. As she ran her fingernails up his penis, he tried desperately to stop his knees banging the back of the seat in front of him, clenching his buttocks and thighs to try and control the pressure building up in his genitals as he became more agitated. She was still looking straight ahead, her face a picture of passiveness in the dim light. It was driving him mad. What a clever ploy he thought, what a sexy bitch! She increased the pace of her hand as she wrapped her fingers more firmly round his shaft and began fully masturbating him. He looked down and saw her hand moving up and down, the swift movements catching little shafts of light from the projector. He felt his blood pounding, his body becoming tense as he strained hard not to make a sound. He could feel the explosion coming and was trying to hold his breath, trying to stop himself crying out or groaning with ecstasy. As her hand moved even faster, he braced himself. His hands gripped the armrests tightly as suddenly his semen pumped out, his relief slightly tempered by feelings of guilt at being detected, but the person three seats away still seemed unaware of what had happened for which he was very grateful. Expertly, Françoise had reached over him with her other hand and neatly gathered his cum in a handkerchief which she left gathered around his now limp dick so that he could mop himself up.

On the screen Marianne was climaxing with her lover. Chris glanced at Françoise again, she was still looking straightahead but now he detected a faint smile of satisfaction and her lips were slightly open. Only then did she turn to him, coquettishly, half smiling, her eyes catching the light briefly as she looked up at him through her long, dark eyelashes. 'Was that nice for you?' she whispered in his ear huskily. 'You are a bad boy!'

'For Christ's sake,' he replied, 'you're the bad one. You're a very sexy lady. That was fantastic.' He squeezed her hand and kissed her lightly on the lips. He could feel the sweat gathered under his armpits, his body glowing with the warmth of his exertions as a great sense of relief seemed to flood through his body after the intensity of the arousal Françoise had stimulated in him. He determined to give her a good time when they returned to the flat later that evening. 'Wait 'til the boys hear about this,' he grinned to himself at the thought. 'A bird unzipping my pecker and wanking me off in the bloody cinema, can you believe that boys?' He could hardly wait to tell them both when he got home but, right now, he felt exhausted. His body seemed lifeless and his arms, legs and buttocks were still aching from the strain; within five minutes he was sleeping like a baby.

He was woken up twenty minutes later by Françoise when the film had ended, 'Wait 'til I tell the boys,' he smiled again to himself as he held her hand and led her from the cinema, feeling no sense of annoyance at all that he had missed most of the movie.

70

Chapter Eight

Gathered in their local pub, the 'Live and Let Live', one night, the three flatmates each agreed that the eighty-odd acceptances to attend their party were enough to handle. One major problem when holding a party in Cambridge on a Friday or Saturday night was the number of students and young people wandering the streets hoping to find a possible party to gate crash, so keeping the number of invited guests down helped to avoid problems at the door.

Mike recalled an incident a few weeks before when he had attended a party in a three storey house in Jesus Lane where so many people had gate crashed that he had been trapped by the crowd on the second floor. Luckily he had met a gorgeous black student from Nigeria who had actually latched on to him when she had become a little panicky on realising that the house had become so dangerously overcrowded. They could not even get downstairs to replenish their drinks. The pungent smoke from numerous cannabis joints hung heavily in the air whilst there seemed to be a slight air of menace pervading the drunken crowd. They had both decided after some time to make an effort to leave, but it had taken twenty minutes to push and shove themselves through the solid, heaving mass of sweating bodies overcrowding the small house. Emerging gratefully into the street, bruised, shaken and dishevelled, the girl found she had lost a gold necklace in the mêlée without a hope in hell of retrieving it. There was no way that they could go back inside to search for it. Despite Mike's efforts to console her, she was so upset that she went off home alone sobbing disconsolately even though an hour earlier, trapped upstairs in the top room, she had danced closely to him while he had gently nibbled her ear. She had responded by kissing him softly and sucking his lips sexily with her strong, white teeth. She had reacted positively to his suggestion that they spent the night together and he had become very excited at the prospect of her firm, dark body lying beside him. Then it had all gone wrong!

After this lesson, Mike was adamant that he would not want their party to end up as overcrowded as that, with all its attendant fears and problems. The others agreed that gatecrashers were definitely not wanted at their party and so resolved to keep the door locked all the time to make sure that no-one got in who was not invited.

They had all worked extremely hard to make certain that their party would be a success and there was general agreement that the time spent in preparing the flat had been worthwhile. The general detritus left by the lady living there previously had been thrown out and the proliferation of her pictures, vases, china and glass had been cleared. Mike had gathered up some battered old gilt picture frames from a builder's skip across the street and they now hung along the hallway, while some old, dusty, Victorian lampshades, complete with tassels, from the same source had replaced the nasty plastic shades that had been there initially.

'It looks really brilliant now,' said Mike to the others one evening, pleased with their efforts. 'The flat's got a really weathered, lived-in look, like the comfortable face of an old sailor. I'm very happy with it.' He had been brought up in a succession of old houses which his elderly parents had never had enough money to decorate properly, nor to replace the worn-out furnishings so he was used to this look, it made him feel at home, more secure. The others seemed to like it too, especially now they had all decorated their own rooms to their own taste. The odd thing was that Mike had not spent nearly as much time on his own room as the others had on theirs even though he had certainly pulled his weight in decorating and cleaning the communal areas. Chris could never understood Mike's attitude and why his room was always so untidy and messy.

The Friday evening before the party saw the three boys putting the final arrangements into place. Raz had set up a fine music system in the lounge, using his coveted Leak amplifier with the large valves, complemented by a couple of enormous speakers over four feet high borrowed from his office. These speakers were so powerful that they were mainly used for outside communications work such as conferences, rallies and shows.

They had cleared a space for dancing in the large red lounge, shoving the battered sofa and the armchairs against one wall. There was still a faint but perceptible odour of fresh paint so Raz burnt a few joss sticks around the flat, a trick learnt from his parents who always used them to banish any smells of curry from their home after cooking. Chris had purchased some large church candles from the religious shop on King's Parade which they placed at strategic points on the window sills and shelves. All the light bulbs were changed for low wattage red or orange ones in order to create an atmosphere, as Chris put it, 'of sexual allure.'

Inspecting the lighting effects that evening before they walked to the Six Bells for a few beers, they congratulated themselves on the dark, sultry atmosphere that they had created. Between them they had assembled an enormous quantity of records and Raz had recorded some of them on his Grundig tape recorder so that several hours of varied music could be played non-stop. There was everything from Sinatra to the Beatles and the Beach Boys to Nat King Cole. 'You've got music to dance your bollocks off, or music to cream your pants by,' explained Raz who was an expert at judging the mood of a party and matching the music to suit that particular mood.

Saturday evening arrived and Mike and Chris had a few laughs admiring each other in their 'toga' outfits as they paraded around the flat showing off to each other. 'Christ, it's a bit cool round my goolies. Now I know what it's like to be a Scotsman,' said Mike who had decided not to wear underpants. 'I don't want to spoil the line,' he told the other two.

They set to work creating an enormous bowl of Sangria, chopping up cucumbers, apples and oranges and throwing in sprigs of fresh mint. Several bottles of lemonade were used as the base for the punch, mixed with seven bottles of red wine, together with some remnants of various bottles of spirits, including port and vermouth that they found laying around. These were all poured in together and stirred around with some sticks of cinnamon and several cloves. For good measure, some ice was added. Mike's tasting every couple of minutes was accompanied by 'mmms' and 'aahs' as he sought to obtain the perfect mix. Eventually, with the bowl almost overflowing, he was satisfied and asked Chris for his opinion. 'Oh, that's brilliant Mike,' said Chris delving the large spoon into the punch again and sipping another mouthful, immediately realising the strength in the innocuous looking dark liquid. 'Raz,' he called down the hall, 'come and taste the punch Mike's made. It's brutal.'

Raz, who had been sleeping, ambled out of his bedroom, pulling on his underpants as he entered the kitchen. 'Try this,' said Chris offering the spoon to Raz.

Raz, who was becoming very excited and was really looking forward to the party, took the spoon and tasted the Sangria. 'Wow, that's really nice. You can tell it's got some oomph in it. That should get people going nicely,' he said enthusiastically.

'Let's hope it gets the girls wanting our bodies rather than falling downstairs or spewing up in the loo,' said Chris seriously, who had suffered the experience of both disasters at various times in the past.

Raz went off to get dressed while Chris and Mike lit the candles set up around the flat and put out bowls of various nibbles. Mike had drunk so much of the strong punch whilst tasting it, that he suddenly found himself feeling extremely light headed. When the doorbell rang and the first of the guests noisily arrived to cheers and laughter as everyone came face-to-face with their sheet-encased friends, Mike made a mental note to slow down a little otherwise he realised that he would be pissed out of his brains before anyone else had started drinking. He began ladling the punch out into the wild assortment of glasses and cups that the boys had amassed between them. He was amazed as he glanced around at the guests crowding into the room how much trouble some of them had gone to with their leather sandals and sashes tied loosely around their waists. Some of the men had even made rings of thorns to wear round their heads.

As the Beatles song, *This Boy*, played gently in the background, the volume of conversation and laughter increased as more people began arriving and crowding the room.

Mike had often thought that much of the success of a fancy dress party was due to the hilarity caused to most of the party goers at finding their friends dressed up and looking so different to normal. The immediate conversation and excited laughter instantly created a great atmosphere. He glanced around at the crowd enjoying themselves and decided with some satisfaction that the party was taking off rather well.

Chris and Raz roamed amongst everyone, making introductions and attempting to put people at their ease, always an important task when large numbers of people who have never met each other are herded together. Chris had a theory that parties were occasions where people meet each other, but to overcome the initial misgivings that many people had when they arrived, the more people you introduced to each other, the more at ease they would all feel and the more successful the party would become.

The party seemed to be going well and, as ever the joker, Chris had attached a rather obscene looking pink, flaccid pork sausage to the front of his y-fronts, hidden by the front of his toga. Whilst chatting to a trio of French girls, one of whom had immediately taken his fancy, choosing his moment carefully, he suddenly stepped back and flipped his toga way above his waist, exposing the limp sausage hanging grotesquely from his underpants. The impact was immediate. The girls stopped in mid-conversation, completely taken aback, their eyes opened wide in astonishment and their mouths dropped open. They were utterly speechless for a couple of seconds, but as the realisation of what had happened crept into their brains, huge self-conscious smiles erupted over their faces as they doubled-up shrieking and laughing hysterically. Groups of people standing nearby turned around to see what was causing the uproar and soon noticed Chris, who was now violently gyrating his hips, swinging the pork sausage from side-to-side. They too joined in the raucous laughter. The dim light made it difficult to discern that the object of laughter was indeed a pork sausage rather than the real thing, which was one reason why Chris so loved this joke. It never seemed to upset people although occasionally people could be mildly embarrassed, but the spontaneous outbursts of good natured laughter all helped to create a good party atmosphere.

'What if I'd stuck my own todger out, that would have shocked them even more, if they'd known. Mind you, I'd have trouble competing with the size of that pork sausage, so perhaps I'd better leave things as they are,' Chris told Mike later on. 'It's better to have the pork sausage as the joke rather than my own apparatus. I know it's juvenile, but if it gives a laugh to people why not?' Chris knew from experience that most girls love a man who makes them laugh and jokes like this would always give him an edge, particularly where there was a girl he fancied, as was the case here with one of the French girls.

Raz meanwhile found himself downstairs at the front door (being the bulkiest of the flatmates) letting the invited guests in but keeping out the crowds of gatecrashers who'd heard about the party taking place and were gathered outside trying to bluff their way in.

Already several people had arrived at the party who had been properly invited but who had not made the effort to wear togas, which slightly annoyed Raz as it was such a simple fancy dress, requiring little trouble to sort out. Suzi, a friend of his from the office, arrived with her sister Caroline. Raz noticed appraisingly that the girls were beautifully turned out, both of them had long blonde hair with their togas slanted across their chests to show one bare shoulder and a little cleavage. They each wore gold sandals and sashes to complement their fairly short togas, which showed off their long, slender legs perfectly.

'Would it be OK for Tony to come in?' purred Suzi, indicating a dark, handsome character with black curly hair standing behind the two girls. He was wearing jeans and a T-shirt and looked rather sheepish.

'Who is Tony?' asked Raz, peering indifferently behind the girls at the tall dark man who stood patiently on the step.

'He's a very old friend,' replied Caroline. 'You'll like him Raz. We've know Tony for ages.'

'I've got two bottles of sparkling if that helps,' said Tony stepping forward and holding up a bottle of champagne in each hand.

'Please Raz, let Tony come in with us,' pleaded Suzi. 'He's great fun, honestly,' she added in a whisper.

'OK,' said Raz, still wary of the tall dark Tony, but swayed by the girls pleading and the two bottles of champagne waved in his face. 'Surely the guy couldn't be too bad with a gesture like that,' he decided and ushered them all into the small hallway and up the stairs. 'Barbara Ann' boomed out as the Beach Boys did their stuff. The conversation was becoming louder and some people had started to dance in the lounge whilst others were singing along to the music and enjoy the congenial feeling of excitement and fun of the party.

Mike had long ago given up handing out drinks but was still ensconced in the kitchen, squeezed in with about twenty others. He was enjoying a good-natured argument with a friend he'd invited from his office who was known for his staunch Conservative views and a champion of Edward Heath, Leader of the Opposition. Mike was a Labourite through and through and believed that the Socialist leader, Harold Wilson, was doing a good job. They both loved to argue about politics until they were blue in the face, even though they respected each other's views. His friend eventually wandered off to the loo, so Mike managed to edge through the crowd and pour himself another Sangria.

'Why do people always congregate, like sardines, in the kitchen at parties?' asked a pretty girl. 'Is it purely because the booze is usually kept in the kitchen?'

'I think that's probably right. They arrive and get themselves a drink and somehow once they're talking to people they know, they never get out of the kitchen at all,' said Mike, wondering who the girl was with.

Raz pushed his way slowly through the crowd in the lounge, dragging the two blonde sisters behind him, with Tony following. He found Mike still in the kitchen drinking sangria and talking to the pretty girl. He introduced the two girls to them and then turned and took the bottles of champagne from Tony and introduced him to Mike as well. 'Hi Mike,' said Tony shaking hands. 'I hope you don't mind me coming uninvited but I called round to see the girls tonight and they said they were coming to this party. They insisted that I come along to meet you all this evening. I'm sorry I'm not dressed properly'

'That's OK,' replied Mike, who was now drooling at the two gorgeous blondes standing beside him. 'What do you do Tony?' asked Mike who had decided that he must be the boyfriend of one of the girls.

'I'm a ladies hairdresser,' replied Tony. 'I've done the girls hair this evening especially for your party tonight.'

'Well, you've done a pretty good job,' said Mike

approvingly, scarcely able to take his eyes off the two blonde girls, particularly Suzi the slightly smaller one.

'Yes, Tony's a brilliant hairdresser.' assured Suzi. 'You're always winning competitions aren't you Tony?'

'Well, sometimes, if I'm lucky,' answered Tony modestly. 'If I cheat a little or bribe the judges,' he added, his eyes glinting mischievously.

'You've certainly made your flat look good for the party,' said Suzi, turning appraisingly to Mike. 'How many of you live here?'

She has a really husky, sultry voice thought Mike. It was the type of voice that reminded him of whisky, cigarettes, night-clubs and louche living in general. It was very sexy and very appealing.

'There's three of us at present,' replied Mike. 'Raz, who you know, myself and Chris, who's somewhere around. We're hoping to find one other person as we've got a spare bedroom at the moment.'

'Oh,' said Suzi, 'I think that Tony might be looking for a place,' she smiled at Mike warmly and turned to Tony who was conversing with Caroline. She tapped his shoulder gently and raised her voice slightly so that he could hear her above the hubbub. 'Tony, aren't you looking for a room in a shared flat?' she asked him, arching her eyebrow and indicating towards Mike.

'Yes I am,' he replied with interest.

'We've got a spare room here,' said Mike 'but we haven't done anything about it. If you're interested we could let you know next week after we've talked it over, when we're sober and we've had a chance to talk to you in more detail.'

'That's fantastic,' Tony cried, a broad smile breaking out over his face. Mike thought that he detected a faint accent coming through, Italian perhaps? He looked Italian. Most hairdressers are Italian anyway decided Mike straining to hear what Tony was trying to say to him above the noise.

'If you would consider me, I'm completely housetrained, I'm clean and tidy and I can cook. I don't snore or leave rings in the bath or turds in the toilet and I don't piss on the seat. I do great hair. I'm solvent and I love women.'

Everyone laughed. Mike confirmed again that they would talk about it during the next week. He glanced at Suzi, noticing the look of interest on her face as she smiled demurely back at him. He took the opportunity to ask her to dance, still wondering whether she was with Tony or not, so he turned and asked her, 'which one of you is with Tony?', hoping fervently that it would not be Suzi.

'Oh, neither of us. We've just known Tony for ages. We grew up with his sisters at school,' Suzi replied, a smile playing around the sides of her mouth.

As they moved across to the lounge, Raz caught Mike's arm. 'Take care of Suzi please, otherwise my name will be mud in the office on Monday,' he teased, speaking loudly enough for Suzi to hear. He laughed, giving her a sly wink, his eyes beaming in delight as he turned to walk over to change the music.

Mike leaned over, managing to grab Raz's arm and whispered in his ear, 'A slow one this time if you please my man.' He nodded his head slightly towards Suzi so that Raz fully understood his meaning.

'Ah, message understood,' replied Raz nodding his head and turning away again. As the record ended Mike smiled appreciatively down at Suzi. What a gorgeous bird she is he thought to himself. Just then the husky sound of Ketty Lester singing *Love Letters* enveloped the hot crowded room. 'Oh, great record Raz,' he smiled to himself as he put his arms gently around Suzi, feeling the outline of her shoulder blades and smelling the sweet tangy perfume of her hair. He felt a slight tightening sensation in his stomach and a faint stirring in his loins. 'Christ, I've only just met her. I've hardly said a word to her. Don't let me get a hard-on and spoil it too soon,' he prayed. He looked dreamily into her eyes and felt he could sense an instant attraction on her part too. 'Your voice sounds a little like this,' he told her, 'sort of husky and sexy.'

'Thank you, that's very sweet of you to say so,' she replied, her blue eyes catching the reflection of a light somewhere as she reached up and gently pulled Mike's face towards her, down until his lips reached hers and she gave him a long, warm, lingering kiss. He knew then that he was in and there was no need to worry about any arousal taking place down below, in fact, she was already pulling him closer to her, her hips gyrating slightly against him.

'Happy Flat Warming,' he thought to himself, smiling down at Suzi happily. Oblivious to the noise and the people crowded around them, he was feeling on top of the world and as they held each other tightly, he could not have been more contented.

Chapter Nine

Much later the next morning, as they sat amongst the debris of the previous evening, the general consensus amongst the three boys was that their house warming had been a great success. The stink of cigarette smoke, of stale beer and rancid wine still hung heavily in the air. Assorted wine bottles, glasses, beer cans, plates of unfinished food and overflowing ashtrays lay scattered everywhere. Some of the candles had burnt down and damaged the surfaces they stood on, spilt wine had stained the carpet in places and, oddly enough, even some of the walls were stained where wine had somehow been splashed over them.

Chris was suffering with a mighty hangover and between alternate glasses of water and mugs of tea, was trying to sober up whilst making some half-hearted attempts to clear up the mess. Raz had emerged from his room with one of the French girls from the Bell School. Both were complaining bitterly of terrible hangovers. For once, Raz's flashing smile and wide-open eager eyes had been replaced by a tight, pained look, distorting his face. His bloodshot eyes attempted to peer out through slits in his tortured greyish countenance. He looked like death - and felt like it too! He attacked the aspirin bottle with relish, offering some to the girl, both of them gulping down the tablets with the help of strong mugs of hot, sweet tea.

Chris, although feeling dreadful himself, could not stop smirking at Raz; to observe him in this unusual state was just such a contrast to the man he and Mike were getting to know so well. The 'Party Animal' was usually the life-and-soul of any gathering, today he was obviously suffering badly, his tail was between his legs, that was for sure.

'Oh, my head,' groaned Raz holding his head in his hands. 'I feel bloody awful. I blame it on that bloody punch of yours, Mike.'

'Well, I must say, I feel pretty good myself,' said Mike

impishly, lying quietly entwined with Suzi on the sofa. She gave him a doey-eyed look and squeezed his arm playfully.

'It's OK for you Mike, you two went to bed just after one o'clock, just when the party was warming-up nicely,' chimed Chris from the kitchen as he started the washing up.

'It was already warm enough for me,' replied Mike as Suzi, lowering her eyes in embarrassment, tightened her grip on his arm and sniggered foolishly. 'Anyway, how did you get on Chris?' asked Mike. 'I saw you showing your pork sausage to some of the French birds early on. Raz ended up with Françoise here. What happened to you? You're not losing your touch are you?' he teased as Raz started to moan once more, his hands clutching his head, while the French girl plied him with more strong tea and put her arm around his shoulders sympathetically.

'Christ, you wouldn't believe it,' said Chris coming to the doorway of the lounge. 'I pulled one of those girls from the Bell School too. She was really nice, but at 7 o'clock this morning she jumped up, pulled her clothes on and shot off to the early-morning mass at the Catholic church. I do not understand these bloody religious freaks!' he told the others, obviously exasperated. 'I suppose she went off to confess to God that she'd just engaged in a bloody good shagging session.'

Mike and Chris had found out one very important mutual factor in their short relationship. Both were confirmed atheists and they both had a fairly irreverent attitude to most religious beliefs. Chris's outburst merely caused Mike to nod his head in passive agreement. To his astonishment, he felt Suzi's body tightening as Chris finished speaking. She suddenly sat up and pushed herself vigorously away from him. 'Look,' she said angrily, 'I'm fairly religious myself. I think you guys have to respect other people's beliefs. I don't think you should trample over someone like that because they believe in God.'

'I agree with Chris,' said Mike, seizing the opportunity to back-up his friend but also wondering how Suzi would react, especially if he wound her up a little. 'I think it's a load of bollocks. The girl's jumped out of bed after Chris had asked her to spend the night with him and she's gone off to confess her bloody sins at the church when she should have stayed here and done the fucking washing-up!'

Even Raz, nursing his raging hangover couldn't help laughing out loud at Mike's outrageous statement. In fact, he had to try and verify in his own befuddled mind that he had heard Mike correctly. 'Raz, you don't believe in this shit as well do you?' cried Suzi unbelievably. 'I didn't realise you were such a male chauvinist pig. I just can't believe that you all mean what you've just said,' she glanced severely over at Chris and turned to glare back at Mike.

'Seriously Suzi,' said Raz gently, seemingly trying to defuse the situation. 'They're only trying to wind you up, although I must say I agree with everything that's been said,' he added mischievously.

'Exactly,' said Mike, eager to see how far Suzi would go before she exploded.

'Oh, so you're agreeing that everyone who's religious is a bloody freak are you?' shouted Suzi, slapping Mike in the chest.

'No shouting please Suzi,' pleaded Raz holding both hands up to his throbbing forehead. 'Let's have a bit of give and take everybody, please.'

'Yes, it's not nice what you say about my friend,' the French girl said to Chris. She was looking uncomfortable and somewhat bemused.

'Don't worry my dear, they're only playing with words,' said Raz. 'They don't really mean it.' He glanced at Suzi imploringly. 'They're just trying to wind you up Suzi, rather like people do at the office on a bad day, just to get a reaction from you.'

Chris sat down on the sofa to explain. 'Look, all I'm trying to say is forget the freaks bit, that's a little out of order, but the trouble with religion is that it gets such a hold on you, like the French girl having to jump up and run off like that because it's supposed to be the right thing to do. She would probably have preferred to stay here, relax and have more fun but she's been processed by the Catholic religion to make sure that every Sunday she has to confess her sins. It's just such a hypocritical act to me,' explained Chris, trying to placate Suzi's anger and feeling guilty that he'd upset Raz's girl.

'What is pathetic is the bloody way you and Mike see the feminist issue, as though all women should be at your beck and call and have no beliefs of our own. We're not just slaves to be summoned when you want to eat or fuck. We've got brains and minds of our own. We don't just have to bear kids and slave over hot stoves for you men any more. We can even, thanks to the Pill, decide how, when and whom we want to shag. That French girl might have had enough of you for all you know Chris and just made up her mind to attend confession as an excuse to get up and leave. It's your bloody ego that's been hurt, isn't it?' Suzi asked him vehemently. 'All bloody men are the same, aren't they?' she added angrily, glancing across at the French girl for confirmation.

Mike sat watching attentively, admiring Suzi's fire and spirit. He was suitably impressed as she had attacked first Chris, then himself and, also, Raz, her office colleague. He realised Chris was still slightly drunk, although he was obviously not feeling as bad as Raz. They had all delivered some facetious comments but Suzi was certainly a feisty lady and he could only admire her spirit and vigour and the way she had stood up for women in general.

Unexpectedly Chris chimed in. 'Look Suzi, maybe I was out of order. I absolutely accept what you've said. I liked the way you stood up against us. You're obviously a lady with a lot of balls and I respect you for that, so may I apologise for sounding like a chauvinist twat.' He winked at her and raised his mug of tea. 'Here's to Suzi, who has most certainly and convincingly put me in my place.'

'Anyway, it was a great party,' said Suzi raising her own mug and leaning over to clink Chris's mug whilst trying to disguise the satisfied grin that spread easily across her face.

Chapter Ten

A couple of days after the party, when their hangovers had receded, Tony was invited back to the flat which still smelt faintly of stale beer and cigarette smoke. Undeterred by the grilling of the three flatmates and having passed the tests set up by the trio, which were basically to answer correctly their more intimate and probing questions to decide whether his lifestyle would fit in with theirs, they unanimously agreed that Tony was the perfect person to join their mad sixties lifestyle with its pursuit of hedonistic tastes. Tony told them that he was, as he put it, a 'crazy bloody Italian,' and had satisfied himself that he would be comfortable living with such a happy group of reprobates.

He moved in two weeks later and brought with him, much to the amazement of the others, his collection of three female mannequins. Tony enjoyed dressing them up in saucy underwear and placing them around his room like statues. Chris soon commandeered one and began simulating copulation with it in the lounge, which caused some amusement to the others. One was then strung from the ceiling in the bathroom much to the surprise of later guests who, when answering calls of nature, were often startled out of their wits to find the naked mannequin gazing down at them.

After the first few weeks, Tony had settled in happily and life at the flat was back to normal with women coming and going all the time, while the boys tried to keep the flat relatively clean and tidy. The group had established a rota for the general cleaning; these arrangements worked well with everyone pulling their weight and there were few disagreements. Mike and Chris, having lived together previously in their small flat, had already sorted out their own trivial problems. Mike had never even made his own bed until he lived with Chris. Chris, who was very methodical and tidy had tried to ensure that Mike became tidy and shared the housework. At the new flat in Mawson Road, the rules of cleanliness and tidiness were only attached to their shared living areas so what happened in their own rooms was up to each individual. Mike soon reverted to leaving his bed unmade and his room untidy so Chris named his room, 'the fucking tip;' there were clothes strewn all over the bed and chucked on the floor, remnants of left-over meals congealed on plates, books and records were scattered everywhere and empty beer cans covered every conceivable surface. Chris could never come to terms with Mike's untidiness. Because Mike was so methodical and deep-thinking about everything else in his life, Chris could never understand how he allowed his room to become such an unholy mess.

Meanwhile Tony had soon converted his room into a shrine to his hairdressing abilities. The walls were covered in photographs of award winning hairstyles he had designed, atop his selected models. The mantelpiece was crowded with the numerous cups and medals that he had won in various competitions. His suits and shirts were hung in colour sequences on a long moveable rail against one wall, while his socks and underpants were all carefully laid out in separate sections of his chest of drawers. He always had fresh flowers placed in a large white vase on a small round table in the corner of the room. His pride and joy was a magnificent Bang and Olufsen stereo, with all his records stacked neatly on a special shelf he had made in an alcove. A silver drinks tray sat on a cabinet next to his bed, replete with bottles of red wine and assorted spirits. He made sure there was always a freshly laundered dressing gown hanging beside his own ready for use by the next lady that he invited back to his room. The gowns were draped over the two female mannequins that he had brought with him. They both stood anonymously in the corner of his room, like silent voyeurs. Occasionally one of his female companions would turn them so that they faced the wall. His background was evident in the Italian flag and pictures of Rome, from where his family had originated, that were placed around the room.

Raz worked longer hours than most of the others, sometimes not returning home in the evening until 8 or 9 o'clock so, inevitably, he tried to excuse himself for not completing his full share of the household cleaning. But after a couple of minor altercations with the others, resulting in a half-hearted demand from the rest that he pull his weight, Raz disappeared from the room with a somewhat guilty grin on his face. From that point onwards, the Sikh carried out his share of the household duties with gusto and none of the others had to reprimand him ever again.

One evening shortly after Tony had moved in, Chris called a meeting of them all to discuss any potential problems that might occur, such as one of them losing their jobs and thus becoming unable to pay the rent, or, even someone leaving the front door open by mistake, allowing a thief to get in. One problem Chris put to them all, concerned women. There were already hordes of girls passing in and out of the flat. One of the neighbours had even enquired whether the flat had now become a language school as there were so many foreign females coming and going all the time. Chris also perceived that there might be a problem if two of the boys coveted the same girl or, as he put it, 'jealousy might rear its ugly head' if one of the girls someone had brought home started flirting with someone else. Chris had decided months ago that life after Jane left no room for falling in love, there were just too many women available in Cambridge to have fun with. Chris put forward a motion to the others that if any problems occurred over women in the flat, there would be an immediate vote amongst them all and if they voted by majority that someone or something was out of order, that decision would stand with no arguments. 'We don't want our friendship or the community spirit fucked up by fights over a tart do we?' Chris appealed to them. There was general assent that they did not.

They also agreed that the voting system would apply to their rent and all the shared bills, such as gas, electricity and the 'phone if any of them got behind with their payments. At the end of this meeting, sustained by plenty of beer and fish and chips from the local 'chippy', there was a general consensus that Chris had instigated a very fair system, and so it proved. During the entire period they all spent together at Mawson Road over several years, there were never any problems with sharing the bills and no jealousy or bickering over any females that came through their door. The pact brought the four flatmates closer together, it was a bond of sharing, no-one had an excuse not to pull his weight and it really gave to each of them a feeling of fairness knowing that any disagreement would be sorted out by popular vote.

Shortly after this high-spirited session an incident occurred that demonstrated how astute Chris had been to present the idea to them. Tony, who let it be known that he had a special penchant for light haired ladies, had met yet another attractive Swedish blonde passing through his salon. She informed him that she was studying English in Cambridge and was working as an au pair for an academic family in Hills Road. He had cut and styled her hair, then taken her for a coffee during his lunch break. He learnt that the family she worked for had gone away for three days to visit relatives in Manchester and had left her in charge of the house. Tony, with his Italian background ensuring that he had never been a shy or retiring type, immediately suggested that he call round that evening with a bottle of wine. She had already warmed to him and being absolutely delighted with her new hair and also finding his sense of humour much to her liking, happily agreed to his suggestion.

So, that evening, which she had told him was the last before the family returned home, Tony called round to see Anita, accompanied in his usual generous manner with not one, but two bottles of wine. They happily consumed these over the next three hours, in between a great deal of kissing, cuddling and minor foreplay before ending up in the academic couple's bed and, according to Tony later, 'having a high old time.' Indeed, he liked Anita so much that he invited her to call round to the flat at Mawson Road to spend another night with him. He suggested Wednesday, a couple of days ahead. He gave her his spare key and explained where his room was so that if she arrived before him she could wait there if none of the boys were around. He was out that night but expected that he would be back to the flat by about 11 o'clock. She explained to him that she would have to leave her room very quietly when the family were asleep and return before they awoke the next morning in order to look after the children.

That Wednesday found Tony dancing at the Taboo Club with Raz and Mike. During the evening they had all become completely enamoured with the new scantily dressed dancers, both from Holland, who danced extremely provocatively in special cages on each side of the bar. Tony, who was drinking and having fun with the others, had somehow completely forgotten his arrangement with the Swedish au pair.

Chris, meanwhile, had been out on a date with Joanne, a pretty secretary who worked at the Norwich Union insurance office. They had been out for a meal and some drinks and he had persuaded her to return to the flat. He'd put on some soft music in his room, turned the lights down low and managed to ensconce her in the dentist's chair, where she had gently but firmly repelled all his advances despite all his skills in trying to seduce her. 'Look, Chris. I'm not that sort of girl although I really like you,' she insisted, 'it's really nice just kissing and cuddling.' Even the tipping mechanism and the gentle mechanical movement rising up and down did not seem to win her over, even though she obviously found it highly amusing.

The unforeseen culmination of the evening's activities occurred when, whilst kissing Chris passionately, the bottom of her blouse (apparently her favourite hand embroidered one), which Chris had slyly succeeded in pulling out of her jeans in his desperate attempts to fondle her breasts, became caught in one of the wheel mechanisms operating the levers. Her blouse was suddenly pulled taut as he leaned down and kissed her ear whilst straddling her body, pulling the lever to tilt her body backward. Unaware of her predicament, Chris suddenly became aware of the girl's blouse tightening abruptly as he pulled the lever. There was the sound of material tearing as several buttons popped off with the sudden force exerted on the trapped material. Joanne cried out in horror. Mistaking this for desire, thinking that she had torn her blouse open with a new-found passion for him, and faced with a fine pair of breasts peering out from her brassiere, he leant down to kiss the top of her breasts. Joanne, convinced that Chris had torn her blouse off and was about to rape her, brought her knee up sharply, hard into his groin, whilst slapping him fiercely around the face with her right hand. Chris let out a yell of pain and half fell, half slithered off the footwell of the dentist's chair. He sank to the floor on his knees in anguish, clutching his throbbing testicles. 'Jesus Christ,' he groaned, 'what the fuck was that for?'

'Look at this, you bastard,' she screamed at him vehemently, trying to extricate her trapped blouse from the somewhat oily mechanism under the lever. 'This is, or was, my best blouse and now you've bloody ruined it just trying to get your end away, you wanker!'

Chris looked up slowly and realised what had happened. As she extricated the edge of the blouse from the mechanism, he could see it was now torn to pieces and covered in oil. He slowly realised how the blouse had burst open and why he'd been mistaken. She had obviously thought that he was responsible and that was why she had kicked the hell out of his goolies. He suddenly felt very guilty, after all, she was obviously a nice girl, not like some of those tarts who couldn't wait to get their clothes off. Having a fuck with them was just like drinking a cup of coffee. 'Look Joanne, I'm really sorry. Let me buy you a new blouse, please Joanne,' he pleaded crawling on his hands and knees collecting the buttons that had been torn off.

'You bastard,' she yelled at him, tears filling her eyes. 'You've spoilt my evening and ruined my blouse. I told you I didn't sleep with any old Tom, Dick or Harry. I have to get to know someone first. I'm not like all the other tarts you have up here, all those easy lays. I've more respect for myself than that, you shit head!' She sprang to her feet, leaving the blouse trapped in the oily mechanism, grabbed her jacket from the bed, put it on over her bra and ran to the door. She slammed it hard and ran down the stairs, slamming the front door even harder. He could hear her heels clitter-clattering down the street as he struggled to get up from the floor. He groaned again and clutched his groin. 'I'll have to have a look at my balls and hope she hasn't severely damaged anything,' he mumbled to himself.

She was probably right, he was a shit, but he had only been trying to entice her to sleep with him by using all his seduction techniques. Often the girls that said no ended up saying yes after all. Most girls loved his chair too. Maybe he should have started off more gently with her, waited until another time maybe? It wasn't his fault her blouse had become tangled up in the bloody machine. Shit, in the morning he would ring her up and apologise profusely, send her some flowers and certainly buy her a new blouse. 'Christ, I don't need her running around telling everybody I tried to rape her, that not only wouldn't be fair but it could ruin my reputation,' he reasoned to himself. He winced with pain again, but managed to pull himself up into a standing position. He then painfully limped to the bathroom where he examined his privates in the mirror. Luckily he could see nothing wrong, not even any bruising. His face was rather blotchy where she'd whacked him though.

With the pain in his groin slowly subsiding, he undressed and went back to the bathroom where he rinsed his face and brushed his teeth. Feeling tired and upset, he decided to go to bed. 'It wasn't often he was in bed alone by 11:45,' he smiled grimly to himself.

Laying quietly in bed with the pain slowly ebbing away, he thought about the unfortunate events of the evening. He often encountered girls like Joanne who would timidly explain that they did not sleep with guys they didn't know, but he often changed their minds and it was part of the fun of seducing women. The chase was often more enjoyable than the sex act itself, all womanisers agreed with that. A vision of Joanna's face swam blearily into view, contorted in anger as she wrapped her ripped blouse around her waist. 'I must ring her tomorrow to apologise and most definitely buy her another blouse,' he reminded himself as drowsiness began to cloud his mind over and he felt himself drifting off to sleep.

He became vaguely aware of a stirring in the bed beside him and the sweet smell of perfume gently assailed his nostrils. He felt slightly confused, was he dreaming this? He started as he felt a smooth, naked body snuggling up to him and was immediately aroused from his tiredness as a small hand circled his penis, whilst a soft tongue gently licked his nipple. He turned on his side, now fully aroused from the lethargy of sleep. The small lithe female who had invaded his bed wrapped her arms around him, kissing him passionately. Bewildered, he responded to her attention, feeling her breasts pressing against his chest, desperately trying to decide who this woman was. It certainly wasn't Joanne. This woman was smaller and thinner and smelled completely different too.

'I'm sorry, I'm a little bit late, but I had to wait for the parents to go to bed,' she whispered in his ear, biting his earlobe gently.

Chris thought he detected a slight foreign accent. Who was this? He was intrigued as to which of the girls he knew was now in his bed. He gently pulled her over onto her back, trying to discern in the faint moonlight that shone through a small gap in the curtains who she was. She certainly had a fine body and he saw that her long hair was blonde as the faint light caught it flowing on his pillow. He really had to know who this was, so he reached over the girl and pulled the cord on the bedside light. As the light flashed on, there was a sudden jolt beneath him and he felt the girl's body turn instantly rigid as she stared back at him in horror. 'Oh, my God,' she exclaimed. 'I thought you were Tony. I've got in the wrong bed.'

Chris, completely stunned at finding the lovely blonde was a complete stranger to him, gasped in mild amusement as she struggled free from beneath his body. Pulling a pillow round her body to cover her breasts, she extricated herself from him and jumped off the bed, gathering her clothes up from where she'd thrown them on the floor. Chris lay looking at her admiringly, still feeling completely astonished and even more sexually frustrated.

'Look, I'm really sorry about this. I thought this was Tony's bed,' she explained. 'At least we didn't get to make love, that would have been even more of a mistake,' she spluttered.

'Well, as far as I'm concerned, that would have been a nice mistake to make,' replied Chris, meaning it. 'Tony's room is next door,' he told her. 'I don't know if he's back yet, but just go in and make yourself at home until he returns.' The girl rapidly put her clothes back on whilst Chris politely averted his gaze, though not before he had glimpsed and appreciated what a fine body she had. 'Lucky old Tony' he thought to himself. 'The bastard!' he muttered in mock envy.

'Look,' she said, 'I'm so sorry for what happened. Please, it would make me feel better if we kept this to ourselves,' she pleaded.

'Look, I'm Chris and you have no worries sweetheart, I won't say anything. Anyone could make a mistake like this,' said Chris soothingly.

As Anita opened the door, the sound of Tony's voice came to her down the hall. The other three had just returned from the Taboo club and were making coffee in the kitchen. Tony came out of the kitchen as she closed Chris's door. His face registered surprise as he suddenly remembered that she was calling to see him that night but, also, at finding her leaving Chris's room. 'Anita,' he asked. 'What's going on?'

'I came as you asked, but I went to the wrong room. Chris is in there, in bed. He told me that your room is next door. I got the rooms mixed up, that's all.'

'I'm sorry Anita, if you've just met Chris then you're very lucky to get out of his room alive, I reckon. This is Raz and Mike, my other flatmates.'

They gazed admiringly at Tony's companion as she smiled cheerfully back at them both.

'Let's go to my room,' said Tony taking her arm and guiding her down the hallway to his room. 'Funny Chris going to bed so early. Has he got a girl in there with him?' asked Tony curiously as he shut the door of his bedroom.

'No,' replied Anita still feeling shocked at her surprising encounter with Chris.

'I bet that gave him quite a shock with you walking in and waking him up,' said Tony.

'Yes, I think perhaps it did,' replied Anita meekly.

The following day, desperate to make amends with Joanne, Chris had extricated the torn remnants of her oil covered blouse from the mechanism of his dentist's chair. He had wrapped it in a paper bag and taken it along to Joshua Taylor's, the most exclusive and expensive ladies fashion shop in Cambridge. 'I was wondering if you could duplicate this blouse?' he had casually asked one of the glamorous, over made-up assistants.

She had grimaced at the contents of the bag and carefully, with the tips of her fingers, checked the size and makers name. She had then sorted out two similar blouses for him to consider. After a minute or two he had decided on the one that appeared to match the discarded blouse most closely. The assistant wrapped it up for him and he set off for the Norwich Union whose office was three hundred yards away on Downing Street. He asked at the reception desk where Joanne worked and was told to take the lift to the second floor.

As he stepped out into the corridor, he felt vaguely apprehensive, but also rather pleased with himself for taking the trouble to make amends. After all, he had told himself, the girl should not have to buy a new article of clothing because he had ruined it. As he passed into the New Business section through the swing doors, he saw Joanne standing at the counter, while behind her sat forty or so girls at their desks busy typing or writing.

Joanne's face expressed surprise but then she pursed her lips in annoyance as she watched him walking up to the counter. He placed the package on the counter before her. As she glanced down at it, her face softened slightly, as she noticed the distinctive look of the JT bag. He knew that she had realised what he had bought her. She seemed about to speak but Chris raised his hand, palm facing her as if to say, 'let me speak first Joanne'. 'I just came to say how sorry I was about last night. I realise now that I came on a bit strong and it wasn't very nice for you. I've bought you another blouse at JT's. I hope that it's OK, but they said that you could change it if it's not suitable.'

She stared vacantly down at the package Chris had placed on the counter in front of her, but now she seemed unable to say anything.

Sensing that she was warming to him again and that she was probably overcome by his kind gesture, Chris decided that if he wanted to see her again and try to bed her, now was the time to ask her. 'Look Joanne,' he said to her quietly, 'I was wondering if you would care to see me again? Who knows, you might even get to like my dentists chair!'

Thinking about the incident later, he wondered why he had added the bit about the bloody chair. He could not explain to himself, the words just seemed to tumble out of his mouth quite naturally. It was like showing a red rag to a bull. Her face turned bright red, her features contorted with anger, and without warning she had leant across the counter and swung her right hand hard against Chris's cheek. The blow was so loud that the sound of the impact caused almost every one of the typists sitting below Joanna to glance up from their desks in alarm. Several of them rose to their feet when they heard Joanne begin shouting at Chris. 'Now get out of here and don't you ever bother me again,' she screamed at him.

Chris, his face stinging with pain from the resounding blow, felt his face turning crimson as he became aware of the sea of faces staring at him. Feeling severely humiliated, he decided that discretion was the best policy and turned to walk away, fully aware of forty pairs of eyes boring into the back of his head. He heard Joanna yelling loudly behind him, 'and you can take the bloody blouse with you, I don't take bribes from creeps who just want to sleep with me.'

Chris felt the package hit the back of his head and vaguely heard the high pitched laughter and cheering as he escaped through the door, choosing to run down the stairway rather than wait for the lift. When he was out on the street, he could feel his cheek swelling up and smarting painfully, and he was surprised to find that he was shaking nervously and that his heart was pounding quite fast. His ego felt severely deflated, he knew that he had made a real mess of the attempt of reconciliation. Obviously he would not now get to bed Joanna, which seemed a pity after all the trouble that he had gone to. Still you can't win them all he said to himself, but there's plenty more fish in the sea.

He walked off down the road to find the nearest pub, so that he could console himself with a nice pint of beer, there might even be a bird to pull as well, he smiled, that would certainly be some compensation for the debacle that he had just endured.

Chapter Eleven

Chris, who had been relentlessly searching for a worthwhile job with some good prospects, had spotted a vacancy advertised in the local newspaper with an office equipment supplier. The job entailed working with companies in Cambridge and the immediate area surrounding the city and the salary seemed to be attractive. Chris had been asked to attend an interview which had gone swimmingly and he had accepted the job when it was offered to him. What he particularly liked was that he could work in his own time, sometimes in the office and at other times out in the field. There was an attractive commission system on sales and, although the company was small with a staff of only twenty people, there appeared to be room for advancement. He found himself in an enjoyable job which not only gave him a great deal of free time, but also paid him well. There was the use of a firm's car, but unfortunately for Chris, it was only for business use as the car was shared by several employees.

Chris had been drinking at the Eagle pub in the centre of Cambridge with a couple of friends one lunchtime to celebrate his new job when he spotted a couple of likely looking girls sitting in the courtyard of the old coaching inn. He could tell by their clothes that they were foreign, their simply cut skirts and expensive leather bags and shoes stood them apart from the local office girls and students. Chris and his friends had wandered out into the courtyard and introduced themselves to the two students who, although they spoke English very well, were both studying the language at the Davis School of Languages in Bateman Street. Both came from Milan. Chris was immediately attracted to Caterina, a dark haired beauty with high cheekbones and a Roman nose. She was also blessed with long legs and a trim athletic figure. She told him that her father was a diplomat at the Italian Embassy in London and, though she liked Cambridge very much, both she and her companion had found English people very reserved, unlike her home city where people were much more friendly.

'We're certainly not as shy as you imagine,' Chris told the two girls as he poured out glasses of wine for everyone. He had the distinctly odd feeling that he wanted to lean over and bite one of her ears. She was wearing large gold hoops hanging from her earlobes, every time she moved her head they bobbed around wildly. The old-style gypsy look always excited him and this girl was certainly stunning. He imagined her lying in his bed, her hair would look fantastic lying on his pillow, he'd have to work his magic on her, he decided.

One of his friends had to return to work so Chris suggested to James, his other pal who was a successful self-employed illustrator, that they show the two girls around King's College and the famous chapel, and then take them down to the 'Backs' where the river glided slowly through the city; they could sit on the well-tended grass bank and watch the punting activities, always a source of merriment on a summer afternoon as sometimes one of the inexperienced punters, mainly tourists, would lose their balance and fall into the river to be greeted by outbursts of laughter from the amused onlookers.

They bought another bottle of cold wine when the pub closed at 2:30 and ambled down to King's College. They looked in at the beautiful chapel and strolled lazily through the grounds which impressed both girls who were used to the wonders of Italian architecture and were very appreciative of the old buildings around the college. They reached the 'Backs', where the grass was dry and, although the afternoon was hot and sunny, the bank was not overcrowded so they found a quiet spot under a tree and settled down there.

Chris had noticed that James was getting on very well with Maria, Caterina's companion. He had produced a battered sketch pad and was drawing some quick sketches of the punting scenes evolving before them. It was evident that Maria was impressed with his artistic skills. Chris snuggled up to Caterina and soon learnt that she was on a year's course in Cambridge, of which three months had already passed. She was then planning to return to Milan to study at university. She was just twenty-two years old and had five brothers and two sisters, most of them younger than her.

The group were becoming nicely intoxicated, the warm sun and the effect of the cold wine had made them all feel happy and relaxed. Chris sensed a chemistry between himself and Caterina. He flicked away a strand of dry grass caught in her hair and, as he did so, leaned over and gently kissed her earlobe. She smiled and he leaned over again and kissed her lips gently. Her eyes danced and sparkled in the sunlight and he kissed her again, longer and harder. He could feel her breasts, soft and warm beneath the underside of his arm as he reached across and held her. He could smell the lemony sweetness of the white wine on her breath and noticed the sunlight catch one or two minute hairs on each side of her mouth. She had a small scar on her right cheek which she explained had been caused when she had accidentally fallen in the street whilst playing with her brothers when she was younger. He touched the scar gently with the tip of his forefinger and, when she had finished her story, he kissed the scar gently as though to tell her it was a lovely feature and was part of her beauty.

Caterina lay back on the grass and looked up at Chris, squinting slightly. She surveyed his face thoughtfully for several seconds, then reached up and pulled him down to her, her tongue thrusting into his mouth as she kissed him lovingly. The sensual kiss brought out slight beads of perspiration on Chris's brow. He leant down to her again, their bodies moving closer together as they kissed passionately. Once again Chris could feel her breasts pressing against his chest and her fingers moving gently in the back of his hair. A bead of sweat ran from his forehead, across his eyebrow and into his eyes. He felt the sweat sting his eye as he felt her ribs straining under his hand as he held her firmly around her waist. He moved his hand higher and gently cupped her breasts. She allowed it for a second or two and then quickly moved his hand away.

She smiled coquettishly at him. 'Naughty English boy, you are supposed to be shy boys, you English boys.'

Chris laughed. 'I told you that my friends and I are not shy boys at all,' he said his eyes widening in mock horror.

'But you are a naughty boy, I can tell,' laughed Caterina

suddenly sitting up and giving him a quick kiss on the cheek.

Without warning, there was a tremendous splash and an enormous cheer went up from further along the grassy bank where a dozen or so students were lounging. Chris sat up quickly and saw a hapless man trying to regain his footing onto the back of the punt that he had fallen from. Covered in mud and slime, he looked a sad figure as other punters and various onlookers sitting on the banks laughed cruelly at his misfortune.

'Yet another cunt who can't stay on his punt,' said James dryly, used to watching the tourists punting and having seen the same thing happen countless times before.

'Poor man,' said Caterina, even though she had laughed at the incident. 'It must be hard to learn to do this. I think it must be nice to go on the boat but not to push it along.'

'It's called a punt. Perhaps we could go on the river one day and I could teach you how to do it?' said Chris who did not particularly like punting although he was quite good at it. He knew that the more you promised a woman, the more she would usually give in return.

'Oh yes, that would be nice,' exclaimed Caterina. Again she took his face in both hands and gave him another quick kiss, this time on the tip of his nose.

James and Maria, who had been deep in conversation, suddenly rose to their feet, brushing the dead grass from their clothes. Maria looked a little self-conscious thought Chris, realising that James had something else planned. He'd known James since he'd first arrived in Cambridge two years ago and knew that he was a smooth operator with the women.

'We're going off for tea,' James told Chris and Caterina, his arm around Maria's waist. 'See you later on maybe,' he nodded and winked at Chris who nodded and winked back certain that James's intention was to take Maria back to his flat. The two girls kissed each other on both cheeks and spoke a few words of Italian to each other. Maria then took James's proffered arm and they walked off happily hand-in-hand. Maria turned briefly to call 'Ciao' to her friend. With a wave they disappeared through a college gate.

'Swift bastard,' thought Chris approvingly as he turned back to Caterina. 'Well, what would you like to do, some tea maybe, or a drink? I could show you my flat where I live with my friends and we could have a drink there,' he suggested, eager now to have some privacy with the girl.

'Oh, naughty boy, but I will come with you if you are a good boy,' she replied reaching for his mouth and touching his lips briefly with her forefinger.

Chris was sure that he had detected a twinkle in her eyes. That twinkle to a man like him, experienced with women, usually meant that she was ready and willing to succumb to whatever he had in mind because she desired him just as much as he wanted her. He could almost feel the hormones racing around his body as he helped her up from the grass. He snuggled against her and nibbled her earlobes again as she let out little short gasps of pleasure. He was elated, his desire for her was so exciting. He recalled sitting with Mike on the evening of the day that they'd decided to take the flat, the day he'd been rejected by Jane. Mike had told him all about Cambridge, about the women that were available and what fun the city could be. Gazing intently at Caterina, a real dark beauty, he remembered Mike's words and how enthralled he had been at the time. It was all true. Caterina was proof of that. He'd only just met her and he was sure she wanted him as much as he wanted her.

One hour later they arrived at the flat, it was quiet and peaceful as the others were all at work. As soon as they entered his room and he'd kicked the door shut, they had begun kissing passionately. Standing in the middle of the room, he began frantically to unbutton her blouse as she pulled his T-shirt roughly over his head. He flipped his slip-ons off and, as he backed her against the wall, he expertly unzipped her skirt, deftly pulling it down her legs until she could step out of it. She was excitedly licking and sucking his chest and nipples whilst unbuckling his belt. He pulled her tights off roughly and then his hand was inside her panties, gently rubbing her moist clitoris. He pulled her panties down as she kissed him more passionately, pulling his mouth down to hers. He unhitched her brassiere with one quick, expert movement of his hand behind her back, causing her large breasts to tumble out. He noticed a pattern on her skin where her straps had been as he lowered his head and sucked gently on her nipples. She was moaning a little and her breath was coming in short gasps. She pulled his pants down round his knees and began caressing his cock, one hand round the shaft and one gently fondling his balls. He felt his whole body stiffening with pleasure, feeling wild with excitement as he gripped her buttocks from behind.

He lifted her urgently onto the edge of the large Victorian washbasin jutting out from the wall next to them. She took his rampant cock, opening her legs wide and inserting him into her wetness. He drove into her hard, revelling in the smell of her skin, the smoothness, the softness, the desire. He held her tightly, balancing her bottom as she moaned and gasped, pulling him into her fervently. He could hear himself crying out, 'Oh fuck, oh fuck,' as the feeling of pleasure intensified. She gripped him even harder, tightening her legs around his body. Suddenly, there was a dreadful crashing sound as the washbasin, loosened by their frantic sexual activity, was torn away from the wall. Lumps of plaster cascaded onto the floor creating billowing clouds of dust.

Caterina, having nothing to support her bouncing buttocks, fell down heavily backwards as Chris fell on top of her. He tried vainly to find a foothold as they both collapsed in an awkward heap but the momentum of the collapse of the basin had caught him unawares. Unfortunately the old lead pipes attached to the taps twisted dramatically and tore open as the washbasin plummeted to the ground. Immediately water gushed out of the broken pipes with amazing force. It spewed over the shocked lovers, swamping the carpets as it flowed rapidly across the room.

As Chris struggled up in shock and pulled Caterina from the wreckage, he noticed that she had grazed herself badly on her buttocks and her lower back where she had fallen onto the washbasin and collided against the taps. Where his forehead had collided against hers as they fell, some ugly bruising was already evident and she was sobbing hysterically for she was obviously in pain and badly shaken up. Chris began to panic as the water streamed around his ankles, desperately wondering what to do first. He sat Caterina on his bed and picked up a pair of socks from a drawer in his chest of drawers and tried in vain to stuff them into the end of the pipes to stop the water. The flow was too strong and simply forced the socks out of the pipe. He ran naked down the hallway noticing that the water was about to seep out of his bedroom into the hall. He rushed into the kitchen, frantically pulling open the cupboards under the sink to try and locate the stopcock to turn the water off. He couldn't find it there, so he ran into the bathroom where in the cupboard under the sink he found two taps. One turned easily but the other was stuck, he simply couldn't move it. He ran down the hallway. The water was now streaming over the bedroom sill into the hallway. As he entered the bedroom he saw Caterina still sitting on the bed desperately attempting to put on her sodden clothes which she had retrieved from the floor where they had been thrown during their recent passionate encounter. She was crying hysterically and obviously very distraught. Chris wasn't sure whether to comfort her or not, but as he noticed the water level was rising, he decided his priority had to be to try and turn the water tap off quickly. He remembered the old steel Victorian poker lying by the fireplace in the lounge and sloshed down the hallway to collect it. He rushed back to the bathroom and desperately hit the obstinate tap as hard as he could, attempting to loosen it. He dropped the poker and, using both hands, made a supreme effort to turn the tap. Suddenly he felt it move a little, then, just as suddenly, it freed as he strained to turn it further. Within seconds he had managed to turn the tap off. Hoping beyond hope that he had turned off the correct tap, he ran down the hallway, the carpet already sodden with water streaming from his bedroom. As he entered his bedroom he was relieved to see that the water had stopped pouring out of the wrecked pipes.

He turned to console Caterina who was still sobbing uncontrollably, partly with the pain from her swollen forehead after the collision with Chris's head and partly from the severe bruising she had suffered on her back and buttocks where she had fallen on the taps. The obvious trauma caused by the disastrous culmination of their sexual activity had not helped either. Chris himself felt utterly exhausted and dejected at the unforeseen incident. Just as he was about to begin mopping up with some towels he heard the loud ringing of the door bell. He realised immediately that it must be the neighbour who lived in the downstairs flat, so he ran down the stairs and nervously opened the door. He was confronted by a very large, very irate man who was covered with an alarming selection of tattoos on his hairy arms. Chris recognised him as their neighbour, although he had only ever said good morning to him once.

'What the fuck is going on up there?' the man demanded angrily. 'My fucking lounge is completely flooded with water pouring through the ceiling. It's like fucking Niagara Falls in there,' he screamed at Chris, his eyes narrowing to slits in his angry red face as he shook a very large hand dangerously in the direction of Chris's nose. The man was glaring up and down at him in a very strange manner.

Chris suddenly realised that he was standing there completely stark bollock naked and soaking wet, whilst from upstairs came the sound of Caterina's tortuous sobbing. Chris was not about to explain what had really happened, but realised that he needed to give the man some explanation. Otherwise he could sense further trouble. He tried to unearth a plausible reason for the calamity from his befuddled brain whilst realising how odd the whole scene must appear to the angry man standing before him.

'And what's going on up there then, that lady crying?' the neighbour demanded, motioning upstairs with a nod of his head.

'Look,' said Chris slowly, trying to ignore his question. 'I am really sorry, really sorry. The water pipes suddenly split when I was about to have a shave. I turned the basin tap on and water gushed out underneath from a terrible split in the pipe. It took me some time to find the stopcock to turn the water off.' Does that really sound feasible enough Chris wondered. Pretty weak stuff he thought to himself, I could have done better.

'Are you telling me that you take all your fucking clothes off to have a shave you clumsy cunt?' shouted the irate neighbour. 'What the hell was all that banging and shouting up there before the flood started then?' he demanded ferociously, little spots of spit hitting Chris's face as the man came near to him. It seemed to Chris that he was like a rabid dog, spitting and snarling.

'I really can't explain the noise,' Chris replied shakily, feeling very vulnerable in his nakedness, trying to cover his genitals with his hands. 'Then the washbasin came away from the wall when I tried to stop the water, but I did manage to find the tap and turn the water off before too much damage was done.

I'm sure the landlord's insurance will pay for any damage,' he continued, wondering what the landlord would say when he found out about this catastrophe.

'Well, I've got water pouring down my walls and my fucking carpets are soaked, and so is my fucking three-piece suite, so it bloody well better pay compensation,' cried the neighbour pointing his finger menacingly at Chris. 'Otherwise you'll have to!'

'Again, I'm really sorry. I'll try to mop up and get in touch with the landlord. Hopefully, I'll sort it all out very quickly,' said Chris wishing he could just vanish into thin air.

'You fucking better or I'll have your bollocks for my dog's dinner,' cried the man. 'I'm going to mop up in my flat, you make sure you ring the landlord and get the pipe repaired and clear the water upstairs so that I don't get any more down here,' he yelled. He then turned and entered his own flat, slamming the door behind him so hard that Chris was amazed that it stayed on its hinges.

Chris trudged upstairs, feeling extremely cold and miserable now, and found Caterina, who was now fully dressed in her soaking clothes, just leaving his bedroom and squelching along the hall. 'Caterina,' he said full of concern for her now that he could attend to her without any distractions. 'Are you OK?'

'No. I leave. I see myself out. I get a taxi and go home to bed,' she replied edging past him and trudging down the stairs, rubbing her back painfully, the bruise on her forehead now turning very purple.

Chris stood watching her in astonishment as she descended the stairs. 'Caterina, when will I see you again? Can I see you home? I don't even have your number,' he called down to her. She did not reply. As she opened the door he called to her again, 'Caterina it wasn't my fault this happened, don't go like this,' he pleaded. But she was already out on the street, oblivious to his anguish, slamming the door behind her. Chris winced, hoping desperately that the neighbour would not reappear to confront him about the door being slammed. He stood stunned, devastated that the passion between them, that had felt so strong, had evaporated and feeling disbelief that Caterina so obviously blamed him for the unfortunate accident that had occurred and that she had run off like that in such a heartless manner.

'Half an hour ago I was in heaven, now I'm in the middle of a bloody living nightmare,' he muttered to himself as he looked up the landlord's number in the phone book before getting to work to clean up the mess.

He was still shaking an hour later when the landlord called round to inspect the damage. Chris then became involved in another row when the landlord demanded to know how the washbasin, with its sturdy six inch screws sunk so deeply into the wall, had managed to work its way off the wall. Eventually the landlord had been persuaded by Chris to call a plumber round to repair the broken pipes and screw the washbasin back onto the wall, but only after he had agreed with Chris to be paid some compensation for the damage at the end of the tenancy of the flat. Chris retreated to his room, both physically and mentally exhausted, and lay on his bed to recover.

The others returned home from work to find the hallway, landing and stairs still saturated. The water had even penetrated under the doors of Raz's and Tony's rooms, soaking the carpets and some of their belongings lying on the floor. Despite demands from the other three, Chris was at first reluctant to explain exactly how the incident had happened, but later that evening when they had all helped Chris to clear up the remaining water saturating the carpets, and the plumber had been round and mended the pipes, they had all gone out together for a drink to the 'Live and Let Live' where Chris decided to come clean and he related to the other three the incidents that had led up to the flooding of the flat.

'You bastard,' exclaimed Tony in admiration.

'Giving her one on the washbasin, surely she was in danger of finding a tap up her arse, wasn't she?' asked Raz, trying to picture the scene.

'What's up with you Chris, are you getting so kinky that you're not into using your own bed anymore, or even your bloody dentist's chair? Why did you have to shag her on the edge of the wash basin?' asked Mike incredulously.

'I just don't know why, it just happened that way in the heat of the moment. You all know what it's like when you get a bird who's really hot and passionate, ordinary thoughts go flying out of the fucking window, all you want to do is give her a bloody good shagging. I'd got no idea that the basin would come off the wall and I'd have all this hassle. In fact I wasn't thinking about anything but the bird at that point. It's going to cost me a fortune when we eventually move as I've got to pay for the repairs then. I was worried that the landlord would kick me out, or worse, ask all of us to leave. I don't think I'd have been too popular with you all if that had happened.'

'Well, I feel sorry for you that the bird fucked off like that,' said Mike.

'Yeah, so do I,' said Chris still feeling terribly upset that Caterina had walked off after the incident and wondering why her feelings had changed so drastically and so quickly. 'Anyway, I know one thing for sure,' he said to Mike.

'What's that?' asked Mike.

'The bloody guy underneath us isn't too happy either,' smiled Chris. 'Not too happy at all.'

Chapter Twelve

As with many young men, cars were frequently a favourite topic of conversation amongst the boys. They grouped them into several categories. There were the very expensive and most coveted prestigious vehicles, then there were the fastest and most desirable sports cars and then the run-of-the-mill derisory cars. The boys own modes of transport all came within the latter category and they each had a love-hate relationship with their own vehicle according to how well it was behaving.

Raz drove a small, green MG sports car, a 1939 TA. He had owned it for over three years and invariably drove it with the hood down, even in the most severe weather, which didn't always go down well with his girlfriends. He was insistent that keeping the hood down was the only way to enjoy a sports car. The MG was not always reliable but Raz had the Indian's seemingly natural mechanical aptitude and was almost always able to fix any problem that occurred.

Mike owned an old Ford Consul saloon inherited from his ageing father, whilst Tony had a sleek, much coveted, Austin Healey 3000 sports, albeit heavily dented and scratched, mainly due to his exuberant driving habits. It soon became clear to them all that Tony was not a very good driver, in fact the others avoided accompanying him as a passenger as often as possible, not wishing to be scared witless by the completely unpredictable manoeuvres he carried out in his vehicle. In short, he was an utter menace on the road.

Chris, on the other hand, since arriving back from the USA and deciding to stay in Cambridge, had managed without a car of his own for some time. He initially found it easy to get around the city by walking or cycling like many other young people. When he badly needed a car, he would usually borrow Mike's rusting saloon. However, he decided that this was not always convenient, so now that he had a new job and could not use the company vehicle for his own purposes, he decided to save enough to buy his own means of transport. It had to be something original, a bit out of the ordinary, something to satisfy his extrovert taste.

So, it was with some exhilaration that arriving at Hammond's auctioneers one day for the weekly preview, he found a Rolls Royce hearse covered in dust and cobwebs, sporting a sign on the window which read, 'This vehicle is being sold without warranty on Thursday November 24th at 12 noon and without reserve.' Apparently the vehicle had stood neglected for over a year. Enquiries in the office informed him that the vehicle had travelled only 27,000 miles from new. It was a 1954 model and was being sold by the undertaker's widow whose husband had only recently died after a long illness. The auctioneers informed Mike that they expected the vehicle to sell for about £100, but hinted that being a hearse, the demand would not be as strong as for a more conventional Rolls Royce saloon.

Chris became very excited, examining the vehicle more closely. The sweeping lines of the coachwork, coupled with the impressive chrome headlamps and the enormous radiator were all very aesthetically pleasing to him. Opening the door, he noted with pleasure the fat leather seats and the walnut dashboard. It seemed to Chris rather like a large estate car with plenty of room for carrying goods, or ideal for taking groups of friends on jaunts into the countryside. There was a dais behind the front seat, running down the rear of the hearse, where the coffin would have lain, with black curtains tied at the corners of the windows. He could smell the leather, but there was something else, a faint, musty, acrid smell and, wondering about it, he realised slowly that many of the dead bodies that had been carried in the rear would have had various diseases and ailments. His brain conjured up visions of rotting corpses, their malodorous fluids dripping from the bottom of their coffin, impregnating the interior of the hearse with the odd odour that he could smell. Trying to banish these thoughts from his mind, he could also visualise the vehicle as the ultimate passion wagon. There was an old mattress lying in the attic at their flat, left there by the landlord. He could put that in the rear and, with the curtains drawn, his mind ran riot, the birds would absolutely love it, and a Rolls Royce at that. 'Christ,' he thought, 'they would be queuing up and, what with his dentist's chair, he could almost become notorious. I hope that I'm not becoming completely kinky. But,' he reasoned, 'a guy has to try and stand out from the crowd. Look at Brian Brown, he lives off his father and he's got an E-type Jag and pulls birds all the time and he's an ugly bastard. I don't have that amount of money, so I have to do it within a limited budget and this Rolls would certainly be worth buying just to pull the women, especially if I could get it for a low price.' He rationalised that with a really good clean-up and some good quality odourisers to clear the inside and eliminate the unsavoury smell, the Rolls would look a million dollars. After all, a couple of his friends had converted ancient ambulances into camper vans and God knows what had happened inside those in their time.

Chris could hardly contain his excitement that night over beers in the Six Bells as he sat with Mike and Raz animatedly discussing his proposed purchase. Tony was absent, out on a date with a supposed Italian heiress, who was studying at the Bell School of Languages. According to Tony, he had told the others that evening that she had the most perfect globular breasts that he had ever seen filling a blouse and he could hardly wait to get his hands on them.

'Chris, a real Rolls Royce,' exclaimed Raz incredulously. 'Well, you could be dead lucky and get it cheap.'

'Dead being the operative word for a hearse,' replied Mike with a big grin.

'At least you didn't say that with a deadpan face,' said Chris, to jeers from the other two.

'It doesn't come with a coffin in it?' asked Raz lightheartedly.

'No, but it smells a bit iffy,' said Chris, still slightly worried that he might not be able to eradicate the odd odour if he did manage to buy it.

'I don't know that I could use it knowing that all those dead bodies had lain inside,' said Mike. 'It could be a bit spooky!'

'Well, they were only passing through, they didn't really have much choice, did they?' replied Chris. 'We've all got to bloody die and be carried somewhere to be buried or cremated, haven't we?' In Chris's mind, the vehicle almost belonged to him already and he was a little aggrieved that the others appeared to be rather negative about it. He decided to tell the other two about the idea that had occurred to him when he was looking around the Rolls. 'I thought I might put a mattress in the back and use it on occasions as a mobile shagging wagon,' he told them hoping that they would agree that it was a brilliant idea.

'What kind of bird is going to want to be shagged in a fucking hearse?' asked Mike in astonishment, nearly spilling his drink and dropping his cigarette. 'You've already got the fucking dentist's chair for Christ's sake.'

'Yes, but with a hearse the birds won't have the discomfort of any bloody levers getting entangled in their clothes, or washbasin taps caught up in their fanny's,' said Raz. The incident where the girl's blouse had been torn off when Chris was trying to seduce her in the chair still delighted the boys when they sat around discussing life sometimes, it had been hard for Chris to live the unfortunate incident down, with the others still ready to bring it up and tease him about it.

'It seems to me that I'm the only chap in the flat who is going to have to rely upon his personal charm and charisma, with only his good, old-fashioned bed to take them to,' said Raz with a superior wrinkling of his nose.

'Jesus, I can't believe you said that when all we can hear when you're entertaining birds in your room is the thunder and lightening from those bloody tapes of yours, whilst you're screwing inside a flaming tent set up around your bed,' replied Mike somewhat aghast at Raz's hypocritical remark. 'I think that I'm the only one of us who doesn't have to rely on all these artificial devices to impress the women,' he added, with a conceited grin.

'Yeah, and look what a tip your room is,' said Chris. 'Very impressive indeed for the ladies. What ever do you say to them, "come up and see my rubbish"?' Chris was always berating Mike for the squalor in his room.

'Maybe I'll attach a cement mixer under the mattress so that I can compete with you boys in the "oh so fucking different" shagging stakes,' said Mike. 'I personally think that giving a girl

110

a good time in bed depends on what you do with your dick, however big or small it is, and not on what sort of elaborate fantasies you can create or what kind of amazing machinery you can dredge up to impress them. After all, look at the Karma Sutra, there's hundreds of positions but I don't recall the use of lavish sexual aids in that little number.'

'Yes, I agree with you Mike, but there's no harm in having a little extra fun, by doing things a bit differently sometimes, that's all,' said Raz.

'Well, Chris will certainly be a bit different running around Cambridge asking every girl he meets if she'd like to be shagged in a fucking hearse,' said Mike.

Chris laughed at Mike, he had already imagined himself doing just that with great success.

'Chris, you could always stick a coffin in the back and make yourself up like Count Dracula, with a white face and a long cloak, and see if you could pull any vampires,' said Raz.

Mike took half-a-day of his holiday the next day so that he could go to the auction with Chris who had suggested that he ought to accompany him as Mike had never attended an auction in his life. Chris was convinced that he would enjoy the atmosphere, besides there were occasionally some very tasty birds to be found there.

Finding difficulty in sleeping later that night, Mike had mulled over their conversation that evening. He thought about Raz's remark suggesting that Chris could dress up as Dracula. He recalled some of the old vampire movies, where coffins were always being carried around in horsedrawn hearses, always at night, everything was very black with the pall-bearers and coachmen dressed in long tailcoats and tophats, but without exception their faces always had a deathly white pallor, contrasting eerily with their dark surroundings. He felt some odd ideas fermenting in his mind, where the group of them were all sitting in the hearse, trundling around town with ashen faces and top-hats but, finally, sleep had taken over and he had drifted off into oblivion, and the fantasy had been erased from his mind.

The next morning they arrived at the auction some thirty minutes before the hearse was due to be sold. They found several people gathered round inspecting it, the bonnet was raised and a small close-cropped man in a flashy suit and tie was lying down at the rear of the car, inspecting the exhaust system and placing his hand over the exhaust pipe whilst his larger colleague revved the engine. 'How is it?' the large man called out.

'Seems fine to me,' replied the suit, rising clumsily to his feet and kicking the rear tyres.

'Obviously a bit of competition for you Chris,' said Mike warily, eyeing another character who was rolling the carpets back in the front passenger footwell and surveying the floor intently, banging it with a large spanner.

'Don't worry about all the flannel,' said Chris quietly in Mike's ear. 'Some people run things down and pretend there's terrible things wrong just to put the other punters off.'

They bought two mugs of steaming hot, sweet tea from a little refreshment stand in a small room adjacent to the auction. They stood at the rear of the room drinking and chatting, casually watching the various goings on as the auction progressed around them. There was the usual rag-bag of antiques, collectibles and household goods, but Mike was impressed how quickly the items were put up to auction and then knocked down to the purchaser.

As noon approached, Mike felt his stomach tightening a little with anticipation, his heart seemed to pound a little faster as the time for the auction of the Rolls drew nearer and nearer and he began to realise why people found auctions so addictive. At approximately five minutes to twelve Lot 80 was announced and the auctioneer explained a few details of the sale, including the history of the vehicle and why the vendor was selling it.

Mike found himself tense with excitement but he realised that Chris was thoroughly composed and was confident that his friend knew exactly what he was doing, what he could afford to spend and that he would not spend more than the amount he had decided on beforehand.

The bidding commenced at £30, the auctioneer pushing the bidding along in bids of £2, but at £66 the bidding stuck, then suddenly restarted, but at £78, being Chris's final bid, the auctioneer took a careful but cursory glance around the room. 'Any more bids?' he asked the crowd? His gavel crashed down and Chris had become the proud owner of a 1954 Rolls Royce hearse with one previous careful owner. Chris punched Mike's arm playfully in delight at his success.

An immediate buzz of conversation broke out around the room. Mike carefully strained his ears to hear the various snippets of conversation taking place around him. He was glad that the general consensus of opinion seemed to be that it was 'a bit of a bargain'.

'After all the crap I took from you guys last night I hope that now I've got the bloody thing, we can all have some fun with it, then you'll all have to eat your words,' said Chris gleefully.

'We were only taking the piss,' said Mike. 'I think you've got yourself a useful bit of kit there.'

'Shall we go and celebrate?' asked Chris.

'It would be a crime not to,' replied Mike, who was really ready for a beer after all the excitement.

They walked to The Globe in Hills Road, about a hundred yards from the auction house. When they arrived in the pub, Chris was surprised to recognise the girl working behind the bar. He had tried to date her a few days earlier at the Deja Vu Club but she had bluntly told him to get lost and not to bother her again. Never one to leave a lost cause alone, Chris decided to try and chat her up again. Unfortunately, as she walked along the bar to serve the two friends, she recognised Chris and pulled a hideous face. 'Oh God, not you again,' she said caustically to Chris as he stood smiling at her.

'Two beers please,' said Mike turning to catch Chris's expression of dismay as the girl ignored him.

'What's wrong with me?' asked Chris innocently. 'I only asked you out the other day, surely that's not a crime?'

'Look, I know all about you,' said the girl placing two pints of beer on the bar.

Mike noticed she was pretty, obviously Irish with that accent. She had long copper hair, green eyes and masses of freckles covering her arms.

'You just want to screw every woman you can and I don't fall for that shit. I like a little respect from a man,' she said to Chris. 'I wouldn't have gone with you for a million dollars the other night.'

'No problem,' replied Chris smirking arrogantly and supping

113

his beer. 'I had a bird lying in bed waiting for me that night anyway.'

'Well, I just hope that she had her guide dog with her,' retaliated the girl vehemently, turning on her heel to serve someone further down the bar.

Mike was almost choking in his beer with amusement, the girl certainly had some spirit.

'Charming,' said Chris, somewhat taken aback. 'She should be on the stage.'

'She soon sorted you out Chris, you've got to respect that. She's a feisty woman. Let's face it, it's very difficult for women because all we want to do is fuck them and I think that quite often we despise them afterwards simply because they allowed us to sleep with them so easily. It's probably why love is such a difficult thing between men and women, we all want different things in a relationship. She sussed you out for what you are. I think that's bloody clever and it certainly takes some guts to tell someone to their face.'

'Mmmm, you're probably right,' replied Chris, somewhat reluctantly eyeing up the redhead as she worked away behind the bar laughing and joking with some of the other customers. She certainly had a nice arse, that's what he had first spotted when he had initially noticed her at the Deja Vu. She caught him staring at her and glared sternly back at him as if to tell him not to mess with her again.

Mike noticed this brief exchange of glances and drained his beer. 'Come on Chris,' he urged, 'let's go and sort that hearse out.'

'OK,' said Chris placing his empty glass on the bar. He couldn't resist a parting shot. 'See you again,' he smiled across at the girl who was pulling a pint for someone.

'Not if I can bloody well help it,' she shouted back, not even bothering to glance back at him.

Chris grinned to disguise his slightly deflated ego, feeling a little embarrassed as some of the customers glanced along the bar to see who was the subject of the barmaid's put-down. Chris turned away from their grinning faces and followed Mike out into the street, leaving the peals of raucous laughter behind them as he heard the girl say something about him to her customers. 'Oh, well, you can't win them all,' he shook his head regretfully, 'and more's the pity.'

The following Sunday the whole household decided to help Chris to clean the hearse. They washed and polished the bodywork, cleaned the carpet and the leather seating and tied the black curtains neatly at each window. A special upholstery cleaner was used on the headlining to clear away the odours that several people had complained about.

After two hours hard work, they stood back to admire the results. The hearse now shone, the black bodywork gleamed and the chrome almost dazzled them as the sun caught it. At Chris's insistence they had all piled inside for a sedate ride to the centre of town to show off the car. They rolled all the windows down, peering out and gesticulating at passers by. Occasionally they would spot a pretty girl and everyone immediately leant over to that side, blowing kisses and yelling through the open windows.

Later that evening they were going to a party in a village just outside the city and Mike suggested a prank which they all heartily agreed with, harking back to his dream. Whitening their faces with powder and painting red lipstick on their lips, wearing tophats and black clothing, they rode out to the party in the Rolls. 'The idea is we must all sit there with deadpan faces and no-one must laugh at anything,' ordered Mike.

When they arrived at the party that evening, which was being held on the lawn of a lovely country house, Chris drove the hearse very slowly down the grand drive and caused great consternation amongst the sixty or so people assembled on the lawn. None of them knew that Chris had just bought the hearse and to see four men arriving with deathly white faces and black funeral clothing was not only a very macabre sight, but somewhat alarming to the uninformed host and his guests.

From that point onwards the hearse was used to convey them all to and from parties. They found that they could cram ten to twelve people into the vehicle, so it became very useful indeed. They even had occasion to sleep in it several times when they were too drunk to drive home and, of course, Chris who used the vehicle occasionally for seduction purposes, kept a roll of foam under the front seat which he could roll out to use as a mattress.

Raz and Chris made a make-believe coffin out of some old

115

drawers they found in a skip. Chris used it to hold odds and ends in the back, but the dais could still be raised and the 'coffin' laid on it, with its brass handles from the drawers fitted on the side, so that it appeared very realistic to onlookers.

It was the ultimate all-purpose vehicle as far as Chris was concerned and he never regretted purchasing the Rolls although it sometimes raised a few eyebrows when people found out that he owned it. 'How great,' they would say to him. 'Yeah, it's certainly something to die for,' he would answer with a solemn expression.

Chapter Thirteen

One cool summer evening the four boys had gathered for a drink after work at the Six Bells in Convent Garden, a favourite little backwater not far from their flat. They sat outside the pub on a bench taking advantage of the last of the evening sun. They smoked and debated, often arguing repeatedly over a range of subjects from girls to football, politics to cars, music and, of course, shagging.

Tony particularly wanted to discuss something that had been bothering him recently. He had now settled down well within the group but he'd been severely pestered recently by a young girl that he had asked to model for him in a national hairdressing competition. He had made love to her briefly on a couple of occasions and it was after these couplings that she had become completely obsessed with him. He had restyled her hair, altering it from a rather frumpy, old-fashioned style into a style reminiscent of the new 'Twiggy' look, short and cute. The change in her character had been immediate and overwhelming. She had confided in him that when she looked in the mirror she realised that the new hairstyle had changed her face completely and given her a new confidence and self-assurance. She saw reflected back at her an attractive woman, bright-eyed and vivacious, a person that she had never believed that she could be. Gone was the old lank hair style that had covered her face for so long; she had in fact hidden behind her fringe and her personality had suffered, increasing her self-consciousness. After sleeping with her, Tony had inevitably moved onto someone else, but she, being very young and completely infatuated with him, had not been able to understand why. Feeling as she did, with compliments flying her way all the time on her new looks and self-confidence, she was baffled and upset that Tony, her 'creator', did not want her any more. She had taken to constantly 'phoning him at the salon, sometimes twenty times a day, interrupting his work with his usual clients. She would hang around forlornly either outside the salon or the boys' flat waiting for him to appear. She had taken to ringing the bell of the flat on odd occasions late at night. This had severely displeased some of the others when it had disturbed their sleep or, on the odd occasion, when they had been caught inflagrante. Tony had done his best to resolve the issue, even resorting to a visit to her parents to explain the problem to them. Unfortunately both the girl's parents, on being told that their daughter had slept with him, went berserk and he ended up being slapped and punched by the pair of them in their sitting room as they berated both Tony and their daughter using the foulest language he had ever heard. Tony eventually made his escape and, apart from a few bruises, was none the worse for wear. He decided that hopefully, the girl wouldn't be a bother to him again once her ghastly parents had finished with her.

Tony was a good-looking heterosexual man working in a ladies hairdressing salon surrounded by attractive females all day and was used to being chatted-up and sometimes pestered. God knows, he had done enough of it himself. But this particular incident had upset him a great deal, especially as the girl was only seventeen, and he'd had severe difficulties coming to terms with the problem. 'I'm actually getting a bit pissed off with women these days,' he announced to the others, 'especially after the fiasco with that young tart recently. I felt I couldn't move without her being on my tail. Besides, there's no challenge any more with these birds, it's just too bloody easy.'

'How do you mean, too bloody easy,' retorted Mike who thought he knew what Tony was boasting about but wanting to hear more on the subject.

'Well, you know what I mean, all of you do. It's just screw this bird and screw that one, la-de-da-de-da, and half of the time you don't even know their bloody names or anything about them at all,' complained Tony.

'Well, as long as they've got big tits, or long legs, or a cute arse, who cares?' cried Chris, a big grin spreading across his face.

'You might have a few nightmares if you knew too much

118

about some of them,' added Mike.

'Or paternity suits,' added Chris with a wry smile. 'Luckily we've all kept our slates clean.'

'Your problem is that you're surrounded by pretty women all day, Tony. You're bound to get a bit fed up at times. Why don't you try and pull an ugly bird for a change?' said Raz guffawing loudly. The others joined in his laughter at Tony's expense.

'Some of the girls I've seen you with late at night haven't always exactly been candidates for Miss Universe have they Tony?' added Chris mischievously.

Raz began laughing uncontrollably, his eyes rolling. He often laughed more at his own jokes than anyone else. 'Have they been a substitute for when you've got bored with the pretty ones?' he queried.

'Let's face it, we've nearly all woken up next to a dog in our time, if we're really truthful,' said Chris glancing around at the others for confirmation.

They all laughed in agreement with his statement, they had reached the stage where their comradeship bonded them together in the knowledge that all good friends share, aware that all the incessant leg-pulling and ribaldry amongst themselves was purely for fun. The teasing they indulged in was never malicious and there was a limit to how far they went and those boundary lines were never crossed. Each of the group knew how far to goad one another in their normal tomfoolery, yet they all were aware that each one of them had his own particular frailties and that the others would rally around instantly with the necessary support or comfort if one of them needed it for any reason. British humour is well-known throughout the world because of its ability to make fun of everything and everybody. Self-mockery can be a very endearing characteristic and it was certainly well to the fore in the lives of all the four individuals living at Mawson Road.

'Seriously though,' said Chris, who had an idea beginning to churn around in his mind. 'Tony, you mentioned earlier that you felt that you aren't being challenged any more, so why don't we raise your philandering to new heights and present you with a new challenge, or set you a new goal to attain with women in mind. Perhaps we could sort out some really ugly females as a challenge? What do you think Tony?'

'I'm really not about to start pulling any pigs!' exclaimed Tony, his face contorted in disbelief. 'What do you take me for?'

'Well, you said you felt there weren't any challenges any more and that pulling birds is too predictable. Why don't we set you a challenge where you would have to pull an ugly one that we would select for you?'

'Christ. I didn't mean that I wanted to go out and start pulling ugly birds,' growled Tony, 'just because I'm pissed off pulling pretty ones.'

'Well, what about us all competing against each other then?' Raz interrupted. 'We'd all have to go out and pull the ugliest or fattest bird that we could find, maybe throw a party where we could vote for the worst one, or would that be the best one? The guy with the least ugly bird would have to pay a fine or a forfeit or something like that, so that there's a proper incentive to pull a real pig.'

'That's a brilliant idea,' cried Chris his eyes shining with exhilaration. 'We could each pay something into a kitty and the winner takes all, the loser would have to take us all out for drinks one night, or clean the flat or something like that. What about doing everyone's cleaning rota for a month, we all hate the bloody cleaning?'

'Great idea,' Tony and Raz agreed loudly. Everyone really hated the cleaning.

Mike, who had been sitting pensively and who was usually the last to agree to some of the crazier ideas embarked upon by the others, spoke up quietly, his glasses glinting in the low light. 'I know that this idea sounds very amusing, but are we all absolutely certain that we're totally happy with the idea before we carry it any further forward.' He glanced around at the others noticing how keenly they had reacted to Raz's unusual idea. He was not entirely convinced that this would be a civilised way in which to behave towards women. 'I mean woman have feelings, especially the ugly or fat ones that we are talking about. I just feel a little bit uneasy about this idea of Raz's. I think most women would be appalled at the idea, for obvious reasons, and I think if we are truthful to ourselves, we'd all actually agree on that fact.'

'I don't agree Mike' said Chris firmly. 'It's just an idea for us all to have what could be a bundle of laughs, a party just for one night only. The women aren't going to realise anyway. I mean, that's one reason we all got together, isn't it, to have fun,' he asked Mike. Turning to appeal to the others he added, 'It's why we live together like this, isn't it?' He knew Mike's character very well now, he was sensitive and inoffensive in many ways and this presented him with certain problems when it came to some of the excesses and extremes that were occasionally engaged in by the others.

'OK, Mike,' said Raz quietly, draining his glass and then rising slowly to his feet. He leaned forward towards Mike, his big hands firmly grasping the edge of the table, 'I know what you are thinking and I know what you are saying. You're not entirely happy with the idea and I understand your reticence, but,' he wagged his index finger slowly at Mike and smiled warmly, 'this is something completely different. We're four chaps sharing a flat to have fun and laughs together. If the fat birds were coveted as much as thin ones, you'd be after them like a shot. But they're not, so I suggested this as a test for Tony because he's come out with this crap about being bored with pretty, thin girls. We're basically doing these ugly birds a favour because they probably never get invited anywhere. Do you not see that Mike?' he asked sitting back down in his chair and patiently waiting for Mike's reply.

Still not entirely convinced, but sensing the exhilaration that the others felt about the idea, Mike smiled weakly back at Raz, 'OK Raz, I'll agree. I'm sure it will be fun,' he replied, nodding slowly, giving in to what he could tell was the unanimous wish of the others.

Raz beamed, his mouth opened wide to reveal his white teeth shining brightly as he extended one of his huge smiles to Mike. 'Good man,' he grinned.

Chris returned from the bar with a tray of four beers. They each took one and got to their feet and taking a large swig they raised their glasses and clinked them merrily together.

'OK, we're agreed, here's to our pig party, details to be arranged,' cried Chris.

'Oink! Oink!' they all roared loudly. 'Oink! Oink! Oink!'

Chapter Fourteen

'We really need to set a date for the pig party if we're going ahead, but I think that we've got to decide exactly what the rules should be,' Mike stated gravely to the others.

It was early evening and the quartet were gathered in the lounge moaning and groaning about the trials each of them had experienced during their working day. Tony in particular had experienced a day he wished to forget. He'd decided to cut a good length of hair off a young woman who had grown her hair long for ten years. When he had finished the cut, reminiscent of the new Twiggy look which was becoming very popular, the girl had burst into tears and, despite Tony's efforts and the efforts of the girls in the salon, she could not be consoled. One of the girls had taken her home sobbing whilst Tony had not even been paid for his work. Later that afternoon, a colour job went hopelessly wrong when an academic from the university, who had asked for a simple dye job to cover the few grey hairs in her short brown hair, ended up with bleached blonde looks, much to her obvious dismay. Tony was amazed to hear that the angry academic's vocabulary could certainly match that of the most vociferous squaddie from the local barracks.

'The girls have got to be really different, the type of girl you wouldn't normally think of dating, such as the grotesque sort, or too fat or too skinny, boss-eyed, two heads, four feet, that sort of thing,' Chris suggested to the others.

'You're talking about fucking freaks,' cried Tony. 'And you ought to know, Chris,' he teased.

'Piss off Tony, when have ever seen me with a rough bird?'

'Plenty of times, especially late at night when you're half-cut and any chick will do to satisfy your primeval urges.'

'Yeah, we've seen and heard you smuggling them out of the flat really early in the morning, real dogs that the rest of us wouldn't be seen dead with, eh fellas? said Mike mischievously, glancing around for signs of confirmation from the others.

'I reckon he's been in secret training for this fucking freak show, putting in some advance training at pulling pigs. What about the other bloody day, with the washbasin woman? What the hell was she like for Christ's sake?' Tony asked, his hands upturned in a quizzical manner. 'We never got to see her did we?' he said scornfully.

'Actually, she was an absolute cracker and you can confirm that with James when you see him,' Chris replied smugly.

'Oh, yeah!' they all chorused mockingly, trying to wind Chris up.

'We've heard all that before,' gloated Raz. his big eyes blazing mischievously as he mocked Chris playfully, despite knowing that it would be most unlike Chris to entertain a girl if she was not of a pretty high standard.

'Right,' said Mike taking charge again, 'let's get down to business. Chris has mentioned that we need unusual girls, but you've all suggested that the bigger and uglier they are the better. In the pub the other day we talked about a fine or forfeit for the loser, who will be whichever one of us that brings along the best looking pig. Are we all agreed that the loser, decided by voting amongst us all after the party, will have to clean the flat for a month and take over everyone's chores? Also, after the party, one evening we'll all go out on a binge and the loser will pay for all our drinks. Whoever brings the ugliest pig will be the winner, again by popular vote, and he will receive £5 donated by each of us into a kitty, which I'll take charge of if you like.'

'Sounds fair to me,' Raz exclaimed.

'And me,' added Chris.

'Me too,' agreed Tony.

'Well, as this has all been organised because you're fed up with pretty girls, I hope that you are satisfied with the idea,' Raz told Tony.

Tony nodded reflectively. 'Yes, I'm certainly quite looking forward to it now that it's become a competition between us all. It's certainly going to be different!'

'I mentioned this to Mark and Johnny and they both thought it was a brilliant idea too,' added Mike. 'I'd like them to come, then they'll be six of us, which means twelve at the party, which makes a nice round number. Does everyone agree that's OK?' he asked, removing his glasses and cleaning the lenses with his handkerchief.

There was general agreement to this suggestion as Mark and Johnny had become the group's best friends and lived just around the corner in a spectacularly squalid bedsitting house. They often spent time together with the crowd at number 110 Mawson Road.

'So, let's set the date then. What about Saturday the nineteenth of July, that's about six weeks away and gives us all plenty of time to look around for likely candidates.'

The format of the party, the competition rules and the date had been set - all the group had to do now was to invite their guests but that was to turn out to be not quite as easy as they had all expected it to be.

Chapter Fifteen

During the next few weeks, there was a great deal of joking and horseplay amongst the boys about the forthcoming party, mainly to conceal the trepidation that most of them felt about finding the 'the pig of their dreams' as Chris decided to call the boys ideal partner for the party. The main problem which none of them had the foresight to comprehend was that, although they were all fully conversant with meeting and coming onto pretty girls, none of them had any experience of chatting up the huge specimens that each of them needed to pull if they were not to lose face at the forthcoming party. In fact only Raz, after the initial moments of inspiration, had paused to give the matter some serious thought. People did pair off with fat or ugly people, he reasoned to himself, but the problem was that he and his friends always had it too good and too easy because of the superfluous number of pretty, shapely females available to them in Cambridge. On reflection, he decided that Tony had made a valid point, they had all become very blasé about women in general. In fact, Raz could recall a statement he had pronounced one night some months ago when he'd been at a disco with some friends from work. They had been eyeing up the talent from the sidelines. Raz had been astonished when one of his compatriots that night had mentioned that he rather fancied one of the girls dancing together on the floor. She seemed to Raz to be badly dressed, overweight and very unattractive. 'Why pick an ugly bird, when there's plenty of good looking ones available?' he had asked his friend. Nevertheless, he knew that if he'd been living with his family in India, a bride would have been procured for him, as his religion decreed, and he could have ended up with a really ugly woman as his wife. Thank God he'd escaped from all that and now enjoyed all the freedom he could desire, together with the companionship of such wonderful friends.

Chris had also spent several sleepless nights anxiously worrying where on earth he was gong to meet a woman suitable for the forthcoming party. What if some of his other friends around Cambridge spotted him chatting up a really rough bird? He had ventured into some very seedy pubs and bars recently in search of an unusual girl to ask to the party, most of these places being establishments that he would normally have been fearful of entering. He had exchanged snippets of information with the others, but everyone was becoming extremely secretive about their search for a partner. This meant that they were all taking the party very seriously, no-one wanted to lose this competition, that fact was becoming very evident.

On Friday evening when he would normally have had a date, or at least have been at one of his usual haunts, either a pub or a disco, looking out for a new beauty to pull, Chris's quest took him into the 'Cow and Calf', a seedy, run-down pub in the Castle Hill area of Cambridge. This pub was the hangout of a richly assorted bunch of locals, low-lifes, American GIs from local bases, heavy drinking Irish navvies and, occasionally, a few reckless students. The place had gained quite a reputation due to the number of prostitutes who gathered there touting for business.

He entered the noisy, overcrowded pub, immediately encountering a heavy haze of tobacco smoke, noting the grimy nicotine-covered walls covered with tattered flyblown 'Playboy' centrefolds. One glance around the room made him even more aware of the salty clientele that he had heard so much about.

He slowly pushed and weaved his way through the crowd to the bar. As he cast his eye along the bar he noticed two huge, obese, blonde haired girls, both heavily made-up, wearing cheap gaudy clothes, smoking and chatting together. His spirits leapt as he realised that either girl would be an ideal candidate for the forthcoming party. He excitedly drained the first pint that he'd ordered and bought another, for some Dutch courage. 'I'll finish this one and then casually move along the bar to talk to them,' he decided. 'Maybe ask them both if they would like a drink? Perhaps they were prostitutes, they could certainly pass for ladies of the street,' he thought, but if they were, 'would they ever go out to the cinema or to a party if it means losing a night's work,' he wondered.

He began to feel very uncomfortable hemmed in at the bar by the vast crowd. The excessive noise and the heat and smoke did not help. He'd never been much of a lone drinker and this dirty, overcrowded pub would not normally have been somewhere he would have chosen to drink in at all. He had to concentrate on his sole reason for being there and from time-to-time he glanced in the direction of the two girls, hoping that one of them might notice and acknowledge him with a smile, even a nod, giving him a chance to move over and have a chat with them.

He ordered his third beer, becoming aware that he was feeling a little light-headed. The beer was very tasty and obviously pretty strong. He had often thought to himself that drinking alone made a person drink faster somehow because there was no conversation to help pace oneself between drinks. He knew that he was drinking too fast but he felt the need to especially in this pub with the oppressive heat and the noisy crowd jostling around him, it certainly made him very aware that he was alone. Finally he managed to catch the eye of one of the girls. He smiled and nodded at her and she held his gaze for a couple of seconds, tossed her hair, took a quick drag of her cigarette and turned back to her friend. He decided that he had to cast aside any apprehension that he felt and ordering yet another beer, he pushed his way through the crowd over to where the two girls were sitting. Interrupting their conversation as he suddenly loomed over them, they looked up at him strangely, noticing his tousled hair and flushed face. He felt perspiration start beading on his upper lip.

'Hi,' he smiled down on them, hoping they did not suspect that he was feeling quite drunk. 'Is this pub always so hot and crowded?' he asked them, trying to appear casual. 'There's so many people in here tonight.'

'Yeah, that's why we like it here, don't we Viv?' said the largest of the two blondes.

'S'right,' Viv answered. 'You can always have a good laugh in here and they stay open after closing time. It's always packed here at week-ends.'

'Oh, I've never been here before,' Chris replied feeling worried that he might not be able to summon up the courage to ask one of them to the party. 'Can I buy you both a drink?'

'Wouldn't say no,' said the larger blonde. 'I'll have a G and T please.'

'I'll have a Babycham and port please,' replied Viv.

'Right, coming up,' said Chris catching the barman's eye and ordering the girl's drinks with yet another for himself. He handed the drinks to the girls and, as he drank a deep swig of his beer, he suddenly experienced a floating sensation enveloping his body. He felt slightly sick and light-headed and could tell that he was swaying a little so he placed one hand on the bar to steady himself. The cheap perfume that the girls were wearing assaulted his nostrils and he could feel beads of sweat breaking out on his forehead with the oppressive heat. 'Cheers,' he said raising his glass somewhat erratically.

'Cheers,' chorused the two girls, raising their glass amicably towards him.

'D'you both work in Cambridge?' he asked them.

'Yup,' replied Viv. 'I work in Boots Chemists and Madge works in accounts at Eden Lilley's Department Store.'

Chris received this news with some relief as, if they both had jobs, they were less likely to be on the game, but then looking at these two huge, fat women, who would want to go with them anyway he wondered.

'Do you live in this area?' asked Chris trying to control the nauseous feeling welling up in his stomach.

'Yeah, we've got a flat just around the corner,' replied Viv.

'No wonder you're in here all the time, then,' said Chris. 'It's lucky you're within staggering distance if you get too pissed in here.'

'Oy, you, cheeky, who said we ever get pissed?' giggled Madge, dragging deeply on her cigarette and draining her G & T with one mighty swallow. 'Would you like another one, then, and what's your name, and have you any mates with you?' she asked him in a friendly manner.

'I'm Chris,' he responded. 'I live across town in Mawson Road with three friends, but I'm on my own tonight. I'm in selling, I sell office goods,' he told them. 'And, yes, I'd love another beer, but just a half this time.'

He'd had time now to make a hazy appraisal of the two

women. Viv had long dyed blonde hair, which was very straggly with some of the black roots showing through. She wore a badly fitting red chainstore suit with red stilettos. She appeared to Chris to be about five feet six inches tall, weighing maybe fourteen or fifteen stone. He nails were disgustingly bitten and dirty, bearing small traces of a red nail varnish. Her friend, Madge, was the one that Chris decided excitedly was an absolute certainty to be the prize winner at their party. She had a flabby face which looked a bit piggy-like thought Chris delightedly, surveying her coarse face. Her eyes were just narrow slits, almost buried in the depths of her overblown features. She had roughly camouflaged several spots around her chin. She had shorter blonde hair than her friend and Chris noticed a reddish tinge to it, he wondered if it was dyed. She was wearing a crumpled navy suit with a white blouse, revealing a little of what appeared to be a massive cleavage. Chris estimated her height to be about five feet three inches. She was so fat and heavy looking that Chris reckoned she must weigh at least eighteen stone. Her legs were as solid and hefty as tree trunks. God knows what the size of her thighs were he winced. She certainly was a frightening prospect, but would she play Cinderella and come to the ball, he wondered?

He felt nauseous again as his head began spinning faster when Madge handed him his beer. He could feel his body swaying and clutched the bar more tightly to steady himself. He knew that he should make some excuse and leave before he passed out or fell over. He'd drunk several strong beers and the heat and noise were making him feel even more uncomfortable, coupled with the tension he felt inside as he steeled himself to ask the big question. He decided that he had to ask them both at this stage. If they both accepted, he would single Madge out on her own by calling her next week. 'Pull yourself together, you arsehole,' he told himself. 'Ask the question, get a 'phone number and get out of here quickly before you make a fool of yourself.' He kept glancing around at the crowd, worried that someone he knew might see him with these two gross women, although it was unlikely that he would find any of his friends in this hell hole.

Viv interjected his thoughts. 'Does your job get you about a bit?' she asked blowing a plume of smoke towards him in an attempt to be sensual; had she watched too many Hollywood movies he wondered, lighting a cigarette himself.

'Yeah, I work in my own time. It's quite exciting,' he replied.

'Must be nice to work when you want to,' said Madge.

'Yeah, it's OK, I guess,' said Chris decided that it was now or never. 'Tell you what, would you be interested in a party next Saturday?' he asked, realising that he had blurted the question out rather too quickly, hoping that they would not detect the eagerness in his voice.

'Might be,' said Madge narrowing her piggy eyes even tighter. 'Where is it?' she demanded brusquely.

'It's at our flat in Mawson Road. It'll be really good fun, good music, good food. It's a sort of house warming,' he lied. 'We haven't been there too long.'

'Sounds as though it could be OK,' replied Madge in a voice that sounded slightly suspicious to Chris.

'Christ, as if you should be so fucking lucky,' he thought, amazed that she had reacted to the invitation as if it was a regular occurrence. 'Do girls like this get invited to parties all the time,' he wondered. 'Look,' he said loudly trying to think straight but being forced to raise his voice to be heard above the general mêlée, 'I've arranged to meet a friend at ten-thirty in the city centre, so I must go now, but if you'd let me have your 'phone number, I'll confirm the time and address of the party during the week.' He noticed that he was slurring his words badly and wondered if either of the two girls had noticed. Mind you, they had both downed a few drinks anyway and would probably get through quite a lot more if they stayed on after closing time. They would be used to dealing with drunks.

'We've got no phone in our flat, we've only got our work numbers,' said Madge.

'OK, put your number down on this beer mat and I'll ring you on Tuesday,' he told her.

Madge wrote her number down on the mat and passed it over to Chris. 'There you go,' she smiled her shifty-eyed smile at him. She was quite a frightening prospect he decided, you would not want to get on the wrong side of her. God knows what could happen. He drained his glass, trying hard to hold himself upright. He was now feeling extremely inebriated yet somewhat euphoric as he clutched the mat with her telephone number and was sure his search was over as long as Madge decided that she would come on Saturday. 'Nice to meet you girls, look forward to seeing you again soon. I'll ring you on Tuesday, Madge,' he mumbled and, with a slight wave, he was off, lurching through the crowd and out into the welcome coolness of the street. The relief of the cold air was short-lived as his head immediately began spinning wildly. He let out a whoop of triumph, causing several people walking by to peer at him curiously and to veer warily away from him as he bounced against a wall.

He swayed unsteadily down the street singing, 'I've met a prize winning porker,' to the tune of Gerry and the Pacemaker's song, *How do you do what you do to me?* Somehow or other, and well over two hours later, he managed to arrive home and stumble up the stairs without waking anyone. He fell heavily onto his bed, fully clothed, and fell into a drunken sleep.

When he awoke late the next morning, it took several minutes for his head to clear and to recollect what had happened the previous evening. He began to feel very apprehensive as to whether Madge would actually agree to come to the party, as he had sensed a certain reluctance in her manner in the pub.

As promised, he rang Madge on Tuesday morning although it had taken several attempts because his courage kept failing him at the last moment. Each time he dialled the number she had given him, on hearing the ringing tone, he had promptly chickened out and replaced the receiver. His stomach kept tightening up and he was sure his heart was racing much faster than normal. 'This is fucking ridiculous, this isn't the girl of my dreams. She's the stuff of nightmares, so for God's sake pull yourself together' he muttered to himself, trying to steel himself to actually talk to her. He had to admit to himself that he was really scared in case she refused him, he would never find such a suitable candidate for the party again, of that he was certain. Eventually, he gritted his teeth, drew heavily on his Pall Mall, lifted the receiver and dialled her number for the tenth time. He recognised her deep, dry voice and his guts started churning, but after a few pleasantries she had agreed to attend the party although he had to resort to some quick thinking because she wanted her friend Viv to come with her. 'Christ, imagine looking after both of them,' he thought to himself with some alarm. He explained to her that the invitation was for a restricted number and that it was couples only, which was in fact the truth. Somehow he felt good that he'd told her the truth about that at least; sometimes he felt a bit uneasy about this crazy idea of Raz's. Mike had been right really, this party was an outrageous idea, but what the hell, 'you only get one life, you might as well enjoy it,' he decided.

'I'm sorry Viv can't come, but maybe another time we could all get together,' he heard himself consoling Madge down the line with another white lie. 'Christ, she should think herself lucky that she's been invited out at all,' he said to himself quietly as he put the receiver down, wondering what she would do and how she would react if she ever became aware of the true reason for his invitation.

Chapter Sixteen

The four flatmates had been greatly intrigued a couple of days previously when they had heard that their friend Johnny, a real Don Juan, had been seen hanging around the YMCA building on Tuesday evenings. Johnny was a real ladies man, with a penchant for lissom Swedish blondes, but it seemed the attraction for him on this occasion was an exercise class for larger women run by Weight Watchers. He had been seen in the bar, eyeing up some of the more obese members of the class as they relaxed over a much needed drink, still hot and perspiring after their showers at the end of the class. The mutual friend who had offered this piece of gossip to the boys had been amazed to come across Johnny eagerly chatting up several of these large ladies. Apparently when the mutual friend had approached him to say hello, Johnny had coloured up, looking very sheepish indeed before making it clear that he did not want to talk. He had clearly been extremely embarrassed at being seen there.

The group had enjoyed the story but could not offer any reason for Johnny's unusual behaviour as they were all sworn to secrecy and an explanation would have given the game away about the forthcoming pig party.

Mike and Chris had been discussing everyone's attempts to pull a bird for the party and were both intrigued by the fact that Raz had been spending his weekends in London recently with some of his old university colleagues. 'Maybe there's more chance of pulling an ugly piece of totty in the Smoke than down here,' said Chris, 'but it might intrigue his friends to find out that his taste has suddenly changed so drastically from the pursuit of pretty dolly birds to big old ugly ones!'

'I think it's because he doesn't want anyone to catch him chatting up a fat old tart in Cambridge,' replied Mike.

'We're all in the same boat, aren't we? None of us actually

wants to be seen with an awful bird,' said Chris. 'Anyway Mike, how's your search coming on?'

'You'll just have to wait and see,' smiled Mike, wishing that he had managed to find someone even though he still felt uneasy about the whole idea. Ever since Raz had conceived the notion, Mike had been unhappy with what he perceived to be a tacky, almost cruel, proposition but his views had been outvoted by the others so now he was attempting to go along with it. Once the day of the party came round and he had actually found a girl for himself, he hoped he would enjoy himself as much as the others, but sometimes lying in bed at night, he would conjure up gross charactures of various fat women jumping around the flat, the unknowing victims of a dubious night of hilarity for himself and his friends. It was upsetting but the arrangements were too far advanced now, he just had to tow the line and hope that eventually his conscience would be absolved of the feelings of guilt that he harboured at the present time.

Excitement grew steadily amongst the flatmates and their two friends as the date of the party loomed closer and closer. Each of the group was endeavouring to discover whether the others had managed to obtain a suitable porker. Who she was, where she lived, how enormous was she? These were the questions on everyone's mind but, of course, they were all playing dumb with each other. It was like an adult game of cat and mouse.

For some relief from the tension generated by the forthcoming party, Raz and Tony had bought tickets to see The Yardbirds, a particular favourite of both boys, who were playing at the Corn Exchange. They were both aware that neither of them had found a suitable girl for the party, but maybe something would turn up at the concert.

The atmosphere that night when they entered the huge old wooden floored building was bursting with excitement. The band were very popular and the number of bodies crammed together made the hall uncomfortably steamy and sweaty. As the boys made their way through the throng to the licensed bar, it was a relief to start introducing themselves and begin talking to their usual prey, the pretty, attractive, mini-skirted dolly birds that they loved to chat up. But Raz suddenly stopped in his tracks having spotted two extremely large and unattractive girls sitting together at a small table near the bar. 'They're bloody horrendous' gasped Raz who could not quite believe his eyes. 'Look at those two Tony, they're unbelievable. They are just what we need. I don't know which one's the worst.'

'I wouldn't even touch mine with yours,' replied Tony, eyeing the girls with alarm over Raz's shoulder.

'But they're just what we're looking for,' replied Raz excitedly.

'Well, I'm game if you are,' Tony said to Raz, completing ignoring the two pretty girls they had just started chatting up.

Feeling extremely self-conscious, they sidled over to the two massive girls and asked them if they would like a drink. After chatting awkwardly for a minute or so, the girls agreed to have a drink, so the boys went up to the bar and returned with two port and lemonades for the girls and two beers for themselves. They sat down opposite the girls, with their backs to the main area, hoping that no-one would recognise either of them talking to these grotesque women.

Raz leaned forward and took a mouthful of the cold beer. As he was about to talk to the girls, he was suddenly conscious of someone tapping him on the shoulder. He half turned in his chair and looked round to find two tall, unkempt looking blokes, both with long straggly hair, staring menacingly down at him. They both wore studded black jackets and dirty jeans. The tallest one who had tapped Raz's shoulder had a jewellers shop window full of large gold rings on his stubby fingers. Tony also turned around, alarmed at the threatening attitude adopted by the two men standing behind them. Out of the corner of his eye he noticed the two fat girls were now huddled together, whispering and giggling.

'Can I help yo....' Tony said, suddenly being grabbed hard by the collar of his jacket and hauled right out of his chair by one of the yobs. Caught completely by surprise, he had no time to defend himself as a ring-studded fist crashed against his nose causing him to stagger backwards against the small table, sending their drinks flying. He lost his balance, falling onto the floor and clutching his damaged face. He vaguely sensed a commotion going on around him but was too badly confused and shocked to take it in. His nose hurt like hell and his vision had been completely distorted by the blow. His eyes were full with tears of pain and he was vaguely aware of blood on his hand and felt it running down his face and dripping off his chin onto his freshly-ironed shirt. Then, almost immediately it seemed, he felt himself being dragged roughly to his feet by someone obviously quite strong. He vaguely thought he heard Raz's voice over the shouting and jostling, then he felt himself being propelled across the room. His glazed eyes could not perceive much, but he heard some banging sounds and then he was out into the coolness of the street where he realised that Raz had dragged him through the emergency exit.

Despite his blurred vision, Tony saw that Raz was bleeding profusely from a cut above his eye. He also appeared to have a split lip that was already starting to swell up. Still confused and frightened, Tony pulled out a handkerchief to try and stop the blood flowing from the cut on the bridge of his nose. He wondered if it could be broken, it was certainly throbbing badly. He noticed that Raz's shirt was covered in blood, whilst his face was swollen very badly, he looked a real mess.

They stumbled along the pavement, Raz holding Tony around his shoulders to keep him upright. 'You OK?' Raz asked hoarsely, spitting blood.

'Not exactly. I feel terrible, but what the fuck happened to you?' asked Tony incredulously, still dazed and beginning to shake with the shock and trauma of the sudden disturbance.

'Well, apparently the two ugly birds were meeting those two equally ugly and unattractive arseholes in the bar. Unfortunately for us, we didn't know that and the two blokes didn't like us chatting up their amazonian ladies. Blokes like that usually have an IQ of about ten between them anyway,' explained Raz. 'They're just ignorant bastards.'

'So what happened after I hit the floor,' asked Tony eager to know, but feeling guilty for not having taken part in any of the action apart from getting hit.

'Well, I shot up off my chair and kicked one of the bastards in the goolies so hard that he went down like a log. The other guy, the one with the rings, hit me really hard and split my lip. He then hit me again several times and split my eyebrow open. I managed to get a good right hand to his eye, but then all hell broke loose. All the people standing around grabbed the guy and shouted at me to get you out of there quickly. Apparently he's a real thug and shouldn't be walking the streets. So, I hauled you up off the floor and dragged you out quickly and here we are, both beaten to a pulp!'

'Christ, I wouldn't mind so much for getting picked on for chatting Miss World up, but for two fucking old slappers like those two, it really takes the biscuit. It's fucking unbelievable,' moaned Tony clutching his nose again.

As they lurched across the Market Square, people passing by gave them a wide berth as they were both completely covered in blood. They made their way to the gents toilets in the middle of the square and Raz led the way down the steps into the soulless white cavern. He turned on the taps of two basins and they both washed the blood from their hands and faces, using their handkerchiefs to help clean up.

Tony wondered again about his nose but, after a close inspection, Raz decided that it was not broken, just badly bruised. Already the skin around Tony's eyes was beginning to discolour and darken. 'You'll have two great black eyes in the morning,' said Raz. 'You'll match my complexion then,' he laughed.

They clambered unsteadily up the stairs and managed to find a taxi almost immediately. When they arrived home, they each checked their wounds in the bathroom mirror, undecided whether or not to go to Addenbrooke's Hospital for stitches. Although both of their faces were badly bruised, the wounds did not seem quite as bad as they had feared, so they made some strong coffee and sat for a while in the lounge discussing their spoilt evening. They hadn't even got to hear The Yardbirds play anything at all. Raz decided that a good night's sleep would benefit them both, so they each went off to bed.

The next morning, Tony's eyes were black with a yellowish tinge around them and his nose was swollen badly. Raz had used sticking-plaster to cover his cuts, while his facial swelling had gone down a little overnight but when he tried to smile his swollen lips took on a grotesque appearance.

When Mike and Chris arrived home from their overnight stay with a couple of girls they had met the previous evening, they were both horrified to find Raz and Tony calmly eating toast and drinking coffee at the table in the kitchen, with their battered and bloodied faces clear evidence that they had been involved in a fight. Mike was particularly sympathetic to them both, clucking around like a mother hen. 'Tony, you ought to have your nose looked at by the accident department at Addenbrooke's or you could end up with a distorted conk,' he advised.

'Well, that could make him look a little better,' said Chris who, although initially commiserating with the battered duo, couldn't resist taking the piss out of them both. 'You both look as though you had almost as much action as we did last night,' smirked Chris playfully.

'Piss off, Chris. We were attacked by these two bloody wankers without any provocation from us at all,' cried Tony.

'Yeah, we were only talking to their ugly girlfriends,' said Raz. 'Not that we knew who they were at the time,' he added ruefully.

'And weren't they ugly?' said Tony. 'You'd have thought those guys would have paid us to take them away,' he added.

'Ah ha,' cried Chris gleefully, his eyes wide with realisation as he nodded across at Mike. 'These two were after a couple of pigs, were you not Raz?' He turned to Raz, awaiting a reply.

Raz drained his coffee, sat back in his chair and placed his hands on the table. 'Yes, that's partially correct. We went out to see the Yardbirds, but then we had an opportunity to pull a couple of birds for the party. These birds were ideal, but I think next time I'll be a little more careful and I think Tony will too. I've never had so much trouble in finding a bird as I've had trying to pull one for this party,' said Raz as he checked his watch and stood up ready to leave. 'And its all your fault,' he wagged his finger and grinned at Tony with his swollen lips. Raz put on his jacket and trooped off to work, wondering what his colleagues would say when they saw his bruised face covered in plasters. God knows what they'd say if they knew that he'd got into trouble trying to chat up two of the ugliest, fattest birds they had ever seen! To cap it all, there were only two weeks left for him to find a girl for this wretched party. 'Oh God, what a nightmare this is becoming,' he thought to himself. 'I think I'll go to London again and see what I can find there.'

Chapter Seventeen

The long awaited Saturday arrived at last and found the boys trying to do their best to clean the flat in readiness for the party, a task met with little enthusiasm at the best of times by any of them.

The long dining table in the lounge had been polished and layers of dust were duly removed from objects and surfaces throughout the flat. The high ceiling in the lounge was clustered with cobwebs and spiders but Mike persuaded the others that they gave the room real character and should be left alone, even though he knew most women hated spiders; indeed many girls invited back to the flat cringed in fear if they happened to glance up and notice the ancient cobwebs strung about the lofty room.

The kitchen was stacked with crates of beer and the ancient fridge was stuffed to overflowing with lager and white wine. They had bought a couple of cases of the brain deadening Hungarian Bulls Blood, an extremely powerful rough red wine that had became a particular favourite of the four flatmates. It was cheap, strong tasting and very potent, often with disastrous effects on the uninitiated who could easily drink too much of it when being misled in the boys company.

Chris had procured a small amount of marijuana, but none of them were really into smoking dope, apart from the odd occasion. Many people in Cambridge used drugs, but most of the boys considered them a waste of time, preferring instead the pursuit of women and the intake of large quantities of alcohol, which they all considered far more pleasurable.

A motley collection of glasses of every shape and size was lined up on the table, many of them having been spirited away from various pubs in the area. They had bought a huge hunk of cheddar cheese, together with various assorted tins of biscuits and several loaves of bread. 'Nothing too substantial in the food line,' said Raz, 'alcohol is the important commodity.'

'Absolutely right, eating gets in the way of drinking,' laughed Chris, picking a piece off the corner of the Cheddar.

Mike had brought out his prized Dansette automatic record player and had set it up in the lounge, relaying the music through Raz's borrowed speakers that they had used at their flat-warming party. Raz had performed minor miracles with some strings of coloured fairy lights they had found hidden away in a cupboard with some old Christmas decorations. He had strung them erratically across the room, together with a string of tattered Union Jack flags that they had unearthed somewhere. Bundles of balloons were placed in the corners of the room, together with an assorted array of candles on most of the flat surfaces.

Raz and Mike had sorted out a large selection of records for dancing, including some of their favourites by The Beatles, The Rolling Stones and The Kinks. Tony noticed Raz glancing through some smoochie records by Johnny Mathis, Nat King Cole and Julie London. 'I hope that no-one gets pissed enough to want to put those slow numbers on tonight,' he told Raz, a sense of panic running through his sensory system as he conjured up an image of the huge girl that he had invited to the party, the thought of dancing close to her made his legs go numb. Good grief, she could probably crush his ribs to bits. She was almost twice his size and the thought of smooching with her almost sent his brain into orbit.

They had set the polished table against a wall in the lounge and the cheese and biscuits, together with the bowls of nuts and nibbles were arranged along the table.

'Looks bloody good now,' remarked Raz, surveying the final decorations approvingly, his face beaming and his huge eyes sparkling with delight. He was, as usual, eagerly anticipating the excitement, the music, the dancing, tempered of course this time by the imminent arrival of the horde of fat and ugly girls. 'I think we're in for a real laugh tonight, let's hope these lucky girls really appreciate it,' he said to the others, trying to imagine how the girls would look together in the room.

Mike had once remarked to Chris that if life was a twenty-four hour party, then Raz would be there most of the day, every day, singing, dancing, drinking, pulling birds and just enjoying himself. Chris had mentioned to Mike one day that Raz had told him that he had been so relieved when he and his family had managed to leave Uganda safely during the xenophobic campaigns in that country just before the brutal dictator Idi Amin had come to power and expelled the Asian community and that every day since then had been a bonus. Sometimes behaving like a sixteen year old delinquent was just an excuse for Raz to let off steam, and parties gave him that excuse.

The four flatmates, accompanied by Johnny and Mark, met up for a late lunchtime drink after they were all satisfied that everything was in order for the party that evening. Mike had organised the meeting at the Live and Let Live in order to finalise the 'kitty', to make sure that everyone paid into it and that they all understood the rules. Once again Mike felt some uneasiness stirring itself in his mind, but it was too late, there was no stopping now.

Mike, recognised as the most serious and able of them (after all wasn't he soon-to-be qualified as an accountant?), was the unanimous choice to look after the 'book' and to finalise the rules. 'Right,' he announced firmly, pushing his spectacles up the bridge of his nose, 'the rules that we agreed on that night in the pub when we all decided to proceed with this bloody pig party are these: one, we all put £5 into the kitty and later on tomorrow, when we're all sober, we'll have a vote as to which one of us had the worst pig, by that I mean the ugliest. That person takes the whole kitty - OK? So, rule one, obviously no-one can vote for their own pig; rule two, the person who brings the best looking bird has to clean our flat, taking over everyone's rota, for two weeks. That includes Mark and Johnny as well,' Mike indicated the two friends from the flat round the corner, who both nodded in agreement. 'And, three, the loser has to buy each of the others beers all evening once a week for a month. Is that OK?' He surveyed them all, examining their faces, hoping that there would be no problems. After all, it was simple enough, surely, even for this lot of reprobates to understand?

Luckily everyone chorused approval, although there were several furrowed brows, each person now anxiously wondering how their choice of partner would stack up against the rest of the women, £30 was well worth winning.

'Let's have your fivers then,' demanded Mike, taking a five

141

pound note from each of them and placing them all into a Barclays Bank linen money bag, sealing the top by tightening a rubber band around it. 'That's for the winner of the Ugly Bugs Ball,' he told them; 'and may the worst woman win'.

Everyone relaxed a little and cheered his final statement. Chris raised his glass and looked around at them all. 'Here's to a great laugh tonight boys. May I suggest that we have a toast to Tony for being so blasé about women that we've had to resort to this party, and also to Raz for coming up with the idea. From my point-of-view, it has been a bloody terrifying ordeal and I know from what you've all said, it's been the same for each of us. After tonight, I think we'll go back to the easy bit, pulling the best looking birds in town as usual.'

'You can say that again,' said Tony ruefully rubbing the faint red scar on the bridge of his nose. 'I shan't open my big mouth in a hurry again, especially after Raz and I were done over in pursuit of a couple of pigs.'

They laughed uproariously together, draining their glasses enthusiastically. Each of them was now eagerly anticipating the evening ahead, but all of them were equally experiencing severe misgivings as to how their partner would measure up in the contest. No-one wanted to lose face to their fellows. Besides, there was all that bloody cleaning as a forfeit if one lost, not forgetting the amount it would cost to pay for the others to drink themselves into oblivion. Losing the contest just did not bear thinking about, so each of them tried not to, they were all just looking forward to the exciting evening ahead.

Chapter Eighteen

Chris drove the hearse slowly across Cambridge, but unfortunately he ran out of petrol on the Backs, a tree-lined road running parallel to the River Granta at the rear of several of the colleges. The petrol gauge had the annoying habit of showing empty when full and, likewise, showing full when empty. Chris had thought he was safe with the needle on the gauge pointing at a quarter full, but the damn vehicle had still managed to totally confuse him. Swearing like a trooper, he foraged through the paraphernalia that he kept in the rear of the Rolls packed in the makeshift coffin, eventually finding the petrol can that he kept there, luckily he found that it was half full. He poured the contents into the tank, jumped back into the Rolls, which started easily and five minutes later he arrived at 20 Merton Street, the address Madge had given him.

It was a narrow, two up, two down little terrace house built of the local yellow Cambridge brick and just as she had told him, located just around the corner from the Cow and Calf where he had initially met Madge and Viv. He gingerly rang the bell and heard the sound of her heavy footsteps descending the stairs through the thin panelled front door. Moments later the door was flung open to reveal Madge dressed in a violet, short-sleeved dress with a vee-neckline, exposing a deep cleavage between the tops of a massive pair of breasts which were obviously straining to burst out of the top of the dress. Her bare arms seemed to Chris to be thicker and more muscular than the average Irish navvy, but as he lowered his astonished gaze, he had to smother a gasp of horror as he took in her short, fat legs emerging from the bottom of her too short dress. She had piled her hair up in a sort of fashionable beehive. He could smell the coarseness of the cheap hair lacquer that she had used to glue her hair in place. The hairstyle only served to emphasise the squat bulbous nose squeezed in-between her little piggy-slit eyes.

'Good God,' exclaimed Chris silently to himself, so taken aback he was completely speechless. 'If we weren't going to a party, we'd be going to the market,' he decided with horror. Recovering his composure, he steered her quickly across the street where she was flabbergasted to find that Chris's mode of transport was a hearse. Reluctant to get in, she began pacing around it with a steely glare, bending down now and then to peer inside whilst uttering sighs of deep dissatisfaction; causing Chris some concern that she might bolt for home.

'What the fuck is this thing you're driving? This is for bloody funerals,' she shrieked at him eventually, stooping to peer inside the back window at the heavy black curtains and made-up coffin.

'This my dear Madge is a Rolls Royce,' said Chris proudly touching the huge gleaming radiator grill and pointing out the RR symbol on the front.

'I don't care what it is, I'm not getting in this fucking hearse thing. It gives me the creeps. You've even got a coffin in the back,' she roared with disbelief, her nostrils flaring as she stood glaring at Chris, her hands clamped on her hips.

'Can I explain, Madge. It's not a hearse any more. It's my own private vehicle,' said Chris soothingly, trying to placate the incensed woman.

'What the fuck's that in the back then, if it isn't a bloody coffin?' she bellowed at him.

'No, no. I mean, yes. It is a coffin, but it's there just for fun. It's made up to look like a coffin from old bits of wood. I just keep bits and pieces in it. Look, I can draw the curtain across the back of the seats so that you won't even see it,' he said leaning over the seat and drawing the curtain across the rear of the seats. 'Is that OK for you now Madge?' he asked desperately trying to reassure her, he certainly did not want to lose her now, not his prize porker.

He glanced across the road at the passing traffic, concerned that someone he knew might catch him trying to persuade this enormous hulk of a woman to enter his vehicle. How much street cred would he lose, he wondered, if that got around Cambridge?

'Oh well, I s'pose I'll have to get in, it'll have to do but I've never heard anything like it. Wait 'til I tell Viv that you turned up in a fucking hearse, she'll never believe it.'

'You can tell her that I turned up in a Rolls Royce, that's more to the point, my dear,' said Chris relieved that she'd stopped arguing and that they were going to leave.

Madge clambered uneasily into the passenger seat, now complaining there was not enough room for her legs. She slammed the door so hard Chris thought that the glass might shatter. He breathed a sigh and silently pleaded with the gods that there was enough petrol in the tank to get back across the city, the bloody vehicle guzzled the stuff and he could not bear to imagine how Madge would react if he did run out. He had already been shown evidence that her tolerance level was not that great and, as for berating his beloved hearse, that was unbelievable. Since when did girls like her get taken to parties in a Rolls?

Luckily they made it back to Mawson Road without any further mishaps and he parked in the road almost opposite their flat. Chris had decided on the way back that Mike and Raz had made the better decision, arranging for their girls to make their own way to the party. Accordingly, they had stayed in the flat attending to all the last-minute preparations, lighting the candles, opening the red wine and sorting the music, 'and probably getting pissed before anyone else arrives,' smiled Chris to himself.

As they climbed out of the hearse, Chris heard the faint beat of Buddy Holly and the Crickets song *Maybe Baby* emanating from the bowels of their flat. Madge, who seemed to have calmed down on the ride over, now appeared far less agitated and, on hearing the music, remarked to Chris that it was one of her favourites. Chris opened the door of the flat and they walked up the dusty stairs and along the dimly lit corridor. Raz had changed the normal white light bulbs for red ones which gave out a warm glow and helped to disguise the worn furniture and tattered carpets. Chris decided the hallway looked extremely inviting for their 'guests'.

Chris and Madge could hear peals of raucous laughter rising above the music. The Rolling Stones were now pleading, 'Hey you, get off of my cloud,' as they stood in the doorway of the lounge, peering through the dim red glow, the flickering candles dotted around producing little pools of soft light on the walls, barely enough for Chris to discern who was who in the murkiness.

Chris could hardly bear the suspense. What girls had the others brought along? How big or ugly where they? Where and how had they met them? As he desperately tried to focus on a couple of people talking together that he could vaguely see through the gloom, he was suddenly doubled up by Madge's left elbow thudding hard into his stomach. Caught completely by surprise and badly winded, the intense pain caused by the impact of her elbow caused him to fall almost to his knees. 'Aagh!' he gasped, his eyes watering profusely. 'What was that for?' he spluttered, his mouth gaping open as he struggled to breath properly, having to lean against the wall for support.

'What's your game?' she demanded brusquely, her nostrils flaring menacingly as her eyes narrowed even further into inquisitive little slits. 'What's going on here?' she demanded angrily, her hands clamped firmly on her hips as she nodded in the direction of the barely discernible forms in the room.

Chris could focus on things better now that his eyes had adjusted to the gloom and he could just make out a couple dancing together at the back of the room. The female was huge, obscuring the view of whichever one of his friends he was dancing with. 'My God,' he thought, 'the others have also brought some crackers along,' as he desperately tried to pick out which of the crowd was dancing with the Amazonian lady.

Madge glared at him angrily. She appeared to be shaking a little as she waited for him to answer, seemingly oblivious to the pain he was obviously feeling.

'I don't understand what you're getting at,' groaned Chris, trying hard to regain his composure. The force of the blow had made him feel physically sick. 'It's a party and, hopefully, we're all going to have a great time.' 'My God,' he thought, 'she's sussed it all out. This could mean big trouble.'

'This is just very odd, something doesn't seem right to me,' she said, turning around to gaze disapprovingly at the forms across the room.

As if on cue, the situation was suddenly calmed when Raz

lurched over and began to introduce himself to Madge. Chris noticed that he was slurring his words and realised that Raz must have been getting stuck into the booze whilst he'd been out collecting Madge. Raz handed Chris and Madge two glasses of the punch that he'd just finished making. 'Well, I must say it's lovely to meet you Madge and, as one of Chris's flatmates, I hope you'll have a lovely time at our party tonight,' beamed Raz, laughing out loudly, unable to contain his natural enthusiasm, even for the unorthodox party they were all giving tonight.

'What woman could resist him when he's on such outrageous form. He just loves parties,' Chris said to Madge, noticing that she was smiling sweetly back at Raz. He had obviously made her feel more relaxed. She had already drunk most of the glass of punch in one great gulp, but he noticed thankfully that she had calmed down and had stopped shaking.

'Are you OK, Chris,' Raz asked with a note of concern, having noticed that Chris was leaning heavily against the wall still trying to recover from being hit in the stomach. Chris was trying to stop himself from retching and felt like throwing up.

'Yeah, I'm OK, thanks Raz,' replied Chris hoarsely, unable to explain to Raz what had just happened with Madge standing so close by. She was still casting her eyes warily around the room as she drained her glass noisily. 'How's it all going?' Chris asked Raz anxiously, attempting to take his mind off the pain in his stomach.

'Just brilliantly,' replied Raz happily and loudly. Lowering his voice to a soft whisper and making sure that Madge was still looking around the room, he spoke excitedly to Chris, 'Yours is a cracker, she's so fat and ugly. Tony's got a great porker too over there dancing.' His shoulders juddered as he finished talking, then they began heaving up and down and Chris realised that Raz was having great trouble containing himself from a bout of uncontrollable laughter. The sight of all these fat women in their flat was obviously becoming too much for his sense of humour.

Chris glanced across the lounge again and noticed Tony dancing with a large blonde woman. He realised that they were the couple he'd tried to distinguish earlier. The woman was so large that she seemed to envelop Tony completely. She was wearing a bright emerald blouse above a pair of tight black trousers, both of which bulged with rolls of fat fighting for freedom in every possible direction. She was leaning so heavily on Tony's shoulders, swigging wine from a large glass, that Tony's legs were almost buckling under the weight of her enormous bulk. Tony was perspiring heavily and laughing loudly at everything the woman said. Chris realised Tony must be well on the way to being drunk even though it was still comparatively early. As the staggering pair bounced off the wall, looking as though at any moment they might collapse together in a heap, Chris hoped for Tony's sake that he wouldn't fall beneath her, he wouldn't want to watch his friend suffocate to death.

'Where's your bird?' asked Chris turning back to Raz who had been endeavouring to engage Madge in some friendly conversation.

'She's in the kitchen talking to Mike. I'll go and fetch her, so prepare yourself,' said Raz triumphantly as he staggered off uncertainly to find his girl.

Chris then noticed Johnny, who had obviously been sitting out of sight at the end of the room, dancing with a woman who had the most extraordinary angular legs and arms. She was so tall and gaunt that she seemed to Chris to be like a giant stick insect. She had some type of brace on her front teeth and she wore thick, round, pebble glasses. She did not look much more than seventeen or eighteen. He decided to try to talk to her later on. Just then he caught Johnny's eye and winked, giving him a discrete thumbs-up sign. The girl reminded Chris of a character from *The Beano* comic called Dilly Dream, or was she more like Olive Oil, the girlfriend of Popeye?

Just then Mike appeared, dragging by the hand a very short, very fat girl dressed in a mini-skirt made of what looked like black plastic. She had an enormous chest which she had tried to disguise by not wearing a bra and letting it hang beneath her blouse. 'I'd like you to meet Juanita,' said Mike, introducing her to Chris and Madge. He explained that she was from Mexico and was in England on holiday for two weeks. Lowering his voice he whispered to Chris that he had met her in The Eagle only a couple of days ago when he had been absolutely desperate to find someone. Mike moved past Madge's bulk, grinning round at Chris, before dragging Juanita to the dancing area. Chris was

148

astonished to notice the Mexican girl's huge buttocks falling below the hem of her short skirt, as she danced they wobbled like jelly, but then every bit of the girl wobbled anyway.

His thoughts were interrupted by Raz roughly grabbing hold of his arm. Still nervous after Madge's blow to his stomach, he was badly startled until he realised who it was. Raz had a huge muscular woman in tow, or so Chris hoped, for 'surely she wasn't a man in drag, was she?' he wondered, fascinated by her masculine features. She was wearing a long azure blue dress which contrasted severely with her long, straight, red hair which was cut straight across her forehead just above the eyebrows. She wore too much garish make-up and her thick bright red lips seemed to be almost too large for her face. Endowed with enormous hips and hefty muscular arms, she cut an awe inspiring figure. She was certainly no beauty, her face reminded Chris of a picture of a dragon that he remembered from a book of fairy tales that he had read in his childhood. As she extended a chunky, bejewelled hand and gave him a bone-shattering handshake, he decided that the comparison with the dragon was pretty accurate. Raz introduced the dragon to Madge and Chris. Her name was Rita. Chris noticed Madge staring intensely at Rita, taking in every detail about the odd woman and, for one fearful moment, he feared Madge might throw another wobbly.

Madge poured herself another drink and Chris watched with concern as Raz introduced the two girls. Rita greeted Madge with a loud clinking of glasses, 'Here's looking at you kid!' she said, laughing at Madge and draining her glass. The two ugly fat women were soon in intense animated conversation, punctuated by bouts of hysterical laughter. Raz was a real trouper decided Chris as he refilled their glasses from a freshly opened bottle of Bulls Blood, he often amazed Chris with his boundless energy and enthusiasm for life. Raz was such a dark horse, but where the hell had he managed to drag the dragon up from? He winced slightly, his hand was still suffering from shaking hands with Rita. 'Maybe she is a man,' wondered Chris again. 'I'll have to investigate later,' he decided as he wandered across the room to chat to Mike who had left his girl dancing while he selected some more records from their collection.

'How's it going Mike?' asked Chris taking a swig from his

beer, unsure whether to mention his concern about Madge's volatility to him.

'Absolutely great. This party is such a hoot,' said Mike taking off his spectacles and wiping them with his handkerchief. 'I just can't stop myself laughing at all these fat birds prancing around. I know I was against this whole idea at first Chris, but it really is fun. I reckon the more booze we can ladle into them, the better it'll be.'

'Yeah, but for Christ's sake don't upset any of them or we could have a mutiny on our hands. If any trouble started here, these women could slaughter us,' said Chris still feeling the effects of Madge's elbow and Rita's handshake, but pleased that Mike was enjoying himself so much.

Finally, Mark, the missing member of the group, arrived to cheers and yells from the others eager to check out the girl he had chosen. He introduced Vanessa to everyone. She was yet another enormous woman who seemed to dwarf her lightly-built companion. She was dressed in a combination of black and white, an absurdly short mini-skirt showing off her enormous calves and thighs and revealing a pair of knees that would not have shamed a Scottish caber thrower at the Highland Games. Glasses of punch were thrust into the newcomers hands as the boys checked Vanessa out with sidelong glances. Now that all the girls had arrived, it was easier for them to decide which of them had brought along the prize winning porker.

The flat was becoming very warm as more people began to dance, in between consuming drinks at an alarming rate. One or two of the girls were beginning to glisten as their make-up suffered in the heat. For some reason known only to himself, Raz climbed uncertainly up onto the lounge table and stood swaying, waving his hands in the air, drunk and excited, as he tried to conduct the others to accompany The Searchers singing, *'Sweets for my sweet, sugar for my honey.'* Unfortunately, Raz, in his enthusiasm began treading all over the sweating Cheddar cheese and crushing the assorted biscuits that had been carefully laid out on the table. No-one seemed too worried as by this time, everyone appeared to be too inebriated to care. Raz's face glowed with delight, his red bow tie twisted at a crazy angle, giving him the appearance of a mad professor as he led the others in chorus, using his hands as though he was wielding a conductor's baton.

Chris, surveying the others from the doorway, noticed that Madge now seemed to be having the time of her life, her enormous bulk thudding up and down as she danced and flapped about with the other girls. They reminded Chris of a group of caged rhinoceros that had just been given their freedom.

Tony appeared from the kitchen with yet another bottle of wine and topped up Chris's glass. They stood together, surveying with amusement the odd assortment of women gyrating their enormous hips to the pulsating music. They both turned to say something and suddenly collapsed against each other, laughing hysterically as they held onto one other for support, both very drunk and thoroughly elated at how well the party was proceeding.

Madge appeared in front of them, now dancing vigorously with Rita. As Rita, her back to Chris, danced her way in front of him, she reached down behind her back and, without warning, grabbed his balls firmly in her hand. She turned round quickly and grabbed his shirt front, pulling her to him against her large chest. 'Mmmm, you've got a lovely set there Chris,' she grinned wickedly, then slapped him in the chest and turned to continue dancing with Madge.

'Christ,' he breathed shakily, turning to Tony who had not even noticed anything as he was still engrossed in watching the girls dancing. The incident had only lasted about five seconds, but Chris realised thankfully that she had not squeezed his balls as hard as she had squeezed his hand earlier on.

Raz staggered over and draped his arm loosely around Chris's shoulder. 'This is a really good fun night, it's such a crease up, Chris,' he mumbled drunkenly.

'Yeah, it certainly is,' agreed Chris. 'That bird Rita that you brought along, she's pretty forward, isn't she? She's got a grip like a professional wrestler.'

'You're absolutely right,' said Raz. 'She'd tie you up in knots as soon as look at you. I met her in London at a party. That's how she makes her living.' He gazed at Chris's face with amusement, looking for his reaction. He could tell, even in his drunken state, that Chris thought he was taking the piss, but wait until they were sober and he would prove it was true.

Larry Williams was belting out the rocking *Short fat Fanny*. Chris and Raz looked incredulously at one another, both amazed that Mike had the affront to play that record. All the girls seemed oblivious to the words and continued dancing enthusiastically to the rock music.

'Are you sure she's female, Raz? She's already tried breaking my hand and just now she squeezed my bollocks so unexpectedly I almost jumped out of my skin,' said Chris.

'Oh, that's just Rita. She likes to have fun,' laughed Raz.

'Well, I can believe that, but I still don't know whether you're pulling my leg,' said Chris uncertain whether Raz was teasing him. 'I think I'm a little dubious about your friend.'

Mike came over, a bottle held in each hand, and topped their glasses up again. 'Whose got the best pig then, have we decided?' he asked them eagerly.

'Sssh, keep your voice down,' said Chris peering round nervously to make certain that none of the girls had overheard Mike.

'Well, it's not as though we're likely to see any of them again, is it?' said Raz, 'unless this party turns one of us onto big girls.'

'You're bloody right,' agreed Mike. 'My blood pressure couldn't stand dealing with this crowd again.'

Tony stood there swaying, drunk and happy, listening to the music, when suddenly he became aware that Madge, who by now was extremely inebriated, was clambering unsteadily up onto the table. The first chords of The Rolling Stones boomed out as Mick Jagger sang, *'Let's Spend the Night Together.'* The song obviously had some kind of impact on Madge as she began strutting her stuff in time to the music, taking little short uncertain steps backward and forwards whilst making jerky arm and hip movements. Mike, watching Madge swaying about up on the table, became concerned that she might overbalance and fall off and flatten someone, or even possibly injure herself. He moved nearer the table, praying that he wouldn't have to try and catch her if she did lose her footing. 'Christ, she must weigh six or seven stone more than I do,' he decided. 'She could seriously damage my health if she fell on top of me.' As she strutted and preened, everyone gathered around the table cheering and clapping, shouting words of encouragement to the manic obese woman gyrating above them. Mike began removing the remains of the biscuits and cheese previously trampled over by Raz when, suddenly without warning, Madge pulled the shoulder straps of her dress down over her shoulders. She then expertly flipped the top of her violet dress down to the waist, exposing two huge pendulous mounds of shuddering white flesh. These enormous forty-eight inch breasts bounced and flopped as Madge shook her hips and wriggled her huge body back and forth, her eyes blazing fiercely in drunken delight. Pandemonium broke out, even the other girls were cheering and yelling, stomping on the floor as Madge pulled her dress halfway up her thighs, trying to emulate the Can-Can that she could vaguely remember she had seen Shirley Maclaine dance in some movie.

As the record ended, to much applause from the excited spectators, the party goers suddenly became aware of the incessant ringing of the front door bell; someone seemed to be leaning on it continually whilst pounding on the door extremely hard.

Madge immediately pulled her dress up to cover her breasts whilst there was some consternation amongst the boys as to what was happening at the front door. Mike was uncertain as to whether it was more likely to be gatecrashers or the neighbour beneath them complaining about the noise level and went careering down the stairs to investigate. He cautiously opened the door, aware that it could be gatecrashers but, as he had feared most, there stood their neighbour from the bottom flat, whom Chris had previously upset when he had flooded the man's flat. He stood there clad only in his pyjama bottoms, his unshaven face contorted with rage. His dark eyes glowered menacingly at Mike, even his wiry brown moustache appeared angry to Mike as he took in the huge expanse of muscled, hairy chest and the heavily tattooed forearms bristling before him. The man was completely covered in a layer of white particles and powder which seemed very odd to Mike. He looked as if he had been in snowstorm.

'Listen, you four-eyed git,' he spat at Mike, jabbing a huge banana-like finger into his chest. 'Not only are you lot up there making too much bloody noise at three o'clock in the morning, but the stomping about up there has just cracked all the plaster in my bedroom ceiling and it's all fallen down on top of me and my wife in our bed. It looks as though there's been a fucking blizzard in our bedroom. What the fuck have you got up there, a herd of cows?'

Mike stifled a laugh, coughing so hard he almost choked himself. Conscious of the sniggering of the others watching in suspense upstairs, he hoped none of the girls had heard the remark and read anything into it.

'First of all one of you floods my fucking flat and now you're knocking the fucking place down on top of me,' he yelled at Mike, his face reddening with anger. 'I've almost had as much as I can stand!'

Several of the party goers had gathered in a small group at the top of the stairs where they could not be seen by the irate neighbour and were trying desperately to smother their spasms of laughter as tears rolled helplessly down their cheeks with convulsive laughter. Mike was still desperately trying to placate the man, who was waving his arms angrily, looking rather like a mad snowman. The group peered down at him from their vantage point, all of them drunk and delirious with silent laughter. Mike's conversation floated up to them. 'Sorry about the noise, we had no idea it was so late and as for the ceiling falling down on you and your wife, may I say how very, very sorry we all are. May I suggest that we all come down tomorrow and help you clear up. We'll bring you a bottle of something nice to apologise for all the inconvenience.'

'Well, you fucking better - and shut the fuck up with your noise now, do you understand?' shouted the angry man. 'You're just a load of wankers. Any more aggro and I'll break your bloody door down and I'll be up there to sort you all out, one-by-one.' He turned away fuming, then entered his own flat and slammed the door forcefully behind him.

Mike carefully shut their own door and traipsed ashen-faced back up the stairs where he was surprised to find everyone crouched down at the top of the stairs. He felt slightly embarrassed that they had all listened to the severe chastisement that he had just suffered, but he'd had to accept it on behalf of all of them. He'd really had no choice in the matter, it was not as though any of them could have known that the ceiling below would disintegrate beneath them all. And, as for the lateness of the hour, Mike was as surprised as anyone that it was already three in the morning, they had obviously had a great time, both the girls and the boys. It seemed unbelievable that the party he had been so against had turned out so well, apart from the damage to the flat below.

'I'm really sorry everyone,' announced Mike, 'but the chap downstairs is obviously not very happy as the ceiling in his bedroom has collapsed on him and his wife downstairs and I value my health too much to antagonise him any further, so I'm sorry but the party must come to an end.'

'I'm not bloody surprised about the ceiling with the weight of this lot,' muttered Johnny quietly in Raz's ear. 'It's a miracle the bloody floor didn't collapse, then we'd all have joined them in bed downstairs.'

Mark, who was the most sober of all of the men, appeared from the kitchen carrying a tray full of steaming mugs of strong coffee which were handed around to everyone now gathered in the lounge, surrounded by the debris of the party. Several of the girls had become definitely the worse for wear, though they were still managing to laugh at the crude jokes that they were telling themselves.

Mike took Chris aside to explain that they had to get the girls out of the flat as quickly and quietly as possible. It seemed odd to think that normally they would try every trick in the book to persuade the girls to stay the night, this time they couldn't wait to get rid of them. 'OK girls,' said Mike trying to assume a sense of urgency and clapping his hands together sharply several times. 'Time to drink up.'

'Oh shit,' groaned Rita, 'can't we stay here?'

'No,' grimaced Chris, a little alarmed at Rita's request. 'We want to go to bed as soon as possible, but we can give you girls a lift home if you want one.'

'Let's stay and have one more drink,' slurred Madge followed by grunts of approval from the other girls.

'Oh God,' said Chris quietly to Mike. 'They've had such a good time they really do want to stay. We don't want them all turning nasty and rampaging around the flat, this lot would present an army regiment with a problem.'

Raz had been sitting quietly, nicely drunk, sipping alternatively from a bottle of beer and a mug of coffee. Now he leaned over to Mike and Chris and in a hushed whisper told them that he had a solution to get the drunken girls out of the flat.

'You haven't got a flame-thrower tucked away in your bedroom, have you?' asked Chris.

'Leave it to me,' Raz assured them, rising uncertainly to his feet. 'OK, girls,' he addressed them all, his arms spread wide as if he wanted to encompass each and every one of them. 'I'm sure you'll agree the party has been great, but we have to avoid any further conflict with our neighbour and especially the Police if he calls them, which he may do if we make any further noise, so may I suggest that you all finish your coffees and leave, then we can do this again sometime as its been such a brilliant evening!'

Chris groaned quietly, holding his head in his hands in disbelief. Mike frowned and shook his head slowly from side to side. 'Surely he doesn't meant that,' he said quietly to Chris. But Raz's request had worked. It seemed that the girls had understood. They all finished their coffees and began collecting their coats and searching for various handbags that had been mislaid. In no time at all they were all trooping uncertainly down the stairs and out into the street, drunk, tired and immediately feeling worse as the cold night air enveloped them.

Chris and Mike managed to manhandle the now almost comatose Madge into the rear of the hearse, together with Tony's girl, Rita, who proved even more difficult. She was so drunk she felt like a dead-weight. Tony had to enter the rear of the hearse, where he leaned over Madge with his hands under Rita's arms and, with much sweating and cursing, managed to pull Rita aboard. Mike stumbled and giggled as he pushed Rita's body forwards whilst Tony pulled her in from inside the hearse. Eventually, with both the huge girls safely ensconced in the rear, Tony scrambled out over Rita's bulk and slammed the rear door shut. Immediately she slid heavily against the inside of the door, her face flattened against the glass. Tony surveyed her grotesque features, her make-up streaked all over her face. She was obviously oblivious to the world as she commenced snoring heavily, immediately falling asleep in a drunken stupor.

Chris clambered unsteadily into the driver's seat, calculating that he should just have enough petrol to get the girl's home and return to Mawson Road. He shook his head vigorously from side to side, taking several deep breaths, trying desperately to clear his alcohol ravaged brain, wishing to hell that they did not have to take these bloody drunken women home when he would rather be in bed asleep.

Just as he started the engine, Rita's snoring changed into a rasping, snorting growl, rising to a crescendo that rattled the rear window. Tony sat uneasily next to him, red-eyed and tousle-haired, wishing that Chris was not so drunk but still knowing that he was a good driver whatever condition he was in at the wheel. He lit two cigarettes and passed one over to Chris as they set off down the road. Chris swore at a cyclist passing by without any lights before realising that his own lights were not switched on. He turned them on guiltily. He motioned to Tony with a nod at the two girls in the back, 'Christ, have we got a pair of sleeping beauties,' he said. 'We'll never live it down if we get stopped by the police.'

'Still, it was bloody good fun while it lasted,' giggled Tony. 'It's a pity about the neighbour's ceiling though. Let's hope he doesn't complain too much to the landlord. We could really get kicked out this time.'

Chris was fighting the wheel, his eyes narrowed down to deep slits in his tired face, the cigarette dangling from his lips, as he tried to keep the hearse's wheels from clipping the kerb. 'Yeah, too right,' he replied. 'But in fact he probably did us a favour as his complaint gave us an excuse to get the women out, otherwise they might have stayed all night.'

'God help us, the way they were carrying on, they might have ended up raping us,' exclaimed Tony. They both laughed together at the madness of the whole evening.

Tony turned round to survey the two big girls lying comatose in the rear of the hearse and remembered how the idea had stemmed from his original remark about being fed up with pulling pretty girls. Raz's idea had been a great success, they'd all laughed themselves silly at the cavorting women, but the nice thing was that all the pigs had enjoyed themselves too.

'Oink! Oink!' said Chris to Tony, knowing the slumbering girls couldn't hear him. 'Oink! Oink!' they chorused drunkenly, glad to be nearing Madge's flat so they could drop her off. Rita's home was only half a mile away and then they could both get home and sleep, hopefully for most of the day.

Chapter Nineteen

Mike rose fairly early the next morning as the incident involving their neighbour in the flat below had played on his mind and had upset his sleep. Despite a raging hangover he had decided to face the music on behalf of all of them by going downstairs hoping to placate the angry couple, taking a left-over bottle of wine as a goodwill gesture. Being Sunday, he had certainly not wanted to wake him up too early and arouse any further anger in the man, but he had heard him closing his front door several times, so he knew that he was already up and about. It turned out that the man had been carrying the larger lumps of plaster that had fallen off the ceiling out to the dustbins in the garden. His wife was vacuuming up the thick layer of white plaster dust that seemed to have covered everything in their bedroom.

Mike was dismayed to be shown several large cracks across the ceiling, culminating in a large hole about three feet by four feet directly above the couple's bed. By now the couple had almost cleared all the debris, so there was nothing Mike could really help them with. 'Look, I can only apologise again on behalf of us all, but may I suggest that I have a friend who is a very good plasterer. I can ask him to repair the damage this week. I'll ring the landlord and explain, but we'll pay for all the damage repairs ourselves,' Mike suggested, pleased that the neighbour's temper seemed to have quietened down this morning.

'OK, as long as it doesn't inconvenience my wife and I too much, but I'm telling you this, if anything else occurs, I don't know what I'll do,' the man told Mike bluntly.

'It sounded like a herd of elephants up there last night,' added his wife.

'Yes, I'm very sorry,' replied Mike, peering uneasily down at his feet, deciding that she was not very far off the truth.

Relieved to get out of their flat intact, Mike went back upstairs and put the kettle on for tea. He turned the radio on and lit up a bedraggled fag from a crumpled packet left lying on the table, reminding himself to ring Alex, his plasterer friend, later that day regarding the flat below.

Twenty minutes later Raz appeared, looming bedraggled through the kitchen door and yawning incessantly, closely followed by the other two.

What a motley unkempt crew they looked thought Mike, gazing around at the others as they sat yawning and wheezing, tousle haired and stubble faced, white tongued, with the smell of last night's cigarettes and stale booze on their breath.

Now that everyone in the group had surfaced and when the hot sweet tea and cigarettes had begun to revive them, the group's main topic of conversation was the dreadful girls they had brought along and which of them had won the contest: Who had brought along the ugliest? Who had brought the prettiest? Who had won the prize for the best porker?

Mike rang Johnny and Mark and asked them to get round for breakfast. They appeared ten minutes later having walked around the corner wearing only their dressing gowns. They joined the others and sat chatting and joking about the antics of the girls during the previous evening.

Mike called for a vote and handed out six pieces of paper on which they all voted twice, one vote for their choice of the best girl - for the person who most of them decided had brought along the best looking girl and who would now have to pay the fine and do the cleaning for a month and pay for all the drinks when they all went out together; and one vote for the "best pig" - which was for the person deemed the winner!

When the votes were in, Mike read each one in turn and added the votes up. With a smile playing around the corners of his mouth as he neared the end, the others sat restlessly awaiting the verdict. 'OK,' he said when he had checked the sixth paper, 'its a unanimous vote for both. Chris has won the competition for best pig with Madge, so he wins the thirty pounds.' There were some mock jeers and boos from the others as they teased Chris playfully. 'There was one vote for Rita, Raz's girl. But the wooden spoon for the best looking bird goes to Johnny who scored five votes, so it was a unanimous decision from the rest. Johnny must have voted for my girl!'

Mike passed the bag containing the £30 over to Chris, while Johnny sat disconsolately in his chair and let out a groan of mock displeasure and held his head in his hands. 'Oh no,' he muttered, 'that means I've got to come round and clean your bloody flat!'

'Absolutely correct,' said Mike gleefully, 'and buy us all drinks one night each week for a month.'

'Yahoo! Well done Johnny,' said Raz.

'That'll keep you fit,' said Mike as they all convulsed jeering and laughing at Johnny's expense.

Chapter Twenty

The ancient activity of punting on the River Cam soon became a favourite summer pastime of the boys once they had become established in their flat. It was a very pleasant and civilised manner in which to spend a leisurely afternoon, but they soon came to realise that the offer of a 'trip up the river' was a great way to pull the birds. Many of the foreign girls had never even seen a punt before, let alone experienced a trip in one. When they observed the punts on the river for the first time and saw the confusion and havoc wreaked by the many inexperienced tourists trying to manoeuvre themselves along the river, the offer by one or two of the boys to take them for a free trip was hard to resist. Often they took along a cooler box with a bottle or two of wine and some glasses as an additional incentive.

On one memorable occasion Chris and Mike had bought an old wind-up gramophone and some 78 rpm records, including Glen Miller and Lonnie Donegan. They had met a couple of lively Australian girls who were travelling around Britain and they had taken them punting up the river, playing music along the way. They had dressed up in their coveted straw boaters and striped boating blazers which they had bought from a second-hand shop in Cambridge. Both of the girls had been extremely impressed with the authentic 'boating' look. The boys had also taken along several bottles of wine and later that afternoon they had moored up at a secluded spot on the river bank at Grantchester where the group had sat drinking and talking together. After some initial amorous advances they had paired off and both couples had discreetly retired behind the bushes and long grass to make love in the late afternoon heat, after which they had all swum naked in the cool river, laughing, screaming and splashing each other like a bunch of naughty schoolchildren.

The great advantage of punting, from the boys point-of-view, was that once the girls had been punted for a while and shown the beauty of the ancient colleges with their immaculate lawns running down to the river's edge, that was usually enough to assure the girls that they had made the right decision and so they became more grateful to the boys for the unexpected invitation. 'Aren't you glad you came with us now?' Chris would ask after some time, knowing that they were already completely enraptured by the sights. Mike also had a theory that a person's character could be determined after a couple of hours punting on the river, but Tony dismissed this as a half-baked idea.

'We only use our punting abilities to try and charm the pants off the ladies, literally, so what the hell does character matter? It's big tits and long legs and a stunning looking face that we're after initially, isn't it? Their character can come into play later,' insisted Tony. 'But amongst us all, who really cares?'

'But I don't just mean with women, it's how men react as well; some can cope with punting and enjoy the experience, but others get pissed off and disagreeable, especially when the river's packed with bloody tourists,' insisted Mike. 'Then their real character comes out.'

'With girls we're only interested in drooling over their bodies for a couple of hours, trying to impress them enough while they're trapped in the confines of a fifteen foot punt so that we can get them into bed later, but we don't seem to worry about their characters. It's all a bit superficial, isn't it?' said Tony condescendingly. 'If they've got a brain I guess that's a bonus.'

'I'd like to know what the hell these girls think of us sometimes after we've fucked them and left them, especially the one night stands,' said Mike who was never as demeaning towards women as the other three could be.

'They think the same as we do,' replied Chris. 'Look Mike, they all want to get into our pants, don't they? We don't force them, we ask them nicely. Sometimes they make it so obvious, we don't have to try very hard, but we could be their one night stand too, don't you see?'

One particular Saturday lunchtime, Mike and Tony had been drinking at the Baron of Beef for a couple of hours, having arranged to meet up with Chris later at Magdalene Bridge. The pub was run by an amazing character, Bob, a loveable ex-sergeant major in the army with an extensive vocabulary of expletives. It was popular with a vast array of locals, academics and tourists, all of whom enjoyed the lively ambience. Consequently, the boys often spent many happy hours drinking there and, knowing many of the regulars of the place well, they usually emerged after a long drinking session feeling very merry, which they did on this occasion, tumbling out of the pub and making their way along to Magdalene Bridge, just two hundred yards away.

Next to the Bridge was a mooring area, adjacent to which was an office from where punts could be hired. When Chris arrived he found Mike and Tony ensconced on a bench regaling four pretty Swiss girls with jokes and stories. He knew immediately on hearing their slightly loud, slurred voices that they had consumed a good few drinks. Tony was busy promoting his hairdressing skills, trying to persuade the girls that, with his expertise, he could change their hair to make each of them 'even lovelier than you are now.'

'Yuk,' said Chris, simulating to Mike and the girls the fingers down the throat pretending to throw-up joke.

Tony's slight Italian accent and dark, continental good looks often won the girls over, but he occasionally used the ploy of 'doing their hair' to gain even more favour with a girl that he fancied. The boys had heard it all before and, though none of them ever felt jealous, they could certainly become bored and restless if he used this chat-up line too often in front of them.

Chris was introduced to the girls by Mike. There was Anna, who seemed to be the leader of the group, then there was Heidi, Christianne and Marianne. 'Would you like to come punting with us on the river?' asked Mike, casting his eye hopefully over the four girls to gauge their reaction, trying to decide which one he fancied the most.

'Yes, but we don't know how to do it,' replied Anna. 'We 'ave no boats like this in Switzerland.'

'What about your navy?' asked Chris cheekily.

'Oh, wise guy,' said Mike, dragging out the words. 'You haven't even had a drink yet Chris.'

'There's no need to worry girls, we'll show you how to do it,' said Tony.

'In more ways than one hopefully,' said Chris quietly in Mike's ear.

'What if we fall in the water?' enquired Anna.

Chris's eyes and mouth opened wide in mock horror. 'You'll get very wet.'

'But we'll save you from drowning,' said Mike.

'They can bloody well save themselves, it's only three feet deep,' cried Chris laughing out loud, enjoying the clowning around with the girls.

'And I will give you the "kiss of life",' said Tony to Marianne, placing his hand gently on her shoulder and squeezing gently.

'Tony's made his selection pretty damn quickly,' thought Chris admiringly. 'He's such a smooth bastard, one has to give him his due, there's no holding back with our Tony.'

After a brief discussion amongst themselves, the girls eagerly agreed to join the lively trio on the river and everyone trooped into a nearby off-licence, emerging with a dozen bottles of beer and three bottles of dry, white Macon. Mike had procured a length of string from the shop assistant to tie around the necks of the bottles so that they could be lowered into the water to keep cool, rather like a portable ice bucket. 'Make sure you tie those bloody bottles tightly,' said Tony to Mike, remember a fiasco that had occurred a couple of months previously when Tony, Mike and Raz had taken three German girls out punting. They had bought some wine but alas, Mike, too eager to attend to the frauleins, had not paid enough attention to tying the bottles securely. When they eventually decided to pull into the river bank at Grantchester Mill to enjoy the cool wine and, hopefully, to begin seducing the girls, Tony had pulled in the strings and had been shocked to find nothing on the end. This had resulted in an infantile argument between Mike and Tony, whereby the German girls, despite Raz's entreaties, had given their hasty apologies and upped and left, leaving the three boys arguing with each other like school children.

Luckily on this particular day, the queue for the punts was short especially as it was such a pleasant afternoon and the group were soon climbing unsteadily into a punt as the boatman held it hard against the quayside, endeavouring to stop it rocking too much in the water as each person stepped in.

Chris, being the best punter of the boys, besides being the only sober one, was designated to start off as Mike, having securely tied two bottles together with the string, lowered them gently into the water at the side of the punt. He produced a corkscrew from his penknife and opened the remaining bottle of wine, handing round some paper cups that they had bought at the off-license.

Chris took the twelve foot pole from the boatman and jumped gracefully onto the platform at the rear of the punt as it was pushed carefully away from the quay by the boatman. Chris pushed the end of the pole hard down into the murky water, using the bottom of the riverbed as a lever to propel the punt along. As the punt glided forwards, he used a hand-over-hand motion to push the pole down. When his hands reached the halfway mark, he lifted the pole up out of the riverbed, hand-over-hand again, until it was halfway above his head, the end still trailing in the water acting as a rudder to steer the punt away from the bank and keep it in a straight line. The movement was then repeated and the punt continued gliding forwards. As many of the punts were in the hands of complete novices, he had to take great care to avoid collisions. Sometimes, especially at weekends, the river could become a nightmare with masses of tourist's punts becoming jammed together with no-one capable of navigating their own punt away from the confusion. Balance was most important for the punter with the rear platform being only three feet long, so an unexpected collision could cause the unwary punter to overbalance and fall into the river.

Chris punted them along the 'Backs' of the colleges, past St. John's, then Trinity College and the famous library designed by Sir Christopher Wren, one of Cambridge's most spectacular buildings. He eased the punt under the bridge at Caius College to reveal the expansive manicured lawns and beautiful buildings surrounding King's College, with the mighty splendour of the world famous chapel, it's majestic turrets reaching up to the sky. Between them the boys gave a running commentary to the girls and Mike kept the paper cups topped up with wine.

They glided slowly under the famous mathematical bridge,

built originally by Sir Isaac Newton, past Queen's College, then under a road bridge into a large open area known as the Mill Pond, overlooked by two old pubs, The Anchor and The Mill. The girls had been entranced by the beauty of these surroundings and appeared pleased that they had been entertained along the way. They were obviously enjoying the boy's company.

Chris, who was feeling hot and thirsty after his exertions, suggested that they tie the punt up at the green near the pubs overlooking the Millpond and sit and enjoy some drinks and conversation in the warm afternoon sun. He pushed his pole down to propel the punt towards the river bank whilst Anna and Marianne rose uncertainly to their feet in readiness to grab some outgrowing tufts of long grass hanging from the high bank, so they could pull the punt round against the bank. Unexpectedly the end of the pole suddenly stuck hard into the thick mud and silt lying on the bottom of the pond, causing Chris to overbalance. As he struggled to regain his balance and wrench the pole from the mud, the punt leaned heavily to one side and, with a cry of anguish, Chris fell head over heels into the water. The two girls standing at the front of punt were caught completely unawares by the sudden lurching and, with a cry of alarm, Anna fell heavily against Marianne, who grabbed hold of Marianne's arms, clutching for support. Unable to keep their balance, they too both toppled over the side into the dark, dirty water.

The remaining occupants of the punt were both astonished and amused, whilst a loud wave of cheering and laughter emerged from the crowds of students and tourists lying around lazing on the green. Chris stumbled round the punt, desperately trying to keep a footing in the thick mud and silt so that he could help the girls up onto their feet. He managed to tie the punt to an old tree trunk on the bank and then helped the two girls scramble up onto the top of the bank. He then assisted the other three out of the punt. Unfortunately Heidi tore her skirt a little, catching it on a rough edge on the side of the punt, which caused a couple of Swiss swear words to emerge from her pretty mouth. Meanwhile a fellow punter had retrieved Chris's pole from where it had stood straight up in the water and passed it up to Chris on the bank.

They all sat in a circle in the sun, Tony having seen fit to

167

carry the last bottle of wine and the beers up from the punt, whilst Anna and Marianne removed their wet shoes and stockings hoping that the sun's warmth would soon dry out their clothes. Both girls seemed to accept the unfortunate incident with good heart and they were soon laughing and joking with the others. As some consolation, Heidi had managed to photograph the girls when they hit the water. She had an expensive Leica camera and had been taking lots of photographs and the girls decided that at least that particular photograph would be worth looking at!

'So, what happened there Chris, leaving your pole stuck in a hole?' teased Tony.

'I thought we were the drunks on this trip,' said Mike sarcastically.

'Piss off,' said Chris. 'That could happen to anybody and you both know it.'

Mike had carried up a rug that was supplied with the punt in case the weather changed and the girls used it to rub their hair to help dry off the muddy water. Mike nudged Tony, he had suddenly noticed that the water had caused Marianne's white blouse to become completely transparent, showing off her superb bra-less breasts. Tony became transfixed as they appeared to strain the wet material every time she moved. Neither of them could stop ogling, yet Marianne seemed oblivious to the excitement she was causing them both.

Mike caught Chris's eye and nodded in Marianne's direction with a slight raising of his eyebrows above his glasses. Chris glanced over, frowned slightly, blinked twice, then pursed his lips and let out a long exclamation. 'Phew!' he breathed harshly. 'Nice tits,' he thought to himself, glad that Mike had brought them to his attention.

As the warmth of the sun soon started to dry their wet clothes, they passed the last of the wine around, the boys were now drinking beer. Tony, who could stand the strain no longer, decided that he had to move over next to Marianne whom he had made advances to earlier, but his interest in chatting to her was now greatly intensified and stimulated by her transparent blouse and the beauties inside. He took the rug from Anna, who had finished drying her hair and went and sat by Marianne. He began gently rubbing Marianne's hair until it seemed almost completely dry. He then took her hair in his hands and began expertly running his fingers through it, pulling the hairs apart to stop them tangling. Marianne moaned a little as Tony continued to finger-comb her hair. After several minutes he began to massage her scalp. She sat with her eyes half-closed, emitting little groans of pleasure as he teased her scalp with his fingers and nails. He muzzled her right ear and gave her lobe a soft kiss. She opened her eyes slowly, feeling tired and relaxed after the massage. As she looked up at him and giggled shyly, he looked into her eyes and knew that she wanted more.

Mike seemed to be deep in conversation with Anna, whilst Heidi had stopped taking photographs and had fallen asleep on the grass.

Chris pulled the leg of his flared jeans up so that he could inspect a large bruise on his left knee which had turned an ugly blue-black colour. He had clipped the knee on the edge of the punt when he had fallen into the Mill Pond.

'Oh my God, it's a bad bruise. I will pour some cold water on it to stop ze swelling,' said Christianne who had seen him examining his leg. She went over to the river bank and immersed a lace handkerchief in the water, then returned to Chris's side and laid it softly over the bruised area.

'Oh, you're a sweetie,' said Chris, touched by the kind gesture. He leaned towards her and put his arm around her shoulder, then kissed her lightly on the cheek.

She smiled back at him, then laughed as she thought of something. 'It was so funny when you fall in ze water, it was like a slow-motion movie,' she told him. 'Then I turn and my friends are falling in ze water too,' she giggled again at the recollection, then rose and wet the handkerchief in the river again.

She carried out the manoeuvre several times and although Chris did not notice much of a reduction in the swelling, he was thoroughly enjoying the attention and affection that he was receiving from the soft touch of Christianne. He lay sipping his cold beer, the sun's rays warm and his clothes drying out, surrounded by his friends and this quartet of lovely girls. They were without a care in the world, what more could the lusty group of friends wish for?

Christianne placed yet another cold, wet handkerchief on his knee, this time he could not resist pulling her gently to him, kissing her firmly but softly. 'That's nice,' she smiled at him, her blue eyes flashing prettily as they caught the sunlight. He kissed her again, still softly but longer this time, revelling in her smell, her skin, her hair, the taste of her.

'I want to make love to you,' Chris told her, already feeling his body stirring a little. He searched her eyes for any reaction.

'That would be nice too,' she giggled, batting her eyes at him sexily. She glanced around quickly to make sure her friends attention was elsewhere. 'But you must wait until we are somewhere else together, but without our friends around.' She reached out and touched the end of his nose with the tip of her finger and leant towards him. In a half-whisper so no one else could hear, she told him, 'My mother used to tell me that all good things are worth waiting for.'

'Oh God,' he sighed, realising that she was gently teasing him and also indicating that she would be happy to sleep with him. 'Utopia? Heaven? Who cares, this is just pure bliss,' he decided hugging Christianne to his side, pleasantly excited as his mind ran riot, thinking about the sexual encounter that lay ahead.

Chapter Twenty-One

Cambridge, set on the edge of the flat lands known as the Fens, was surrounded by RAF bases, many of which were left over from the Second World War, and had become rundown and deserted, but several of the more prominent bases had been leased by the American Air Force (USAF) and some had grown into quite extensive communities of American life and culture. Chris and Tony, in particular of the group at Mawson Road, had made friends with some of the American personnel who were stationed at the surrounding bases, such as Lakenheath in Suffolk or Alconbury in nearby Huntingdonshire. The Americans liked to journey into Cambridge, especially at weekends, looking for girls and parties and other diversions to enjoy where they could let their hair down.

Chris had made close friends with several Americans in the USAF who lived off base in Cambridge. They particularly liked the Hills Road area near the centre of town. Bateman Street was full of terraced four storey Victorian town houses, many of which had been converted into cheap flats. The street had a certain cachet as during the Second World War many of the city's prostitutes had lived and worked there. Somehow this tradition had continued with many of the occupants of the flats being 'good time' girls, together with a cosmopolitan mix of students and young working people. The American servicemen like the salty, somewhat bohemian atmosphere and some of them had moved into rented flats in the area.

Jerry O'Hara and Bill Callahan were two jovial, hard drinking Irish-American GIs who shared a notorious flat at No. 10 Bateman Street. The flat consisted of the whole of the first and second floors and had gained its fame from the wild parties that the duo liked to organise every two weeks or so. Jerry and Bill had achieved the reputation of being particularly generous hosts, probably aided by the fact that booze, cigarettes and certain foods were available at absurdly low prices to service personnel from the subsidised PX stores on the American bases.

Somehow the two servicemen had managed to squeeze two huge old General Motors fridges into the confines of their small kitchen. One fridge was stacked absolutely choc-a-block with Budweiser beer, whilst the other was stocked with ice, Cokes, Dr. Peppers, Pepsi-Cola and mounds of huge steaks, hamburgers and hot dogs. The cupboards on the walls were jammed full with spirits, including Jack Daniels, Wild Turkey, Old Kentucky and various tequilas, rums and oddments for mixing cocktails. At their wild parties the spirits were gathered together onto a large table in the kitchen, together with a stock of US government plastic cups and glasses and all the guests were simply expected to help themselves to whatever they wanted to drink.

Jerry would string coloured fairy lights around the walls of their lounge, which consisted of two rooms knocked into one leading off the kitchen. They had two old, battered sofas which were pushed against the walls, leaving a good-sized area for dancing. A huge Stars and Stripes linen flag covered one entire wall. Another wall was covered by a huge collection of ancient American car registration plates. The remaining two walls were covered with *Playboy* magazine centrefolds; as Jerry had told Chris one day, 'We're purely tits and ass boys, Chris, fuck the culture, we'll get that when we're a little older, when we can't get any pussy!'

The room was barely lit by the fairy lights, so they had fixed a couple of wall lights on the end walls which gave off a red glow from some low wattage red bulbs. Chris had decided that the decor was all very tacky the first time he had seen it, but his opinion had mellowed since. Hell, it was a great party room and somehow it seemed to give off a kind of sexual frisson when full of people enjoying themselves.

Chris had met the two Americans at a dance in Cambridge shortly after their arrival in England. The next day he had taken them both to the historic Eagle pub in Bene't Street where, during the Second World War, the US flight crews had written their Squadron Initials over the ceiling using the sooty flames of their Zippo lighters. His new friends had both been impressed by

172

the legacy left by their predecessors, but over several beers in the old coaching inn, Jerry had explained their own philosophy of life to Chris. 'Hell Chris, we're over here in Great Britain courtesy of the US government and while we're here, Bill and I intend to have a hell'va lot of fun. We wanna' make as many girls as happy as we can. We sure love it here and I for one will be very unhappy when I'm put back on that plane to the good ole U.S. of A!'

Since then Chris had enjoyed many good times with the two amiable Americans but he especially enjoyed their riotous parties. One particular Saturday night, Chris and Tony had been invited to yet another party at the Bateman Street flat. Tony had decided to take along a raven-haired Italian girl called Maria whom he had met the night before at the Dorothy Disco. They had spent a very passionate night together, extending into most of the Saturday. Tony was so enamoured of her that he had 'phoned the salon and lied that he had a sore throat and would not be in to work. 'What I've really got is a sore cock. She's a real goer!' he boasted to Chris later when the three of them had gone to the Eros restaurant for a Greek meal of moussaka and kebabs, accompanied by plenty of Retsina.

About 11 o'clock that evening Chris had driven them in the hearse to the party where they had managed to park nearby, but the American's flat was so overcrowded that large numbers of people had spilled out into the street, or were sitting drinking on the steps leading up to the entrance of the house. The trio had to push and shove their way through the throng, past various assorted drunks and smooching couples gathered on the stairs leading up to the flat. When they finally reached the lounge, they found it to be unbearably hot and humid. With such a mass of sweating, drunken bodies jam packed tightly together, they found it was difficult to breathe. As Chuck Berry belted out *'Go Johnny Go'* and the smell of toasted American tobacco and human sweat filled their nostrils, they eventually managed to squeeze through the crowd into the adjoining kitchen where they found Jerry holding court, his right arm around the shoulders of an attractive Scandinavian girl (both Tony and Chris were experts at telling the nationality of most girls at a glance by now), while Jerry's left hand waved a can of Budwiser erratically in the air as he conversed amicably with several of his guests. 'Introvert was certainly not a label that one would stick on Jerry, mad was probably a more accurate description,' smiled Chris to himself. 'Hey you guys,' Jerry cried enthusiastically as they squeezed themselves into the centre of the room, his eyes lighting up as he noticed Maria. 'Chris, Mike, how ya'll doin'? Just you help yourselves to anything you desire, OK? Bill and I made a fantastic punch tonight, if you'd all like to partake, it's highly recommended and it's waitin' in the tub in the bathroom.'

Maria looked up at Tony with surprise. Tony thought that sounded odd too, but Chris who knew the Americans best, merely nodded his head. Tony introduced Maria to Jerry, who told her to try the punch. 'It's really awesome,' he told her. 'You will love it sweetheart,' he added, giving Tony a wink of approval after appraising Maria up and down.

Jerry straightened up and moved over to Maria, gently taking both of her hands in his, 'Sweetness, where ya' from?' he asked her in his Southern drawl.

'From Roma in Italy, like Tony,' she replied, unsure of the big man standing before her. Jerry leaned down and gave her a quick peck on each cheek, 'You be sure and have yourself a real good time now, ya' hear?' he told her. 'I know Tony and Chris will look after you.'

'Thank you,' said Maria, feeling more assured by Jerry's friendly manner.

'Thanks Jerry, catch you later,' said Chris as Jerry turned to continue the conversation with his other guests.

Tony led the way as they pushed their way through the crowd to the bathroom, where Maria was astonished to find the old roll-top bath two-thirds full of a bright red liquid with bits and pieces of fruit floating around on top. At first sight to Maria, it looked like a bathful of blood, but Chris had seen it all before. Sometimes their American hosts filled the bath with iced beer and coke, other times they mixed up coloured punches like this one, sealing the waste pipe up at the bottom of the bath.

Jerry's buddy, Bill, came into the room, pleased to see them all and handed them paper cups. 'Guys, just dredge up a cup of that mother, it was full to the brim at eight o'clock, it's Hawaiian Fruit Punch, which is a combination of eight fruit juices with strong Vodka mixed together. It'll grow hairs right out of your arsehole if you're not careful.'

'Hope there's no vampires around tonight,' Tony told Bill after Maria had mentioned to him that it looked like blood.

'Well, if there is, they'll certainly love this mother, believe me guys,' replied Bill scooping another cupful for himself.

'Veree nice,' said Maria, cautiously sipping her cup of punch. 'It's very strong, I think,' she added, glancing at Tony for agreement.

Tony just smiled at her, he had suddenly had a vision brought on by Jerry's remark. He'd had his hands around Maria's beautiful smooth, firm bottom only a couple of hours ago, now he saw her drinking the punch naked, sprouting great hairs out of her arse. He tried to regain his senses and to dismiss the grotesque vision from his mind. He choked on his punch, trying to suppress a laugh, and spilt a few drops of the red liquid on his clean, white shirt, much to his annoyance. Maria thoughtfully grabbed a handful of serviettes from a pile by the bath and tried to remove the stain from his shirt front, giving Tony a kiss to stop him swearing.

Chris meanwhile had spotted an interesting looking girl through the crowd on the far side of the lounge. She was smoking and sitting alone on one of the sofas, so he made his way round the mass of dancers and when he reached the sofa he bent down and asked the girl if she'd like to dance. As she stared up at him, he noticed that she was even more attractive then he'd thought but the tell-tale glazing of her eyes immediately told him that she had drunk a great deal. She had some difficulty in standing up from the sofa, so he helped her up gently and put his arm around her shoulders to steady her. He immediately noticed the tightness of her breasts when she leaned heavily against him as they began to dance slowly together. The Platters were singing *My Prayer*, which was one of Chris's favourite ballads, besides being an intimate, slow number.

'It's a great party,' said the girl. 'They're really nice, Jerry and Bill, aren't they?' She was having trouble co-ordinating her feet so Chris had his work cut out to keep her standing upright.

'Yeah, they're great people,' replied Chris. 'How do you know them both?'

'My boyfriend introduced me,' she told him, slurring her words slightly.

'Oh, where's your boyfriend then,' Chris asked feeling pissed off that she was with someone. He had to hold her more tightly when she missed her footing completely and almost fell over, very nearly toppling Chris over with her.

'He's fucked off with another girl,' she told him in a matter-of-fact way.

'I'm sorry about that,' replied Chris feeling better hearing that news and wondering if they'd had an argument before or after she'd become as drunk as she was now.

'Well, I'm glad. He wasn't very nice to me anyway and I'm glad he's gone. I'm free as a bird now to do as I wish and I'm going to have lots to drink,' she slurred, laughing up at him. He noticed again the vacant look in her eyes, she was unable to focus and her smile appeared to be caught in a freeze frame as though she had no facial movement at all. She really was very drunk decided Chris, feeling upset as he couldn't envisage spending the rest of the night with her. 'She won't even be able to talk soon in the state she's in, she's just a liability,' he concluded sadly, wondering whether he should order a taxi for her immediately and send her home before she collapsed completely.

'I must find the toilet,' she mumbled interrupting his thoughts, suddenly grabbing hold of his sleeve to prevent herself from falling over. The momentum caused by this sudden movement caught Chris off balance and they were only saved from collapsing in a heap together by lurching against another dancing couple, whereby Chris was able to recover his equilibrium and keep them both upright.

'Look angel,' he told her gently, 'you're very drunk. Are you sure you're going to be OK? I can call a taxi for you if you like.'

'Thanks,' she replied, 'but I'll be OK. I'll just go to the toilet.'

Nevertheless, he still had to half pull, half carry her through the mass of smooching dancers. He reached the bathroom and plonked her on the seat of the WC whilst he ushered a canoodling couple out of the room. 'Sure you'll be OK?' he asked her again.

'Yeah, I'll be fine thanks,' she replied as a bout of hiccups started, causing her to jerk her head back sharply.

He shut the bathroom door and put the engaged sign that Bill had fitted on the door up and then he pushed through the crowd again to retrieve his drink. He stood watching the dancing mêlée through the smoke and the gloom. He certainly fancied the girl but, unfortunately, she was pretty far gone. There was nothing worse than being with a pissed girl and having her collapse on you, or worse still, having her puke all over the car or somewhere in the flat. 'It's a bloody shame really,' he thought to himself. 'She's nice looking, she's got great tits and good legs but I can't hack drunken women.' It would be best to call her a taxi before she gets worse, he decided, she's unlikely to sober up now.

He weaved his way through the crowd and tapped on the bathroom door. 'It's me,' he called, hoping that she could hear him above the loud music. 'Are you OK in there?' He couldn't hear an answer and tapped again. 'Hey sweetheart,' he called, louder this time. 'Are you OK?' Concerned that she might have passed out, he opened the door just in time to see the top of her head protruding above the Hawaiian Punch in the bath, the red liquid gently sloshing over the side of the bath and small bubbles popping on the surface of the punch. 'Christ, she's fallen in the fucking punch,' he cried rushing to the bath and reaching under her body and grabbing her underneath her armpits. He dragged her right out of the bath, causing a wash of punch to slop heavily over the side. As he laid her out on the carpet she spluttered and coughed. He pulled her up to a sitting position and slapped her back hard, trying to force out any liquid that had entered her lungs. The carpet was oozing with the red punch and the bathroom had suddenly become full of drunken, excited people, alarmed by Chris's yelling, all peering down at the girl over Chris's shoulder and offering advice and encouragement.

'She's been swimming in the goddam' punch,' said one.

'Its not a suicide attempt, is it? Her boyfriend fucked off with someone else,' remarked another.

'I hope she's not got any contagious diseases,' said another casually scooping two cups of punch from the bath. 'Can't waste this stuff.'

'At least she wasn't sick in it,' said another voice.

'Yeah and let's hope she didn't piss in it either,' came another

177

voice from the back.

'Wise guys,' said Chris under his breath as he pulled the girl over to the washbasin. He dunked her head under the cold tap as she spluttered and groaned in protest. 'What happened,' she asked, spluttering drunkenly as Chris began towelling her face and hair dry.

'Don't worry about it,' he said. 'We'll get you home to sleep it off.'

Tony and Maria came pushing through the crowd having heard the commotion. Chris was holding the girl upright as she was having trouble standing unaided. Tony immediately noticed the girl's dripping, red stained clothes. 'Christ, is she OK?' he said, alarmed at the state of both the girl and Chris, who was now also covered in punch stains. 'What the hell happened?'

Chris explained the sequence of events, which had Tony almost doubled up with disbelief and laughter. 'I'll have to take her home or call a taxi, she needs to sleep and get out of these wet clothes,' Chris added.

Maria stood watching silently, completely astounded by such odd goings-on, she was certainly learning a great deal about British behaviour.

'Yes, you'll have to squeeze her out of those wet clothes, she'll look like a red, wrinkled prune under there,' quipped Tony smirking at Chris. 'And no taxi's gonna take her wet through like that, staining the bloody seats red, are they?'

'Yeah, you're right,' agreed Chris, realising how true that was and glad that Tony had mentioned it, for it saved him the hassle of ringing a taxi for the girl and then getting turned down for the ride. So he manhandled her down the crowded stairs and out into the street. He felt exhausted on the way down the stairs as everyone had some smart remark to make about the drunken girl who by now was falling into a stupor. When he reached the hearse, he bundled her into the back and found an old blanket and wrapped her in it. 'At least she hasn't been sick,' he muttered to himself. Then, suddenly realising that she might well vomit in his vehicle he thought, 'Oh God, I'm being the Good Samaritan here. How the hell did I get caught up in this? There were plenty of other good looking girls up there,' he thought regretfully as he started the car. Suddenly realising that he didn't know where the girl lived, he looked over his shoulder to ask her, but saw that she had fallen asleep, breathing heavily, lightly snoring. He couldn't wake her up now, it was better to let her sleep it off. 'Oh well, there's nothing more I can do for her now,' he decided. 'I think I'll just go up and rejoin the party, leave her sleeping here and just keep a check on her every now and again to make sure she's OK.' As soon as she wakes up I'll find out her address and get her home.

He clambered out of the hearse, locked the door and realised that he needed a good, stiff drink. He hurried back up the stairs to the flat, eager to sample another cup of Jerry and Bill's Hawaiian Punch cocktail from the bathroom. 'It's a funny life,' he thought to himself, 'a very funny life.'

Chapter Twenty-Two

One of the main tests of the strength of the group's friendship occurred one Saturday night at the Dorothy Ballroom where Raz, Chris and Tony had gone together to see the Spencer Davis Group. Unfortunately, Mike had to stay in to revise for an impending examination that he was taking the following week.

The venue was completely full, for the 'Dot' as it was known locally, was the largest place for dancing in Cambridge with several rooms on different floors offering either disco or live bands. The place even had a proper ballroom with a resident orchestra. The boys always enjoyed the 'Dot' as it was always full with hundreds of pretty girls, a factor that helped make the place so popular, ensuring a packed house every week.

That night they were crammed together like sardines in the 'Oak Room', waiting for the band to appear. The oak panelled walls were streaming as the crowd sweated and strained. Soon a half-hearted chant commenced in a section of the crowd, 'Why are we waiting,' they ranted in a rather jocular, ragged manner, becoming louder and louder as more people became impatient and joined in.

Raz had been dying to get to the toilet and had made his way over to the cloakroom, having to push and shove his way across the room. Some minutes later Tony noticed him across the crowd talking to a pretty girl by the door. He nudged Chris and motioned in Raz's direction. 'Our boy doesn't waste much time, does he?' laughed Tony. 'We've only just got here and he's already pulling birds.'

They could just make out the head of the girl Raz was talking to, the crowd was so dense and animated that they could only partially see the top of her face. 'She looks like a real cracker from here,' said Chris admiringly, standing on tip-toe to try and catch a better glimpse of the girl.

At that precise moment, a great cheer went up as the Spencer Davis Group took to the stage and launched into their opening number. The crowd started clapping and swaying and a few couples began dancing at the back of the packed room. Chris gazed over the heads of the crowd across to the door to try and catch Raz's eye. He noticed that Raz and the girl had been joined by a man. He was alarmed to notice that the man appeared to be rather animated, thrusting his hand with his forefinger held straight out towards Raz's face in a very heated manner. The group were then joined by another man who also seemed to stand beside Raz in a threatening manner. Chris could vaguely discern from Raz's expression that he was in an uncomfortable situation. Nudging Tony sharply in the ribs, he said, 'I think Raz may be in a spot of bother. Let's go and see what's happening over there.'

Chris began pushing his way through the cheering audience, Tony immediately falling in behind him. They managed to push and weave their way through the crowd, now enthusiastically clapping and dancing to *Keep on Running*, but when they reached Raz they found one of the men menacingly grasping the lapel of his jacket. 'Hi Raz, everything OK here?' said Chris, trying to appear to greet his friend casually, but worried that they could become involved in something violent. The two men had turned in surprise when Chris and Tony appeared out of the crowd to stand side-by-side with Raz. Chris noticed the girl he had admired appeared to be rather subdued and downcast, whilst also noting that both the men accosting Raz were broad, tough looking, hard-faced types, not the types to choose to mess with if it could be avoided he decided.

'Are you friends of this Paki,' spat one of the men, his eyes narrowing aggressively as he glared ominously at Chris.

'Raz is not a Paki, he's an Indian and he's a great friend of ours,' said Tony desperately trying to stop his voice quavering. 'What's the problem?'

'Well, I'm gonna give the black bastard a good hiding for chatting up my bird,' the man said, tightening his grip on Raz's lapel and trying to pull Raz round in front of him.

'Leave it,' said Tony, pushing the man hard in the chest making him fall back against the wall.

'Right, you cunt,' yelled the other man aiming a punch at the side of Tony's face, catching him hard on the side of his ear. Tony stumbled, caught off balance and barging against the girl standing by his side. She let out a shrill cry of 'No, Johnny, don't.' With arms all akimbo she tried to restrain the man.

Chris, not normally a fighter, quickly realised that there was only one thing to do and, summoning all his strength, he hit the man who'd punched Tony in the face. There was a cracking sound as he connected with the bridge of his nose. The man fell forward clutching his hands to his face. Tony pulled the girl away and hit the man again on the back of his head, his survival instinct coming to the fore. He instinctively opened his hand and wiggled his fingers; he couldn't operate in the salon with a broken hand. A crowd had gathered round the meleé as Raz was now tussling with the girl's boyfriend. He had already taken two hefty blows to the face but had managed to capture the man in a headlock. The man was swearing oaths and profanities at Raz when the crowd suddenly parted and three burly bouncers appeared. They grabbed hold of Raz and ordered him to release the man. They quickly ushered the two groups outside into the corridor where they stood separated, glaring at each other. Chris realised that he was shaking badly and that he felt physically sick. On top of that, his right hand felt completely numb where he had connected with the other man's head. Violence had never been something that he enjoyed, it had always made him feel sick and afraid and the shock of the confrontation had deeply upset him. He noticed Raz's face was beginning to swell up painfully from the blows he had sustained.

Raz started trying to explain to the bouncers what had happened, but they did not seem to care, after all they had heard and seen it all before. The girl stood behind the two trouble making oafs, mute and sullen. Chris decided that, as the girlfriend of one of them, she was probably quite used to such violent and moronic behaviour. Mind you, he could not blame Raz for trying, she was certainly a nice looker, in a slutty kind of way. He hoped that the boyfriend would not beat her up later because of this incident, most bullies needed a scapegoat and she was probably it.

The bouncers issued stern threats to them all. 'Any more

trouble and you're out, and we won't be gentle next time,' the two groups were told bluntly. 'Now piss off and enjoy the concert.'

The two yobs and the girl turned and walked off down the corridor to the bar, turning to glance back at the other three, muttering threats and obscenities under their breath.

'How's the face, Raz?' asked Chris concerned at the heavy swelling.

'It feels like it's twice the normal fucking size,' joked Raz. 'And I forgot to ask the bird if she fucks.' They all fell about laughing and trooped off to the cloakroom, where Raz threw cold water over his badly bruised face, whilst Tony bathed his battered hand and swollen ear, which had now swelled up considerably and felt very sore and painful. Chris had not suffered physically, but he was very conscious of a sickly feeling churning in his stomach and he was still nervously shaking a little after the confrontation.

One of the bouncers followed them into the toilet, 'I think it might be better for you all to leave,' he told them, 'rather than getting involved in a fight with those prats again. It's obvious that they won't leave the matter alone,' he advised them. 'Besides I don't reckon you guys would enjoy it much getting those bruises battered again,' said the doorman. After a brief consultation, they all decided that it would be prudent to take the bouncers advice although it meant missing the concert. None of them fancied becoming entangled with the yobs again, so the helpful bouncer showed them down the corridor to the fire exit so that they could leave the building without going back through the crowd.

'I'm really sorry to bugger up your evening,' Raz apologised to the others. 'I had no idea that bird was with that prick; he just appeared out of the blue and told me he didn't like blokes chatting his girl up, particularly black Paki fuckers. He told me he was going to do me over, but she tried to intervene and then the other arsehole turned up. Just after he grabbed me, you two arrived, so thanks to you both for sticking up for me. I'm sorry you got bashed about too.'

'Look Raz, you're family now, you're special, we're like brothers and no-one gets away with crap like that. We'd have stood up for anyone but especially you because at Mawson Road, we have to look after each other. Mind you, I bet you're pissed off you didn't get to take his fucking chick. She was gorgeous. Makes you wonder what the hell she was doing with someone like that prat,' said Tony.

'There's no accounting for taste. That's why fat girls, hairy girls, smelly girls all end up with someone, 'cos someone out there like's them,' replied Chris, chuckling at his own remark.

'At least none of us is badly hurt, we've just a few cuts and bruises between us,' said Tony, flexing his bruised fingers again to satisfy himself they were still working.

Chris put his arms around the shoulders of both his friends. 'Let's call in the Six Bells on the way back and have a beer,' he said cheerfully. 'We can drown our sorrows there.'

'Good idea,' replied Raz and Tony spontaneously.

'But, I mustn't be too late, I've got a Swede calling round at 12 o'clock and I don't want to turn into a pumpkin,' added Chris feeling better now that he'd remembered the girl, it would be something to take his mind off the dismal experience he'd just had with his friends.

Chapter Twenty-Three

Directly opposite the house where the four boys shared their flat in Mawson Road, lived an academic couple in their early fifties together with their two pretty daughters. The general consensus amongst the guys was that they were both about seventeen or eighteen years old. Mike had his own opinion which he kept to himself for he had decided that they were possibly one or two years younger. 'Possible jailbait,' he used to think to himself sometimes as he watched them coming and going from their semi-detached Victorian house. The girls were certainly very attractive, they both wore their dark red hair long and they always dressed alike in tight sweaters and jeans.

Chris, whose bedroom on the first floor contained a large bay window which looked across at its equal in the house opposite, often observed the girls in their room. He assumed it was their bedroom. They could often be seen sitting at a table in the window studying or reading, much to the consternation of the boys who would gather in Chris's room trying desperately to attract their attention, waving and smiling through the window. Unfortunately for the boys, their constant attempts to impress the two girls were met with complete frostiness. Their parents had seemingly made it absolutely clear that they wished to have nothing to do with the inhabitants of No. 110, despite the initial attempts of the lads to be friendly and neighbourly. Indeed, any greeting offered on the street by one of the boys to the couple or their daughters would be met by an averted gaze, no verbal response whatsoever and a quickening of their steps to distance themselves. It was as though they thought the lads had the plague.

So perplexed had the group become by the family's hostile behaviour that, urged on by one another, they became frantic to establish some contact with the two stuck-up daughters and so they went out of their way to establish friendly relations with the family opposite.

Mike, despite his protestations, was one day despatched across the road bearing a large bunch of daffodils which Tony and Raz had picked the night before from another neighbours garden. The point of the flowers was as a goodwill gesture to the parents and, hopefully, if the gift was received with good grace, they planned to invite the family over for a meal, obviously with the intention of ingratiating themselves with the two girls.

Chris, Tony and Raz arranged themselves together behind the curtains of Chris's room, staring intently at Mike's back as he knocked on the door of the house opposite. There were gasps of appreciation as the door opened to reveal one of the girls standing there. 'Oh God,' they all groaned, each wishing they had elected to take the flowers over as they drooled at the sight of one of the pretty girls talking to Mike.

'What's he saying,' muttered Tony in frustration as he stared across at the girl smiling and chatting animatedly to Mike. They watched in earnest as Mike continued chatting, then they saw him hand the flowers to the girl, who turned and disappeared from view, leaving the front door ajar. Mike turned around and squinted up at their window, smiled and gave them a thumbs-up sign.

'It seems to be going well so far. I'll be really pissed of if he gets invited in,' said Chris.

'You're just jealous,' retorted Raz.

'Yes, you can't mean that Chris, we've just coerced poor old Mike into going over there to try and entice them over here, just so that we can meet the bloody girls. You can't have it all ways,' said Tony.

Suddenly the door opened wide and the mother appeared, her expression was stern and angry and she was carrying the bunch of daffodils which she roughly thrust at Mike's chest. The silent watchers gasped as she delivered a tirade of abuse at Mike, they could only stare forlornly at the back of Mike's head as he stood on the doorstep in disbelief, probably making a serious effort to stay calm while she berated him. Finally, having exhausted herself, she slammed the door in Mike's face. He turned, glanced up at the three faces staring anxiously down at him and, with a shrug of his shoulders, meandered back across the road carrying the battered flowers. As he trudged up the stairs, the bewildered trio came out of Chris's room and gathered on the landing.

'What the hell happened there with the sour old bitch,' asked Chris, feeling sorry for Mike now.

'Well,' said Mike, 'as you saw, one of the girls answered the door. I had a chat with her and she told me that she and her sister would like to be friends with us but they've been forbidden to have any contact with us by their parents. I explained we wanted to ask them all over but she said she didn't think the parents would come as they disapprove of us too much and they think that we're all promiscuous and irreligious and that we drink too much and probably take drugs, so we'd be a bad influence on their daughters. That's why they're not allowed to talk to us. But she said she'd take the flowers in to see what her parents would say. Well, now we know! The mother came out and simply confirmed what her daughter had said but in a rather nasty manner.'

'What a cow, she must be a mind reader, too,' smiled Chris.

'What do you mean?' enquired Raz.

'Well, let's face it, the bloody woman's right. We would be a bad influence on her daughters, all any of us really want to do is to get them both into bed.'

Reluctantly they came to the conclusion that any further attempts to meet the girls, especially to placate their parents, would be doomed to failure.

One Saturday morning, a couple of weeks later, following what the boys would always call the 'Daffodil Incident', Raz knocked gently on Chris's door. 'Are you awake yet, Chris?' he called, 'I've just made some tea.'

'Oh great stuff Raz,' Chris groaned. 'Come in, that's just what I need to get the brain working again.

Mike had gone to London to spend the weekend with a female accountant that he'd met there whilst on a recent one week course preparing for his exams, whilst Tony had gone to spend the weekend with his Italian parents in Bedford.

Chris and Raz had been out the previous evening at the Deja Vu club where they had met two lively student nurses who lived and worked at the nearby Addenbrooke's Hospital. When the club had closed the girls had invited them back to their flat in the high-rise hostel where they both lived on the twentieth floor. After several drinks, some joke telling and then some bawdy kissing games, they had paired off and gone to bed. At 4:30 in the morning they had all been startled to hear the fire alarm ringing, piercing through the thin walls. The two girls, fully conversant with the fire drill, had quickly ushered the bewildered boys down the twenty flights of steps to the ground floor and out into the courtyard where the inhabitants of the building were massed. Luckily there was no real fire, but one of the nurses informed Raz that they had a fire drill every six months or so and that they often had to wait an hour or more before the all clear was given for them to return to their rooms.

Feeling conspicuous amongst the hordes of female nurses, although there were several other males milling around, the boys lit a cigarette and chatted to the girls. Raz felt rather uncomfortable as in the excitement he had put his trousers on inside out and this highly visible mistake caused some sniggering amongst many of the nurses. After waiting over an hour, the boys decided that they would return home to the flat, so they made the lame excuse that they had to get up early, kissed the girls goodnight and drove home to sleep what was left of the night.

'That was a bloody fiasco last night,' said Chris sitting up in bed, propped up by pillows, and feeling himself come to life as he drank the mug of tea and ate the toast and marmalade that Raz had made for him. 'Mind you, there were some great looking birds down in that courtyard weren't there? Some of them had hardly anything on, did they? It left very little to the imagination'

'I was really pissed off, I can tell you,' explained Raz. 'I was on the job when that bloody alarm went off. I was so surprised that I inadvertently let out this huge fart which made me start laughing and then she started laughing. The next thing I knew, I was being hauled out of bed, my clothes slapped in my hand and then we're off down the stairs with everyone else. And, of course, when we got down to the bottom I found I'd put my trousers on inside out, which was bloody uncomfortable and she was laughing even more!'

Raz looked a comical figure thought Chris as the big man

gesticulated wildly, clad only in his underpants as he prowled about the room telling the story. 'Hey, there's the two birds in the room across the road,' cried Raz gazing out of the window. 'They look as though they're into some studying.'

Chris who was also wearing just his underpants, jumped out of bed and they both peered across at the two girls sitting quietly at their usual place by the window. One of the girls raised her head and seemed to be looking out of her room, contemplating the sky. Chris stayed partly behind the curtain to conceal his near nakedness and waved his hand slowly at the girl. She took no notice and Chris wondered if she was trying to make it obvious once again that they just weren't allowed to acknowledge the boys, or maybe she really had not seen him and was deep in concentration. 'How many times have we stood here like lemons trying to attract their attention?' complained Chris bitterly.

'With such snotty parents, it's not really surprising,' said Raz. 'They've laid down the law to those girls that they're not allowed to have anything to do with us and I guess that's it. If we were all rich and famous it might possibly be a different story.'

'Changing the subject, have you heard the new Beatles LP, *Sergeant Pepper's Lonely Hearts Club Band*? I bought it yesterday, it was the last copy in the shop,' said Chris.

'No, but I've heard it's brilliant,' enthused Raz. 'Let's play it now Chris please, it should wake us both up properly and get us ready for the weekend.'

Chris carefully pulled his new prized LP from its cover, which Raz examined enthusiastically. Chris carefully placed the record on the turntable. Suddenly the strident tones of the Sergeant Pepper album filled the room, at which point they both became spellbound by the Beatles music.

'Oh, it's great,' beamed Raz his face erupting into a huge smile, shining with pleasure at the amazing new sounds. He jumped up in excitement, gyrating his hips to the music, his hands above his head waving in time to the heavy beat, oblivious to everything but the raw energy and excitement of this new revolutionary Beatles album.

Chris joined in too, unable to suppress his own appreciation of the music and the great new songs. They danced around the room, still clad only in their underpants, arms waving and bodies shaking to the exciting music. As the track of *Lucy in the Sky with Diamonds* ended, Chris thought he heard a loud banging completely disconnected from the music and, as the next track started, he happened to glance out of his window and saw to his surprise that the two girls opposite were now standing at their window waving and shouting. They stood giving the thumbs-up sign and Chris suddenly realised that he was standing in full view of the girls and that they must have been watching Raz and himself dancing around the room.

'Look Raz,' cried Chris, 'the bloody girls are going crazy. They've spotted us dancing around semi-naked and they've suddenly come to life.'

'It's the sight of the bananas in our skimpies, that's what's got them going,' laughed Raz. 'Let's call them over to join us.' He moved to the window and beckoned with his forefinger for the girls to come over.

Chris mouthed through the glass at the girls, 'we're having a party, come and join us.'

The two girls stood at the window, still laughing hysterically at the two boys standing somewhat self consciously at the window, beckoning to them through the glass. They shook their heads negatively at the boys, but neither of them could stop laughing.

'I reckon their parents are either away or they're out, otherwise they'd never be as friendly as this,' said Raz.

'Why don't we moon at them,' suggested Chris wildly, 'just for a laugh. Are you game for it Raz?'

'Well, I'm always ready for a laugh,' said Raz and went over to the gramophone and turned the volume up high. He returned to the window and smiled over at the two girls. 'This'll shake them up,' he said, waving both hands across at the girls.

'Or put them off men for ever,' replied Chris. 'Shall we go?'

Raz nodded in reply, they both turned their backs to the window and, as one, they pulled the backs of their underpants down exposing their naked buttocks. They simultaneously pressed their bottoms against the inside of the large window and one pair of black cheeks and one pair of white cheeks became flattened against the glass. They began gyrating in time to the loud music and, as Raz half turned to glance over his shoulder across the road, he could see the two girls almost collapsing with hysterical laughter, tears running freely down their cheeks, as they desperately clung to each other for support.

Spurred on by the sight of the girls enjoyment, the two friends gyrated their bottoms faster, their bare flesh pressed against the glass creating a peculiar squealing sound which they could both hear above the music. Glancing over their shoulders they saw that the girls had now pushed the sash window up and were leaning out over the sill, whistling and cat-calling across the narrow road at the two mooners.

All of a sudden, the girls voices stopped and the boys heard a loud piercing scream, made even louder as the first side of the LP came abruptly to an end and the music stopped. The angry voice continued raging incoherently. Raz and Chris ceased their gyrating simultaneously, both quickly pulling their pants up over their buttocks before turning to find out who was causing the commotion. Looking down onto the street, they both instantly recognised the girls' mother who was standing on the pavement outside the house opposite. Her face was contorted into a mask of utter fury. She was shaking her umbrella violently up and down and as she stamped into the middle of the road, a small flat hat fought to stay on her head and a little hairy grey dog on a lead ran nervously around her feet. Her movements were so animated, she reminded Chris of a clockwork toy. 'You filthy bastards, you complete animals,' she screamed up at them. 'You dirty stinking perverts, trying to corrupt my daughters, sticking your stinking arses out of the window, you're nothing but scum and filth.'

Raz, somewhat amazed at the genteel woman's vocabulary, glanced across at the two girls in the opposite window. They stood cowering behind the curtains, obviously completely shocked at their mother's sudden appearance.

Chris decorously pulled his underpants higher up his waist, opened the window and leaning out to peer down at the irate woman. 'Sorry madam,' he said sweetly, 'we were only have a little fun. Perhaps you'd care to come in for a cup of tea to discuss the matter?'

At this amazing statement, Raz found he could not control himself. He almost collapsed in hysterics, bent double and shaking with laughter.

'You perverts haven't heard the last of this,' the woman screamed. 'I'll have your guts for garters.' She turned abruptly and stormed swiftly back across the road, dragging the unfortunate little dog behind her, it's feet pawing wildly at the ground as it tried to keep it's balance. She wrenched her front door open, dragged the poor dog through and slammed the door loudly.

The boys looked across at the opposite window, but both girls had disappeared from view. 'Oh God, I bet they're both in for it! I don't think I'd like to be in their shoes right now,' said Raz. 'The old goat looked pretty wound up to me.'

'The trouble is, if a man's bare arse can get her that worked up, imagine what could happen if she saw a dick. She's probably one of those women that puts the light out before sex, I bet she's never actually seen a man naked, even though she's got two kids.'

'If those girls do get into trouble, it's really our fault, that's why I feel a bit sick,' said Raz disconsolately.

'Yeah,' replied Chris, 'but what are we in this life for Raz, why are we sharing a flat together, going to parties, drinking, pulling birds? Because we want fun, that's F.U.N. We didn't hurt anyone just then, did we? I don't think we contaminated those girls by mooning at them, it's their parents behaving as they do that will cause them problems. Once they leave their clutches, they may rebel so much they could go completely off the rails, like some of the convent girls do, cooped up for years with all that Catholicism shoved down their throats and having to cope with all those weird Catholic morals, and then, wham, suddenly the girls are let loose and go fucking mad! And as for us, in a few years we could all be settled down with a couple of kids and a wife, we'll never be able to live like this then, 'cos then we'll have too many responsibilities, with pensions, life insurance and all that crap.' He walked across to the record player, turned the Beatles LP over to Side 2 and, as the music started, they began dancing again, energetically waving their arms and legs around like manic puppets.

'Yeah, yeah, yeah,' they sang as they moved in time to the music, hips gyrating frantically.

Chris sang a little ditty that he made up on the spot, to the tune of the old GI recruiting songs:

'That old bitch across the road,

She is such a slimy toad,
With two daughters we'd like to screw,
She's made it clear just what we can do.'

'Maybe she'll chastise them so badly, they'll both do a runner and come over here seeking refuge,' shouted Raz over the music.

'And if they did, we'd have to send them home to their crusty old Mum and Dad, wouldn't we?' said Chris.

'But perhaps only after they'd had their wicked way with use,' chortled Raz.

'Yeah, yeah, yeah,' they chorused as the Beatles belted out their new songs. 'She loves you, yeah, yeah, yeah!' they sang together over the top of the Sergeant Pepper album, screaming with laughter again at the image of the woman across the road yelling up at them, just a few minutes before.

Chapter Twenty-Four

Tony had been experiencing some problems whilst urinating. For several weeks he had endured some severe pain, as though a red hot needle was being forced down the middle of his penis. He had also noticed a faint yellowish discharge seeping from the end of his glans.

On several occasions at work, he had been forced to rush off extremely rapidly to the toilet, having muttered some half-hearted excuse, leaving his clients with half-cut, cold, wet hair. Once ensconced in the toilet, he had sometimes had to spend several minutes sitting on the pan, his trousers and pants lying around his ankles as he held his cock tightly, trying to suppress the feeling which felt like razor blades zapping away inside. He would pop several painkillers, sometimes he had resorted to lobbing his throbbing penis into the washbasin and running cold water over it to try and erase the pain.

As young men are inclined to do, he had put off seeking advice from the doctor, but eventually the pain had become so severe that he had made an appointment at the surgery where he had rather self-consciously explained the symptoms to his doctor. Lying on the couch for examination, Tony was subjected to the doctor prodding and pulling his penis, whilst relating all the problems that he had experienced. The doctor took a specimen of the discharge and two days later phoned Tony to inform him that an appointment had been made for him at the Venereal Disease clinic in the Old Addenbrooke's Hospital in Trumpington Street.

On arrival at the clinic, although anonymity had been promised by his doctor, on entering the door marked 'Men', he was astonished to find at least a dozen, mainly young men, sitting reading and talking in the waiting area. Unfortunately, he realised that he knew several of them.

'Hello Tony,' said Peter who was a disc jockey in a local disco. 'Surprise, surprise, been dipping your wick in a bit of rough then?'

'Well, err...' Tony stuttered, unsure of himself.

'I'm surprised I haven't seen you or any of your friends up here before, the way you lot throw your salamis around,' chided Peter.

'Yeah,' said Tony trying to recover some composure. 'We all get plenty if that's what you mean. I just didn't want a dose of the clap, if that's what I've got,' he added dejectedly.

'Anyone can get VD,' piped up a bespectacled young man sitting reading a copy of *Varsity*, the student newspaper. He was about nineteen or twenty and Tony decided that he was certainly a student. 'It's just the luck of the draw as to whether you get it or not,' he told Tony matter of factly.

'Well my luck's obviously not good,' replied Peter. 'This is the third time I've been to this clinic in the past year. My fucking todger will be falling to bits soon if I'm not careful.'

'What have you been in for?' asked Tony.

'I've had gonorrhoea and N.S.U.,' replied Peter. 'But a friend of mine had syphilis and that rotted his cock away. There's several hundred have died of the syph this year, you certainly don't want that mate! Some of the things they do to you to try and cure it are unbelievable. Christ, they stick a needle thing with something like an umbrella end right down the middle of your prick, then pull it out to try and scrape the infection out. It's a fucking killer in more ways than one, I can tell you.'

Tony began to feel increasingly alarmed as he digested this information, wondering what was in store for him. His mouth felt like a dust pan, really dry and unpleasant. He was dying for a drink. As he was about to find the cloakroom so that he could drink some water from the tap, he heard his name called out and looked up to find a large, stern-faced, middle-aged lady, who ushered him into a small cubicle with two chairs and motioned to him to sit down. She began reading his doctor's letter that he could see pinned to her clipboard. She told him that she was the Sister-in-Charge of the clinic. She certainly looked the part, thought Chris, noticing her immaculate starched uniform and tall white cap.

'I want you to take this slide,' she told him, handing him a small rectangle of glass, 'and put the end of this spatula,' handing him a small flat wooden spoon, 'into the end of your penis and obtain any discharge and place it on the slide. Don't let your fingers touch it. I'll be back shortly to collect it for examination.'

She swept out, shutting the cubicle door behind her. Tony completed the task and five minutes later she rapped on the door and took the slide from him, labelled it and placed it on a small tray. She left Tony sitting in the small cubicle for some twenty minutes. When she reappeared, she seemed even more reproving. She sat down and told Tony that he had gonorrhoea. After the story Peter had related to him in the waiting room, he was almost relieved that he had not got the dreadful syphilis and that his cock wasn't about to rot away.

'Well, have you any idea where this came from?' she demanded, nodding her head slightly in the general direction of his genitals.

'No, not really,' replied Tony truthfully.

'Do you have a steady girlfriend?'

'No, not really,' he said.

'Well, I'd like to know the names of any girls that you've slept with over the past six months.'

'Mmm, that's quite difficult. I can't really remember them all,' replied Tony blushing deeply and feeling extremely uncomfortable. Some of his conquests he'd only known by their first name and, indeed, several of those he'd only known for a few hours - during which time they had performed the dirty deed with him - and then he'd said goodbye. He'd never seen them again. He tried hard to remember all these girls, but they just seemed to blend into one another in his memory. There were a couple that he'd gone to bed with when he had been very drunk. He had been unable to make love to them, or had he done so eventually? He almost remembered the failures better than the others due to his embarrassment at the time. He vaguely recalled the story Chris that had once told him, when he'd had to leave a job because of a girl that he'd had problems with in that field.

'Come on, come on,' she said irritably, interrupting his thoughts.

'Oh God,' he sighed, feeling guilty. 'I will try to remember some of them.'

He gave the Sister a somewhat vague list, so vague that several girls were listed very simply; there was Maria from Pisa in Italy, that French girl he'd known as Tramp who had told him that she was studying or working in Cambridge and an English telephonist - was it Bet or Beth? She had been on a week's training course in Cambridge, she came from Bristol. She was a dirty cow, he recalled, never wore any knickers and she liked having knee tremblers in dark alleys or in people's front gardens. It had excited her to know that they might be discovered whilst they were shagging. He'd never felt comfortable being with her, that wasn't really his scene.

The Sister's sharp voice interrupted his thoughts again. 'Are you aware that some or all of these young women that you have had sexual intercourse with might be a carrier of this disease, or perhaps they may have caught it from you personally?'

Tony certainly had not thought about it before and shifted his feet uneasily. He blushed again and felt beads of sweat gathering on his brow. He felt that he should be experiencing a sense of shame, but somehow he did not feel that way. He felt distinctly uneasy, the Sister's stern attitude made him nervous but, after all, she had a job to do and it couldn't be easy for her dealing with people like him. But, was it his fault? After all he hadn't known that he was carrying the disease. All the girls these days were on the Pill, so no-one wore contraceptives, although he had to admit he always carried a battered Durex packet in his wallet. He certainly felt embarrassed sitting with the Sister, because she had made him much more aware of the implications of his promiscuous behaviour and he had never worried about screwing around before.

'When you catch this disease, you often don't realise that you have it and then it becomes rather like a pyramid,' explained the Sister. 'You commence with one person who has the problem, unbeknown to him or her. It is then passed onto someone else, and within a couple of weeks its been passed down to several others, and then another couple of weeks and it's passed down to many more. The only time that anyone realises they've got it is when they have a discharge, or itching, or problems going to the loo, as in your particular case. By then, of course, it's too late, it's been passed along to many others who

197

have passed it on to even more people, just like a pyramid structure. Unfortunately in your case the pyramid stretches out to people we just cannot locate to warn them.' She stared angrily at him. Having admonished him, she appeared to be looking for signs of contrition. He reddened again as he began to fully understood what she was trying to tell him. Several of the girls he had slept with had taken all his powers of persuasion to get them to succumb to his advances. These girls had not taken such actions lightly and now, thanks to him and his lust for their bodies, they could be running around with a dose of the clap. Shit, it was unbelievable. He had never given any thought to all this before. The Sister had begun to make him feel extremely bad. He felt she must perceive him as being completely immoral in his sexual attitude towards women and he realised with a certain amount of horror that she was probably correct.

'Right,' she interrupted his thoughts yet again and passed him a small package, 'Here's some tablets for you. I want you to take one each day for twenty eight days and you should be OK. I'll make an appointment for you to come in and obtain the all clear. In the meantime, no beer or spirits, only fruit juice, water, tea or coffee. Definitely no intercourse and if there are any girls on this list whose address you may remember, let us know; and all the ones you do know, you must tell them to report to the clinic or at least go and see their own doctor for their own sakes. Is that clear?' she demanded, giving him yet another reproving look.

'Yes it is,' replied Tony weakly, feeling humiliated and depressed. He rose slowly to his feet, wondering how he was going to survive without alcohol. 'Christ, I could murder a pint right now. And girls, no sex. Must be like being in prison, I guess,' he decided somewhat vaguely.

The Sister showed him out through the side door so that he did not have to pass through the reception area again, eliminating the possibility of further humiliation if he saw anyone else he knew. Gossip could easily get passed around Cambridge. 'I bet that bloody Peter will tell everyone he knows that he saw me here. That could be really bad news, I could easily become ostracised. I might not get a shag for years.'

He walked slowly deep in thought back to the flat. There was a slight drizzle and a chill hung in the air which added to his gloom.

'Shit,' he said to himself, drinking a glass of water and taking the first of his tablets. 'Shit! Shit! Shit!'

Chapter Twenty-Five

Tony soon discovered that there was something else to suffer besides the lack of alcohol in his life and the abstinence from sex, albeit for a short period only. Once he'd announced to the others in the flat that he had the clap, he was constantly teased and humiliated by them and although he understood that this ribbing was good-natured and entirely without malice, it began to grate on his nerves, to the point where he'd often stay in his own room to read or watch TV to get away from the piss taking.

One Friday though, he was persuaded to go out with them all to the Turks Head, a large Berni Inn situated right in the centre of town. The fake Tudor beamed inn was highly regarded by the boys as the best pick-up place in the city. It seemed to attract an abundance of pretty girls, with its four different bars and two accompanying restaurants serving good value steak and chicken dishes.

At 8:30 that evening, the whole building was absolutely heaving with young people out on the razzle. As they entered their favourite room, the Duck Bar, they were enveloped in a cauldron of hot air, cigarette smoke and body heat. They pushed their way through the mass of bodies, recoiling at the occasional whiff of body odour or pungent perfume, until they managed to reach the bar to order their first drinks of the evening.

'What are we all drinking lads?' asked Chris. 'Beers all round except for our socially diseased friend Tony who will no doubt favour orange juice tonight.'

Tony looked glum but managed a weak smile as they waited eagerly for Chris to hand the beers around. Chris turned from the bar and playfully called to Tony, 'Did Doctor say it was OK to have ice in your orange?'

'Lay off, you silly bugger,' replied Tony, feeling pissed off with these silly remarks from his macho friend.

They stood together chatting and drinking in a tight group at a table near the bar, occasionally casting an expert eye over the girls in the room to see whether they could catch the eye of any available girls they might fancy. Mike had already established eye contact with a couple of girls sitting together on an upholstered banquette set on a raised area at the edge of the room. They were both dark haired and busty. One of the girls was wearing a white blouse that seemed to be held in place by two buttons above her waist, the rest of the top fanned out to show off her large cleavage. 'Phew, look at the mammaries on her,' breathed Mike, nudging Chris. The whole group turned round to stare. The girls turned their eyes away and pretended not to notice the crowd of boys ogling them.

'Very nice,' replied Chris, 'but I bet when you take that uplift bra off, they'd drop down to her waist.'

'Tits are very odd things,' said Raz authoritatively, taking a mouthful of beer. 'Some guys like droopers like hers. In fact, I do, they're always so nice and soft and floppy. They're sort of warm and comfortable. There's something about huge breasts with blue veins lightly running through them that makes them seem sort of vulnerable and fragile. They make me feel that I need to protect them so, of course, I do if I get the opportunity.'

'Oh shit,' cried Tony. 'I hate blue veined tits, they remind me of a couple of great blue cheeses. I'm a sucker for little pert tits with small nipples, just a nice handful. They're my favourites.'

Mike, who had caught the girl eyeing him again across the room, was hoping that she and her friend wouldn't realise what the boys were talking about. 'I'm with Raz on this issue. I like big tits, but I do prefer them nice and firm. I especially like black girls breasts because they often have those cigar butt nipples.'

'Yeah, that's right,' agreed Raz. 'And a lot of Indian girls have larger nipples than white girls,' he added.

'What about inverted nipples,' interjected Chris. Sometimes, no matter what you do to them, you wonder if they're ever going to come out to play.'

'I've actually got a fantasy based on tits,' said Mike. 'I'd like to have about an acre of them, all different shapes and sizes and colours. Then, I'd arrive naked and bounce about on top of them all, gently rolling about on them, grabbing, kissing, licking,

201

sucking and slithering and sliding all over them.' He waved his hands in the air, clutching at an imaginary breast floating in front of him. 'Christ, what a thought,' he said to the others, 'I feel quite horny just telling the story.'

The others laughed, amused by Mike's revelations.

'Just one pair at a time will do me fine. I like to concentrate on the job in hand,' smiled Tony.

'What seems really odd to me about women physically, leaving aside their tits, comes from another fact. As men we've all got these amazing preferences about what type of breasts we prefer, big or small, soft or hard, big nipples or small nipples, but if the girl's skin isn't right, doesn't smell nice or doesn't even feel good to touch, then your own individual sensitivity can turn off so you don't fancy her anyway,' added Raz.

'Especially if she's got BO,' added Tony. 'That's a turn off for most people.'

'Ugh! But it's the same for girls too, I'm sure,' said Mike. 'Things about us can turn girls off.'

'Well, you'd know all about that, wouldn't you Mike?' said Chris seizing an opportunity.

'How do you mean?' asked Mike not understanding fully, but ready for the one-liner.

'With that little winkle of yours, you must be used to rejection by now,' said Chris jokingly.

They all laughed loudly at Mike's crestfallen face as Chris put his arm around Mike's shoulder. 'Only joking old buddy,' he told him as Mike hissed back at him, 'Bastard!'

Raz pushed through the crowd to the front of the bar again, ordered another round and passed the glasses carefully back over people's heads to Chris's waiting hands. He knew one of the barmaids intimately and had managed to get served very quickly.

'Well, that's given breasts a good going over,' said Mike. 'I think I'll see them in my dreams tonight.'

'I do every night anyway,' sniggered Chris, 'especially when I haven't got any real ones to play with.'

'Aah, so that's what those battered old copies of *Playboy* are for is it?' jeered Raz.

'Bollocks,' muttered Chris. 'Anyway, at least I've got a cock to be proud off and, as far as I'm concerned, there's nothing wrong with polishing your own helmet occasionally.'

'Look, just because you're the only one who's circumcised here,' cried Tony. 'You helmet must get polished just banging against your thighs when you're walking down the street.'

'Let's not get into cocks, just because we've had a session on tits,' said Mike, concerned that the conversation might deteriorate even further.

They all turned to stare at him in amazement. 'And who started it?' demanded Chris jokingly.

'Yes, OK, I did, er, sorry about that,' said Mike quietly, unable to say anything to defend himself, realising that Chris was correct.

The noise level in the crowded bar was becoming noticeably louder as the evening progressed and more drink was consumed, releasing people's inhibitions. The boys ordered some more beers and extricated themselves from the small table by the bar and thrust their way round the outside of the crowded room, making their way to an area near the top of the stairs. Here, cooler air floated up from the open door to the street, but they also knew from experience that they could 'inspect' the talent as the clientele passed up and down the stairs.

Raz had been attracted to a pair of attractive blondes and started to chat them up, but was warned off by Tony who whispered in his ear that they might be prime candidates in the carriage of social diseases as he knew the girls and was aware that half of the male population of Cambridge had been with them. Tony had suddenly become very worried about VD since catching it himself and, after his dressing down from the Sister at the Clinic, he had thought more about the implications of the disease. The knowledge of how easy it was to catch the clap had come as a shock to the group and, although it had not exactly made them paranoid, it had certainly made them think more about their promiscuity. Although Tony had been getting some stick from the others, in reality they all felt sorry for him, especially as he was the first one of the crowd to catch VD. Raz listened intently to Tony's whispered message and immediately decided it was better to be safe than sorry.

'Nice to meet you girls, see you around,' he told them both

as he turned away, winking saucily at each of them in turn. 'After all, a chap had to keep his options open, disease or no disease,' he thought to himself, wondering how much effect Tony's dose of the clap was going to have on them all, were they all going to end up becoming extremely paranoid about screwing women? 'Shit,' he exclaimed to Tony, 'you're not pulling my leg are you, you rotten bastard.' They were all so used to pulling each other's legs, that sometimes some conversations that they had with each other had to be taken with a pinch of salt.

'No, seriously Raz, I heard in the salon yesterday that Don, one of my friends whose been with both those girls, has caught a dose. It may not be them, but is it a coincidence or what?' asked Tony.

'Bugger,' replied Raz. 'They're both really gorgeous so that news has really pissed me off.' He leant back casually against the wall, but immediately his body jerked forward as he felt something hard painfully prod him in the back. As he half-turned to inspect the problem, he suddenly saw out of the corner of his eye what looked like a red snake shooting foam and bubbles into the crowded room from over his shoulder. It appeared to his astonishment that the masses of thick soapsuds were spurting out extremely rapidly.The surprised crowd became frightened and over-excited, pushing and shoving each other as the swirling torrent of foam began to cover people completely. 'What the hell's happened?' cried Raz trying to wipe his eyes free of the foam that was beginning to envelop him and was covering everyone nearby in thick white suds.

'You must have hit the top of the fire extinguisher and set the fucker off,' yelled Mike, trying to make himself heard over the pandemonium.

The crowd was now shrieking and shouting in the commotion caused as the red snake continued whirling this way and that, shooting foam across the room as people pushed and shoved each other trying to escape down the overcrowded stairway. Raz turned to the wall and decided to try and locate the extinguisher which he vaguely remembered hanging on the wall nearby. He could not see the red snake, which was obviously the hose of the extinguisher, as now there was too much foam piling up everywhere. As his hands groped around through the foam, he felt the metal container on the wall. He grasped it, trying desperately to locate the knob or whatever he'd inadvertently pushed to try and turn the spurting monster off. But as his hand frantically tried to find the on/off switch or knob, he slipped on the foam covered floor and, as he fell, he instinctively clutched at the fire extinguisher, tearing the container off its brackets on the wall, and feeling it heavily and painfully bounce onto his right foot as he sprawled on the floor.

The unseen snake now began maniacally whirling in circles with the force of the foam as it poured out over the excited crowd. Raz, completely covered in foam, clutched at his throbbing foot. 'Aah! Aah! The fucking thing's landed on my fucking foot,' he screamed between mouthfuls of the soapy suds. None of the others could see him writhing in agony on the floor as they were all now completely covered in foam themselves, surrounded by a cacophony of sound from the room full of screaming, yelling people. Tony and Chris were in absolute hysterics at the scene developing before them, both leaning against the wall to prevent each other from falling over in the general mêlée, whilst Mike was down on his hands and knees desperately searching for his spectacles which had been knocked off his nose in the confusion.

All of a sudden the foam stopped spurting as the supply exhausted itself. The commotion had probably only lasted fifteen or twenty seconds but to Mike, who had now found his spectacles, thankfully unbroken, it had seemed like fifteen minutes. He began crawling through the foam desperately searching for Raz. He found the extinguisher on the floor and then came across Raz lying in front of him clutching his foot and swearing. He helped Raz to his feet, emerging through the foam to the cheers and yells of the remaining crowd, most of whom had thoroughly enjoyed the spectacle of the frenzy created in the few seconds of mayhem.

A black suited man immediately appeared through the foam, an angry expression spread across his face. 'Did any of you louts let this off?' he demanded, glaring around at the group. 'I'm the manager and my bar staff tell me you lot were standing by the stairs here.'

'Yeah, I must have done it,' admitted Raz trying to ignore his painful foot. 'But it was a pure accident, it was not done maliciously. I must have leaned against the wall and somehow set it off. I'm really sorry about all the mess, but all I've got to show for it is probably a broken toe where the bloody extinguisher fell on my foot when I tried to turn the thing off.'

Cheers and shrieks were still issuing from the excited crowd left in the room, though the bar staff were trying to quieten them all down and asking them to leave the sodden premises as quickly as possible. The manager shrugged his shoulders, for he could now see that Raz was clearly in severe pain. 'OK lads, I'll take your word for it, we'll just have to clean up the mess. You ought to go to the hospital and get an X-ray on your foot,' he told Raz, feeling somewhat sympathetic towards him now. 'Come on Raz, let's get out of here,' said Chris, beginning to feel uncomfortable in his foam-soaked clothes.

Mike put his arm round Raz's right shoulder and Chris took the other shoulder as they stumbled down the foam-soaked stairs and out into the street. Mike's old Ford was parked almost opposite the entrance, so they helped Raz to settle into the back seat.

'Jesus Christ, what a scream. You certainly know how to give the boys a good time, Raz,' said Tony. 'Let's get you to the hospital.'

'No, I think it's just badly bruised,' replied Raz groaning softly. 'If it's really bad in the morning, I'll have it X-rayed then. Let's just get home and change out of these soaking clothes, shall we?' he pleaded with the others, slightly annoyed that their evening had ended so abruptly and that he had injured his foot, but enjoying the image of the bar filling with foam and the madness that had ensued during those few seconds of fun that he had caused purely by accident.

Chapter Twenty-Six

Some week's later, a highly amusing escapade happened to Tony that gave the other's something to laugh and talk about for weeks.

One Sunday, Tony had gone out for the day with Peter, a friend of his who was in the Merchant Navy and had returned home on leave. Peter had brought along two pals from his ship who were also on leave and who were both staying with him at his parent's house in Cambridge. The group had walked into Cambridge and trawled their way though a number of pubs, becoming highly inebriated in the process. After closing time, they had found themselves back at the terraced home of Peter's parents who were away on holiday in Norfolk. They had continued drinking heavily, raiding the elderly couple's drinks cabinet and consuming the remnants of several bottles of assorted spirits. One of Peter's friends suggested that they play some games, one of which was a risqué activity that they sometimes indulged in on board ship as a diversion to while away the boredom of a long voyage.

The idea was loudly and drunkenly explained to Tony by the others all talking at once. The game loosely involved each of the participants lowering their trousers and pants and attempting to force out farts that would ignite a lighted match held directly behind the arse of the contestant. The bigger and longer the fart the better the flame, with a particularly lively breaking of wind sometimes causing a flame that roared like a jet engine. The obvious objective of the game was to attempt to produce the most spectacular lighted fart.

The drunken quartet had agreed to play, but first they turned all the lights off, just leaving a table lamp glowing in a corner, in an attempt to create an even greater spectacle. A couple of the boys started off, showing Tony the basics of the game so that when it came to Tony's turn to participate, though he had never played it before, he was sure his enormous intake of alcohol during the day had caused him to build up a fair amount of gas. He let out a wonderful lengthy fart that caught light extremely well, but for some reason it seemed to blow back as though it had been mysteriously sucked inwards towards Tony's braced buttocks. Unfortunately Tony's rear was extremely hairy and, within seconds, there was a crisp crackling sound as these hairs caught alight. The acrid smell of burning hair assaulted Tony's nostrils as the sensation of pain penetrated his drink sodden nerve endings. The flames crackled across his posterior and quickly enveloped his scrotal sac, causing Tony to leap forward in pain and anguish. Unfortunately his brain did not register that his trousers and pants were now lying round his ankles. He tripped, losing his balance completely, legs entangled in his underpants and trousers. Unsure of his surroundings in the dimly-lit room, he fell heavily, head first against the edge of the television set which was knocked backwards off its stand with the impact, crashing heavily to rest upside down with Tony's body lying irregularly on top of it.

At first the others had gasped in admiration at Tony's amazing fart, then they had begun laughing out loud when his posterior caught fire, but now they realised Tony was in trouble, hearing his cries of pain as he tried to move. They sprang into drunken action. Someone switched on the lights. Peter, trying to think quickly, poured a bottle of beer over Tony's arse, which hissed and steamed as the foaming liquid gushed over it.

Tony lay writhing in agony, moaning and cursing as he slipped awkwardly off the upturned television set to sprawl on the carpet. He lay holding his face and as he turned towards them, the others could see he was bleeding profusely. Blood was pouring out from between his fingers and running down his face, dripping from his chin. Two of the boys helped Tony to gingerly and carefully extract his legs from his pants and trousers as Tony's cries of agony became louder and harsher. The singed flesh and hair on his arse gave off a very strong acrid smell. Peter could see Tony's bottom was pink and burnt as they turned him over onto his side. As he inspected Tony's face, he could see that his eye was badly split across the brow and there was a cut on the bridge of his nose where his face had smashed into the top edge of the TV set. His face was noticeably swelling, so whilst one of the boys mopped the worst of the blood from Tony's face, Peter, now sobering up very quickly, told Tony that he was going to ring for an ambulance. He was very concerned that Tony might have broken something in his fall, but his angry looking pink scrotum and bottom obviously needed immediate medical attention. There were some blisters forming there already, noted Peter unhappily, taking a quick look at Tony's bottom.

Fifteen minutes later Tony had been given an injection for the pain and was being carried ignominiously from the small terraced house on a stretcher by the bemused ambulance crew. The shock of the accident had sobered the others up, as each of them now realised that Tony's injuries could be quite serious and they became concerned for his well-being.

Peter accompanied Tony in the ambulance and, on arrival at the casualty department at Addenbrooke's Hospital, he had to undergo the humiliation of explaining to the staff nurse on duty how the accident to Tony had occurred. He tried to clarify the details as simply as possible, but found himself getting deeper and deeper into trouble, becoming more embarrassed every time he opened his mouth.

'Letting off wind and trying to ignite it. My God, whatever next?' exclaimed the staff nurse indignantly. 'Haven't you people got anything better to do with your lives? And what about his facial injuries?' she queried.

'Well,' said Peter uncomfortably, wondering if she thought they had been playing homosexual games. 'It's as I told you, his trousers were round his ankles and he tripped and fell and hit his head badly.'

'Well, he'll have to go to X-ray to make sure he hasn't broken anything. Once we've sorted his lower parts out, we'll send him off there.'

Peter hung around the casualty waiting room, occasionally diving into the men's toilet for a drink of cold water from the tap, trying to dampen down his raging hangover and overcome the dehydration caused from the surplus of alcohol. He had a raging headache, but he was more concerned for Tony, desperately hoping that no long-term damage had been done to his privates, knowing his reputation with the ladies. He decided that he'd better ring Tony's friends at the flat to inform them what had happened, even though it was an inconvenient time.

Mike, woken up by the 'phone ringing, had padded sleepily down the hallway to answer it, wondering who on earth would be calling at this ungodly hour. 'Burnt his arsehole badly and he's in hospital,' cried Mike incredulously. Is this some kind of joke you're playing? Do you know what fucking time it is Peter, 4:30 in the morning and I've got to get up for work in a couple of hours.'

'No, it's really true,' emphasised Peter. 'I'm at Addenbrooke's now, he's having an X-ray too because he fell over on his face. They think he might have broken something.

Chris, who had been woken by Mike's voice loudly exclaiming to the person on the phone, joined Mike in the hall. 'What the fuck's going on?' he asked irritably. He had just had to endure a tough two hours of sex with a relentless pneumatic blonde German tour guide who was sharing his bed. He had only managed half-an-hour's sleep before being woken up and was not too happy about it.

Raz also appeared in his silk dressing gown, rubbing his eyes and yawning ferociously. 'What's the problem, is anything wrong,' he asked anxiously, his eyes puffy from being woken up from a deep sleep.

'It's Tony. Apparently he's got really pissed and ended up playing some stupid game. He's burnt his bum and bollocks and damaged his face badly. He's at Addenbrooke's right now,' explained Mike.

'Sounds like he's been shagging a really hot bit of stuff to me,' replied Raz dryly, somewhat impervious to the seriousness of the matter.

'Seriously Raz, it's true. Peter's on the 'phone right now,' insisted Mike, still a little unsure as to whether Peter and Tony were trying to pull a stunt. The truth was that one or other of the crowd were always playing practical jokes on each another, and this could be yet another game they were playing.

On the other end of the 'phone, Peter implored the others that he was telling them the truth. He then noticed Tony being wheeled back along the corridor towards the clinic, a young doctor striding along beside his trolley. 'I'll ring back with more news. Tony's just back from X-ray,' said Peter hurriedly, slamming the receiver down and walking over to the cubicle where Tony's trolley had been deposited. He looked down at his friend and saw Tony's eyes peer up at him from over a large plaster strapped across his nose. There were bandages round the top of his head, covering the swollen eyebrow where Tony had fallen onto the TV set.

The doctor was talking down to Tony, who tried to wink at Peter from behind his bandages. 'We've reset your nose, which will join up quite happily, it's not a bad break and we've tidied up your posterior and your privates. You've got a cream to use on your lower regions and a supply of bandages, they pin on like large nappies. You'll need to lie quietly for two or three days, but then you can get up and move around. It will be painful initially, for a week or so, until the burnt tissue has had time to recuperate. We'll make an appointment to see you again in a few day's time.'

The doctor turned to Peter, staring at him with little attempt to conceal the contempt that he must have felt. 'May I suggest that you both refrain from playing such sordid little games like the one that caused this,' he said, motioning his head down at Tony's groin. 'There are many people brought into hospital with terrible accident damage or life-threatening problems, treating people like your friend just wastes time that we should be spending on more important issues.'

Peter stood there, tired and humiliated, wishing that the floor would open up and devour him, until the doctor turned and flounced off along the corridor.

The clinic arranged for an ambulance to carry Tony home to Mawson Road where he was carried unceremoniously on a stretcher upstairs to his room, where the ambulance crew deposited him painfully onto his bed. The others crowded round, shocked to see him covered in plaster and bandages and eager to ask questions. The pain was evident on Tony's face as he lay on his back looking up at their startled faces. As he self-consciously explained to them what had happened and why, they fell about the room laughing unsympathetically, they just could not help themselves, if only they had all been able to see it happen, it was like a comedy show!

'Look, I'd really appreciate it you guys if we could keep this matter to ourselves, it's so embarrassing. I must have been pissed out of my brains to get involved in such a stupid game. But if one of the girls in the salon got to hear about it, the story would be passed around like wildfire and then every bloody person in Cambridge would know, and I'd become a laughing stock. I'd never live it down,' pleaded Tony.

'Well, you would certainly be an object of some derision,' chuckled Mike.

'What I want to know is, how the hell are you going to have a shit?' asked Chris, with some interest.

Tony groaned up at him. 'Oh God, I really don't even want to think about it,' he said quietly.

'Oh, well, we'll leave you alone to get some rest Tony. Hope you're OK and just call out if you need anything,' said Mike. 'We're all in tonight.'

They left Tony alone, retiring to the lounge where, needless to say, they could not help discussing Tony's antics for some time, dissolving into fits of laughter from time to time as they tried to imagine the scene when the accident happened.

After a few weeks, Tony had soon made a speedy recovery, both top and bottom, but he became the butt of the other's jokes for quite some time afterwards, although they did of course respect Tony's wishes, and it was never mentioned to anyone outside their own four walls.

Chapter Twenty-Seven

The traditional May Ball week in Cambridge was eagerly awaited by the thousands of exam exhausted, daylight deprived student population, most of whom had been revising for several months leading up to the May examinations and badly needed an excuse to let their hair down. Many of the 'townies' also enjoyed taking part in the end of term festivities, particularly the May Balls. These balls were rather oddly named as they always took place during the first week in June just before the students started to 'go down' for the summer holidays.

Each college surreptitiously competed against the others, not only for the honour of being voted the 'Best Ball', but in an intense rivalry to lure the best bands and groups, as long as they could be obtained within the confines of the college budget which were presided over by May Ball committees set up by the students themselves. Some of the larger and wealthier colleges, such as St. John's and Trinity, were in a stronger position to stage larger, more dramatic balls than the lesser colleges, such as Downing and Pembroke. Their larger revenues enabled them to hire more prestigious groups and entertainers to produce the more spectacular balls.

Tickets for the events were usually put on sale many months in advance of the actual ball and, for the more popular colleges, tickets could soon be in short supply, particularly when a popular band was playing. Chris and Mike had decided, soon after beginning to share their first flat together, that the actual purchase of tickets was an inconvenience that they both deemed unnecessary and expensive. The May Balls were surrounded by strict security arrangements which the friends had decided presented them both with an interesting challenge. That challenge was how to obtain entry to the Ball without actually purchasing a ticket, known simply as 'Crashing the Ball'. This method of entry had long been a tradition amongst some 'townies' and undergraduates alike, who either because of limited finances or simply because of the challenge, decided that they had to try and gain illegal entry to a ball.

During the summer before meeting Chris, Mike had crashed several Balls. This was completely out of character, but he had a friend in his accountancy firm who had issued him with a challenge - to see which of them could gain entry into the most Balls. Mike had tried several ruses that had worked well. Once, by pretending that he was a roadie in one of the bands, he had brazenly walked into the ball with a coiled electric lead wrapped around one arm and an old microphone swinging from his hand, briefly explaining to the porter that he was in a hurry to get through so that he could fix an amplifier that needed repair.

'Hurry up son, they'll be waiting for you to fix that, they're due on in twenty minutes,' the porter had told him, ushering him through the crowd of gowned and dinner-suited couples waiting patiently with their tickets.

'Fucking brilliant, so simple,' cried Mike as he strode into the mêlée, cheekily accepting his first glass of champagne from a tray held by a waiter.

On another occasion, he had approached the Porter's Lodge at King's College, this time immaculately attired in his dress suit. He had made up a sob story, complete with a few tears, explaining to the porter that he'd come from London for the Ball but that he had been waiting outside the college for his girlfriend who was in charge of the tickets. In conversation with a local, he had been informed that King's College was further down the street, but he had unfortunately been waiting outside St. Cath's College. 'She must have tired of waiting for me and gone into the Ball with her friends,' he told the porter. 'You probably saw her, she was in a long, white dress with blonde hair. She would have been accompanied by another couple.'

'Sir, with all good faith, there are countless girls here that answer that description,' replied the porter.

'Yes, but surely you must have seen her, she must have been waiting outside for over an hour. Perhaps she's left a message for me?' he suggested.

'No sir, we've been very busy here, but I know that we've

received no messages from young ladies,' assured the porter.

'Oh God, what can I do?' mumbled Mike, forcing tears into his eyes again.

'Well, I don't see how we can help,' replied the porter who seemed to becoming slightly more sympathetic to Mike's plight.

'May I just pop in for a few minutes to see if I can spot her, if not I'll return here and wait outside to see if she comes out to search for me,' he suggested.

'Well, sir, I uugh...' The porter was interrupted by Mike offering his pièce de resistance. Mike took his arm and spoke in a hushed voice, 'Between you and I, this evening was going to be special.' He took out a small ring to show the porter, it had a large white stone and sparkled in the light. 'I was going to ask her to marry me tonight,' he choked, tears filling his eyes. He put the ring back into his pocket, a worthless ring that he'd found in a Christmas cracker some years ago and had held onto for no known reason. Tonight it was going to be worth it's weight in gold.

'Oh, I see, Sir,' said the porter who appeared to be feeling a little more charitable. 'It's highly irregular, but I can see you're very upset, so I'll let you in sir, just to see if she's there. If she is, then may I wish you good luck with your proposal. If not, please come back, and I'll keep an eye out for the young lady in the meantime.'

'Oh, thank you so much. That's very kind,' smiled Mike, suppressing the desire to jump for joy. He had felt jubilant at first as he entered the first large marquee and accepted the free glass of champagne, obligatory at the Balls. But as he sipped his bubbly, taking in the heady atmosphere, he began suffering a few misgivings and then, unexpectedly, a strong sense of guilt overcame him. He suddenly felt extremely uncomfortable because he had blatantly lied to the aged porter. He had relied on the elder man's compassion, the porter had believed his story because he had trusted Mike, and now his conscience was pricking at him, which he had not expected when he had planned the ruse several days previously.

Mike strolled through the marquees with various bands playing, enjoying the musicians dressed as clowns, noting the fairground rides, the disco music, the countless bars serving juices, beer and champagne. After an hour he came across a pretty girl with dark hair sitting on a wall. At her feet, propped against the wall lay an undergraduate, his dinner suit splattered in vomit and dirt; it appeared to Mike that he lay exactly where he had fallen. Mike started to talk to the girl who looked very unhappy. She explained that she was American and that the drunk was an undergraduate at Kings; apparently he had met her a couple of weeks previously and invited her to the Ball. Unfortunately, after his exams had finished he had engaged in a sustained bout of heavy drinking for a couple of days before the Ball and he had been extremely drunk when he had collected her earlier that evening. On arrival at the Ball, he had continued drinking heavily, resulting in a nasty argument between them. She had felt incredibly let down, having looked forward to going to the Cambridge Ball. She had even telephoned her folks back home to tell them all about it and how excited she was about attending the event. The student had then collapsed in a drunken stupor and someone had helped her prop him against the wall.

Mike could sense that he had a chance with the pretty girl who was obviously extremely upset and feeling so let down. He listened sympathetically as she disconsolately told him the sad story, sobbing quietly as she did so. Her cheeks became heavily streaked with mascara. He took out his handkerchief and tenderly dabbed her cheeks dry. Then, without warning, he felt a hand grabbing his leg whilst a torrent of abuse poured out of the undergraduates mouth, who had suddenly woken up. The girl, whose name he'd found out was Susie, clutched his arm in despair. 'Please take me away from this goddam schmuck, I cannot stand this behaviour any longer,' she whispered earnestly to him.

Mike pulled away from the undergraduate's grip on his leg. As he did so, the drunk collapsed against the wall again, incoherently rambling away to himself. Mike and Suzie had then walked away together. After a short trip to the powder room where she had repaired her face, they had danced in every marquee and drunk endless glasses of champagne, even staying for the 6 o'clock breakfast and the photograph of the 'all night survivors' of the ball. Still harbouring guilt feelings, he had not forgotten the kindly porter and, having related the story of how he had deceived the old porter to get into the Ball, which had

216

shocked Susie somewhat, he had asked her if she would mind calling in with him just to thank the porter, so that he could pass Susie off as the girl he had been looking for, basically this gesture was to relieve his conscience. The porter was delighted when Mike appeared in his office with the girl, although Susie could not comprehend the porter's remark just as they were returning to the Ball. 'Hope everything will be wonderful for you both in the future my dear,' he'd told her quietly, with a smile and wink as she had left the office with Mike, hand-in-hand.

Mike then had to explain to her that he had told the porter he was going to ask the make-believe girl to marry him that evening. Susie was even more astonished at the elaborate scheme that Mike had thought up, especially when he showed her the ring from the Christmas cracker, which he immediately gave her as a keepsake.

After the Survivor's Breakfast, the pair had hit it off so well that Susie gladly returned home with Mike where, after some rather pathetic drunken attempts at lovemaking, they had both fallen soundly asleep and had not woken up until eight o'clock that evening when they had consummated their relationship. Mike had taken her home to her lodgings in a much happier state of mind than when he had met her the evening before.

'So, I've done it before and we can do it again,' he assured Chris one evening as they sat drinking beer and smoking whilst watching a re-run of the Cassius Clay/Henry Cooper fight on TV. 'It's just a question of which Ball we want to crash and how we do it. If I can do it, I reckon anyone can,' he added modestly, puffing smoke rings up to the ceiling.

'Why don't we try and get a party together,' suggested Chris who was always keen to push ideas to their limit. 'We could take some nice girlies with us, because surely the majority of girls there are going to have partners with them, aren't they Mike? If we could invite the girls we would like to be with, that would be better wouldn't it?'

'Christ!' retorted Mike. 'It's hard enough for blokes to crash the Balls, let alone tagging your own harem along with you. Women think differently, they wouldn't get the same buzz out of something like this. The only balls that women want to crash are those little soft ones that hang between our legs.'

Chris was not convinced, he was sure that there were plenty of women who would take the risk just for the fun of the escapade. He thought back to Françoise, who had returned to France sometime ago, and what she'd done to him in the cinema - she'd be up for it, that's for sure.

'I'm sure if we put ourselves out and invited the right girls, we could get some to come along. Let's face it, you were lucky at that King's Ball, meeting Suzie, who was ready to leave her drunken partner, but chances like that can't happen at every ball,' said Chris trying to sow some doubt in Mike's mind.

'Well, if we could get some girls to come along, we'd have to plan it very carefully as they'd all be wearing fucking great ball gowns and high heels,' said Mike. He knew that he'd been very lucky in his success at bluffing his way into the Balls, but he was not blasé about it. He knew others who had succeeded, but he also knew of several people who had been caught and severely beaten by the security staff. Another group of friends had tried a complicated method of gaining entry to a ball by crossing the river Cam on a Heath Robinson-type raft. Made of an intricate arrangement of poles and oil drums, it had capsized in midstream. Several of the party had fallen into the river in full dress suits, one of them nearly drowning in the process. Another friend had suffered a broken ankle after scaling a wall at Queen's College and jumping down to the other side. To make matters worse, a gardener's rake had been left lying in the longish grass and he had landed on the prongs at the end, the long handle had shot up and given him a hefty crack on the forehead, which had eventually needed seven stitches.

The more Mike thought about Chris's idea, the more feasible it became. They would however, he reasoned, need to plan such a manoeuvre with almost military precision. The ease with which he had managed to stroll into the Balls he had crashed could not possibly be emulated with a group of people. It was a challenge and he knew it would be difficult, but he liked demands made upon his mental prowess, after all that was why he was training to be an accountant. As they sat mulling the idea over, Tony arrived home from work, As always he gave off aromas of hair lotions and shampoos. He collected three beers from the fridge and joined the others in the lounge, handing a

218

bottle to each of them. They both explained the latest crazy idea that they had come up with. Mike was still slightly reticent, but Chris's enthusiasm had almost won him over.

Tony could tell by the way they were both leaning forward in their chairs as they explained the plan, together with a great deal of arm waving and earnest head nodding, that they wanted his seal of approval. Since he had lived at Mawson Road, he had seen and been involved in many new crazy ideas germinating in the flat, but knew that most of these madcap schemes would fade away to nothing unless there was enough unbridled enthusiasm generated in them at an early stage by a majority of the four flatmates.

'I reckon that we could get away with about eight or ten people as an ideal number, I mean in for a penny, in for a pound. What do you think Tony?' asked Chris.

Tony smiled at them, feeling tired from standing all day at work. He kicked off his shoes and rubbed his chin, feeling the stubble that started to break through in the early evening. He registered the sparkle in their eyes and the eagerness in their faces as they waited for him to answer. He took a swig of the cold beer, he always savoured this moment, after a long day, when he could finally relax and take the weight off his feet. 'I think it's really a great idea. Count me in. I've never been to a May Ball and I'd love to go. But I'm not really very good at planning things, but you two could do it. I know that you've crashed Balls before Mike, so you obviously know what goes on.'

At that moment Raz arrived and, after drinking a cold beer with the others, it didn't take long to convince him, the ultimate party animal, that it was a great idea. They had begun to realise that it was almost impossible for Raz to refuse an invitation to anything social at all, however far-fetched it might appear.

So, that evening they all agreed to crash a May Ball and that they would invite along some girls who were game to try a large-scale attempt to get into one of the Balls without paying. Mike said that he would organise it, as long as the others gave him some help if and when it was required.

They had a period of six weeks before May Ball week, so Mike and Chris quickly began some research, pouring over the local newspapers and student magazines for information about the Balls. They wanted to find out which groups were playing, how big each ball was intending to be and which was the most desirable event to attend that year. Eventually, they whittled the list down to the Jesus, St. John's and Magdalene balls. Evaluating all the pro's and con's of these, by a serious process of elimination, Magdalene College was finally chosen as their target.

They were ultimately swayed because of the location and by what Mike laughingly called 'ease of access'. Magdalene College lay on the north side of central Cambridge, surrounded by high red brick walls on three sides and by the river on the other. Two of the walls fronted busy roads which met at right angles at a junction. One of these, Chesterton Road, was a pretty tree-lined avenue, where a wide pavement adjoining the college wall jutted out about one hundred yards before a set of traffic lights. Situated on the other side of this wall was the Master's Garden, forbidden to undergraduates but accessible to the main areas of the college either through the Master's Lodge or through a heavy wooden door, used only by the gardeners. Mike had spent some time looking at this area and had decided that if they could get the group over this wall, they could find their way to the door and crash the Ball. The great advantage of this scheme was that no-one should be in the garden when they would be entering it, late on the evening of the ball, when it would be dark.

Mike knew that Raz had an Indian friend who worked as a bartender in the rowdy college bar at Magdalene and explained the plan of action briefly to Raz indicating that the plan would only work if they could gain entry through the garden door and so they would somehow need to obtain a key. Mike told Raz to confide in his friend to find out whether he could obtain a key from one of the college servants. If not, the scheme would fold.

After some gentle persuasion from Raz, his friend agreed to talk to one of the younger gardeners, who thought it was a brilliant idea and happily agreed to lend his key for a couple of packs of American cigarettes that Chris and Tony often bought from their American pals, Jerry and Bill. The college gardeners apparently had to live with the knowledge that the Master's Garden was only accessible to the Master and his family and a few Don's in the college, as other members of the college and the general public were never allowed in. Most people were probably not even aware of the garden's existence and so all their hard work was appreciated only by the privileged few. Consequently, one or two of the gardeners had a bit of a grudge against the college hierarchy, although the young man who had agreed to lend the key probably had no idea that so many gatecrashers would be passing through in the dark on that particular evening.

Mike and Chris had invited their close friend Johnny to make up the group, so there would be five couples in all. Mike decided to call a meeting to outline the plan to everyone, so one evening in early May they gathered in the Baron of Beef and took over a large table in a quiet area at the back of the pub. They sat smoking and sipping their pints slowly, as Mike pulled a folded piece of paper from his pocket, carefully unfolding it and spreading it out flat on the table. They moved forward in their chairs to study the rough, pencil drawn outline of the college. 'Right,' said Mike pointing, 'this is Magdalene, and this is Chesterton Road where we start.' His finger traced the outline of the road, while they all listened intently. 'We're going to need a van or small truck with two ladders about 12' high, and an old mattress. That's all the equipment we need. I think Stuart Haig, the window cleaner, might help. He has a pick-up truck and some ladders, so I'm going to ask him if he would help us out on that score. This is how the plan works: on the night of the Ball, the truck drives along Chesterton Road to this point here, which is a quiet area with a wide pavement, whilst across the road there are some large trees. The truck stops here on the pavement. The first person places the ladder against the wall and climbs up almost to the top of the wall. The mattress is then passed up by a second person and hauled onto the top of the wall to cover the broken glass embedded in it. OK so far?' he enquired looking round at them all. They all nodded in agreement. 'OK, the person on the ladder then straddles the wall, sitting on one end of the mattress, and the second ladder is then passed up to him. He pulls it up and over the wall and lowers it down to lean against the wall on the other side in the Master's Garden. This should take no longer than thirty seconds and, hopefully, the traffic will just carry on passing by completely disinterested. The truck will be parked mainly on the wide pavement anyway. The rest of the party, in the meantime, have been waiting in all their finery across the road under the trees. They cross the road quickly and proceed one-by-one up the ladder, over the wall and down the other side. Whoever is on the wall, and I think Chris should be that person as he is probably the strongest and most athletic, will help everyone over.' Chris made a show of flexing his arm muscles.

Mike ignored this and continued, 'once the last person is over the other side, the second ladder is pushed back over the wall to our helper, who then packs it in the truck, pulls the mattress off the top of the wall and into the truck together with the first ladder and drives off pronto. The group are all now gathered together in the Master's Garden,' he continued pointing at the exact position on the map, 'with our trusty key to the inner door here, leading to our Ball in the college. Hopefully, getting over the wall will take us about three minutes only.'

'What if the police arrive when we're all going over the wall, or someone sees us?' asked Johnny.

'Good point. If they do, then we could be fucked,' replied Mike shrugging his shoulders and extending both hands, palms upwards, as if to emphasise that point.

'It'll be the same if someone from the college sees us and reports it, but let's face it, students are always doing odd things and, having the girls with us, most people would just think we're just pissing about,' said Chris. 'After all, it is May Ball week!'

'Yeah, it's the chance we take. It's never going to be one hundred percent certain, but this is as easy as we can make it. We just have to hope that in the period when we are climbing over the wall, when we are at our most vulnerable, that no-one spots us and rings the college,' added Mike.

'What if its raining?' asked Raz innocently.

'Then we get fucking wet, you prat!' laughed Mike. 'I can't really control that Raz, I'm very sorry. I will have a word with God though,' he quipped, looking up at the ceiling, whilst placing both hands together as through he was praying.

'Let's not look on the black side, er, sorry Raz,' said Chris in fun, laughing at his Indian friend.

'How high is the wall, 'cos I'm not much good with heights?' muttered Tony. 'I'm not even very good on ladders.'

'Christ, are you a man or a mouse? It's only twelve feet high, it's hardly Mount fucking Everest, is it?' exclaimed Chris.

'Yeah, but I can't help it. I get vertigo just standing on a chair,' replied Tony.

'I got felatio the other day sitting in a chair,' cried Chris to the groans of the others, as they laughed at his crude announcement.

'Look Tony, we could get a ladder set up against the wall in our garden and you could practice on that. I'm sure that we night have to do that with some of the girls just to get them used to climbing up and down ladders quickly.'

'I'll hold the ladder for their practice if that's the case,' volunteered Chris.

'You dirty sod,' said Raz. 'I know what your game is. If those girls have any sense, they'll wear jeans.'

'Right chaps,' said Mike, banging his hand on the table to cut out the wisecracks. 'As long as that's reasonably clear, I'll get the ball rolling and have a word with Stuart Haig about the truck and ladders. Just make sure each of you has a glamour babe ready with a bit of adventure in her for that night and we should be able to have some fun at the Ball.'

Mike drank his beer with relish, almost draining his glass, feeling pleased that his plan had gone down well with the others. Raz stood up and knocked his glass down twice on the table, then raised the glass in his big right hand and contemplated the group. 'Friends, let's raise our glasses to Mike for all his hard work putting this scheme together for our benefit. Let's hope that it works out successfully.'

They drained their glasses as one and Raz went over to the bar to order another round. He also wanted to chat to the new barmaid that he'd noticed whilst Mike had been talking.

Mike got up for a leak. Whilst urinating in the toilet he felt very pleased that it had gone so well, no-one had asked any awkward questions nor put forward any opposition to his plan. He felt more confident now that he had explained it all to the others. Yes, he felt it was really going to work. He had a gut feeling, an anticipation inside him, that seemed to be telling him that everything would be all right on the night.

Two days later Mike called round to see Stuart Haig, the

window cleaner. Sometime ago, they had played badminton together at the YMCA for about a year and had become good friends. Mike had got to know Stuart well enough to know that he was a reliable and trustworthy character who would not let anyone down. Mike outlined the plan in confidence to Stuart who thought it was hilarious and was only too pleased to help out. He knew Mike now lived with some other crazy characters in their fairly notorious flat. He admired the way Mike seemed to have overcome his initial shyness, which had been very apparent when Stuart had first met him.

They agreed that Stuart would drive his pick-up truck and bring his two light-weight aluminium ladders and that Mike would provide the old mattress. They then went over the plan in detail. Mike showed Stuart where he needed to park and where on the wall the ladder was going. Stuart said that it should be a doddle and ought to take no time at all to get everyone over the wall.

Later in the week Mike went along to the student bar at Magdalene College with Raz, who introduced him to his friend Jimmy. He had obtained the key from the gardener and Mike decided that it would be prudent to test the key in the big wooden door. They left the bar and walked through the college to the Main Court, neither of them feetling conspicuous as they looked like two ordinary students, although maybe just a fraction older admitted Mike to himself with a wry grin. They passed down an ancient stone passage and into a smaller court, where Mike, who had thoroughly researched the layout of the college, indicated the heavy door to Raz.

'Stick the key in the lock quickly, there's no-one about,' said Raz, glancing up and down the passage.

'OK, just keep an eye out,' said Mike, pushing the heavy iron key into the keyhole of the old studded oak door. He turned the key, gripped the iron handle and pulled. The door squealed open slowly. Mike stepped inside and looked around at the garden. It was beautiful. The lawns were immaculately manicured, the hedges and shrubs were artfully trimmed, the gravelled paths were raked and there was a profusion of beautiful flowers. 'This really is a secret garden,' he whispered to Raz who was peering around the door. 'It's such a shame that most people will never ever get to see it. That's why the gardeners must get pissed off, because only a very few privileged people get to enjoy this.'

Mike looked over the garden to the red brick wall fronting Chesterton Road, the wall they were going to scale to get into the Ball. He observed large clumps of shrubs and groups of flowers in the border adjacent to the wall, but could see that there were plenty of spaces between some of the plants where they could lower the second ladder to make their descent into the garden. Having satisfied himself on the rough layout of the garden, he turned back into the courtyard and locked the door.

'Phew, what a gorgeous place. It's like paradise in there,' said Raz, taken aback a little. 'It all seems to be coming together very well. I must congratulate you Mike on sorting it all out for everyone.' He was very impressed with the way in which Mike had planned the details of the whole affair so meticulously.

'Let's hope that on the night, everything falls into place,' replied Mike thoughtfully. 'That's the time when you can congratulate me, when we're all inside the college on the night of the Ball, pissed out of our brains and enjoying ourselves. Then we can say it's been a success!'

Chapter Twenty-Eight

On the evening of the Magdalene College May Ball, the group of five men and five women assembled at the flat at 10 o'clock for some cocktails that Raz and Mike had prepared. They all appeared to be in a boisterous mood, though some of the party admitted to feeling a little apprehensive, especially Mike who knew that the others were relying on him to make it into a successful evening for them all. The men looked immaculate in their hired dinner suits, whilst the girls were resplendent in their long ball gowns of varied hues, several with a daring décolletage, obviously all much admired by the males. Johnny, an inveterate womaniser, had joined them with his current girlfriend, an attractive English girl who worked as a secretary for a local publisher. Mike was accompanied by Louise, a friend of his from the accountancy firm that he worked for. She had made her own gown for the Ball, only completing it at 11 o'clock the previous evening. Chris and Tony had invited a pair of well-endowed blonde Swedish girls, both of whom were in their second year at the Studio School of Languages. 'Why the hell they're studying English, I just don't understand,' said Chris to Tony shortly after they had met them at a disco in the town centre, 'they both speak better English than most English people I know.' The girls were both close friends from the University at Uplands Varsby in Northern Sweden and when the boys had invited them to take part in the illicit scheme, they had excitedly agreed to go along with the idea thought up by these mad English men that they had become involved with.

Raz had invited Madhur, an Indian girl that he had known for a number of years and with whom he seemed to enjoy, what seemed to the other boys, a very agreeable relationship. Occasionally, perhaps every three or six months, one or the other would ring to say hello and check how the other was. They would arrange to meet up and have a lovely evening with dinner, culminating in a wild night of passion. Their relationship continued without any ties or demands on each other and suited them both admirably. Mike and Chris had both attempted to emulate Raz's arrangements in one or two of their own relationships without much success. They had both found that most girls would become intensely jealous of other girls intruding on their particular relationship, especially when they knew that sexual activity was involved.

Raz and Madhur had obviously taken some trouble to compliment each other colourwise. Madhur had a plum coloured ball gown with matching accessories, while Raz was wearing a plum coloured tuxedo with a matching bow tie and cummerbund. He seemed more at ease in his ensemble than the other men, probably because he often wore bow ties, an affectation left over from his college days.

Chris had volunteered to drive them over to Chesterton Road in his hearse and, after a couple of cocktails each and four bottles of champagne between them, they left the flat and managed to squeeze themselves into the hearse. The girls had a little difficulty with the skirts of their gowns, which billowed out and seemed to take up an enormous amount of space. Nevertheless, they managed to cram together and, by now in a relaxed but still quietly excited mood, Chris drove the crowd across town. He parked in a side street off Chesterton Road and as they all struggled to free themselves from the confines of the hearse, they became aware of the loud music emanating from the Ball which had started at 8 o'clock. Mike smiled at the sound of the music, knowing that it would produce the usual batch of irate 'phone calls from disgruntled members of the public, especially as the Ball progressed through the night, all complaining that they could not sleep because of the noise. He'd never understood people like that, living in a university city, complaining about a couple of nights a year when the students let their hair down. If they didn't like it, why didn't they piss off to live in Siberia?

A sharp twinge of excitement shot up Mike's back, he thought he could feel the hairs on the back of his neck stand up. He knew from his previous experiences that crashing these balls really got the adrenaline pumping. This time though, it was completely different. The jolly crowd around him were relying on him and his expertise. They had also gone to a lot of trouble with their suits and gowns and he did not want to let them down. He checked the time and led the group along Chesterton Road, gathering at the appointed spot under the trees directly across the road from where Stuart should soon draw up in his pick-up truck. There were a few people about. They could see several couples in evening dress walking further along Chesterton Road towards Magdalene College, obviously on their way to the Ball. Mike glanced at his watch again, there were just two minutes to go. There was an air of expectancy and subdued exhilaration amongst the group as Mike ran over the details again for the girls' benefit, and checked the order that each person was going over the wall. Mike patted his breast pocket to confirm the presence of the iron key to the garden gate and peered anxiously down the road, looking for Stuart's red pick-up to appear. Another couple of minutes passed and then, with a twinge of relief, he spotted the pick-up coming down the road towards them, the metal ladders on the rear picking up the glow of the orange streetlights.

The pick-up drew up opposite the group, mounting the kerb and parked on the wide pavement as Mike had instructed. Stuart jauntily gave the thumbs-up sign to Mike as he pulled down the tailgate of the pick-up and pulled the ladders off their rack. He placed both ladders against the wall, then pulled the old mattress that Mike had given him out onto the pavement.

Mike checked the traffic and the group followed him swiftly across the road and, as planned, Chris quickly climbed up the first ladder, then Mike and Stuart lifted the mattress up to him. Chris manhandled it up the ladder and laid it over the top of the wall, making sure that it was safely anchored, covering the dangerous shards of broken glass. He then climbed off the top of the ladder and straddled the wall, sitting on one end of the mattress to hold it steady. Stuart then deftly passed the second ladder up to Chris, who hauled it up and over the wall, gently lowering it down on the other side in a suitable space between a shrub and some clumps of flowers. Satisfying himself that it was secure, he helped Mike, the first person up the ladder to turn his body at the top and to find his foothold on a rung of the lower ladder. Mike then descended quickly down into the garden.

Stuart, meanwhile, was helping the first girl up the ladder. Chris leaned down and held her arm tightly as she turned at the top, the protective mattress preventing her gown catching on the ancient wall. Mike was ready with both hands outstretched to help guide her down the other side. Then the next girl started up the ladder. Chris, sitting on top of the wall with his legs straddling each side, was very aware of the traffic passing by on the road below him. He wondered to himself what the people in the cars were thinking if they happened to catch sight of the group climbing up the ladder in their ballgowns and dress suits. He knew, as the others knew, that if they were unlucky and a member of the college or the police saw them, that the game was probably up. It was a precarious few minutes, so he tried to put it to the back of his mind and concentrate on the job in hand. It was quite disconcerting enough observing the heaving bosoms of the girls as they clambered up the ladder towards him, their breasts bouncing gently beneath their shimmering gowns.

The girls were rather slower than the men and were not helped by the constrictions of their flowing gowns. One of the Swedish girls was especially nervous, but when she began shaking nervously near the top of the ladder, Chris almost lifted her up and over the wall, waiting patiently until she found her foothold on the descending ladder. Unfortunately, as she descended the ladder, her gown caught under her foot. There was a sharp ripping sound and when she inspected it, she found to her consternation that there was a ten inch gash in the material. Luckily Mike, ever practical, had foreseen such an event and produced two small safety pins with which he pinned the tear together satisfactorily.

Finally the group were all standing together, talking in excited whispers as Chris, the last person, descended quickly down into the garden and then pushed the ladder back up over the wall as Stuart's head appeared over the top. Stuart grasped the ladder, lifting it over his head and lowering it down onto the pavement. 'Good luck,' he called softly down to the party standing below, then disappeared from view.

They heard the metallic banging of the ladders on the other side of the wall as Stuart loaded both of them back onto his truck, together with the mattress. They then heard him drive off with a roar and a parting blip on his horn.

Mike looked at his watch as they gathered around him. 'Brilliant,' he stage whispered, but trying to make sure they could all hear him over the music which sounded much louder now that they were over the wall. 'Four minutes from start to finish, and we're all over the first hurdle. Everyone OK?' he enquired, his eyes passing over the group as each of them nodded in agreement. They could hear people laughing and talking excitedly from within the confines of the college which made them all the more excited. 'Follow me everyone,' said Mike quietly as he led them across the soft manicured lawn and round various flower beds, helped by the light from a half-moon in the sky. They made slowly for the gate that Mike knew was in the far corner, the girls holding the hems of their gowns in their hands so they did not catch on any shrubs or trail on the ground. The half-moon cast an eerie glow over the garden and one or two of the group started in surprise when confronted by a large statute in the middle of a flower bed as they passed by, but in no time at all they had reached the gate. He turned to them as they all gathered round. Mike put a finger to his lips. 'Ssh now,' he told them. 'I'm going to open the gate, then when I've checked all's clear, we'll shoot out in couples, just walk out confidently as if you own the place. We'll meet up in the Champagne Bar in twenty minutes, OK everyone?'

There were silent nods of assent from the others as they stood apprehensively, feeling very excited now they were so nearly inside the college and almost at the Ball itself.

Mike slowly and carefully inserted the iron key into the lock, then turned it, bit-by-bit, trying not to make any noise at all. When he had unlocked it, he pulled the door slowly and gently towards him, then peered cautiously round. He glimpsed a large marquee set up on one of the lawns. Gowned and bejewelled couples were talking and laughing in the courtyard, drinking champagne. He took in the bunting and balloons hanging from the roof of the historic courtyard as various couples passed by the doorway, jostling and laughing. He could not discern any security guards nor see anyone who appeared to be official. It was the ideal opportunity. He turned and beckoned to Chris, who grabbed the hand of his Swedish girl and ushered her straight out into the courtyard where they seemed to melt immediately into the crowd. Mike motioned to the next couple and they too went out through the door, completely unnoticed by anyone nearby.

This was the time Mike had foreseen that his elation, as they finally crashed the Ball, would be clouded by his moral misgivings. He had no intention of spoiling the group's enjoyment, but he knew that a large number of people at the Ball would have paid a great deal of money for their tickets. He felt particularly guilty when he thought about the students, many of whom would have saved for months to pay to go to the Ball. He had organised this group to enter the Ball without paying for their tickets and they were about to enjoy the music, the food and the champagne for free. He knew it would spoil his own evening if he dwelt on it too much, but he had known that these feelings would surface at some point.

Everyone had passed through now, except for himself and Louise. He glanced round the door for the last time and guiding Louise out into the courtyard, he quickly closed the door and locked it. He put his arm around her and gave her a soft but passionate kiss, then pocketed the key and together they strode off anonymously into the crowd.

Twenty minutes later the group met up as arranged in the Champagne Bar, which was set up in a marquee in one of the many courtyards. There was a great deal of kissing and hugging, and some hefty back-slapping and congratulations for Mike who was the hero of the moment. His plan had succeeded without a hitch and when Tony appeared with a bottle of Moet and Chandon and a tray of glasses, setting them down and opening the bottle, popping the cork like a professional and raising his class to Mike, he felt that it had all been worthwhile. 'Here's to Mike everyone,' said Tony delightedly.

'To Mike,' they all chorused as one and drank the first of the free champagne that they would consume all through the night.

'Well, let's go and boogie,' cried Mike as the sounds of Kenny Ball and his Jazzmen playing *Midnight in Moscow*, a favourite with him, floated through the side of the marquee. He loved jazz music, especially for dancing.

'That's what we've come for, isn't it?' asked Chris who was particularly pleased with Mike for having got the party into the Ball, for when he had first mentioned it, Mike hadn't seemed too keen on the idea.

Mike clasped Louise's hand and steered her through the throng of revellers in search of Kenny Ball. Outside the Champagne Bar she pulled on his arm and stopped him. He turned to her to see what she wanted, 'Mike are you OK?' she asked anxiously.

'I'm great Louise, what's the problem?'

'It's just that I know you quite well, having worked with you for nearly three years, and I somehow noticed your mood changed when we'd actually got into the Ball, and I wondered why. Is it an anticlimax for you?'

He was pleasantly surprised by her insight into his mood. 'Surely, he hadn't appeared that morose?' he asked himself. 'It's only my conscience,' he explained to Louise. 'It's silly really, crashing balls is a tradition that's been going on for years, but I just felt a little guilty about gatecrashing like this and guzzling all the champagne and food without contributing anything, especially ten of us, that's a lot of fizzy we're actually stealing if one is blunt about it. But I s'pose the college pay for it in the end, I just feel sorry for the students who've had to save up like mad,' explained Mike.

'Most of the undergrads at Magdalene come from rich families anyway, so I wouldn't worry about it,' smiled Louise, giving him a kiss on his cheek.

'That's true,' said Mike, relieved at having got the uneasy feeling out of his system. 'I'm just being a little silly. One day we'll be too old to dance and enjoy ourselves, let alone climb twelve foot high walls to crash Cambridge May Balls! C'mon Louise, let's dance the night away!'

Chapter Twenty-Nine

Occasionally on Sunday mornings, especially in the summer months, the boys would decide to have a leisurely drive out to the Tickell Arms, a most unusual pub with striking Gothic-style windows located in the village of Whittlesford, about five miles from Cambridge. The pub was owned by a well-known homosexual, a graduate of Trinity College, well known for his flamboyant dress sense and his taste in classical and operatic music. Kim de la Taste Tickell was usually dressed in plus fours and gaiters, often sporting a monocle. The music would be played at full volume whilst he hurried about his business, constantly berating the customers for their dress sense, manners or sexual persuasions. The pub was often overrun with college undergraduates, particularly from Trinity, many of whom were homosexuals themselves. With their uproarious conversation and Wagner at full volume, sometimes even ordinary conversation became difficult, but the outlandish atmosphere made up for it.

The boys preferred to eat in the delightful garden, at least when the weather allowed, where there was a patio overlooking a large overgrown pond stuffed with carp, complemented by a large cascading fountain which generated a wonderfully cooling effect on hot, humid summer days.

On these special Sundays, they usually drove over to the pub each in his own car, together with their current girlfriend or maybe a pick-up from the night before. They would line their assorted vehicles up in the car park outside the pub; Raz with his reliable old MG sports car, Tony with his sleek racing green Austin Healey, with its ever-growing number of dents and scratches, Mike in his trusty old black Ford Consul and Chris in his shiny black hearse. Sometimes Mark or Johnny would join them, with Johnny driving his pride and joy, a light blue Triumph TR2 and Mark in his self-built Caterham 7, which was very fast and powerful. The boys called it 'the bumscraper' as the car was so low the seat bottom appeared to be almost touching the ground. They all liked to give their cars what they called a Sunday airing and, although their vehicles were such an assorted collection, there was never any bitching or boasting about who had the best, or the fastest vehicle, they just enjoyed driving their colourful mismatch of machinery out into the country on idyllic days at weekends.

The various girls they invited along were always impressed by the pub, with its unusual music and the old gargoyles and busts that were strewn around the oddly decorated interior. The boys enjoyed the feisty atmosphere and the chance of a leisurely get-together and to eat, drink and flirt with each others' girls. It was a day to discuss and debate the events and news in the headlines of the assorted newspapers they took along with them, from *The News of the World* to *The Sunday Times*.

On occasions, Squire Tickell as he was known, would venture out into the garden to quieten the group down, haranguing them mercilessly whilst he threw food to the assorted carp in the pond. He would play up to the girls, often making the most bizarre or brazen sexual comments to them, which caused great hilarity amongst the boys, but which greatly intrigued the girls who were not always sure of how to take his mischievous sexual innuendoes.

The papers would be devoured for every lurid detail, which they would then read out aloud in odd accents to each other, which often convulsed them all in fits of uncontrollable laughter. Raz would read out some items in a very loud, pompous Anglo-Indian accent, alternating it with a very comical Indian accent, while Chris would butt in using a Cockney accent, or sometimes a Scottish or Norfolk dialect, which always caused much amusement amongst the group.

The casual girlfriends would often be astounded as the boys conversation became more heated and animated. They could not always comprehend how such good friends could shout and castigate and even jeer at each other with such venom and anger. But the four boys had become that way, they each had their own opinions, whether it was race, religion, politics, women, whatever, and they were damned if anyone, particularly their flatmates, were going to get one over on them without at least listening to their own opinion about particular matters. It wasn't really forcing the others to change their opinion, sometimes they were too dogmatic to consider that, but it was the debate, the variety of opinions and the knowledge one of them would sometimes show on a particular issue, that forced them all to listen and, sometimes, even to change their way of thinking.

The astonishing factor was that at the end of these very rambling, drunken sessions, they would toast each other vigorously, happily content that they ought to be responsible for righting all the wrongs in the world and that by rights they should be in a position so that they could. At the end of one of these alcohol enthused Sundays they each thought that they should be the one to rule the country, if not the world! Unfortunately the debate would then often deteriorate into a lascivious session of dirty jokes until at the end of the afternoon when the squire kicked them out so that he could have some peace and quiet. On one afternoon, Tony had craftily scooped a small goldfish from the pond and dropped it wriggling down his date's cleavage. She had jumped up so quickly in her astonishment that she had knocked Tony off balance as he stood guffawing loudly at his prank. He had fallen heavily backwards into the pond and lay struggling amongst the overgrown waterlilies and assorted carp. The boys and their girlfriends had erupted in inebriated laughter, as indeed, had all the other parties seated around the garden. As Tony had emerged from the pond, covered in mud and algae, he had been greeted by a round of enthusiastic applause from the bystanders, but had been asked to leave the premises immediately by the irate Squire Tickell.

Closing time would find them piling out into their cars with their respective partners, competing to be first out of the car park, everyone trying to keep clear of Tony who seemed to have no worries about increasing the number of dents in his sports car. Once out of the car park, there were about three possible routes home. The slowest route often had hold-ups or roadworks, another had a level crossing and the longest had more traffic lights, so they tended to split up when they reached Shelford, the next village. With a great hooting of their horns shattering the quiet of the peaceful village afternoon, they would each veer off on their own preferred route home. There was no prize for being the first car back to the flat, it was just the satisfaction of reaching Mawson Road ahead of the pack, after such a fun filled afternoon.

'It's like the fucking Brighton Run in miniature,' Mark had said to Raz after the first Sunday that they had decided to race home.

'It's certainly not Le Mans, but it's bloody good fun,' replied Raz.

And that was why they did it, because it was fun. They were drunk, they were irresponsible, but hell, this was their time, their youth, their decision to possibly endanger their lives by competing together. It was just a game, nothing too serious, it was a confirmation of their friendship and camaraderie. It was like a competition, but the game was not to beat anyone as in a normal race, it was the taking part with your friends, the togetherness that made it fun. Their time together always seemed like a party, a continuous party and they all hoped in these heady days that it would never end.

Chapter Thirty

Raz had been trying for some time to assemble all the flatmates together for a Friday night out. They had been having trouble with their itineraries, it was either their different working hours or, in Mike's case, his studies, or one or other of them would be out with a girl, so that it had become increasingly difficult to arrange a time to suit them all. Eventually Raz decided on a date two weeks ahead and they were all pledged to keep it free.

They chose to go to the Eagle that evening and they were all in excellent form, delighted to be out together on a Friday again. It was a warm, sultry night towards the end of August, so they sat at a table in the cobbled courtyard of the inn, debating and haranguing each other, whilst consuming the local Greene King beers at an alarming pace. The courtyard was pleasantly full of its usual mix of students, academics, tourists and foreign language students, together with a staunch crowd of locals who lived in Cambridge.

Tony had started to make himself known to a group of a dozen-or-so American girls sitting nearby, whom he soon learned were studying at the Summer School in the city. Most of the boys had a love-hate relationship with American girls. They loved their vitality and friendliness, they seemed to have an energy and fun for life that seemed to be lacking in many English girls, but they lacked the composure and the finesse of the foreign girls. The lacquered 'big' hair and seeming obsession with their nails and make-up, the gaudy clothes that could only be American, all helped to mark them out from the other foreigners who visited the city. 'You can tell an American from a hundred yards, or my name's not Mark Twain,' announced Chris one day surveying a party of American tourists trooping down King's Parade. It was true, all the boys agreed with him, the Yanks stood out like a sore thumb.

Tony had soon discovered that one of the girls was of Italian extraction but, by then, the other three friends had introduced themselves and were busy chatting up various girls in the group, trying to size up whom they fancied the most. Inevitably, in the groups relentless hunt for women, there would be occasions when two of them would both fancy the same girl. They had decided some time ago, in the vote instigated by Chris, that they would never argue over women, but that everyone was free to try and impress the girl in whatever manner they could. Whoever got the girl in the end, that was the end of it, no sour grapes were allowed. No fighting, no protesting, no bad mouthing, no grievances. It was assumed that the girl would make her choice of the best man, so any competition was then over and done with. As Tony had put it to them, 'there are thousands of gorgeous females out there, and if you miss out on one, there's always another one that will turn up somewhere else.'

Sometimes, maybe at a party or in a pub, they had come across a real stunner, a girl that made them all gasp because she stood out from the crowd and then it had been like bees around a honeypot, each of them trying his best to impress her and gain her undivided attention. Situations like that could be farcical, but they were all very aware of being part of the swinging sixties, they were young and randy and after women, and life was to be enjoyed. They were always ready to accept the fact that the girl might not choose them and, if she chose one of your mates, then it was 'Tough Shit', one of Chris's favourite sayings whenever things did not run smoothly, or according to plan.

Finding this group of American girls fairly agreeable, they soon sorted out two tables, pulling them together on the cobbles and arranging themselves in amongst the girls, introducing themselves with a certain amount of play acting and fooling about, which caused plenty of amusement amongst the girls. The two groups soon established a rapport and there was a great deal of convivial shouting across the table at one another. One of the girls sitting diagonally across from Tony decided to remove her small bolero-style jacket and his eyes almost jumped out of their sockets as he set eyes on her tight beige sweater, showing off a perfect pair of pointed breasts. He could hardly take his eyes away as he listened to the girl by his side telling him about her life back home.

Further down the table, the pair of magnificent breasts had not escaped Chris's attention and he had to close his eyes for a second or two before opening them again to confirm that he wasn't imaging things. 'Look at the tits on that blonde,' he exclaimed in a fierce-stage whisper across the table to Mike, nodding his head in the blonde's direction. He could feel absolute lust flooding through his body as he furtively glanced at her every few seconds.

Mike was also suitably impressed by the blonde's dimensions. He turned back to Chris and surreptitiously whispered over the table, his right hand cupping his mouth so no-one else would hear, 'Phwoar!' he exclaimed sharply, his eyes gleaming behind his spectacles, 'you could keep yourself pretty warm between those on a cold winter's night.'

Chris had become quite agitated by this time, he knew that Tony had seen the girl and would move in if he didn't. He desperately wanted to move over to the end of the table to try and ingratiate himself with the girl who owned the fabulous breasts. Unfortunately, he found himself unable to extricate himself from the attentions of the girl beside him who was bombarding him with a succession of boring questions about life in Cambridge. 'Where were the best places to visit? Where were the best bars? Where was the night life?' She was certainly much less attractive than most of the other girls in the group and instead of the 'big hair' that most of the Americans sported, she had her hair plaited in two long tails, complete with a flowered headband round her forehead in a hippy style. Chris could tell that she was intelligent, she told him that she lived in California and had come over from Berkeley University to study English history at Cambridge for the summer. She was somehow involved in the Flower Power movement and followed a beat poet, the LSD-fuelled American Timothy Leary, and told Chris that she was concerned that Cambridge might not be large enough to stimulate her. But what really annoyed Chris about her, besides wanting to get away from her boring conversation, was that she sat next to him constantly chewing gum and blowing silly little bubbles. It was a habit that he utterly detested. The relentless moronic chomping of her jaws and the sudden pop as the gum exploded when she blew a bubble almost drove him to distraction. It was a habit that would antagonise him for the whole of his life but, in this instance, as the girl droned on it became almost too much to bear. Only once, as a kid when he was about seven years old, had he ever chewed bubble gum. He had, egged on by some other children in the school playground, blown a bubble so big and so pink that when it had eventually exploded, it had enveloped his whole head, clinging savagely to his eyelids and encroaching its sticky residue into his hair and eyebrows. It had taken his parent hours to remove and he had possessed a revulsion for gum ever since. He had concluded over the years that, apart from kids and teenagers, the art of chewing gum seemed to be confined to the lower and less educated classes of society. It was certainly not a sophisticated activity. 'Maybe that's why Americans like it so much,' he mused. As the girl beside him chomped her jaws and rolled the gum around the inside of her mouth as she talked, he felt he was about to explode. He could stand it no longer and excused himself to the girl, telling her that he had to use the toilet, but not without a covetous glance at the blonde at the end of the table, who unfortunately still appeared to be in a deep conversation with the girl beside her. He extricated himself from the crowded table and strode across to the Gents, glad to be away from the barrage of annoying questions.

When he emerged, he was completely taken aback to find Raz standing calmly outside talking with the coveted blonde. She looked even more desirable close up, she had strong blue eyes and nice legs, as well as the breasts that pointed at him from beneath her sweater. 'Ah Chris,' said Raz, taking hold of Chris's arm, trying to hide the impish grin that was trying to form itself upon his face. 'This is Natalie, I thought you might like to meet her, she's from Santa Monica in California.'

Chris, still stunned at finding her standing there with Raz, weakly proffered his hand, trying to avert his eyes from her sweater. 'Hello Natalie, I must say that I noticed you sitting at the end of the table. I was hoping to get around to talking to you,' he said, feeling slightly weak at the knees. 'I just had an interesting conversation with one of your friends, the one with the headband,' he lied.

'Oh, that's Mary. She's a little different, isn't she?' said Natalie, her eyes twinkling a little. 'Your friend Raz kindly rescued me from talking about studies with one of my friends.'

Chris was completely flummoxed as to how Raz had singled Natalie out and was bursting to ask him.

'I must go back to the table and carry on my chat with some of your friends, Natalie. I'll leave you in Chris's capable hands,' said Raz.

'I certainly hope so,' thought Chris to himself, allowing himself another quick glance at Natalie's sweater.

Raz allowed himself a sly wink at Chris. 'How had he known that I fancied Natalie,' Chris asked himself, surely I hadn't made it that obvious.

Chris took Natalie inside to the bar and ordered a couple of beers, sitting on stools at the end of the bar so they could talk in peace away from the main crowd. That was one great thing about American girls, they did love their beer, especially cold lager which was similar to their own light beer back in the USA.

They were soon deep in conversation. Natalie told Chris she was studying at Berkeley University and all about her home in Santa Monica and how her father was British and had emigrated to the States in the 'thirties before the Second World War and then had married an American girl. She herself had ambitions to become a doctor when she graduated from Berkeley.

Chris told her about his life in Cambridge and how much he had enjoyed the USA during his visit. 'It seemed incredible that they might even have been close to each other at some time when he visited Los Angeles,' he told her. They both laughed at that amusing fact and Chris realised that he was making an impression, but what he really wanted was an impression of her body in his bed.

Natalie was talking enthusiastically about her parents and how her father had warned her to be careful on her travels. Something stirred in the inner recesses of Chris's mind, it was something his own father had said to him when he had reached twenty-one. He had taken Chris aside after lunch one Sunday, into the barely used sitting room whilst his mother had gone to the kitchen to do the washing up. 'Son,' he had said, his back to the fireplace and his hands placed in the pockets of his jacket, 'I just wanted to have a quiet word with you.' Life is very short, but at your age, when you've got everything going for you, you think you're invincible, that you're immortal, that it will all last for ever. I thought that too at your age, but let me give you a word of advice, I know that you don't take a lot of advice from your old Dad, but just this once, heed what I say. Sow your wild oats now son, have fun now, do your own thing and enjoy your life, because suddenly, in a flash,' and he'd snapped his fingers hard, 'you'll be thirty, and then forty, and then fifty, and then you'll be coming up for retirement, and you'll look back and say, "where the hell did it all go?" If I look back, it's as though I was twenty-one yesterday. Do it all now son, don't have any regrets.' His eyes had narrowed and they seemed to become very tired and then they had filled with tears. Chris remembered how he had felt that his father was almost imploring him to follow his advice. 'Dad,' he had replied, 'I'll try and remember what you told me today.' And he had remembered, possibly too well, he smiled, thinking of all the women he had bedded. Christ, his old dad would have had a fit if he'd known what Chris had got up to in his short life.

His attention was jolted back to Natalie, who was explaining how well her father had done in America and how he had built up his own successful finance business.

Chris's thoughts strayed again to the remembrance of his father, 'Wild oats,' he had told Chris, 'sow them when you're young, you won't be able to do so forever.' 'Well, he certainly wanted to follow his father's advice today,' he said to himself, unable to keep his eyes from straying to gaze again at Natalie's marvellous breasts. The breasts shuddered a little as she laughed heartily at the story she was telling him; how her father had told her that British people were very reserved, but looking around the table in the courtyard at his friends yelling and laughing, that did not seem to be quite correct.

'Hmm,' muttered Chris, enjoying Natalie's engaging smile, her teeth were white and even, and she had that big wide mouth that many American girls have. 'We'll have to try and show you that not all the British are as your father remembers them,' he told her eagerly, hoping that she would give him the chance to prove that statement.

He noticed Tony across the courtyard, leaning against the wall with his arm around the Italian girl. They seemed to be gazing deeply into each other's eyes and Tony was talking quietly to her, almost whispering in her ear. 'It looks as though Tony's bullshit is working as usual,' smiled Chris to himself, 'he'll be doing her hair in ten minutes, probably in bed!'

He saw that Raz and Mike were in animated conversation with three of the other girls clustered at one end of the table. Mike's spectacles had slipped to the end of his nose, which gave him a mad professorial demeanour, especially with his thatch of long fair hair hanging down thickly over his forehead as he waved his arms around ecstatically, rather like a crazed conductor in front of his orchestra. Chris could tell that he was well oiled, but he was certainly amusing Raz and the girls with some story or other. How he loved having fun like this with his friends he said to himself, 'it's really great to be alive at times like this.'

He noticed Tony and his girl walk over to talk to some of the other girls at the table, then they both walked around the table and mentioned something to Raz and Mike. Chris and Natalie watched Tony approach them at the bar. 'The girls are getting hungry,' he said to Chris, 'shall we all go off for a curry?'

'Sounds good to me,' replied Chris. 'How about you Natalie? I'm bloody starving.'

'I've never had a curry before, but I'd like to try it,' declared Natalie. 'I'm sure the other girls will like to try one too. We have Mexican food in the States, but not Indian.'

'I thought you had loads of Indians in the States,' said Tony, sniggering a little.

'You prick, they're Red Indians, but what did they eat anyway?' Chris asked Natalie. 'Buffalo, I guess, before they became integrated with the whites.'

'I guess they used to,' replied Natalie. 'There aren't many buffalo left now and most of the Indians are on reservations, but I guess that buffalo and corn would have been their main diet when they were free. Now I guess it's hamburgers the same as the rest of us.'

Chris and Tony smiled at that, then Raz joined them, delightedly informing them that all the girls were happy to go to the Kashmir, which was Raz's favourite Indian restaurant.

Some twenty minutes later the noisy crowd of sixteen descended on the restaurant, where Raz was immediately welcomed as an old friend, which indeed he was, having eaten there once a week since the start of his university career in Cambridge.

The girls listened attentively to Raz as he told them a little about Indian food and explained that not all the dishes were hot. Eventually the boys decided to order a variety of dishes to share between them, which they felt would give the American girls a gentle introduction to Indian food. Chris tried to get one of them to order the Madras and Vindaloo curries, but the others dismissed that, calling out to him that he was an evil bastard. Chris thought that it would be great fun to see the girls being initiated with the hottest curries the restaurant could serve though he knew from experience that initiating girls into eating curry could produce the most disastrous results as the curry could act like a laxative to those stomachs unused to the strong combinations of spices, which could put any hoped for sexual liaisons later completely out of the question, so prudently he knew that the others were right to stop him ordering the hottest curries.

An enormous pile of poppadums soon appeared, together with a variety of pickles and yoghurts, whilst cool pints of lager were regularly carried over to their table from the bar. The party was extremely lively and the American girls seemed to be thoroughly enjoying themselves with the fun-loving lads from Cambridge that they had only just met. The food quickly arrived and they all began tucking into the assortment of curries and byrianies, which were passed around the table so that all the girls could sample them. The Americans were soon full of praise for the new tastes, they all agreed that it was even better than the Mexican food that many of them were used to. The girls were astonished at how much the boys were drinking, since they had been in the restaurant, they had each consumed five pints of lager, on top of all the beer that they had drunk in the pub. But, as Raz explained to some of the girls, beer was probably the best drink to have with a curry, because of its coolness against the spices and heat in some of the sauces.

'Maybe we do drink a little too much,' Raz told the girls

truthfully, 'in fact, everything we do is over the top. There are no half-measures with us at all,' he laughed, as the other three boys agreed with that statement, by chorusing their approval.

At the end of the meal everyone ordered coffee, although several of the American girls ordered the inevitable Coca-Cola. The boys main concern now was to invite their chosen girls back to Mawson Road, otherwise they might have to invite the whole crowd of girls back to the flat, thus reducing the chance of getting together with the girl they each wanted. It was sometimes difficult to prise a girl away from her friends when they were in a group, the boys all knew that from experience.

Tony sat quietly with his girl, whose name was Sophia, his arm casually draped round her shoulder, playing casually with the ends of her long dark hair. He had already kissed her briefly several times and she seemed to be attracted to him. He decided that the time was right to ask her before everyone got up to leave. 'Would you care to come back for a drink at our flat?' he asked her as casually as he could. 'Maybe dance a little, or drink some wine or coffee?'

'Oh, I'm not sure what's happening,' she told him, glancing around the table at the other girls as if for help or inspiration.

'We don't have to worry about the others,' said Tony, snuggling up nearer to her and kissing her lips lightly.

Sophia pushed him away gently and smiled coyly back at him. 'No, but they'll think it's kinda odd if I leave with you,' she replied.

'No, they won't mind. You'd like to come wouldn't you?' asked Tony, feeling upset now that he could see her wavering. It always knocked his ego if he was certain that he had pulled a woman and then she backed off.

'I'll have to ask the other girls to see what they're doing,' she said. Leaning across the table to one of her friends she asked, 'What are we all doin' now?'

'Goin' home, I guess. I'm kinda tired now,' replied her friend.

Tony knew from Sophia that all the girls were staying in the lodging houses in Brookside. He glanced across the table at Chris, who was ensconced with the blonde with the enormous knockers. Chris seemed to be getting on well with her, he had his arm around her and they were engaged in what appeared to be a friendly intimate conversation. Their faces were only a few inches apart. Tony wondered what bullshit Chris was giving her in order to get her body into his bed.

Meanwhile, Raz had ordered the bill. The American girls insisted on paying their share. There was a great deal of excited chattering as everyone started to rise from the table and mill around the entrance to the restaurant waiting for the inevitable stragglers in the toilets.

Tony was really pissed off when Sophia told him that she would be going home with the others, but he did manage to scribble down the 'phone number of the house where they were staying, which was better than nothing, but he really wanted to take her home and try to seduce her that night.

Chris, was still sitting at the table with his arm around Natalie's shoulder, desperately trying to persuade her to go back to the flat with him, a task made more difficult as all the other girls had told her that they were all going home together.

'Look Chris,' said Natalie, 'it's been a really great evening, but I do think I ought to leave with the others. Maybe we might bump into each other again?'

Chris's mouth fell open a little in dismay, was he hearing her correctly? They had swapped intimacies and lots of stories with each other. He was sure that she was attracted to him and he had really thought that she was a dead cert, but now she was dismissing all that by simply informing him that they might bump into each other again. Had all his chatting up and seduction techniques gone down the drain? He looked down at Natalie again with longing for those magnificent, tantalising breasts beneath her beige sweater. He decided to try again to persuade her to go home with him. 'Oh, come on Natalie. The night is young, the others won't mind if you come back for a coffee with me,' he insisted, nuzzling up to her softly. 'Please come.'

'No, I'm sorry Chris, but I really do think that I must go back with the girls,' she told him again, this time rising to her feet and reaching for her handbag on the back of the chair. She leant forward and kissed his cheek. 'It's been great meeting you Chris,' she told him as they walked to the entrance, joining the crowd as everyone left the restaurant together.

The two groups gathered outside, saying their goodbyes and

thanking each other, then the girls turned and walked off en masse in the direction of Brookside.

'Jesus Christ,' cried Chris, who was beside himself with frustration. 'I thought I was in there.' He stamped his feet on the pavement and glanced around at the others for a hint of sympathy.

'Fuck me, I thought I'd got it made too,' added Tony. 'I'm really pissed off. In fact, we're both really pissed off, aren't we Chris?'

'Raz and I asked two of the others back and got the same answer,' said Mike disconsolately, passing some cigarettes around as they slouched slowly down the street towards home.

'Well I'm really sorry for you Chris,' said Raz. 'I though you were going to get that pair of breasts presented to you on a plate.'

'Oh, bugger it,' said Chris, dejected and annoyed. He remembered that Raz had picked Natalie out to introduce her to him in the courtyard. 'That was good of you to sort her out for me anyway Raz, but how did you know?' asked Chris.

'I saw you go for a piss when that hippy girl was obviously boring you to death, but I'd seen you staring down at the table fairly blatantly at her tits, your eyes were out on fucking stalks, so I jumped up when you disappeared to the loo, went across to her and told her that she ought to meet you as you were such a nice guy. We walked across the courtyard and there we were when you emerged from the toilet.'

'And now, after all that chatting up, she's fucked off with the others,' said Chris glumly, 'what a bloody prickteaser.'

'Yeah, but don't forget that you can't have your way with every single female that moves on this earth. You've got to be rejected sometimes. Even Elvis Presley can't get every woman he wants,' laughed Raz as the others spoke up in agreement to that.

'Well, I was certain I was going to get lucky tonight,' said Tony emphatically, knowing that Raz was correct. 'I know that it's impossible to pull every girl that you fancy, but nevertheless, it still bloody well hurts when you think you're onto a winner and then they bugger off like those girls did tonight.'

'At least they weren't really prickteasers, like some. They were just a load of girls out for the night and they went home

247

intact as a crowd of girls,' said Mike.

'Intact!' yelled Tony. 'That's exactly how we didn't want them to go home.'

'Oh God, I don't want to think about it any more,' said Chris. For some unknown reason, an image of his mother had appeared in his mind. What the hell would she say if she knew that he was like this, screwing around with women like he did. Then an image of the lovely Natalie unfolded before him, she was naked, her beautiful breasts swaying gently as she opened her arms enticing him to embrace her. As his imagination ran riot, his thoughts were rudely interrupted by some horseplay amongst the others. As they reached the flat and he gloomily followed the others upstairs, at least he had his friends, he thought. He knew they would never let him down. 'Women,' he muttered to himself. 'Nothing but a bloody nuisance,' knowing as he said it that tomorrow he would be out searching eagerly for the next female that happened to take his fancy.

Chapter Thirty-One

After nearly five years together, the inevitable happened, but it took some time for it to become apparent to everyone at Mawson Road. Tony, to the complete astonishment of the other flatmates, had been seeing a very attractive local girl called Christine for some three months. What made this liaison so amazing was that he had barely looked at another girl during this period. Even on the odd occasion when he had seen fit to go out with any of the boys and they had met some girls who had been absolute certainties, Tony had invented some lame excuse about feeling tired and needing to get up early for work. Discussing it amongst themselves one evening, Raz, Chris and Mike were in complete agreement that Tony was beginning to feel a great deal more for this girl than any of them had foreseen. It made them feel uncomfortable because this was the first time that someone had come between the four of them and they had begun to experience an uneasy mixture of jealousy and annoyance, together with an odd feeling of being let down; Mike even suggested to the others that the relationship was almost a betrayal to all they stood for.

Mike managed to persuade Tony to meet up with him one evening after work, fully intending to have a chat with him about his relationship. They ate a pleasant steak meal at the Berni Inn in Trinity Street, after which they sat in the bar enjoying a drink and discussing the merits of the latest James Bond movie which they had both seen recently. Mike had been receiving some serious eye contact from two blonde girls sitting at a table across the room but Tony, as was usual just lately, had not been drawn into the eyeing up game. When one of the girls approached the bar to order another drink, Mike had jumped up and asked her if they would both like to join Tony and himself for a drink. After a brief moment's discussion they decided to do so and joined the two boys at their table.

It emerged that both girls worked in the perfumery department at Robert Sayle's, a large department store in the city centre. Their names were Jane and Mary and they were both beauticians; it showed, they were elaborately made-up and both gave off strong wafts of Chanel. They were both wearing identical tight tops with mini skirts and knee length leather boots. 'Are you sisters?' enquired Mike attempting to break the ice, to which they both rocked backwards in their chairs, laughing out loudly at his question.

'People often ask that if we're together just because we're both blonde. Sometimes we tell people that we are sisters, just for a laugh. A guy the other day thought we were lesbians,' Mary replied, giggling to her friend.

As they chatted and teased the two girls, Mike soon discovered that Mary, the one who had initially been giving him the avid eye contact across the room, was a really horny little thing, consistently interspersing the conversation with some extremely rude and exciting suggestions about what she could do for him later on. Mike happily noticed that Tony seemed to be engrossed with Jane, so when the last orders were called at 11 o'clock, Mike immediately asked both girls if they would like a coffee back at the flat, hoping that Jane was as eager to pair off with Tony as Mary obviously was with him.

'As long as it's not just to see your etchings,' replied Jane seductively, casting her eyes sideways at Tony, her hand on his knee.

'Brilliant,' thought Mike, 'Tony's in as well,' but then he noticed a slightly pained expression cross Tony's face. 'Surely he's not going to give this one the cold shoulder?' Mike wondered apprehensively.

'Yes, you're both welcome to come back for a coffee,' said Tony to the girls, but then, averting his gaze from Mike, he spoke quietly to Jane. 'Unfortunately I've got a long day in the salon tomorrow, so I'll have a quick coffee and then hit the sack if you don't mind, but I'm sure Mike will look after you both very well.'

Jane's expression changed, she appeared completely crestfallen at Tony's obvious dismissal of her and Mike could only stare at Tony in disbelief. 'What was the fucking matter with the prick?' he asked himself. He glanced over at Jane again, she was a really gorgeous bird with a fabulous body and Tony was casting her aside, completely rejecting her despite the fact that she had just made it blatantly obvious that she wanted him.

Later, on reflection, Mike realised that it was at that moment that he knew that something dramatic had happened to Tony. He realised that Tony had actually fallen in love; that was what all this was about. Tony did not want to two-time Christine, so he was now rejecting the need for all other women in his life where previously he would have taken them eagerly and voraciously devoured them. Mike felt a slight feeling of panic envelop him; it was a sense of loss somehow, as though a piece of himself was being prized away from his own body and that he was powerless to do anything about it. Almost five years had passed since he had first met Tony, and shortly afterwards he had moved into their beloved Mawson Road flat. Since then the four of them had enjoyed a really great time together, during which they had shared fun and laughter, wine and women, good times and bad. Those years of debauchery had created a bond, cemented together by the four of them living and sharing everything together, each from different backgrounds, of different race and religion, even their jobs and aspirations for the future were all completely different. 'But that was the problem wasn't it,' he told himself, 'their objectives, their desires, their needs.' Eventually as they all changed and matured, which they all inevitably had to do, their lives had to alter. They had been completely enmeshed in the ongoing party that had been running for several years and suddenly it was about to run out of steam. Maybe they had never bothered to sit down and think about their futures, to make the decision that there had to be more to life than boozing and shagging and a continual round of parties. Mike remembered the headline that he'd glimpsed in the *Daily Express* just the other day, 'This is the advent of the can't be bothered culture.' And it was true, they hadn't been bothered. But why had none of them realised that eventually certain circumstances would pervade their lives and lead inevitably to change? Tony had fallen in love and, although it was a shock to realise that, it could have been any one of them, even himself. It was not an offence for God's sake, that was what happened in people's lives. How could they all have missed the point that they could not continue with the shallowness of their lives for ever more. Mike realised that they were on the brink of something that was going to change their lives forever and Tony, by rejecting this girl that he would joyfully and enthusiastically have bedded just a couple of months ago, had unknowingly started that change.

It was even more strange thought Mike, because Tony and Chris had often played jokes on each other about being in love. Sometimes if they happened to notice an attractive girl in the street, or across a crowded bar, one of them would clap his hands to his heart, crying out to the others, 'Oh no, I've just fallen in love!' It was harmless fun at their own expense, but there was an underlying factor to all that. He could see it clearly now: love was never going to happen to them, love was for wimps. But, of course, there was always going to be the one girl that stood out from the crowd, the one who would make each one of them eat their words. His thoughts were interrupted; Mary and Jane had gathered in a huddle, talking softly together, whilst Tony had gone off to the toilet. As he returned Jane glanced contemptuously at him, then turned to her friend, 'I'll see you Mary. It was nice to meet you two fellas,' she said curtly as she turned quickly on her heel and flounced off through the doorway.

There was an awkward movement as Mike and Tony looked uncertainly at each other, then Mike took Mary's hand and playfully punched Tony's arm. He wanted to tell Tony that everything was all right, that he had suddenly realised how he felt, but he couldn't explain it to him now in this bar with all these people around. He would talk to Tony later when they were alone.

When they arrived back at the flat, Mary went off to the bathroom while Mike opened a bottle of cold wine from the fridge and cleaned a couple of glasses. Tony took the opportunity to confide in Mike. 'Look Mike, I'm really sorry about Jane, but I really do care a great deal for Christine. If she found out I'd been with someone else, I'd be in deep shit.'

'It's OK Tony,' replied Mike quietly. 'I've only just understood that you care that much about her. I'd never realised before that it was so serious, but I guess if you can turn down a cracker like Jane, then it's obviously a big deal for you.'

'To be absolutely honest with you Mike, and I haven't told anyone else, not even Christine, but I think I've fallen in love with her, really! I can't look at other girls at all now. I'm just not interested in fucking about any more.'

'I only guessed tonight that you might have fallen in love Tony,' said Mike quietly, putting his arm around Tony's shoulder, 'and I really hope it works out for you. Christine's a nice girl,' he smiled, his blue eyes feeling slightly misty behind his spectacles. For some unknown reason he felt very sad. He could not understand why, for he was genuinely happy for Tony.

They heard Mary's footsteps coming down the hall. As she entered the kitchen Tony stopped her and with his hands resting on her shoulders, he bent down and kissed her gently on the cheek. 'Good night Mary, it was good to meet you. Would you apologise to Jane for me? She's a gorgeous lady and I would have loved her to come back with me, but I'm afraid that I've just realised that I'm in love with someone.' He turned and nodded to Mike. 'Good night, Mike, and thanks.' He walked out of the kitchen and along the hallway to his bedroom. He wondered if Raz was in but couldn't see a light showing under the door, nor could he hear any music emanating from his room. 'Pity really,' he thought, 'I could have had a chat with him and told him about Christine too, but they'll all be talking about it tomorrow anyway.' He lay in bed trying to allay the guilt that he felt because he knew that the partnership that the four of them had forged together was about to be severed. He felt that he was letting his friends down, not because of his love for Christine, but because he now understood what Mike already realised, that their group would never be the same now that he had met Christine and fallen in love. It was like a body losing a leg or a finger. It would carry on, but things would always be different to how they were before. He was that severed leg, the first part to be lost. Even if they replaced him, the group would never function quite as well as it had before. They had been the modern-day equivalent of the Four Musketeers - 'All for one and one for all!' He smiled to himself at the comparison. The rallying cry had often been yelled out by Chris when they were all together getting pissed in some pub, or at a party together.

His thoughts turned to Christine, she was so different from the other girls, they were ten a penny; but she was special, not just a quick, easy lay. He wanted to be with her, he loved doing things with her. He was proud to introduce her to his friends. In fact he missed her now, even thinking about her made him horny, but there was another ache, emanating from his heart and his brain which told him how much he missed her. He wanted her beside him as his partner and his friend as well as his lover. He'd thought the matter over very seriously for several weeks and had decided that he was going to ask Christine to marry him. He had confided his love for her to Mike, but he wanted more. Only he knew how intense his love was and he was certain that she felt the same way. He could feel it coursing through her body when he touched her. When they made love, they became almost as one and the things she said and the way that she said them were so gentle and kind, she was always so considerate and he loved her for it.

He felt tired and began drifting off as hazy visions of Christine floated through his mind, when suddenly Jane's face appeared, etched with the shock of rejection when he had told her he was going to bed early. Then he imagined Mike and Mary shagging away down the hallway, and the image of them at it entered his mind briefly. Christine's naked body floated before him again as his eyes grew heavy and sleep took him over, a soft contented sleep made easier now that he had happily entered the first stage of a new chapter in his life.

Chapter Thirty-Two

The next morning, as usual, Tony was the first to leave for work. He had to open the salon at 8 o'clock. At breakfast later, Mike had disclosed to Raz and Chris that Tony had admitted to being in love and told them both about the previous evening's episode with the two girls whilst Mary was using the bathroom and out of earshot. Raz and Chris had glimpsed her briefly as she rushed self-consciously down the hallway clad in Mike's old dressing gown, her dishevelled blonde hair and long legs had attracted very approving looks from them both.

'This girl Jane really came on to Tony. She was an absolute cracker. He just basically told her that he was going to bed alone,' said Mike. 'That's really when I realised what had happened to Tony.'

'Normally, the Tony we know and love would certainly have had trouble keeping his hands off a bird like that, especially if she was a blonde,' joked Raz, lavishly spreading a thick layer of marmalade on his toast.

'Christ, I wish I'd been there with you. I'd have had this Jane, I'm sure,' exclaimed Chris feeling exasperated that he had missed out, especially as he had spent the evening with Johnny, flat on his back in a cold garage endeavouring to help sort out a problem with the transmission system on Johnny's Triumph TR2 sports car.

'How was this one, or need we ask?' asked Raz cheekily, showing an almost indecent interest in Mike's girl, jerking his thumb in the direction of the bathroom.

'She's bloody hot stuff,' said Mike leaning towards them both and lowering his voice to a whisper. 'I first noticed these two girls trying to catch my eye in the Turks Head, or maybe they were trying to get Tony's attention at first. Anyway, we pulled them both and established a great rapport with them, but when we got up to leave the bar, I obviously asked them both to come back to the flat. Then Tony told this girl Jane that he had to get up early and that he'd just have a coffee with her if they both wanted to come back here, but making it clear that was all. So she buggered off, obviously not very happy because she fancied him and he's turned her down. When Mary and I got back here, it was a straight into bed job. As soon as I had shut the door to my room she was tearing off my clothes, like a mad woman.'

'So you got to tearing off her clothes too?' asked Raz, his deep laugh booming around the kitchen.

'The trouble with these highly-sexed girls is that it's all very well if they come on to you, but personally I like to take my time and build up to it, rather than plunging in so quickly. Just because they're on the pill, some of these girls seem to think they can take you over,' said Mike thoughtfully pouring himself another strong mug of tea.

'That's why you're an accountant Mike,' quipped Chris playfully, leaning over and ruffling Mike's hair. 'You like to take plenty of time to work on your figures.'

They all laughed uproariously at the in-joke. Mike was used to them all taking the piss out of his job. He guessed that most accountants had to put up with it.

'One question I've always wanted to ask you Mike, is about your spectacles. Do you leave them on when you're shagging and get them misting up on the job, or do you take them off so you can't see a bloody thing?' asked Raz, tittering away to himself. Chris laughed too, because he had often wanted to ask Mike the same question.

Mike had to smile along with the other two, but he gamely took the question in his stride. 'Well, myopia means short-sighted, which is what I am. It means that I can see things close up without my glasses, so I usually start off with them on but, like clothes, they get pulled off and thrown elsewhere. It's bloody funny kissing someone else who wears glasses though, you end up clinking together all the time! But seriously though,' said Mike wanting to continue their earlier conversation, 'let's get back to Tony. There's no doubt that he is a completely changed man and I think he and Christine are now an "item".

We'll just have to see how things progress from now on.'

The bathroom door opened and Mary walked into the kitchen now fully dressed, her hair sleek and golden after her shower. Chris and Raz both stood up together in mutual admiration as Mike introduced them both to her.

'You lucky bastard,' muttered Chris to Mike behind Mary's back as he and Raz left for work.

Mike smiled back happily, placing some bread in the toaster and heating the kettle on the stove to make Mary breakfast.

It was not long after this that Tony and Christine announced their engagement to the other three flatmates on a Friday evening at one of their regular haunts, the Six Bells in Covent Garden. Christine proudly showed her ring off to them, as they expressed admiration and proffered endless toasts of congratulation. Tony could hardly have been more ecstatic and everyone enjoyed revelling in the newly-engaged couple's obvious happiness. Tony revealed that the wedding was already being planned and they were expecting to marry within weeks. This announcement during the evening immediately led to some speculation amongst the others as to whether Christine might be pregnant, but when questioned by Mike, Tony was adamant that she was not. He assured Mike that they simply wanted to be together and the sooner the better, they were just madly in love.

Later that evening, nursing a mild hangover, Mike lay in bed smoking, deep in thought. He blew smoke rings expertly and watched them float slowly upwards towards the ceiling, billowing out and disappearing in long streams of smoke that swirled across the ceiling. He was worried, not just about Tony leaving the flat as soon as he was married, but because certain dramas were unfolding at his office. Since he had completed most of his examinations, there had been hints that several staff might be asked to relocate to a new London office. He was aware that these plans could include him. He had not mentioned it to the others as nothing certain had yet been concluded; it was really only office gossip at present, but he had begun to feel somewhat unsettled. He had never really given any thought to moving from Cambridge since his chance meeting with Chris. With the chaos and madness of the last few years, together with his hard work studying for the endless examinations, it had never occurred to him, but now it seemed that there might be a possibility of his having to relocate and leave the flat and his friends and even his comfortable office. 'We're like a family. In fact, we are a family! What am I going to do without these guys around?' he asked himself. He carefully stubbed his cigarette out, took his glasses off, placed them next to his clock on the bedside table and switched off the light. He turned onto his side, falling asleep minutes later. His sleep was punctuated throughout the night by unsettling dreams, where he found himself alone, searching through a desolate wilderness for the friends that he had so cruelly deserted by leaving them back in Cambridge.

Chapter Thirty-Three

A few days later, Tony had invited Chris into his room early in the evening. Christine was sitting quietly on the bed, looking happy and relaxed whilst she idly flipped through the pages of a magazine. 'Would you like a glass of sherry, Chris?' asked Tony.

'Well I never say no to any offer of alcohol as you should know,' smiled Chris, sitting next to Christine and wondering what Tony had to say.

Tony uncorked a half-full bottle of Bristol Dry Sherry and handed Christine a small glassful. He then poured a large schooner for Chris and another for himself and settled himself onto the Corbusier leather chaise longue that he had recently bought himself. The smell of fresh flowers, the multi-coloured freesias that he had chosen this week, pervaded the room. Tony had once memorably explained to the others that 'a room without flowers was a room without a soul.' He seemed very calm as he fixed his gaze on Chris, smiling and raising his glass.

'Cheers,' the three of them said almost simultaneously. Chris turned to Christine and they clinked glasses before sipping their sherry. Chris was still very conscious of the couple's recent engagement, so he raised his glass again towards Tony, then he turned his gaze to Christine, 'I'd like to wish you both all the very best for the future,' he told them seriously. 'We're going to miss you Tony, old buddy,' he said, then turning back to Christine he added, 'But I think you've made a very good choice, with our Tony here.'

Christine blushed slightly, averting her eyes for a second. Chris could see that her blue eyes were shining as they widened appreciatively and she broke into a shy wide-mouthed smile. 'Thanks Chris, that's really sweet of you,' she replied quietly.

They sipped their sherries again, enjoying the moment of

togetherness, the lovers and their friend. 'Chris,' said Tony, interrupting the silence, 'Christine and I have talked it over and we would both be delighted if you would care to be my best man.'

Chris was slightly taken aback. He had not expected anything like this. 'Does that mean I get to snog the bride,' he asked brazenly, recovering his composure and winking at Christine.

'Just a small one on the day,' replied Tony. 'But that's all you get to do I'm afraid,' he added as an afterthought, trying to keep a straight face.

Christine held her hand over her mouth trying not to laugh out loud. She had very quickly realised during her early involvement with Tony what his flatmates were like, but she had never quite become used to the incessant leg-pulling that was de rigeur amongst Tony and his friends.

'I would be delighted to do that for you Tony,' said Chris demurely. 'How much did you say I get paid?'

It was later that evening when Raz was working happily in the kitchen, dissecting chicken and crushing garlic, preparing a curry for himself and Chris, that Raz came up with a suggestion. Full of his usual joi de vivre, he drained his glass of wine and refilled both their glasses. 'Chris, why don't you offer Tony and Christine the use of the hearse as their wedding car. I think that gesture would be much appreciated, especially as you're the best man anyway,' he said, grinding some spices enthusiastically with his pestle and mortar. 'Tony was telling me the other day that Christine's parents are not terribly well off, so that would save them the cost of hiring a car, plus the fact that it is a Rolls Royce after all,' he continued.

'I wouldn't mind at all Raz, that's a good idea. But I don't know how keen Christine would be, to be taken to the church on her big day in my bloody hearse,' replied Chris. 'But I'll certainly ask them. They may feel fine about it. Maybe one of you boys could drive them to the church. I'll have too much to do if I'm going to be the best man.'

Later, when the couple returned to the flat, Chris asked them both if they would like to use the hearse for their wedding car. Christine seemed very apprehensive about the idea at first, even though Chris tried his best to assure her that the vehicle could easily be transformed into an appropriate wedding carriage.

'I'm not sure that I'd be happy knowing that it's been used for carrying dead bodies. It's kind of creepy isn't it?' she confided to Tony as they snuggled up in bed that night.

The next day, Raz had tried to make the idea seem more appealing to the couple. 'With a length of white ribbon running from the corners of the windscreen attached to the mascot at the front and with some flowers laid out on the rear shelf, everything will look absolutely pukka. You'll never even think of it as a hearse on the day and think of the saving in money terms.' He had given Christine such a broad grin because it seemed to be such an easy decision in his eyes and, although she had smiled, she said to herself that he wasn't the one getting married; he was just trying to please everyone in his own inimitable fashion.

'I just don't want any bad vibes on my wedding day,' Christine replied. 'You're sure there's no weird spirits or presences that might upset things for us?' she asked, still worried about the hearse factor.

Don't worry about anything Christine,' replied Chris, 'we've all had so much fun with the hearse, going to parties and having such good times with it that there's not a hint of bad spirits or spookiness at all. Don't forget, it is a Rolls Royce. Once we've cleaned and polished it for you, it'll look like the bees knees, believe me.'

Tony squeezed her hand, looking carefully over her face for any traces of doubt that she might still harbour. He smiled gently at her to show her that he was happy, besides he didn't want to appear indifferent to Chris's generosity and Raz's obvious enthusiasm.

'OK,' Christine turned to Chris, having made her mind up and feeling happier now that Tony appeared agreeable to the idea. 'Thanks Chris, I'm sure it will be wonderful!' she cried and pecked him lightly on the cheek, glad that Chris's offer had now been resolved to everyone's satisfaction.

Chapter Thirty-Four

The wedding was scheduled for a Saturday two months away and Tony had informed his flatmates that he would be moving out just before the wedding as he and Christine had found a flat that they liked; they wanted to move in and clean it up and perhaps attend to a little decorating when they could find the time, so that it was ready for them both to move into on their return from their honeymoon.

Mike attempted to talk to Chris and Raz regarding the search for a new flatmate. He sensed already that there was a slight feeling of unease permeating their lives at the flat now that their alliance had been upset. When he confronted the others, Chris suggested that they should wait until after Tony's departure before endeavouring to find someone compatible to take over his room.

Mike deliberated on this suggestion later that evening as he lay restlessly in bed, wondering if Chris was simply sweeping the matter under the carpet as he was prone to do sometimes. Mike himself had still failed to mention to the others that there was a possibility that he also might have to leave because of the changes taking place at work. He felt nervous about mentioning it and, not wanting to create any further distress to the other two, he decided to wait until he knew something absolutely positive and keep the dilemma to himself.

Tony began spending more time away from the flat as he and Christine spent their evenings together making wedding plans with her parents. There was the church service to organise; the priest also wanted to spend time with them discussing their marriage vows. There was the guest list to sort out which they seemed to run through a hundred times with both sets of parents before everyone was satisfied, plus all the other countless tasks that Tony surprisingly found to be not nearly as mundane as he had feared. This confirmed within himself that he had made the correct decision to marry Christine and, whilst having a drink with Chris one evening, he confided in him: 'If I can get along with all these preparations for the wedding, and enjoy myself doing it, then the marriage itself will be a real doddle.'

'I'm sure it will be perfect,' said Chris, secretly unsure as to whether it would be. He still felt amazed at the sudden transformation that had taken place in Tony, from the notorious womaniser to the besotted husband-to-be, but he had certain reservations in the back of his mind as to how long the relationship would last, knowing Tony as he did. But, so far, so good. They would all just have to wait and see, only time would tell whether they had been right or wrong.

Chapter Thirty-Five

On the Friday evening before Tony's wedding, the stag party had assembled at the Live and Let Live. The party comprised of Tony's three flatmates from Mawson Road, Tony's brother, Mario, two of his associates from the salon, John and Frederico, Johnny and Mark, who were the flatmate's best friends, and two other old friends from Tony's adolescence, Mathew and Clive. Introductions were swiftly made between those who did not know each other and the beer was soon flowing in true stag night tradition. As best man, Chris decided that a kitty would be in order, so they each handed three pounds over and Mike, as usual on these occasions, was asked to take charge of the money.

Raz, par for the course at any celebration, was soon deliriously happy, even after just two beers, and before anyone could stop him he had removed the yard-of-ale glass from its mooring above the bar, suggesting to the group that it would be a great idea to consume a yard-of-ale each before they moved on.

'That's if we can move afterwards, let alone move on,' said Mario who was unused to drinking such vast quantities of beer and was already alarmed at the speed at which Tony and his flatmates were drinking. Having just consumed three pints of draught beer each, the lesser mortals amongst them, especially John and Frederico, who both rarely drank, blanched a little at the prospect of the yard-of-ale, but egged on enthusiastically by the others, managed to drink passable amounts, oblivious to the fact that their shirts and trousers had become completely soaked in beer.

Tony, as the groom, had been the first of the crowd to try and he drank his yard slowly and surely, barely spilling a drop, much to the amazement of the others who cheered him on with admiration in their voices. The secret was to drink it slowly, keeping the air bubble in the long glass from forcing the beer along the stem too quickly, which could then disgorge over the drinker's face and clothes. The uninitiated also found that the torrent of beer forced out if the glass was tipped too high could cause a severe bout of choking as the beer disgorged itself up the nose of the unlucky participant.

'Good grief Tony,' cried Chris, suitably impressed, 'this is your last night of bad behaviour with the rest of us and you put that yard of ale away like a champion. I mean, look at the rest of the rabble.' He waved his arm round at the rest of the party who were standing in an untidy group, dishevelled and soaked in beer from their mainly unfortunate attempts to drink the yard of ale successfully.

'Well, I couldn't disgrace myself on my last night as a bachelor with you guys, could I?' said Tony grinning warmly at Chris.

A sudden bout of hiccups, caused by drinking the yard of ale and taking air in with the beer, disrupted Tony from continuing further. Raz immediately handed him a fresh pint but Tony asked for some water. Mathew said that he knew a fool-proof method of getting rid of hiccups. He told Tony to stand on one leg with both arms outstretched, while he drank water slowly from a glass. Mathew held the glass to Tony's mouth, tilting it slowly to his mouth as he drank. Much to the general amusement of everyone in the pub, the hiccups amazingly ceased as Tony finished consuming the pint of water. The crowd cheered and whistled, clapping their hands enthusiastically at Tony's balancing act.

Chris suggested that the merry party move on, to begin a relentless cruise that he had planned around the city's pubs, where at least one pint of beer was supposed to be consumed by each member of the party at every pub they stopped at. Mathew and Clive, who were not used to the astonishing amounts of alcohol being drunk, began lagging behind in the consumption stakes. Sometimes one of the group would come across friends and drunkenly explain that they were on a stag night pub crawl, but there was little time for a chat as they were soon ushered off to the next pub by Chris who began to feel rather like a mother hen looking after her brood of chicks.

At about 10 o'clock they found themselves in the notorious

Criterion, a lively spit and sawdust pub secreted down a dark alley and a home-from-home to many of the reprobates of Cambridge. The landlord kept a baseball bat behind the bar, instantly available if any trouble broke out in the place, which it frequently did. By now the party were extremely the worse for wear, being thoroughly inebriated, but greatly enjoying themselves and still able to converse with each other relatively coherently. As they gathered at the bar chatting and joking, Tony was amazed to see Anita, an ex-girlfriend, walking through the bar. She was a medical rep that he had dated several times earlier in the year before meeting Christine and he had not seen her for some time. He noticed that she was clutching something to her chest, it almost looked like a baby to him. She suddenly spotted Tony surrounded by his friends, leaning against the bar and waving at her. She immediately made her way over to him. As she walked across the room towards him, Tony watched her, mentally unclothing her, hazily remembering her well proportioned body and the fun that they had enjoyed together in his bed.

'Hi Tony. I'm glad I've seen you. I've got something to talk to you about,' Anita said, smiling up at him and giving him a peck on his cheek.

Tony stared glassy-eyed at her, trying to force his alcohol sodden brain to function properly, curious as to why she was in a pub with a small baby at 10 o'clock in the evening. 'She can't be married, can she?' he wondered as he tried to pull himself together to talk to her. He could only see the top of the baby's head, the rest was covered by a wrap. It was probably asleep, he decided, steeling himself to talk coherently to his old flame. 'Can I get you a drink Anita? I'm getting married in the morning,' he told her, trying in vain to prevent himself from slurring his words.

'That's why I'm here Tony. I wanted to talk to you about our baby,' Anita told him.

'Our baby!' Tony exclaimed, his eyes widening with astonishment, his drink befuddled brain trying to digest her words. He leant away from the bar and tried to hold himself up straight.

There was a short stunned silence as the others in the group looked uncomfortably at each other, a couple of them uttering gasps of astonishment.

'Are you OK, Tony,' asked Marco, peering into Tony's glazed unbelieving eyes. 'What's going on?'

'Anita. What are you saying to me? I haven't seen you for ages,' replied Tony, feeling totally flustered. He gripped the bar rail hard, trying to prevent himself from sliding away from the bar. He had the awful feeling that his legs could buckle under him at any moment.

'That's right, Tony. You said you were going to call me the very last time we met. As we'd seen each other several times, I really thought you liked me, but you left me high and dry. When I found out that I was pregnant, I went away and had the baby,' replied Anita.

Tony stood crestfallen, mouth agape, trying to fathom out how this could be happening right now and why she hadn't come to him and told him before. He was supposed to be getting married tomorrow and now he was being told he was a father! What the hell would Christine say? He felt shocked, whilst his brain seemed to become numb, unable to function properly, for the amount of alcohol he had drunk was now badly distorting his thoughts. 'How could life be so cruel,' he asked himself. His stag party had suddenly become a bad dream. He looked around at the others, hoping for some sympathy and consolation, but they were all grinning back at him. Chris was doubled up in hysterics, while Raz stood laughing and grinning like a buffoon. 'What was going on?' Even Anita stood there, smiling at him, nonchalantly swigging a lager that Chris had bought her. 'My God, she'd lain the baby down on a bar stool, it could fall off and hurt itself, couldn't it?' Tony stared at the small bundle in disbelief.

As if in answer to his concern, Anita put her glass down on the bar and, with one quick movement, she pulled off the shawl that was wrapped around the child, to reveal a pink, plastic doll. On it's chest and stomach someone had written in large letters, 'Have a Happy Wedding Day - Tony!'. Anita reached up and cupped Tony's cheeks in her hands and kissed him softly. 'Sorry Tony, but I happened to meet Chris two weeks ago and he told me that you were getting married and asked me to help play this trick on you.' She grinned up at him.

Tony felt completely astonished as he gradually realised that they had all planned this practical joke for his stag night. The feelings of shock and despair that he had felt only a few minutes before began to disappear, to be replaced by a somewhat befuddled euphoria. 'You bastards,' he exclaimed, looking around at their gleaming, smiling faces. 'You really had me worried then,' he slurred, his glassy eyes trying to distinguish everyone. He drained his glass with relief, whilst another round was quickly ordered.

Anita finished her drink, gathered up the doll and gave Tony a quick kiss. Not wishing to intrude further on the stag night, she left with a wave and a goodbye to the others.

There was a lot of back slapping and mock sympathy for Tony. Everyone had really enjoyed Tony's discomfort at being put on the spot like that, it had been a good joke, well planned by Chris without any bad feeling on Tony's behalf. Stag parties often turned sour for the groom with the guests sometimes putting the drunken groom into an uncomfortable position during his last few hours as a bachelor. It was like a penance that had to be paid for the privilege of leaving the male fold and all the boozing, birds and bad language that bachelor life entailed. The transition from carefree to careworn, from nights out to nights in, from boys only to couples only and all the other penalties that came with marriage had to be derided by the single friends left behind, so the send-off also had to remind the male getting married of what he would be missing when the inevitable ball and chain was locked around his ankles.

Tony's head began to swim. He was beginning to become very drunk indeed and was somewhat relieved to hear the bell ring for last orders. He was egged on by the others to drink one last pint, topped with a double vodka. This last drink completely finished Tony off and, as the crowd tumbled out of the pub, he swayed uncertainly and grabbed hold of Mathew who was standing next to him to prevent himself from collapsing onto the pavement.

Chris, who had hoped to take the party on to the Taboo Club where several strippers were performing that night, decided Tony was in no state to continue, so they decided to return to the flat and carry on the festivities there. Raz managed to flag down an empty taxi and four of the party managed to clamber in, manhandling Tony in with them. The others said they would find another taxi and follow on.

By the time everyone had arrived back at the flat, Tony was in a terrible state, moaning and groaning loudly to himself, completely incoherent and extremely drunk. Raz was convinced that Tony might become violently sick, so they hauled him off to the bathroom, hung his head over the toilet bowl and left him there while the rest of the party carried on drinking, smoking and telling dirty jokes in the lounge.

Tony could occasionally be heard retching violently in the bathroom. Eventually Raz and Chris ventured into the bathroom and found Tony lying comatose on the floor, having obviously been very sick indeed. They undressed him and threw his vomit stained clothes into a plastic bag, then they carried his naked body unceremoniously into his bedroom and laid him on his back on the bed, where he lay breathing heavily, his mouth agape, with a little trickle of saliva running down the side of his chin. 'He looks just like a baby,' smiled Raz drunkenly.

'A very drunk baby, that's for sure,' said Chris. 'Now for the surprise. He's so far gone, he'll never notice.'

Chris left the room and walked down the hall to the kitchen where he opened a drawer and took out a small bottle. He peered round the door of the lounge where the others were still noisily gathered. 'Do you chaps want to see Tony's pecker change colour, as a little wedding night surprise for Christine?' he asked them in a tone that seemed to say, you would be silly not to.

Mike laughed loudly, having carefully decided on the practical joke after much discussion with Raz and Chris and knowing what was about to take place. Some of the others stared at Chris with a mixture of astonishment and mild amusement in their expressions, uncertain as to what was going to happen.

'Come on, follow me, but please, whispers only as we don't want to wake Tony up,' said Chris, beckoning with his finger for them to follow him.

They all rose to their feet, somewhat unsteadily, and quietly followed Chris into Tony's bedroom where they gathered around the bed. Tony still lay on his back, snoring heavily. Several of the party sniggered at the sight of their friend lying naked, his body juddering with the heavy snoring, while his mouth gaped open lifelessly.

'Did you get the stuff?' Raz asked Chris.

Chris produced the small bottle and undid the lid which had a small wire attached to it with a pad on the end. 'Black shoe dye,' explained Chris in a hoarse whisper as one or two of the others gasped, slowly cottoning on to what was going to happen.

Raz leant down, lifted Tony's limp penis away from his body, then placed a cloth between Tony's upper thighs and underneath his scrotum.

Chris then leant over Tony and using the swab he liberally coated Tony's penis with the black dye. He then worked round the scrotum, his face a picture of concentration as the tip of his tongue protruded from his closed mouth, while he completely covered Tony's genital area with the black dye.

The others crowded round in silence, staring down in utter amazement at the snoring white figure now replete with black genitals, desperately trying to contain their hilarity at was taking place.

After a minute Raz decided that the dye had dried out and let Tony's limp, black penis fall back onto his black scrotum. He then pulled the cloth out from under Tony's balls which had prevented the dye from staining the bedclothes.

Everyone was conversing with each other in stage whispers, trying desperately not to dissolve into riotous laughter, although several of them had tears running down their cheeks. 'Ssh,' said Raz waving his finger at them all. 'We don't want to wake him, let him sleep his hangover off.'

'Christ, will that stuff come off in the morning?' Mario asked anxiously.

'No way,' replied Chris adamantly, 'otherwise Christine wouldn't get her surprise, would she?'

'Let alone the surprise for Tony when he comes to in the morning,' added Raz gleefully trying to imagine what Tony would feel when he looked down and noticed his new black cock hanging between his white legs.

The thought of Tony waking up in the morning to find this out brought the group to almost total collapse, such was the hysteria amongst them all. They could all imagine in their own minds Tony staggering to the toilet to have a piss and finding his genitals had changed colour; oh, if only they could be there to see it. Mike rounded the visitors up and everyone traipsed back into the lounge for a final drink and a smoke, leaving Raz and Chris alone with Tony in his room.

'You don't think we've gone too far Chris?' asked Raz peering down at Tony's genitals. 'It'll take ages to wear off.'

'Look, he's one of us, one of the original gang of four. How could he be mad at us?' said Chris, now desperate for a last drink but secretly hoping that Tony would indeed accept the joke in good fun. 'Let's join the others for a beer. It's already 2.30. I think I'm going to hit the sack soon, otherwise I'll be completely fucked for tomorrow and I have promised to get Tony to the church on time. If I don't, no doubt someone will want my guts for garters.'

Raz took a sheet and covered Tony's body with it. Chris and Raz left the room, Raz closing the door quietly behind them, wondering when Tony would find out; would he wake up during the night and want a piss or would he sleep soundly through the night until he was woken in the morning. Whenever it would be, it was certainly going to be a surprise for the poor old sod, and for Christine too.

As dawn broke in the morning over the City of Cambridge, the sun slowly and majestically appeared from behind a collection of foreboding dark clouds which, thankfully, began to separate over the next two hours. By 9 o'clock the sky had turned into a beautiful light blue, interspersed as far as the eye could see with gentle white clouds that hung like cotton wool balls suspended in the sky. The temperature for later that morning was predicted by the weathermen to rise to a pleasant sixty-two to sixty-three degrees - perfect weather for the big day.

The wedding was scheduled for 12.30 at the Church of Our Virgin Lady on Hills Road. This was the largest and most imposing Catholic church in Cambridge and only half a mile from the flat in Mawson Road.

When Tony was shaken awake by Chris at 10 o'clock, he gratefully took the mug of strong, sweet tea Chris handed him. His head was throbbing violently and he had trouble opening his eyes at first, whilst his mouth tasted dreadful. His mind

271

wandered hazily over the events of the previous evening and, despite the knowledge that all the preparations were in hand, his thoughts began to run riot about the day ahead. He began to feel distinctly nervous as his brain began to start working and to wonder if his body was able to function properly.

'Don't worry Tony, everything's fine,' said Chris sitting on the bed nursing his own hangover and wondering whether they had overdone things regarding Tony's marriage kit, he obviously hadn't found out yet. Tony looked absolutely terrible and Chris hoped that he would be able to sober up in the next couple of hours. 'I'll leave you to shave and shower at your own pace Tony, we've got plenty of time.' He walked out of the room and down the hall to the kitchen where the other conspirators were gathered in eager anticipation. They were all dying to see Tony's reaction to his new set of coloured genitals. They sat listening to the Four Tops, smoking, eating toast and marmalade and drinking hot tea and gulping several aspirins each. They all felt exceedingly fragile themselves, especially Raz, who sat as always when he had a hangover, with his head in his hands, trying to lessen the incessant pounding taking place beneath his forehead.

All of a sudden they heard Tony's door crash open and he came running down the hall, yelling loudly. Chris immediately noticed that he had a white towel tucked around his middle.

'You bastards,' he yelled at them, ashen faced and stubbled, his mouth open wide with horror and surprise. 'What the fuck have you done to me?' he cried out in anguish, pointing down towards his genital area.

'Surprise, surprise,' they chortled back at him, laughing uproariously at the indignation showing on Tony's face.

'What the fuck is Christine going to say? Please tell me that it will wash off,' Tony appealed to them all. 'How can I possibly show my face to Christine on her wedding day with fucking black bollocks?'

'We were hoping you were going to show her more than your face,' said Chris. 'That's why we did it. We thought it would be a great surprise for Christine.'

'It'll be a great surprise, that's for bloody sure,' said Tony. 'I just can't believe this,' he said disappearing into the bathroom as the others doubled up in fits of silent laughter, falling about the kitchen hysterically, holding onto the walls to prevent themselves from collapsing onto the floor.

Tony examined himself in the bathroom mirror, aghast at what he saw there. Tired gaunt eyes, underlined by heavy black circles stared lifelessly back at him. His eyes were heavily bloodshot, sunk into his unshaven face, while his skin was blotchy, pasty and unhealthy looking. 'Oh Christ, I look like shit and I feel like shit,' he groaned, rubbing his stubble with shaking fingers. As he started to shave, Chris knocked on the door and brought him another strong cup of tea and several aspirins. He turned on the taps to run a bath for Tony who gulped the tea and aspirins down before finishing his shave and unwrapping the towel from his middle. He sat on the edge of the bath and examined his painted genitals. 'The bastards,' he said to himself, still not quite believing what had happened and trying to remember to ask them what dye they had used.

When the bath was two-thirds full, Tony tested the water and jumped in. He lay with his knees sticking above the water level, savouring the heat enveloping him. He was nursing the most dreadful hangover that he could remember. Suddenly he began retching and felt sure that he was going to throw up. His head began spinning as he lay groaning and moaning in the warm water, trying not to entertain thoughts about the event later that morning, but seriously uncertain of whether he was going to be able to start the day, let alone last the rest of it.

He stood up in the bath and took the soap and began lathering his genitals, then ducked down in the water to rinse the lather off. 'Christ,' he muttered on further examination, 'there's still no difference!' He took a nailbrush and rubbed some soap on it. Then he carefully rubbed his penis with the brush, but it began to feel painful and he gradually realised that he was not going to be able to remove the colour. 'Oh Christ,' he murmured disconsolately to himself, 'whatever will Christine say?' He had decided to spend his last night as a bachelor at Mawson Road despite the warnings from both his parents and from Christine that it was not a good idea. But he had put his foot down, he wanted to be with his best friends for his final celebration and to stay with them on his final night as a single man. Chris had told everyone that as the best man he would take full responsibility for delivering Tony to the church on time. Predictably he had not exactly stated what sort of condition Tony would arrive in and this vague promise had done little to convince both Tony's and Christine's sceptical parents to cease worrying. Certainly Tony's parents had just cause for concern as during the time that Tony had spent at Mawson Road, they had seen him change drastically. 'Those crazy boys that you live with will lead you astray Tony, with all that drinking and chasing girls and staying up all night, and not eating properly. They will just get you into trouble,' his worried father had told him countless times.

'Believe me Dad, if that's so, it's the kind of trouble that I can handle,' Tony would sometimes reflect on his father's anxiety and realise that it was well meant. 'OK Dad, I'll be careful, I really will. You've no need to worry, they're all really nice chaps,' he would insist, but his father had never been truly convinced. Now as he painfully eased himself out of the bath and dried his white body with its black bits dangling between his legs, with his head throbbing and his limbs aching, he began to wish that he had been a little more prudent. Maybe, upon reflection, he should have held his stag party a few days ago so that he would have had time to recover. That would have been more sensible, but since when during the time spent with his friends at Mawson Road had any of them ever been sensible! The 'phone ringing in the hallway interrupted his thoughts. He decided to answer it but realised that Chris had got to it first for he could hear Chris saying, 'yes, he's fine. He can hardly wait to get to the church.'

'Oh God, such lies,' muttered Tony, struggling desperately to put his necktie on, now feeling as though he was at death's door.

He heard a door bang and Raz came bounding into the room, looking pretty rough but still beaming that smile of his. 'How are you feeling Tony?' he cried, slapping Tony's shoulders vigorously. 'Any more children turned up?' he asked, laughing out loudly at the previous evening's practical joke.

Tony just groaned and sat down heavily on his bed, vaguely remembering how his stomach had turned when they'd played the joke on him and how convincing his old girlfriend had been. Trust Chris to think of a practical joke like that, to completely unnerve him.

Mike wandered in to Tony's room, bare chested and clad only in his suit trousers. 'Not long to go now mate and you'll have that ball and chain around your leg. And, you'll be able to entertain Christine to the *Black and White Minstrels Show* later,' he said as he burst into raucous laughter.

They all laughed together as Tony tried to force a smile back at them all. He could certainly feel his cock now. It was terribly sore where he had scrubbed it raw and had started to throb with pain.

'Only joking Tony. I've just polished your shoes for you,' said Mike, handing Tony the new black shoes that he had recently purchased for his big day. 'Black as your privates are,' he added as Tony grimaced yet again at the mention of his black bits.

Chris wandered in, still in his dressing gown. 'That was your dad on the phone, so I've told him that you're OK, Tony. I reckon we want to leave just before twelve and have a quick one in The Globe just to calm our nerves.'

'Christ, calm our nerves,' cried Tony wide-eyed. 'I feel like I'm gonna be sick at any moment.'

'Exactly, it's a topping up of alcohol that you need, my friend, a good pint of beer will soon settle you down,' said Chris emphatically. 'I'll quickly take my bath and be ready in twenty minutes. Everyone else OK for then?' he enquired, looking round at them all. Mike nodded and Raz belched loudly, while Tony pulled himself up from the bed and staggered down the hallway to the kitchen to pour himself a glass of water. He could hear Chris singing to himself in the bathroom. 'What was that? *Bachelor Boy*, the Cliff Richard number,' Tony thought. 'Charming, is that in honour of my last couple of hours of bachelor status, or is he taking the piss?'

At ten to twelve the four of them stepped unsteadily out of the house, Chris having made sure that he had obtained the ring from Tony and placed it securely in an inside pocket of his jacket. The bright sunlight made them blink uncertainly, but the fresh air felt good as they traipsed along the side streets towards The Globe, feeling conspicuous in their smart suits, particularly as none of them felt one hundred per cent. Each of them had either a headache or felt nauseous, or both. They all appeared pale and tired.

They stepped into The Globe at exactly twelve o'clock. There were only a few regulars, mainly Irish navvies sitting drinking alone at the bar or reading through the *Sporting Life.*

'Four beers please,' ordered Chris.

'I just hope this isn't the bad idea that I think it is,' said Tony who was still feeling incredibly fragile and worrying non-stop about the rigours of the day ahead.

'No, honestly Tony, it'll do you and each one of us the world of good,' advised Chris, paying the barman. 'You know the old expression, the hair of the dog, well this is it. But I would like to say Tony, with this your last drink ever as a bachelor, that it's been wonderful to have your company in the flat and I'm sure we'll all agree to that. You and Christine must stay in touch with all of us and I hope that you'll always remember the good times that we've enjoyed together.'

'Hear, hear,' cried Raz and Mike in unison, raising their glasses.

'So,' said Chris, 'I'd like to wish you on behalf of all of us, all the best for the future Tony, and for Christine too.'

'Hear, hear,' the others chorused again, as they all lifted their glasses and drank deeply.

Despite his reservations, Tony felt that the beer seemed to steady his stomach a little. He looked around at each of the other three standing beside him, glasses in their hands, patiently waiting for him to say something.

'Thank you all so much guys. I've had a bloody wonderful time ever since I met you all at that party when I came along uninvited with Suzi and Caroline. I couldn't have wanted for three better flatmates. Now, you're all my best friends and even though I've got black bollocks and I feel like shit, I want to say thank you all for everything, it's been a fucking brilliant time together, it really has.'

'OK, drink up then Tony. We've got time for just one more for the road,' said Chris checking his watch and draining his glass. 'You'll feel even better after this one Tony.'

Tony groaned inwardly, knowing that he had to drink this one last beer with them, but realising that he might have to pay the consequences later on.

The quartet arrived breathlessly at the church at twelve twenty seven to be met by Christine's mother and Tony's father. 'Where have you been,' his father cried frantically at Tony. Turning angrily to Chris, he added, 'we thought you were never going to appear.'

'Look Mr. Santiago, I said that I'd get him here and I have. Christine will be late anyway,' said Chris, stifling a belch.

'Look at him, he's so white. What have you done to my boy?' asked Tony's father, anxiously scanning his son's haggard face.

'I'm fine dad,' said Tony, feeling nauseous again, but trying desparately to ignore it. 'Come on everyone, let's get in the church and enjoy my big day.'

They all walked into the beautifully decorated church. Tony and Chris walked quickly down the central aisle, smiling briefly at friends and relatives. Tony had a big contingent present who had arrived early that morning from Italy. Others had arrived the day before and had stayed at his parents home, or with friends.

Chris couldn't help noticing the two beautiful girls sitting two rows behind them, but one in particular caught his attention. She had jet black, curly hair, an olive complexion and was stunningly beautiful; completely dressed in black. 'Who's that girl two rows back,' asked Chris nonchalantly as they took their place at the front.

Tony glanced behind and though still feeling very rough, smiled and nodded at his relatives and friends. 'That's my sister, Maria, and you can keep your hands off her. She's engaged and lives in Milan,' said Tony, noticing Chris glancing round again for another look at his sister.

Almost immediately the organ music started and everyone stood up as Christine and her father appeared, walking slowly and elegantly down the aisle. Chris had been worried as to whether the hearse would break down, but having checked it all over thoroughly with Johnny, who had elected to be the chauffeur for the day, he had been fairly confident in the car's ability. 'Thank God for that,' said Chris to himself with a sigh of relief, as Christine drew up beside Tony and he promptly stepped out to stand with his soon-to-be wife.

The service ran very smoothly apart from one bout of hysterical sniggering when Tony and Christine had to kneel together before the priest for the final blessing and a large number of the congregation were soon alerted to the fact that Tony's soles bore a large white R on his left sole, while SOLE was written in large white letters on the other. Tony's parents sat fuming, turning to throw repeated angry glances back at Raz and Mike who both sat straight-faced, looking ahead, seemingly oblivious to the sniggers and laughter erupting around them. Chris too seemed intent on following the service and paid no attention to the seething couple across the aisle.

At the end of the service, as everyone gathered to remove themselves from the church, Mr. and Mrs. Santiago rushed over to Chris and Mr. Santiago grabbed him by the arm. 'You have insulted my son,' he spluttered, glowering with rage, 'with that filth written on my son's shoes.'

'What's happened? Why are you so angry?' enquired Chris.

'You saw what was written on my boy's shoes?' demanded Tony's father, wringing his hands and then waving them again to emphasise his point.

'Well, they're new shoes, so was it the maker's name perhaps? I personally didn't notice anything,' said Chris innocently. 'As I was standing next to Tony, how could I?'

Tony's father pounded his forehead with the palm of his hand. 'This is incredible, it's a bloody disgrace,' he said loudly to Chris, grabbing his wife's hand and storming off up the aisle where Chris saw him gesticulating in front of Mike and Raz. Chris watched as they both stood staring blankly at the ranting couple in front of them, shaking their heads from side-to-side and appearing completely puzzled by Mr. Santiago's ranting and raging.

Outside the church, the usual photographs were being taken of the bride and groom and family. As soon as Chris had finished having his picture taken in a couple of group shots, he gathered Raz and Mike together and they shot across the busy road into The Oak, a small but friendly pub opposite the church, popular with the local Irish community. As they entered the pub, Chris noticed three pints of Guinness standing miraculously in a line. Behind the bar, the landlord stood grinning at them. 'There you go boys,' he said indicating the three brimming glasses.

'How did you know we were coming in?' asked Chris

completely mystified.

'I saw you three lads across the road. I could tell that you'd all been to the service and were probably as dry as parrots without water, so I lined 'em up for you lads,' replied the landlord in a soft Irish brogue, a knowing twinkle in his eyes. 'It happens all the time at these weddings,' he assured them. 'Worse at funerals though, they dry you up the most lads,' he added knowingly.

They reached for their glasses and drank the creamy black nectar with relish. Chris noticed that almost everyone in the place was drinking Guinness and those who weren't stood out like a sore thumb. He glanced at the others and as one, almost as if a signal had gone off, all three of them erupted into spontaneous laughter which they had found it so difficult to withhold in the church when Tony had knelt down, and the congregation had immediately become aware of the letters painted onto Tony's soles by Mike when he had polished them for Tony earlier.

'Did you see Tony's mother and father?' said Mike. 'I thought they were both going to have an epileptic fit,' especially as most of the congregation were helpless with laughter.

'It's only fun, for God's sake. But that was a good joke Mike. I only wish I could have turned round to see everybody laughing,' said Chris.

'He was going to write F.U.C.K. OFF until I persuaded him not to,' said Raz with a snigger at the thought.

'I think R SOLE was perfectly fine,' said Chris, 'though even that's caused enough problems!'

'I think we might have to take a lot of stick for that at the reception,' said Mike, 'especially from the families.'

'Correction Mike, you may have to take some stick,' said Chris. He tapped his watch with his right hand as if to say, 'time to go.'

They drained their pints, said goodbye to the cheery landlord and strode briskly up the street towards the Farmers Club where the reception was being held in the Recreation Room.

Chris was especially eager to try to meet Tony's sister and to enjoy the wedding reception. He felt good now, his hangover had cleared and he was hoping that Tony was bearing up and that he too would be feeling much better.

'We mustn't forget Tony's car,' reminded Mike as they strode along, 'everything's all ready for that.'

They had planned to decorate Tony's Austin Healey to give the couple the traditional humiliating send-off that the bride and groom usually had to endure, and had amassed a bag full of bits and pieces to make sure that Tony's car looked the part!

'Yeah, we should be able to cover up most of the dents on his car. It will never have looked so good since he's had it,' grinned Mike.

Chapter Thirty-Six

The trio arrived breathlessly at the reception hall, where most of the other guests had already been introduced, proceeding first along the line of the immediate families and then to the bride and groom. Now the guests were all milling around in assorted self-conscious groups drinking champagne which was being served by two of the girls from Tony's salon who were acting as wine waitresses for the day. The boys immediately chatted them both up to ensure that their glasses were given priority and kept full throughout the afternoon.

Tony's father had hired a local four-piece band who were accompanied by an Italian accordionist and the music, which had already started, was to range from pop to polka. The band were playing quietly at the beginning of the reception from a small stage at the end of the room. The room was lavishly decorated with vast quantities of flowers, streamers and balloons.

With almost two hundred guests, a great hub-bub of conversation filled the room, punctuated with spontaneous outbursts of laughter erupting from various groups of guests around the hall. As the boys stood chatting and drinking together, their hangovers now miraculously erased, Chris began searching the room for a sight of Tony's sister. Several guests came up to them to chat and ask who was the instigator of the writing on Tony's shoes, it seemed that almost everyone had thoroughly enjoyed the joke. As though on cue, the group noticed Tony's mother and father pushing through the throng towards them. 'Oh, no,' said Chris talking sideways through the corner of his lips, 'you're in trouble Mikey.'

Mike felt slightly alarmed as Tony's parents reached them, an angry expression on both of their faces. 'Whadd'ya do to my son, trying to make him look a fool?' Tony's father demanded, trying to address them all, saliva flecks flying from his mouth as he spoke rapidly to them.

'Look Mr. Santiago, I can see that you're still very angry, but I'm sure Tony will have seen the funny side of it. It was only a bit of fun for everyone,' said Chris, trying to soothe the irate couple down by talking very quietly, he did not want the matter to develop into a scene and spoil the party, even though he knew that he would probably have to take the blame for it.

'It's a terrible for my Tony. You made him a laughing stock in front of all the guests,' cried Mrs. Santiago. 'You were supposed to be the best man, not to play tricks on him.'

Mike decided that Chris was taking the flak for him. He knew that Chris would not drop him in the shit, but he decided that he had to intervene. Trying to appear innocent, he put on what he felt was his 'little boy' look, fluttering his eyelashes behind his glasses. 'Excuse me,' he said politely to Mrs. Santiago, smiling and feeling his cheeks flush with the tension, 'it was nothing to do with Chris. It was my idea and it was me who painted the letters on Tony's shoes. I'm very sorry if it upset you, but I think most people thought it was a joke and it was something we did because we love Tony so much, it was not done to hurt him.'

As if on cue, Tony suddenly appeared beside the group, eyes shining and smiling broadly, his face no longer pale and languid but now flushed with the enjoyment and tension of his big day. He still felt very tired from the previous night, but he was not about to let that spoil things. 'You bastards,' he exclaimed cheerily draping his arms around his three flatmates, 'that was a good one you guys pulled and I was completely unaware of it until I got out of the church.' He noticed the anger showing in his parents faces and realised the reason for it.

'Mum and Dad, these boys have been great to me, don't be upset please. We're always playing jokes on each other, so don't be mad at them. Besides, it's my big day and both Christine and I thought it was a real laugh, so promise me, don't let it worry you both any more. Enjoy the day, my day - please?' He looked down at them both, urging them through his pleading expression to forget the matter. 'What the hell would they say if they could see my black privates,' he wondered, they would probably want to kill the other three. Dismissing the thought because he still did not know how to begin to tell Christine, he listened to his father talking to his friends.

'OK, we forgive you boys,' said Mr. Santiago solemnly, taking his wife's hand. 'It's my son's day after all. Sometimes we old ones can never understand young people these days. Have a good time anyway.' He reached up wearily and patted his son's cheek as though he was still a small child, then turned away in resignation and led his wife away to talk to some other guests in another group.

Christine came over to Tony's side. The boys all told her how beautiful she looked, which was true. She was a very attractive girl and the dress she had chosen showed off her excellent figure whilst remaining fairly traditional. She seemed exceptionally radiant and beautiful as, indeed, most brides do on their big day. She clutched Tony's arm lovingly and glared around at the other boys, 'I must say, I was flabbergasted at Tony's appearance when I joined him at the alter. I wanted to turn round and strangle you Chris. He looked so ill and pale and completely exhausted. But now he seems to have recovered well, so I want to thank you Chris, and Mike and Raz for looking after him. And when we found out what you'd done to his shoes, well, I nearly died. I remember hearing people laughing behind us in the church and wondering why. Anyway thanks to you all for getting him to the church in one piece,' Christine said. She stepped forward and gave each of them a quick kiss on the cheek, then put her arms around her new husband and gave him a strong kiss on his lips. Raz and Mike whistled at this, but Chris just smiled, wondering what would happen when she was confronted with those black genitals. What would she say about them all then? He suppressed a grin at the thought and took a sip of champagne.

A friend of Christine's interrupted them. Chris saw that she was one of the bridesmaids. 'Can I introduce Trisha, an old friend of mine from my schooldays,' said Christine. 'This is Mike, and Raz and lastly Chris who, as you know, is Tony's best man.'

Trisha was a small, auburn-haired girl with nice legs Mike noted and she shook hands gently with them all. When she

283

smiled, Mike realised that it was one of those rare smiles that can turn a plain person into a beautiful one in a split second. She also had fine well-formed teeth which helped to make her smile even more appealing. Mike stood next to her, apparently transfixed, as the group chatted amongst themselves. She must have some kind of inner glow to radiate the happiness that her smile exudes, Mike thought to himself, feeling himself increasingly attracted to her.

Chris meanwhile had spotted Tony's sister chatting animatedly with two other girls across the room, so he excused himself from the group and thrust his way impatiently through the crowd until he reached the trio. As he stood waiting for the girls to finish their conversation, he cast little appreciative glances at Tony's sister, noting that she was even better looking close up, with smooth olive skin and deep brown eyes, her tumbling black hair set off by a simple, short black dress, beautifully cut, showing off her long legs and perfectly proportioned body. She was a real stunner, no wonder Tony had warned him off her. As he waited, one of the other girls turned to him and spoke, 'Hi, you're Chris, Tony's best man aren't you?' making it sound more of a statement than a question. 'I'm Joanna, one of Christine's friends. This is Maria, Tony's oldest sister and this is Gina, Tony's youngest sister. They're both studying in Milan.'

'Hi,' said Chris politely shaking hands with each of them in turn. 'Do you both normally live in England?' he asked the sisters, wondering why Tony had never invited the girls to the flat. He remembered Tony's aside to him in the church and realised that Tony would not have wanted the girls to get anywhere near himself or Raz and Mike, just in case. After all, they were his sisters, so they were special.

'We're both studying at college in Milan for three years and then we'll return to work in England as most of our family now live here. We've just a few older relatives left in Italy,' replied Maria.

'What are you studying?' asked Chris.

'I'm History of Art,' replied Maria.

'And I'm studying Textile Design,' said Gina.

'Well, they both sound very interesting,' said Chris suitably impressed. Noticing that the girl's glasses were empty, with a swift jerk of his head he caught the attention of one of the girls serving the drinks. The group gratefully took another glass of champagne each from the proffered tray.

'Our brother looks pretty rough,' said Maria looking at Chris somewhat accusingly. 'I 'spose that's your doing last night, getting him legless!'

Chris was slightly taken aback by the abrupt manner with which she had mentioned that. What did she think a stag night was, a fucking picnic? 'Well, yes, earlier on Tony looked a bit peaky, but he's slowly coming back to life,' said Chris, desperate to reassure her. 'A few more drinks and he'll be as right as rain,' he added.

'A few more drinks and he'll be past it. He'll be bloody useless to Christine, and on her wedding night too,' replied Maria venomously, her brow furrowed and her eyes blazing as she glared at Chris.

'Look,' said Chris somewhat taken aback, 'I may be wrong, but do I detect a certain family attack against me, or us, if I include my flatmates. We've already had to be rescued by your brother from a tongue lashing that your parents were dishing out to us.'

'Yes, that's because one of your so-called friends of Tony's wrote that crap on the back of his shoes,' snarled Maria.

'OK, that was Mike, but so what?' replied Chris. 'Everyone had a laugh and, despite your parents hostility and now with you ranting on about it, everyone else enjoyed the joke, especially Tony and Christine when they both eventually found out about it.' Chris was beginning to feel upset at this girl arguing with him. He wanted to talk to her, to find out more about her, this beauty that Tony had kept in the closet, and yet here they were arguing like cat and dog.

A loud banging sound interrupted them as Christine's father announced that the buffet was about to be served. Immediately a queue began to form, especially those with small children who were beginning to become hungry and restless. Within minutes the queue had stretched across the room.

'Look Maria,' said Chris, taking her arm and drawing her to one side so the others could not overhear their conversation, while beckoning to the waitress again to refill their glasses, 'I don't know why you've got it in for me, but I am probably your brother's best friend. He's lived with us for several years now and we've been through a lot together and I really don't think I deserve to be castigated by you for enjoying ourselves. All bridegrooms have a stag night and I looked after your brother, made sure he was at the church on time and, OK, so we played a little joke on him in the church, so fucking what? You have no right to be so rude to me and I'm particularly pissed off because, believe it or not, I quite fancied you even though we've never met before. I thought it would be nice to talk to you properly. You obviously think differently.'

With that, Chris turned on his heel and stormed off, angry at himself for losing his temper and for swearing, angry because the bloody woman did not understand the male camaraderie that had bound them all together for so long, and angry because he fancied her like mad and any chance of getting together had now been blown apart. He took yet another glass of champagne from the waitresses tray as she passed by and made his way back through the crowd to join Mike and Raz again.

He could tell from the body language that Mike was now well ensconced with Trisha, while Raz was arguing noisily about politics with an uncle of Tony's that he had just met. 'What happened over there?' asked Mike. 'I could see you surrounded by those three gorgeous babes, but it looked to me as though you were having an argument with them. Aren't they Tony's sisters?'

'Bloody right Mike,' Chris replied, still angry. I went over to talk to the group of girls to find that two of them are his sisters, but one of them started an argument. I was defending our integrity against the seething tongue of Maria, his eldest sister, would you believe.' He glowered over the heads of the crowd in the direction of the three girls and noticed Maria glancing over her shoulder. As he caught her searching in his direction, she must have seen him looking for she turned brusquely away to continue the conversation within her group. He could tell that she had deliberately avoided making eye contact with him.

Christine's father came over and laid a hand on Chris's shoulder. 'Have you got your speech ready lad?' he asked. 'I've got a few telegrams for you to read as well.'

'Yeah, I'm OK,' said Chris suddenly feeling nervous for the

first time. He hated public speaking. 'I'm ready when you are. It's not a long speech anyway.' He was not comfortable in front of large numbers of people and had mentioned to Tony that his best man's speech would be 'short but sweet'.

'I'll get everybody's attention when the last of the guests have been up to the buffet, probably in about twenty minutes, then I'll give you the nod,' added Christine's father.

Chris lit a Pall Mall to calm his nerves and wished that he had brought a joint with him; though he rarely smoked marijuana it might have helped loosen him up more than the alcohol, after all that arguing he really felt on edge. He felt thoroughly pissed off that the bloody girl had made him so angry. It had been a real put down, he was only trying to be nice and chat her up, only to find her spitting at him like a wildcat. No doubt her little group were having a good laugh at his expense right now, probably congratulating Maria for putting the boot in. He noticed the crowd at the buffet had thinned out, most of the guests were standing around talking and eating, though the luckier ones had bagged the chairs at the sides of the room to sit and enjoy their food. He took a final drag on his cigarette and wandered over to the buffet table. It had certainly been a magnificent spread, but the attention of almost two hundred people had made quite a mess of the presentation. He decided he ought to rescue what he could from the destruction, he needed something solid in his stomach. As he reached for the last two sausage rolls his thoughts were interrupted by a woman's voice behind him. He turned around to find Maria standing there alone.

'Chris, I've come to say I'm sorry. I do know how much Tony cares for you all,' Maria said. 'Whenever he's been home, he always talks about you and the other chaps in the flat. I'm sorry I flew at you a bit, it's just that I'm very protective of my younger brother and I didn't want to see him made a fool of. But he's looking great now and he's obviously really enjoying his wedding day. I told him that I'd been very rude to you and he said that I must apologise to you, so here I am.'

'Oh Christ,' thought Chris, now Tony knows I've been talking to her. But still, if he's told Maria to apologise to me, that can't be bad.' He stared down at Maria, completely entranced by her beauty and her dark eyes. He was suitably impressed that she had the guts to stand before him like this and say that she was sorry. He was also curious as to whether this meant that she wanted to become more friendly and decided to put her to the test. 'Maria,' he said sweetly, 'I accept your apology completely, so let's just forget about what happened and enjoy your brother's wedding.' He turned back to the table and continued searching for any morsels still worth eating, but then felt Maria tugging at his sleeve.

'But I can't forget that you said that you fancied me before you walked off,' she said huskily, her large eyes seeming to become even darker and more sensual to Chris as she stared up at him, hoping for signs of interest on his part. She seemed to be almost pleading with her eyes for him to show that his interest in her was still there.

Chris could not believe it, she had reacted exactly as he had wanted her to, he knew that only if she was attracted to him would she have responded in this manner. He was so elated that he felt he really had to go for it now that he had the upper hand. 'And I meant it,' he told her gently. 'I fancied you immediately I saw you in the church. When I asked Tony who you were he told me you were his sister and that I wasn't to bother you. But I couldn't help my feelings, that's why I came over to talk to you just now.'

'Don't bother about my little brother, he's only trying to be protective towards me,' she said. 'I do what I want to do and he does what he wants to do. He's got married today and I'd never do that, I just wanted to be free to do as I wish.'

'But Tony said you were engaged,' said Chris.

'No, that's all over now, finished last week. I realised the guy was not right for me and I got rid of him,' Maria replied. 'I just didn't want to get married.'

Just then Johnny joined them. Chris introduced Maria and gratefully accepted the beer that Johnny offered him. It was a welcome respite from all the champagne that he had quaffed so far.

'I've left the Rolls outside, so when you take it back to Mawson Road you can bring Tony's car back here,' said Johnny handing the keys back to Chris. 'Then we'll do the honours on his car before they leave for the honeymoon. Where are they going anyway?'

'They're staying at a lovely hotel in Devon for a week,' said Maria, 'and then they're having a week at Lago di Como in Italy. My sister Gina and I are hoping to meet up with them when we return to Italy.'

Johnny gathered a few titbits onto his plate. Chris finished eating his sausage rolls and decided that he would not eat anything else until after the speeches and toasts. He noticed Christine's father waving, trying to attract his attention across the crowded room. He was holding his hand up, palm outermost, fingers outstretched. 'Five minutes,' he mouthed silently.

'Christ,' muttered Chris, nodding in assent. He realised how nervous he now felt, within five minutes he would have to read the telegrams and give his speech. He could feel the butterflies churning in his stomach and felt his throat tighten with apprehension, so he took a large gulp of his beer. His hands felt clammy with the tension building up inside him.

'Have you got a good one ready?' asked Johnny.

'Hopefully, short and sweet,' replied Chris wondering if Johnny was referring to his speech or referring to Maria, who stood beside him looking stunning.

'I'm not going to say anything,' said Maria grinning at Chris, 'and if you are rude about Tony, I promise not to say anything about that either. I'm beginning to realise that all of you boys living at the flat had a weird sense of humour!'

The two girls from Tony's salon were passing around glasses of champagne to everyone for the toasts and Chris sensed a feeling of expectancy amongst the guests as the band finished their stint and began leaving the stage for some refreshments. He started to feel quite anxious, hoping that his speech would not upset anyone, especially Tony's parents, and that everyone would accept his jokes in the spirit that they were intended.

A loud banging brought a hush to the room as Christine's father stood at the front of the stage calling for quiet. The guests gathered around, their attention focused on the speaker. A baby immediately began crying and the mother trying to quieten it, rocking it gently back and forth, and finally stuffing a rubber dummy in its mouth.

Christine's father called Tony and Christine up onto the stage as everyone clapped and cheered the happy, but slightly self-conscious, couple. He went on to make a short sloppy speech telling the guests how much he had longed for this day, to see his little baby married and how hard it was going to be for him and his wife to realise that Christine was no longer at home any more. But, he added, they were very pleased that she had found such a wonderful husband as Tony, who had his own salon which he had worked so hard for. There was much applause at this remark, especially from Tony's contingent and as the speech concluded with a toast to the bride and groom, Christine's father called for the best man. Chris bounded up onto the stage and was handed the telegrams to read out. Luckily there were only a few, from friends and family in Italy who had not been able to attend and one from Tony's elder brother in America who was recovering from an operation, but who made an offer that if Tony became too tired during the honeymoon, he would be glad to take over for a while, which raised a few titters in the audience, while Christine blushed a little and shuffled her feet uneasily. She had only met Andreas once. He was short and fat and unattractive and the thought of him offering to do that made her cringe.

Concluding the reading of the telegrams, Chris took a quick sip of his champagne, taking a studied glance around the crowd to make sure that everyone's glasses were filled. The guests stood staring up at the stage where Chris stood, expectantly waiting for his speech. Chris raised his hand to the audience, 'OK everybody,' he said, trying to ignore another baby crying, 'as the best man it is my duty to tell you all a little about the man who has changed his life today by becoming a married man. As he has asked me to be very discreet, I won't be able to tell you everything I know as a quickie divorce might be on the cards.'

There were a few polite laughs from the audience. Christine smiled, still slightly embarrassed at being the centre of attention as she knew that everyone would be looking at her to gauge her reaction to anything Chris might say that could affect her. She was feeling distinctly apprehensive at this point in the proceedings in case Chris came out with some titbit that might really upset her. She already knew much of Tony's past, he had been very forthright with her and she knew that he had been no angel but Chris might still have something tucked away that she did not know about. She listened intently to Chris continuing his speech.

'Now I'm only going to take a few minutes because of my throat.' Chris put his hand around his neck as he added, 'if I go too far then Christine might come over and cut it.'

There was some laughter and muted applause.

'I first met Tony several years ago when he used a couple of girls he knew as bait to gatecrash a party that Mike, Raz and I were having at our flat. When Tony produced two bottles of champagne to bribe his way in, I thought to myself that this guy is either bloody mad or he must be a really nice guy. It didn't take long for all of us to realise that he was both, especially as he moved in with us shortly afterwards. We soon found out that he was obsessed with his hairdressing, as did many of the young ladies that he was to ingratiate himself with over the years. I can certainly vouch that Tony's gives 'good hair' and I'm sure that Christine won't disagree.' There was more laughter, especially from the younger guests.

'On the serious side though, Tony has been a great friend and a great flatmate to Raz, Mike and myself and we are really going to miss him. So Christine,' he turned to gaze directly at her, 'please look after him well.' He turned back to the audience, 'I must tell you that when Tony finally came clean and told us that he was in love with Christine, we were all absolutely amazed. No, we were gobsmacked! Not, I hasten to add, because of Christine, who we all know is a fabulous lady in every respect, but because none of us at the flat could believe that Tony would suddenly change his life for one woman! But change it he has and with Christine by his side, Tony has become a new man. I know I say it for all of us, but only such a beautiful girl as Christine could have brought this transformation in Tony. I have already congratulated Tony. I said to him that you'll always look back on this day as the happiest day of your life.'

He looked over at Tony standing quietly beside Christine. 'That was yesterday, unfortunately the last day of his bachelor life,' said Chris raising his voice towards the end. There was a sympathetic burst of laughter, everyone looked over at Tony, who smiled weakly at Christine, both of them looking a little self-conscious. 'But seriously,' Chris continued, 'Tony is a man of many parts and I hope that at least <u>one</u> is still in working order after his stag party last night, a colourful event by any standards.'

Raz, Mike and Johnny let out little whoops, while Tony became distinctly uneasy at the reference to parts and colour as he still hadn't had an opportunity to tell Christine that he was now sporting black genitals and he was crawling with embarrassment desperately hoping that Chris would not mention it.

'There is a saying that a girl has to kiss a lot of frogs to find her prince and I'm sure that has been true for Christine, how much further she has gone I'm not really sure.' This last sentence drew some 'oohs' and 'aaahs' from the audience as Chris continued, 'Unfortunately Tony has also had to kiss a lot of frogs to find his princess, but not only that, he's kissed loads of spics and spades and wops and God knows who or what else during the time that I've known him.' More 'oohs' and 'aahs', but even louder this time. 'But now that they are joined together, it's been worth it for both of them.' Chris turned to address Christine, 'I can honestly say to you Christine, that Tony is a very good man and I'll say again that he's been a great friend and a wonderful companion and we shall miss him very much because he's become so much a part of our lives at Mawson Road. It's broken up our family; but, now, it's time for him to start a new family with you, so look after our buddy well, Christine. I know that you will.' Chris turned first to Tony and then to Christine, and smiled broadly, 'I wish you both, on behalf of everyone here, the greatest happiness in the future.'

Chris turned to the guests, surveyed the crowd, then turned back to the couple again and raised his glass, 'To Tony and Christine.'

'To Tony and Christine,' the assembly chorused loudly, sipping their champagne as one, then clapping and cheering appreciatively.

After the bridesmaids toast, Tony came over to Chris and clapped him on the back. 'Thanks Chris, that was very nice,' he said, relieved that Chris had not been too severe on him.

Tony then gave a very short thank you speech, which everyone applauded and glasses were raised again.

'That was a really good speech Chris,' said Mike, moving

over to speak to Chris. 'It went down very well.'

'Yes it did. I have to congratulate you too,' said a distinctive little voice behind Chris. He turned and was pleasantly surprised to find that Maria had also made her way back to him. As he was about to reply, Tony reappeared next to him.

'Thanks again Chris,' said Tony, 'that was really good fun. I feel great now too, no hangover at all. I just wanted to say thanks for everything, for the stag party, the car, all the jokes, arranging everything. It's been great, and we both really appreciate it.'

'That's OK Tony,' said Chris pleased that his friend was enjoying his big day. 'Christine OK?'

'Just look at her Chris, she's absolutely radiant. She enjoyed your speech too. We're off to change, so catch you later Chris, and you too Mike,' Tony said. Spotting his sister standing quietly behind Chris, he leaned across and hugged her, then kissed her full on the lips. 'You look gorgeous today Maria,' he told her, smiling broadly at her before turning to make his way back to Christine.

'She certainly does,' said Chris agreeably to Maria, feeling a strong desire for her stirring inside him as he gazed into her eyes. Maria was suddenly spirited off for a dance with Mario, Tony's brother, and Chris stood watching them dance, hoping that Mario wasn't warning her off him. He marvelled at her fine body. She certainly knew how to move it around.

When the newly-married couple had chatted for another few minutes to some of their guests and finished a couple of dances together, Tony kissed Christine delightedly and they took the opportunity to slip off to a small anteroom to change from their wedding finery into their going-away clothes. They were due to leave in about ninety minutes. Chris checked his watch and decided that it would soon be time to take the Rolls home and fetch Tony's Austin Healey back so that the flatmates could get to work on it.

Mike appeared hand-in-hand with Trisha, both perspiring a little from dancing. 'Another beer, Chris,' he said producing two cans from his jacket pocket. 'How are you getting on with Maria?'

'Very well,' said a female voice beside Chris. He turned quickly to find Maria standing there laughing; he felt a surge of pleasure at seeing her come back to him yet again after dancing with Mario. 'You were quite rude about my brother, but he seemed to enjoy it. I thought your speech was fun. I realise now that you must all make fun of each other all the time,' she said, grinning up at Chris warmly.

'Well, at last I've done something right in your eyes,' replied Chris trying not to sound sarcastic. 'You're a great dancer, Maria,' he told her sweetly.

'Don't forget to collect the car Chris,' interrupted Mike, checking his watch. 'I left all the gear in a bag in the hall.'

'OK,' said Chris. 'I'll take the Rolls back shortly.'

'I've never been in a Rolls Royce,' said Maria. 'I couldn't come with you could I?' she asked, her eyes shining up at him expectantly.

Her request made Chris ecstatic as he could now take her in the car and talk to her alone without the noise of the band and everyone else's conversations drowning them out and people interrupting them both all the time. 'Of course you can Maria,' he said. 'It's only a short ride and then I'm bringing Tony's car back here so that he and Christine can drive straight off, but at least you'll be able to say that you've been in a Rolls Royce.'

'It's also the cleanest it's ever been,' Mike told Maria, secretly worried that Chris might land himself in hot water as he could sense Maria was becoming very interested in Chris, and he in her, but for Chris to become involved with Tony's sister on this particular occasion might not be the most prudent move. 'We all spent ages polishing and waxing it and making the leather shine ready for today,' he told Maria. 'Chris doesn't always keep it looking quite like it does at the moment.'

Chris drained his beer, deciding to leave a little earlier than he had planned, eager to spend more time with Maria, hoping that they would enjoy talking together. 'Let's go Maria,' he said taking her arm, pleased that Tony and Christine were still changing in the anteroom and that both sets of parents were happily ensconced with groups of relatives and friends, so that hopefully they would not notice him leaving with Maria. He winked jauntily at Mike. 'See you later, Mike. Look after him, Trisha, get him out on the dance floor, he's a demon out there.'

'Don't be long,' mouthed Mike at Chris as Trisha led him

back to dance. The band had just starting playing a rendition of the Glenn Miller number, *Moonlight Serenade*, in an attempt to entice some of the older guests to get up and start dancing.

Chris took Maria outside where the Rolls sat parked at the kerbside. He shooed away a couple of teenage boys who were peering into the car, and they both got in. Chris drove the short distance to Mawson Road where he parked immediately behind Tony's Austin Healey. He smiled, picturing in his mind how the car would look when they had all finished decorating it. He briefly wondered how Tony would feel when he saw his beloved sports car desecrated; with that and his painted bollocks and the surprise with the plastic baby on his stag night, Tony would certainly remember his wedding, that was for certain!

'Well, at least I can say I've been in a Rolls Royce now,' said Maria happily, patting the shining walnut dashboard.

Chris turned to face her, feeling slightly nervous as he realised again how beautiful she was close up. He could feel his stomach churning as he looked directly into her eyes. 'Would you like to say that you'd been kissed in a Rolls Royce?' he asked her, a half smile playing on his lips as he searched her face for a reply.

Without speaking, Maria leant towards him, her hand reaching behind his neck as she pulled him towards her, hungrily pressing her mouth to his, her tongue probing deeply.

Chris, slightly taken aback by the swiftness of her reaction and surprised by the intensity of her kiss, nevertheless felt pure joy as he returned her kiss. He could smell the cleanness of her hair and the perfume she was wearing smelt exciting, it was a delicate smell, not over-powering like the stuff so many girls wore. They kissed again, harder and more passionately this time.

A family passed by on the pavement, parents with two young girls about four or five and a baby in a pram. The parents tried not to notice the couple in a clinch on the front seat, especially as the car still had the white ribbon strung across the bonnet. From the corner of his eye, Chris caught one of the girls peering in and suddenly felt very self-conscious as he heard the girl's father calling her away. He checked his watch, he had just over an hour before the couple were due to leave. 'Shall we pop into the flat and have a quick drink?' he suggested breathlessly to

Maria. 'Mike's left me a bag upstairs that I have to collect anyway.'

'OK,' replied Maria, checking her lipstick in the rear-view mirror. 'That sounds good, I'd love to see where my brother has lived all this time.'

Chris locked the car and they clambered up the stairs where Chris noticed the bag Mike had left for him sitting in the hall. He took Maria into the kitchen and poured them both a glass of wine from the remnants of a cold bottle of sauvignon in the fridge. She took the glass and wandered into the lounge, interested to look at the place where her brother had obviously enjoyed himself so much. Chris followed her down the hallway and opened the door to Tony's old room. 'This is where your brother lived,' he said. 'We haven't re-let the room yet.'

Maria walked slowly around the empty room, gazing intently at the four walls. It seemed to Chris that she was imagining her brother in the room and attempting to breathe its very atmosphere into her body.

'We each have our own room. Each one is completely different,' said Chris. 'Tony's was always very up-to-date. He had the most gorgeous furniture and he always had fresh flowers in here.'

'Yes, he's always been like that, very clean and tidy. What's your room like?' she asked him matter of factly.

'I'll show you. It's just next door,' said Chris, leading her out into the hall. She followed him as he opened the door to his room and let out a short gasp as she caught sight of the gleaming red and chrome dentist's chair sitting in the middle of the large room.

Chris laughed at her reaction, it was the same as most of the girls. He strode over to his hi-fi and put on a Billy Fury LP, comprising some great rock and several gorgeous love songs. Maria stood at the bay window, looking down into the street at the two cars parked below. She sipped her wine as Chris came up behind her and leaned down to gently kiss the nape of her neck. He felt her body shudder and she moaned a little with delight at his touch. She turned round to face him. He could almost feel the lust oozing out of her. The set of her eyes seemed to implore him to kiss her again. Acting suddenly, in a frenzy of passion, he lifted her up and carried her over to the bed, where he laid her down roughly and immediately they were rolling on top of each other, over and over, almost attacking each other, kissing and biting hungrily, like wild animals, as they pulled and tore at each other's clothing in their eagerness to get at each other's bodies. They flailed around frantically, both breathing heavily and uttering little cries of joy. In an instant Chris had entered her, his trousers caught tightly around his ankles, whilst Maria still had her skirt on, hiked uncomfortably around her waist. With such intense passion impeded by the awkward fumbling with their clothing, they had been unable to strip each other completely naked. Chris roughly ripped Maria's blouse open and enveloped his head between her breasts, kissing and sucking feverishly as she cried out in delight. He pounded into her furiously, shouting out unrecognisable words, trying not to let the discomfort of their half-clothed bodies upset him. Suddenly he realised that he could not stop himself coming and he drove more deeply into her, pounding, pounding until he came violently and intensely, letting out a loud cry of pleasure. He realised that she was coming at the same time. He felt her body rocking maniacally backwards and forwards, beadlets of sweat running between her breasts as her muscles became taut, her fingertips clawing desperately at his back as she strained to hold him deep inside her. Her nails dug into his flesh as she came in several intense spasms, screaming out loudly with the intensity of the pleasure she felt, coursing like hot needles through her body.

They collapsed, spent and gasping for air, sweating profusely, chests heaving. They turned onto their backs, still partially clothed and desperately hot, feeling the warm glow of intense pleasure and relief flooding through their bodies. They lay inert, feeling lifeless, devoid of energy for several minutes until Chris, having managed to regain his normal breathing pattern, leant over Maria and kissed first her breast and then her lips. 'Phew, that was fantastic,' he told her in a hoarse whisper, wiping the tiny beads of perspiration from her top lip and caressing her damp hair.

'And for me too,' she told him softly, endeavouring to pull her crumpled skirt down from around her waist. Her panties lay tangled around her right foot, whilst she had one arm in and one arm out of her blouse, which was now very creased and lying entangled beneath her.

Something jolted Chris's memory, causing a feeling of sheer panic to engulf him. He checked his watch and jumped off the bed and began rapidly pulling up his trousers and pants. 'Oh, shit,' he cried anxiously. 'Come on Maria, we've got to get Tony's car back to the reception in fifteen minutes or I'll be slaughtered.'

Maria had just wanted to lie with Chris and savour the warm feelings flooding through her loins, but hearing Chris's voice interrupt her relaxed mood, immediately understood Chris's urgency and the need for them both to return to the reception, as she leapt from the bed and began dressing herself as quickly as she could. A look of horror crossed her face as she realised how creased her clothes were. She made desperate attempts to smooth the creases as she dressed herself.

Both of them were hot and sweaty and flushed as they tried to make themselves presentable. Chris felt himself shaking, a reaction to the abrupt change of mood that had occurred with them both having to leap up from the bed. He wondered if he had been a little rash in seducing Maria. Or had she seduced him? No, let's be truthful, it had been instant and mutual lust and desire for each other and it had been wonderful! Chris became concerned that they now had to return to the reception, both looking as though they had been rolling around in their clothes. They didn't even have time to iron out some of the worst creases. He helped Maria to smooth and straighten her clothes as best he could and pulled his own clothes along the seams running his hot hands over the creases in a vain attempt to eradicate them. 'Come on Maria,' he urged, giving her a quick kiss on the cheek. He took her hand and led her rapidly down the hall, remembering to pick up the bag of goodies on the way.

They rushed downstairs, slammed the front door and ran across the road to Tony's green sports car. Chris hurriedly turned the key in the ignition. Luckily the engine roared into life immediately and within two minutes they drew up outside the reception hall. They both jumped out of the car and Chris told Maria to go ahead of him, so she hurried back into the hall alone.

Chris gave her about twenty seconds and then followed her into the hall where he desperately looked over the crowd to try and find Mike and Raz. He noticed several people gazing in his direction and wondered if they were talking about him. Surely they hadn't been missed in that short time?

All of a sudden Mr. and Mrs. Santiago were by his side, dragging Maria along roughly, demanding to know where she had been. Her face was still shiny and flushed from the passionate encounter, but she stood her ground well, explaining that she had just gone with Chris to collect Tony's car and that they'd had a little problem starting it. Chris, realising that Maria had cleverly made up the story, backed her up by stating that Maria had helped him push the car to get it going. Mr. Santiago growled and scratched his head, feeling uncertain, whilst Mrs. Santiago stood looking at her daughter in a very concerned manner.

Mr. Santiago turned to glare again at Chris, then rapidly pulled him out of earshot of the others, thrusting a large, banana-like finger under his nose. 'If you have touched my daughter this day, I will kill you,' he seethed. Several of the guests had gathered round them, wondering what was happening.

'It's all right, Dad, Chris has been a perfect gentleman,' cried Maria, butting in between them. For the second time that day, Chris realised that Maria was a strong woman who would not let people step on her. She could certainly stand up for herself that was for sure, he liked that in a woman.

At that moment, Raz, obviously much the worse for wear, staggered over, his smile beaming away as always. 'Chris, old chap, where have you been, I've been looking everywhere for you, you rascal you.'

Chris groaned to himself in disbelief. Raz was plastered and obviously completely oblivious to the situation. Mrs. Santiago glared at her daughter and then glowered at Chris, disbelief etched in every furrow of her face. It was exactly what she had expected of Tony's friends, first bringing her son to his own wedding late, looking ill and haggard and obviously still drunk and only just arriving in time. He'd smelt of beer when he arrived, all those wretched boys had! And now, her beloved eldest daughter was caught up with one of them. She certainly seemed very flustered, but surely nothing could have happened in just a few minutes?

'Raz, I've been to collect Tony's car. Luckily Maria came with me for a ride in the Rolls,' Chris said quickly. 'We had trouble starting it and Maria had to push it,' lied Chris. 'The car's outside now ready for us to do our bit,' he added very slowly for Raz's benefit.

Raz glanced at Maria, noticing her flushed cheeks and creased blouse, and saw the displeasure showing on the faces of Tony's parents. He realised something odd had happened, even though he was so drunk. 'Aah, we often have to push that car, it's very hard work indeed, so well done Maria,' he stammered, trying to do his best to help Chris out. He smiled one of his biggest smiles, the real white tooth flasher and took Mr. Santiago by the arm. 'Chris,' he slurred, 'you've not only given Tony a wonderful night yesterday, lent him the Rolls for his wedding and given Maria a ride in it too, but then you and Maria have both got his car started and delivered it here too so that Tony and Christine can set off on their honeymoon. What a great gesture, don't you agree Mr. Santiago. I think he deserves many congratulations for his efforts.' Raz staggered a little unsteadily and patted Chris heavily on the back as some of the people gathered around them started clapping and cheering.

Mike appeared from the middle of the pack of dancers, perspiration running in rivulets down his face from his exertions. 'Got the bag, Chris?' he asked quietly as he wiped the sweat from his forehead with the sleeve of his shirt, oblivious to what had been going on.

'Yeah, I did,' replied Chris, glad of the opportunity that Raz had given him to change the conversation. 'We've got just ten minutes to go, so may I suggest we get on with it. It looks like they're just about to have their last dance,' he said, catching sight of Tony and Christine taking to the dance floor.' Turning to Tony's parents he added, 'if you'll excuse us, we have one more thing to do for Tony and Christine.'

Mr. Santiago appeared bemused, the wind completely taken out of his sails by Raz's congratulatory praise for Chris. Raz had made some sense, Chris had obviously done quite a bit for his son, but going off with his daughter? He glanced over at Maria, talking earnestly with her friends. She looked a picture of happiness. They could only have been gone for half-an-hour, that was no time at all. Maria would not have done anything surely? OK, she looks a little flushed, but they had both said that she'd had to push the car. 'OK, boys,' he relented, patting Chris on the arm as a friendly gesture, 'don't forget they are leaving in ten minutes.' Lowering his voice, to Chris he added, 'thank you for helping my boy, I'm sorry I got upset.' Then, turning back to Maria who was still chattering away to her friends, he called to her, 'Maria,' raising his arms to embrace her as she came over to him. He told her, 'I'm sorry. Forgive me my dear?' She nodded and kissed his cheek tenderly.

Chris grinned at Mr. Santiago, nodded his head briefly towards Mrs. Santiago and glanced again at Maria, who had returned to chat to her group of friends. She puckered her lips in a kissing motion and grinned back at him happily. Chris turned and quickly followed Mike and Raz out of the hall. Mike delved into the car and brought out the bag. He unzipped the top and brought out a vast selection of items to decorate the car with. Firstly, there was a banner three feet long which he quickly attached to the aerial. The banner read, 'With you in spirit, your pals Raz, Chris and Mike'. There were several bags of marbles which they scattered on the floor of the car and in the boot. They used shaving foam to write messages on the bodywork and strung long strings of old tin cans to the chassis and bumper, which were then discreetly hidden under the car.

Several days before Mike had purloined a smelly kipper from the fishmonger which he now laid on the exhaust pipe and tied in place with wire. Chris and Raz tied long, brightly coloured streamers and ribbons to the door handles and the spoked wheels. With a huge, but unnecessary, JUST MARRIED sign stuck across the boot, the original paintwork on the car could barely be seen. They wrapped some condoms around the bottom of the aerial and a paperback book called *How to Improve your Sex Life* was placed on the passenger seat. On Tony's seat they placed a scrubbing brush, a packet of washing powder and some soap, just to remind him that there was the small matter of his black bits to contend with later.

Chris, who was dying for a leak, went back into the hall to

301

use the cloakroom. As he entered the toilet his heart almost missed a beat when he found Tony standing there having a piss, his black cock looked so odd lying in his white hand, that Chris could hardly suppress his desire to start laughing again. Tony, now changed into a smart blue lounge suit, glanced at Chris in the mirror as Chris stood beside him peeing. 'Chris, thanks for everything. It's been a great day for Christine and myself, and all the guests have had a great time. There is one thing though, I heard you took my sister for a ride in the Rolls. I just want you to tell me that you didn't shag her, that's all.' Tony turned to face Chris, buttoning his fly as he did so, his eyes appealing to Chris to tell him the truth.

'No, of course I didn't shag her,' lied Chris, for it was the only answer he could give, especially at this moment. He could not upset his best friend now, just before his honeymoon. 'I took her for a quick ride to pick up your car and then we came back here.'

'Oh, I knew you wouldn't, especially on my special day', said Tony, relief showing in his eyes as he clapped his arm around Chris's shoulders even though Chris was still peeing. 'Well, it's time for Christine and I to leave, so the car's all ready outside with the keys?' he asked, walking to the door.

'Yeah, it is Tony. I'll be with you shortly,' grinned Chris, somewhat devastated that he'd had to lie to his best friend and feeling pangs of guilt that he had really and truly fucked Tony's sister, not on any day, but on this his wedding day. But, somehow, another feeling crept in to disturb his emotions, it was elation, it was ecstasy! Christ, how he had enjoyed fucking Maria. The suddenness of it all, the lust, the heat, the animal passion, the intensity of his coming and of having her come at the same moment too. It was something he would remember all his life whatever else happened. He looked down at his cock lying limply in his fingers, still red and tender and with the smell of Maria on his genitals rising to catch his nostrils, mixed with the stink of warm urine as he pissed away the day's booze. He wondered how she was feeling now and whether her parents would give her a hard time. But she had proved she was tough. She had denied it in front of them both. She wouldn't let on, he was certain of that. He wondered if he would ever see her again after today, knowing that it would be difficult because she was

Tony's sister and how unfavourably Tony would react to them both if he ever found out. His thoughts turned again to the image of Christine catching sight of Tony's black cock and balls later that evening. He had to stop himself laughing out loud. If only he could be there, Christ, what a laugh it would be!

He zipped up his fly, doused his hands with hot water and straightened his tie, then tried to smooth out a couple of bad creases in his trousers. To calm himself, he took out a cigarette, lit it and took a deep drag, peering critically at himself in the mirror. 'I lied to Tony,' he said. 'You bastard,' he hissed quietly at his reflection in the mirror. Better go and see them off now he decided, then it will be time for another drink with Mike and Raz and maybe I might be able to fix it to see Maria again sometime soon.

Chapter Thirty-Seven

Several days after the trauma of the wedding, Mike and Chris sat smoking and chatting in the lounge one evening wondering how Tony was enjoying his honeymoon and debating about what might have happened when Christine eventually discovered his black dick. They were also keenly discussing the 'Ban the Bomb' marches taking place around Britain and arguing over whether or not they should take part. Raz was well over an hour late and they were waiting impatiently for him as they were all going out to eat at the Eros, a cheap and cheerful Greek restaurant in the centre of town, and both of them were starving.

They heard the front door slam and the pounding of Raz's footsteps as he hurried up the stairs and came down the hallway. As he appeared in the doorway of the lounge, both Mike and Chris immediately sat up in alarm at the Sikh's appearance. His brow was deeply furrowed and his heavily bloodshot eyes gave evidence of some deep anguish. He seemed to be about to break down in tears. He stood staring vacantly down at them, slightly out of breath, holding onto the doorframe for support. Even his clothes were dishevelled, his collar unbuttoned and his tie askew. His mouth hung open, his lips were shaking so badly it seemed as though he would not be able to speak.

Mike, realising that something terrible had happened, jumped up from his chair and put his arm consolingly around Raz's shoulder. He led him over to the sofa and sat down with him. Mike and Chris had never seen Raz like this before. He was always in such a good humour, he was the self-appointed court jester of their group, laughing and joking all the time, flashing his huge smile at everyone.

'What's up Raz,' asked Mike, feeling extremely concerned for his friend. 'What's happened?'

'It's my father. I've just heard that he's gravely ill. He's been diagnosed with terminal cancer,' sobbed Raz, his eyes flooding with tears before they streamed uncontrollably down his cheeks. 'My mother and my young sisters need me there, so I've got to go up to London to help care for him. He could die within a month or it could go on and on according to the doctors.' He buried his head against Mike's chest, his huge shoulders heaving and shaking as the tension inside him poured out in his grief.

Since Raz had become an integral part of their lives, the others had never seen him lose his temper or even become annoyed at anything much and for them to see him so distraught was terribly upsetting for them both. 'Raz, we're so sorry,' murmured Chris, feeling inadequate, knowing that whatever either of them said could not be enough.

As Mike sat cradling Raz's grief-stricken body in his arms trying desperately to comfort him, wishing that there was something else he could do or say, he suddenly realised that this was the final straw - their lives were never going to be the same again. The death knell was ringing for them, their comradeship and their brotherhood was falling apart. The party that they had enjoyed so much was coming to an end. First it had been Tony who had left, now it was Raz being forced to go. He glanced at Chris sitting uncomfortably in his chair, staring at the ground helplessly, obviously terribly upset by the news Raz had received. Mike wondered if Chris realised what was happening to them, he was good at keeping his feelings to himself sometimes. But Chris suddenly covered his head with his hands and instinctively Mike had the feeling that Chris had realised that with Tony gone and now with Raz having to leave in such distressing circumstances, their whole lifestyle was about to change. Their world was literally falling apart, but what was particularly devastating for Mike was the news that only he knew about. That morning at work he had been told that he was being transferred to London together with several other members of staff to set up their new office in Kensington. He had been intending to choose an apt moment to tell Chris and Raz at dinner later that evening but now events meant that those plans would not materialise as Raz needed all their attention and compassion at this sad moment.

Gradually Raz's sobbing subsided. Chris went into the

kitchen and made some strong sweet tea which made Raz feel considerably better as they all sat and drank it together. 'I'm very sorry for my emotional outburst, it's just that my father suffered so much when the family had to leave Uganda. We lost our house and our business and my father had to work so hard to put me through university, but it's very unworthy of a Sikh to show emotion like this,' said Raz, wiping his eyes dry.

Chris noticed the dark rings that had appeared underneath Raz's eyes. 'Don't worry Raz, anyone would be upset at this news, but if there's anything or anyway in which we can help, you must let us know,' pleaded Chris. 'We're your friends and always will be and that's what friends are for.'

Raz's eyes filled with tears again, but he bravely held them back as he took another mouthful of his tea. 'I know, Chris,' he said, looking up at his two friends. 'You and Mike have been so good for me, asking me to share your home initially. We've had such bloody good fun. I'll never forget the times that we've shared together. I hope that I'll come back to Cambridge again someday and we can share some good times again.'

Mike lowered his gaze, looking down disconsolately at the carpet, knowing realistically that things would and never could be the same again. He wondered how and when he would be able to tell Chris of his own impending departure. Now that they had both been so badly upset by Raz's misfortune, how could he possibly follow that up with further bad news? It was bad enough keeping it to himself, but to tell Chris, whom he had shared so much with, who had inspired him and given him all the confidence in the world and who had suggested that they share together in the first place, how would he tell him now? Chris was going to be left alone as everyone else departed for their different reasons. Chris had been like an elder brother to him, forcing him out from under the carapace that he'd hidden beneath. It was Chris who had believed in Mawson Road at first sight, he had somehow known that it would turn out to be the ideal place for them. Then they had found Raz, and then Tony, and it had turned out to be the best years of his life. He knew Chris, perhaps more than any of them, had revelled in the crazy life that they had enjoyed together. He had been the catalyst, leading them, steering them, cajoling them into the mad whirlwind of fun that they had all enjoyed together. Chris had been their leader, although he was a pack animal too, but he still needed people around him, which was why their beloved flat had worked so well, with the four of them linking together so completely.

With a deep sigh, Raz placed his empty mug on the table and stood up slowly. 'Thanks boys,' he said quietly, almost in a whisper, 'I think I'll start packing my stuff and then clean my room. I'll have to leave first thing in the morning. I don't feel up to driving tonight.'

'OK Raz, but if you need any help, just give one of us a shout,' replied Chris.

Raz ambled slowly down the hall as Mike and Chris stared sadly at his retreating back, desperately sorry to see him so upset and unhappy. At that moment Mike suddenly decided that it was the right time to tell Chris that he had to leave. His instinct told him that he had to tell all and get it over and done with before he exploded with the effort of withholding it. 'Chris,' he mumbled quietly, finding it a struggle to meet his friend's gaze. 'I'm afraid I've got more bad news. I'm having to move to London in a few weeks. I'm being transferred to our new office and there's nothing I can do about it. I only heard about it this morning and I was going to tell you and Raz about it at dinner, but now there's no dinner and Raz is going off anyway.'

Just for a split second, Mike thought he saw Chris's eyelid flutter, then his eyes seemed to glaze over for a couple of seconds as he took in the news. His brow furrowed as he stared down at the floor. Mike could tell that he was very upset, but that he was trying to keep his composure. He looked up at Mike and shook his head. 'Oh God,' he groaned, 'everything's gone complete shit-faced now.' He held his head in his hands as he digested this further disclosure from Mike.

Mike shifted uncomfortably. He felt his throat drying up and it seemed that all this extreme sadness had completely engulfed both his body and his mind. He had hoped to feel some relief by telling Chris the news early, but he felt much worse now as he realised the reality of the whole episode; it was completely draining him emotionally and he was powerless to stop it. 'I'm really sorry Chris. You know I don't want to leave or let you down,' explained Mike. 'But it's my future,' he added, shrugging his shoulders almost as though he disbelieved what he was saying.

Chris looked up from the floor, his face looked drained and pale. 'You don't have to explain or excuse anything Mike. At some point it had to happen,' said Chris weakly. 'Let's face it, our whole thing together is finished. Tony's got married, Raz has to leave because of his Dad and you have to move for your work. This place, our life, it's all just come to an end. It could never be the same even if I stay here and get some new flatmates, it would never feel right. People have to move on in their lives for different reasons and I guess now must be the time for me to move on too.' He leaned forward, drained his tea, stubbed out his cigarette and rose up from his chair. 'I guess it's time to become responsible,' shrugged Chris, trying to force a smile. 'I just hope that Raz is going to be OK. Do you think we ought to go down to his room?'

'No,' replied Mike. 'Leave him, he may want to be on his own for a while. He knows we're here for him if he needs us. May be we could take him for a beer later if he's up to it.'

Chris took two steps forward, reached out with both arms and closed them around Mike, engulfing him in a hefty bear-hug. Mike returned the embrace, trying to steel himself to stem the tears that he could feel welling up ready to cascade from his eyes. His spectacles clouded over as Chris held him tightly.

'I'm really going to miss you Chris. We've had such a great time together,' Mike said, his voice sounding husky as he almost choked the words out.

'I know Mike, it's the end of an era, our own era. But we'll always be friends, keep in touch, meet up whenever we can, all that usual bloody rubbish, won't we,' Chris demanded earnestly.

'Yeah, we must,' muttered Mike as Chris relaxed his embrace, their male bonding completed, their future friendship assured in the committed but uneasy manner men have when displaying deep emotions in front of one another.

'So, it's down to the Six Bells a bit later and we'll ask Raz if he feels OK to come along, yeah?' asked Chris, attempting to cheer them both up.

'OK,' replied Mike who suddenly felt an unexpected wave of

relief flooding through him now that Chris knew he was leaving. 'Let's carry on where we left off,' he replied, forcing a strained smile at Chris's back as he carried the dirty mugs into the kitchen. Mike knew even then that it was a hollow gesture, they could never repeat the life that they had enjoyed so much, all they could do was to make the best of what little time they had left together.

Chapter Thirty-Eight

Some thirty years later, one cold February night shortly after the millennium celebrations for the year 2000, Chris lay tossing and turning in his luxury king-size bed, unable to sleep, recalling the memories of the idyllic times spent with his friends during those crazy days of the late 'sixties', as he had nostalgically recalled them a thousand times before. Astonishingly, Chris had remained in Cambridge since the break-up of the group at the Mawson Road flat, apart from an enjoyable period of eighteen months spent travelling around the world. He had often thought of moving away, but something had always pulled at his heartstrings and kept him living and working in the city. He liked the familiarity and the easy laid-back lifestyle of the university city. He had been married briefly at the age of thirty-three to a volatile girl called Elaine Parker, until a traumatic accident where he had flattened her prized Persian cat whilst reversing into his garage one evening, when the cat had apparently been stretching out behind the car. Unfortunately, the cat hadn't heeded the vehicle's approach and unable to see it in the dark, Chris had squashed it as flat as a pancake. The ensuing argument that developed had been so serious, with Elaine smashing almost everything breakable in the house and blaming Chris for everything under the sun, that the incident ended with Chris leaving their house, never to return. They had divorced two years later.

Chris remembered that dramatic day over thirty years ago when Raz, grief stricken with the news of his father's illness, had told Mike and himself that he had to leave to look after his ailing father. Shortly afterwards Mike had also told him that he had to move to London with his job, and he had been utterly devastated for some time afterwards. He remembered sitting alone in the empty flat three weeks later, having just said goodbye to Mike,

310

who had finished packing his belongings in his car and had left for London. There were just the ghosts of the others and the fond memories of their time together to keep him company. He had stayed awake throughout that lonely night, chain-smoking the Pall Mall cigarettes that he often obtained from his American GI friends, and managing to finish a couple of bottles of Bulls Blood, feeling as though he had been torn apart and wondering what the hell he was going to do with the rest of his life. The sense that the other three were still in the flat kept pervading his thoughts. Several times he had imagined that he had heard Raz's bellowing laugh ricochet off the sad walls and resonate down the hallway.

The next day, Chris handed the flat keys over to the agents, who had presented him with a bill for repairs and decoration, including renewal of the wash basin and pipework, which were the result of the damage incurred during the fiasco when he had shagged Françoise on the washbasin a couple of years before.

Chris had moved alone into a small rented flat situated just off Huntingdon Road, keeping on at his job with the office furniture company. He decided that he should save hard for a deposit on a house of his own, so he sold his beloved hearse which was expensive to maintain and bought a small economical Ford. He also sold his dentists chair, which was well past its sell-by date, to a young guy who was setting up a hairdressers business in King Street. Whenever Chris passed the small salon after that, he couldn't help but smile to himself when he saw someone having a haircut and knowing what had happened in that chair over the years.

Within a year he had purchased a small house in nearby Canterbury Street and fitted it out with very modern furnishings. He acquired a bright red E-type Jaguar convertible and resumed his old lifestyle, albeit this time rather more flamboyantly, running around town pulling women and sleeping with as many as he could possibly seduce. He became something of a small-time playboy; he had the money, the house, the car and the charisma. He became bosom buddies with Johnny, the group's old friend, who like Chris, had done well in his career. When his best friend Mark had left to work in the USA, Johnny had bought a small flat of his own. He had also bought himself a

311

flash Jensen Interceptor and, adopting the same lifestyle as Chris, they often went around together, trawling the pubs and clubs like predators, looking for women to pick-up. It had evolved into a lifestyle that Chris could not tear himself away from, it was almost like an addiction.

Chris had wondered on many occasions why he had never felt the need to remarry, though he still felt the urge to flirt with and seduce pretty women, even at his age. Was he immature? Possibly he was. Was it his primitive urges that made him unable to settle down? Maybe he was incapable of settling into a monogamous relationship. Anyway, whatever it was, he had never been able to stifle the excitement he felt when his eyes alighted upon a pretty girl and the incessant desire to seduce women had never deserted him. He had to admit to himself, it was like a disease, he just loved fucking women. These days, if a women wasn't available, he masturbated or rang a number for telephone sex. Hell, was that so bad? A little sad possibly, he admitted to himself. He wondered if his old friends were still as rampant as they all used to be, certainly the married friends that he knew these days seemed to get out of the habit of regular sex soon after they became married. That knowledge had helped to put him off any further long-term relationships, especially since his disastrous marriage to Elaine.

Chris remembered very well that after the group's break-up, he had attempted to keep in touch with the rest of the boys. He had been invited to dinner by Tony and Christine several times, but he still suffered terrible feelings of guilt about his sexual encounter with Tony's sister Maria at his wedding and the lie that he had been forced to tell Tony. He had even seen Maria secretly several times after the wedding to attempt to renew the frenzied passion of their frantic sexual encounter, but eventually Maria had to return to Italy with her sister Gina to continue their studies. The last time he had heard from her, she had become engaged to a fashion designer from Milan. He wondered to himself whether the guilt he felt had helped to distance himself from Tony, but then Tony had changed so drastically since he had met Christine that Chris decided it was nothing to do with his own feelings. Tony was a man completely besotted with his wife, a man so changed that Chris could only watch in disbelief

312

as they fussed over one another in his company. It sometimes made him feel so uncomfortable that he wondered how long such a relationship could possibly last. Tony never even wanted to go to the pub and talk men-talk as they always had in the past. 'Let's just open a bottle here, shall we Chris,' he would suggest, snuggling up to Christine on their sofa at home and passing the glasses around. Within a year of their marriage, Christine had become pregnant and the last time Chris had visited them, when she had just had the baby, a boy, Tony and Christine had sat on the sofa together, billing and cooing like a couple of love-birds. This odd behaviour went on for so long that however much he tried, he couldn't start a proper conversation with them. Their unsociable attitude had made him feel so uncomfortable, almost bordering on nausea in fact, that he had made an excuse and left. After that last meeting he had never been able to come to terms with the change in his old friend and he had not seen the couple since.

At first, Chris and Mike would often visit each other. Chris liked travelling up to London and spending a wild weekend with Mike visiting new bars and discos. In Cambridge, they would trawl around all their old haunts together. But, after a year or so, Mike, now fully qualified, had been offered a unique opportunity in Edinburgh and had decided after much thought to accept the partnership he had been offered. Shortly after moving there, he had met a local girl and within six months he was married. Chris had again been asked to be the best man and had travelled up to Edinburgh with Tony and Christine for the occasion. Unfortunately, Raz had been unable to attend the wedding. Mike had then settled down happily and the couple had two children within as many years.

Shortly after Mike's wedding, the others had all received the news that Raz's father had died, and soon afterwards Raz had been offered a great opportunity in Canada working in the computer industry and he had emigrated there three months later.

Somehow over the years the four friends had all slowly lost contact with each other and, as Chris lay in bed wistfully recalling the old days, he wondered how the others were now, were they happy, were they fulfilled, did they sometimes sit and recall those golden years that they had spent together? Chris had never managed to forget because, since those days, he had never experienced quite the same joy, the same spontaneity, the freedom and the comradeship that had been so much a part of their lives. That period had overshadowed everything else that had followed in his own life. He had certainly enjoyed most of his life since then, but it had never been as exhilarating as those days had been. He often wondered if he had made a mistake by staying in Cambridge where the ghosts of the past were always present to haunt him, or whether it was because he had never remarried and had never been fulfilled in that respect.

Chris had last seen Mike some fifteen years ago when he had journeyed up to Edinburgh and stayed with his family for a long weekend. During those few days, Chris had sensed that relations were somewhat strained between Mike and his wife, but it was alarming to see the change in his old comrade, to see how serious and politically correct Mike had become. It was as though the responsibility of both his marriage and his new job had drained the humorous qualities out of his life. Chris had found it difficult to laugh and joke with him during his visit and it had almost felt like being with a stranger. But how was he today, Chris wondered? Would he seem any happier now? Did he have any more children? Perhaps he would have a bigger house and a more expensive car, but would his enjoyment of life have been erased yet further? Chris felt he would dearly love to satisfy his curiosity, to see dear old Mike again.

Chris's thoughts turned to Tony and Christine. He recalled that in about 1974 Tony had relinquished the lease on his Cambridge salon when the university, who owned the building, had greedily raised the rent to an unrealistic level. Soon afterwards, Tony had been offered an incredible opportunity in Birmingham. A hairdresser who owned two salons had gone bust and Tony had bought the business on a whim. Shortly afterwards Tony and Christine had moved up to the Midlands, taking their two children with them. Chris still exchanged a Christmas card with them every year, but he had made no real contact for over twenty years.

What would the old crowd look like now Chris wondered? They must at least still be alive, surely he would have heard if any of them had died or had contracted some dreadful debilitating disease or illness. Christ, they were all getting on a bit now, anything could happen to any one of them at any time, especially at their age, but wouldn't it be wonderful to get everyone together again, laughing and joking, recalling the women and the parties, the madness and the joy of that time together? What would they all think about life today and all the changes that had occurred? Chris had always held some fairly definite and well-argued theories about most things, he had always loved the constant debate and occasional heated arguments that they had all taken part in during those heady 'sixties years, but the world had changed drastically over the thirty-odd years in between. How had his friends coped with it? Did they yearn for the freedom of the old days, or had they simply taken the many advances in their stride? He wondered why they had not made more of an effort to keep in touch, other than the annual Christmas card? Had they all pushed the memories of him to one side, he wondered, immediately feeling sorry for himself. But he could not stop feeling more and more curious about his old friends and, the more he recalled the memories, the stronger the desire became to try and see them all again.

With his enthusiasm fired up, Chris determined to make an effort to contact the old flatmates and attempt to gather them all together for a grand reunion. He would need to spend some time on the 'phone and arrange a suitable time and place for everyone to meet. God knows what they were all up to now. How the hell would he find Raz, would he still be living in Canada and, if so, where? Still, in the modern world, the world of the computer and the internet, anything is possible, Chris reasoned. But, if he did find Raz, would he want to come all that way to meet his old friends again? That might be a stumbling block, but Chris simply viewed that as a hurdle to overcome; surely Raz would want to see everyone again?

Chris suddenly felt very tired, he lay back in his bed and yawned loudly, then almost immediately fell asleep, dreaming of the reunion and trying to picture what his old friends would look like after all these years.

The following evening, the idea having gained momentum as Chris's thoughts about the reunion became more positive during his working day, he decided to contact Raz first. He looked out his battered address books from that period which he had kept stored away for nostalgic reasons. He found the old address of Raz's parents and though realising that the family would most probably have moved, he rang Directory Enquiries. Much to his surprise and delight he was given a new telephone number for the old address, so obviously someone in the family, possibly Raz's mother, still lived at their old home. He rang the number and a male voice answered, who turned out to be the husband of one of Raz's sisters who now lived in the house with Raz's mother. She was extremely pleased to hear from one of Raz's old friends and after a short chat, she willingly gave Chris Raz's telephone number in Canada.

Much later that evening to take into account the time difference, Chris nervously rang the number. When he heard Raz's distinctive voice answer the 'phone, sounding exactly the same after all these years, Chris felt over the moon as the memories flooded back. After the usual pleasantries and exchanges, Chris found out that Raz had been married but that his first wife had died leaving him with two children, but he had since remarried and had produced two more children. He now owned a small computer company and was just about to retire, but the news that excited Chris the most was that Raz was due to travel to Britain on business in about three months time. Raz was looking forward to visiting England for the first time in twenty years. When Chris explained the reason for his call, Raz's great laugh boomed down the line, agreeing with Chris that it was a wonderful idea. Apparently Raz quite often sat and thought about his old friends and remembered the good old days. He told Chris that he would be both curious and excited to see the others after all this time. They agreed to meet up on the Saturday on the first week in June at their beloved old local, The Live and Let Live, at precisely 11 o'clock when the pub opened that day.

Chris fervently hoped that the other two could be contacted and that both of them would be able to make the agreed date. The following afternoon he rang Mike first at his home, the answering machine informing him of Mike's office and mobile numbers. He rang the office and was immediately put through to Mike who was both flabbergasted and delighted to hear from Chris after such a long period.

'It's really been too long,' Mike said and Chris could tell that he meant it, the affection in his voice was obvious.

Chris explained to Mike what he was attempting to do and Mike immediately accepted the invitation, together with Chris's offer of a bed for the night at his house in Cambridge. Chris did not stay long on the 'phone as Mike seemed to be very busy, so he decided to wait to hear all his news when they all met up together.

Chris then rang Tony, who was also overjoyed to hear from him, while Christine kept butting in excitedly from the extension 'phone which she had picked-up when she discovered that it was Chris on the line. Tony told Chris that he wouldn't miss the reunion for anything but that he would have to make arrangements for someone to oversee his salons; he now had four salons situated in the Birmingham area and Saturdays were his busiest day of the week. Tony began firing questions at Chris about Mike and Raz, but Chris could not really tell him much, not having seen them himself for such a long time. Tony decided that he would turn it into a long weekend so that they could also visit Christine's parents, who had moved to Bedford. Tony told Chris that both his parents had since died. The mention of them immediately caused Chris's thoughts to turn to Maria, but he decided that she probably had a handful of grown-up children by now and might even look like the back of a bus, it was amazing how some people went downhill as they got older.

Replacing the receiver after chatting to Tony and confirming the time and date of the reunion, Chris sat quietly contemplating their future meeting together. He felt extremely excited and very pleased that the other three could all make it. To hear their familiar voices again had been a real tonic and from the brief conversation he'd had with each of them, they all seemed to be fit and healthy and they had all appeared delighted that he had taken the trouble to 'phone out of the blue and arrange the reunion for them all.

Chapter Thirty-Nine

Some weeks later, on the Friday evening just a few hours before the reunion was due to take place, Chris lay uneasily in bed with a married woman that he had met a couple of weeks before, completely unable to concentrate on making love to her. His mind was elsewhere, constantly worrying about how the old gang would get on together after all these years.

The woman began annoying Chris as she desperately tried to get his attention, her mouth busy around his cock, her hands wandering sexily over his body. 'Look, I'm sorry, I've just got things on my mind,' he told her, pushing her firmly away from him, conscious that he was probably hurting her feelings.

'Is it me,' she asked nervously, recoiling from him and covering her breasts self-consciously under the sheet.

'No, it's nothing to do with you love. I'm meeting up with some old friends tomorrow. I haven't seen them for years and I'm bloody nervous about it, that's all. I really need to catch some shut-eye, if that's OK?' Chris leaned over and kissed her tenderly, hoping that she understood. He switched the bedside light off and turned away from her to lie on his front, cuddling the pillow tightly against his face. He lay thinking, apprehensive and uncertain, but still pleased that he had instigated the meeting. He was so nervous and excited that it took some time before he fell asleep and, even then, he dreamt of the many exploits that the four of them had been involved in all those years ago.

Chapter Forty

'Chris!' cried Mike, leaning out of his car window when he spotted Chris about to enter the door of the pub, as he searched for a parking space.

'Hi Mike,' yelled Chris joyfully, turning and striding quickly over to the car and pumping Mike's hand furiously.

Mike found a space and climbed out of the car. Chris noted approvingly the brand new BMW M3, obviously Mike had done well. He looked Mike up and down and noticed that Mike, thinner than Chris remembered him, had kept all his hair, although it was cut short now, and he wore a pair of the new trendy rectangular Armani spectacles. He was dressed casually in a linen jacket and trousers and a button-down shirt.

Chris was dressed in the blue jeans and sweatshirt that he had favoured all his life.

'You look good Mike,' said Chris, noticing that Mike's face was relatively unlined; he appeared carefree and relaxed, a big difference to the last time Chris had seen him.

'And you look pretty good yourself, you old bugger. You've hardly aged at all!' said Mike, smiling affectionately at Chris. Chris still had a good complexion and, although he had a few laughter lines etched heavily into his face and he had put on a little extra weight, he was still in pretty good shape.

Chris and Mike entered the pub, which although almost unchanged on the outside, was now completely different to how Mike remembered it. The radical change had included the demolishing of the small snug bar and the complete relining of the walls with old floorboards and the installation of gas lighting. The walls were covered in bric-a-brac and pictures. It was quite a change from the sad state the pub had been in when they all used it so often in the 'sixties when they had lived only a hundred yards away. 'Wow, what a change,' enthused Mike as

Chris ordered two beers from the selection of real ales at the bar.

The door opened and Raz appeared. The other two were shocked to see that he had become grossly overweight and was seriously balding, with the little hair that he had left peppered with grey. His face had filled out considerably, so that his cheeks were quite jowled and he had developed a double chin. 'He must be at least two stone larger,' decided Chris, in fact he looked to be almost obese now.

Raz was wearing a dark two-piece suit, single breasted and, amazingly, just as in the old days, he wore a flamboyant yellow polka dot bow tie. But when his smile lit up as he spotted Mike and Chris at the bar, they knew he was the same old Raz. The great booming laugh erupted and his eyes shone brightly as he warmly hugged both his old friends in turn.

'It's bloody wonderful to see you guys, you both look so well,' said Raz approvingly, his big hands slapping their shoulders affectionately. 'Unfortunately I've piled the fat on as you can both see,' he grinned, patting his stomach. 'Too much good living and not enough sex,' he laughed at them.

Chris ordered a beer for Raz and they stood in a small group, clinking their glasses together.

'Cheers chaps, it's good to see you both, you old sods,' said Chris.

'Thanks for setting this up Chris,' said Raz. 'I wouldn't have missed this for the world.'

Chris noticed that the back of Raz's hand was badly scarred and seemed to be shaking slightly. He wondered what could have happened to Raz and was about to ask him but the door opened again and two regulars filed in, immediately followed by Tony who greeted them all enthusiastically, shaking hands vigorously with each of them in turn.

'Christ, it's great to see you all,' he said, unable to contain the pleasure that he felt at seeing the old crowd again. The others noticed with astonishment that Tony had become completely bald. They all remembered the mass of thick, dark, well-groomed hair that used to attract so many girls. Nevertheless, he was still lean and straight-backed, meticulously dressed in a designer jacket, V-necked sweatshirt and designer cargo pants. Right up-to-date, even at his age, decided Chris, wondering if he should have made more of an effort. But, hell no, he was comfortable in his old familiar stuff, he wasn't there to please anybody in the fashion stakes.

Chris ordered a beer for Tony, while there was a moments awkward silence before suddenly each of them started talking at once, loudly and animatedly.

'So you've stayed in Cambridge all this time,' said Raz to Chris.

'Yeah, it's fucking amazing really,' replied Chris, 'but I guess it's because I love the place so much, it just became difficult to leave. I got married for a short period, if she'd stayed here after the divorce, I would definitely have left then, but luckily she pissed off to London.'

'What happened?' asked Raz, sensing some acrimony in Chris's tone.

'She was a bloody nutter and what happened reflected that, but unfortunately I only found out after I'd married her. We'd had a few problems, but the end came when I was reversing my car into the garage one night, and I flattened her beloved cat. She went absolute ape-shit when I told her that her precious cat needed peeling off the concrete,' sniggered Chris.

'She could have hung it on the wall, she would have seen it every day and there would have been no need to feed it,' said Mike, making light of the image Chris's story had put in his mind.

'Well, she nearly hung me on the fucking wall after that,' replied Chris, explaining vividly to them both how the irate woman had smashed his hi-fi to pieces and broken all the china in the house.

Raz gasped with amazement at the story and then proceeded to tell them all what had happened in his life. 'I got married in Canada. I went there after my Dad died to make a new start. It's certainly a land of opportunity if you're prepared to work hard. Shortly after arriving there, I met this wonderful girl. She was half-French and very, very beautiful. We had two children, but after we'd been married for four years, we had a terrible car crash, skidding off the road in the snow and hitting a tree. She was killed instantly. Luckily the kids weren't with us at the time.'

The others murmured sympathetic noises as they listened

intently to their old friend. 'I was in hospital for months with a broken leg and pelvis and various internal injuries,' added Raz.

'Christ, is that how you got those scars on your hand?' asked Chris, motioning his head towards Raz's hand.

'Yes, it is, but I came out OK eventually, plus I still had the kids,' continued Raz. 'I carried on with my computer business, but a year later I met a girl from Hong Kong who was living and working with her parents in Vancouver. We got married shortly afterwards and I've got another two kids with her as well. I feel guilty now that I didn't invite you all over for those weddings, but somehow we all seemed to lose touch and I wasn't sure where everyone was. Now I'm about to retire, it seemed an ideal time to come over, do a bit of business and see my family and I was really, really going to try and get in touch with you all. When you rang Chris, it couldn't have been at a better moment.'

'So you've been through the wars a bit,' said Mike sympathetically. 'Well, I've been married twice too. Chris and Tony met my first wife, you both came to the wedding. Then Chris came to visit on his own and shortly after you came to Edinburgh to stay the weekend with us Chris, I discovered, after twelve years of marriage, that the bitch had been having an affair with her office manager. She told me that she had joined a health club, but every time she was supposed to go there, it turned out that she was fucking him in a small flat just down the road, that was her fucking fitness programme! One day one of the kids got ill at school and when I rang the health club to tell her, no-one there knew who the hell she was. Eventually when she arrived home, we had a blazing row and she broke down and told me about the affair. It had been going on for five years. The next day I went over to her office and saw the guy's car in the car park. It was a top-of-the-range Merc. I poured superglue into all the locks, let down the tyres and then superglued the valves. Apparently when he went down to his car, he went up the bloody wall. I wish I could have seen it myself. He couldn't do anything about it though because he was married and, although he must have suspected it was me, he couldn't reveal that he'd been having an affair with my wife or he'd have lost his job. Shortly after that I divorced her and met someone else. I'm now married to Mary. She's only twenty-seven and she's also been married

322

before. She's got a son of seven and my two girls are seventeen and eighteen. It's a far cry from the old days when all we thought about was screwing anything that moved as long as it was female and avoiding having kids at all costs, isn't it?'

'Yes, that's very true,' recalled Chris. 'I remember this girl, Penny James her name was, calling round to the flat late one Christmas Eve to tell me she was pregnant. You'd all gone away for Christmas. She sat on the stairs bawling her eyes out. Trouble was, I had a girl lying in my bed at the time. She was a singer in a band and when she heard this girl, Penny, crying, she got up and came out and cuddled Penny to calm her down. Penny was really pissed off because this other girl was there. Not only that, it turned out she wasn't pregnant at all, she'd just been trying to get at me because I'd also shagged her sister. It ruined my whole Christmas I can tell you.'

The others laughed, remembering how cruelly they used to treat girls in those days when female company had been so readily available to the group of randy young men. It had just been too easy for them. They ordered more beers, enjoying choosing from the selection of real ales available in the transformed pub.

'So what about you Tony?' asked Mike. 'You were the first to leave the fold, what's happened to you along life's pleasant journey?'

'Well, it's all pretty mundane really. I'm still married to Christine. We live in Birmingham and we've got three children, two are at university now and basically I'm very very, happy. I've got no regrets at all,' smiled Tony, almost self-consciously as though he felt that he shouldn't feel that way because of the unfortunate stories just related by the others.

'Bloody hell, to be perfectly honest Tony, you were the biggest ram going. I personally never thought that you would stay married, especially for all this time,' revealed Mike candidly. 'I'm really amazed that you're still married, but I'm obviously very happy for you and Christine.'

'I felt the same at the time,' agreed Raz. 'If I can remember correctly, it just came out of the blue, didn't it Tony? One minute you were fucking yourself stupid, the next minute you were madly in love. Mind you, it took us all a little while to realise that. But I remember one thing Tony, and I've always wondered about it, so I've got to ask you now, what happened on the wedding night when Christine set eyes on your black wedding tackle?'

'Oh Christ, you bastards,' exclaimed Tony, grinning at Raz, feeling a little embarrassed that Raz had brought the matter up. 'Don't remind me of that night.' He still remembered it vividly, even after all these years. 'During the reception, I just couldn't bring myself to tell Christine, so we drove to the hotel and again I didn't know how to explain it to her. We were late arriving, so we quickly got changed and went down for dinner. We had a lovely meal and loads of champagne during which I tried to broach the subject but kept chickening out. Of course, although we were very tired after such a long day, she was still feeling quite amorous, so when we got up to the room I had to tell her then, I had no option. She didn't believe me at first, so she pulled my trousers off and then my pants and she realised then that I wasn't pulling her leg. At first she giggled a bit, but then she became nasty, yelling at me that you were all a shitty load of friends. Then she really hit the fucking roof, flinging things around the room and screaming at me like a mad woman. "Jesus, how can I make love to you when all your so called friends have been fiddling about painting your fucking bollocks on my wedding night?" she shouted. I told her that it was only shoe dye and that it wasn't my fault. "Shoe dye, shoe dye," she screamed even louder,' said Tony mimicking his wife, '"something like that could react on my fanny and God knows what I could catch. This is my wedding night and you're asking to shag me with your shoe-dyed bollocks and black cock."'

The others were convulsed in uncontrollable laughter. Raz had tears streaming down his face, trying to picture for himself the scene as it must have been all those years ago.

Tony continued, 'eventually I managed to calm her down. I think she ran out of steam in the end, but I couldn't get her to make love even though I'd scrubbed my cock and balls almost raw trying to get rid of the bloody dye. It was three days into the honeymoon before she'd let me make love to her and when we did do it, I was so sore because of all the cock scrubbing, I was in absolute agony; and I had to pretend to enjoy it. As you can all imagine, I was not very happy with you lot and if Christine had not been such a strong-minded girl, that little incident could have ended our marriage. Anyway, it's all a long time ago, it's history now. Christine and I have even laughed about it since, but we made a pact that neither of us would ever mention it to anyone at all because it annoyed her so much at the time.'

'Oh God, what a story,' sighed Raz, drying his eyes.

Chris suggested that they move over to a large table in the corner of the room while he ordered some more drinks.

'I'll have to take it easy,' said Raz. 'I'm not used to these real ales any more. Christ, when I remember how pissed we all were most of the time in the old days, and now I'm worried about the strength of a few beers.'

'Yeah,' said Chris, placing the tray of drinks on the table. 'We could all drink forever then. But times have changed so much. Do you remember, we could even park wherever we liked in Cambridge, right outside any pub in town? No bloody parking meters, no breath tests or drinking laws to speak of. It was brilliant. Now in the city they've stuck fucking traffic lights everywhere, every fifty yards or so, it's a bloody nightmare. They've really fucked the place up Raz, you wouldn't believe it. You even have to apply for a pass to enter the colleges these days just to walk around. Do you remember the days we used to spend on the backs at Kings, drinking and pulling birds? Well you can't even sit there any more, it's really terrible, all the old freedom we enjoyed so much has just disappeared. George Orwell just about got it right, we've become a restricted, contained society watched by cameras that follow you everywhere you go these days.'

'Yes, you're absolutely right,' agreed Mike, 'things have certainly changed, just look at our British yob culture that grew up during Thatcher's era, which the Tories did nothing to suppress. Now, every bloody town, village and city is full of these Neanderthals, the animal underclass. They've got no manners, no social graces, no class, no social understanding whatsoever. They're vulgar, terrifying and violent. It's a sort of football and pop culture gone mad. I know it's easy to say, but there was on the whole a certain innocence about our life in the 'sixties, everything was so easy-going. Although we all drank too much and fucked everything in sight and we were certainly no angels, life was more laid-back and natural, it wasn't so in-your-face and predictable, like things are today.'

'It's true. I've got two teenage girls,' said Tony, 'and when they were growing up Christine and I were worried sick. There's so many of these crap magazines for young girls, explaining in full detail how to fuck and do blow jobs and turn men on. These magazines are often read by eleven or twelve year old girls for Christ's sake! And the problem is, that it comes over something like a lesson at school, you have to do this and then you do that, it's all so chemical and synthetic. The pure enjoyment of life seems to have gone out of the window, they've all got to have the latest fashions and designer gear, even young kids want stuff like that these days. Everyone's herded into buying the right thing, just like bloody lemmings. With all the problems around today, I don't think the government does nearly enough to deter young people from having sex at so young an age. Christine and I tried to explain everything to our girls and, luckily, they were very understanding. I think if they do decide to do something, they'll have thought about it properly, but we can only hope!'

'I certainly hope mine will have done the same,' added Mike.

'Hold on though,' said Raz, feeling somewhat bemused. 'Aren't we being a little hypocritical here, after all we were after anything in a skirt in our day, apart from the odd stray Scotsman perhaps?' he giggled. 'Can we really sit here pontificating and say that we had nothing to do with it?'

'Maybe it's our generation who are to blame for what goes on these days,' suggested Chris, taking a long drag on his cigarette. 'I mean we were probably the start of the promiscuous society. What pisses me off is that in those days we could go to any pub in town and there would be loads of girls hanging around waiting to meet guys and get picked-up. These days they all go out in big groups, get pissed and go on to clubs and get picked-up there, when they're complete arse-holed through drink or drugs. The trouble is, that over twenty-five and you're considered to be ancient these days.'

'Aaah,' cried Raz, his face erupting into the beaming smile they remembered so well, 'that my dear Chris is something you'd notice more than the rest of us, because you're still a single man and maybe you're still looking around for something to pick up.

But life is not like that any more in England, older women rarely go out to pubs and clubs to get picked-up, so you've only got the teeny-boppers left and you're just too old for them now Chris,' laughed Raz, as the others joined in with his laughter.

Mike felt a little twinge of sadness as he glanced over at Chris, was he really still running around looking for girls at his age?

'You've also got the problem of AIDS these days,' added Raz to the others, 'we never had to contend with that. Now they've got all these flavoured condoms, and spiky numbers, and glow in the dark things. I don't think any of us ever used a rubber johnny, did we?'

'Oh yes we did,' countered Chris, 'just after Tony got the pox that time, we were all a little worried about catching it but that didn't last long. Besides all the girls were on the pill, weren't they? We just took a chance that we'd never get VD.' Chris remembered how they had taken the piss out of Tony when he had contacted gonorrhoea. It had been pretty unfair really, but it had all been in good fun, like everything had been then.

'If AIDS had been around, our life-style would have been completely different. The other major problem around now is drugs. If I remember correctly, apart from some weed and a few pills, we were never into drugs were we?' asked Tony. 'I can't remember anyone I knew who took a hard drug, or even being offered them anywhere, can you guys?'

'No, I never did take hard drugs,' said Chris. 'I remember James Page, a good friend of mine, getting hooked on Cannabis so badly that he'd just sit around all day with his hippie friends playing Dylan and smoking dope. It took over his life and completely fucked him up. After I'd seen that, I decided that was enough for me and drugs never interested me much after that. Very occasionally I'd smoke some shit, but it was no big deal.'

'But now even hard drugs are being offered to young kids in primary school playgrounds,' Mike stated angrily, thinking about the lectures that he often gave his children about the harm drugs could do to them.

'If I was in control, I'd hang the fucking bastards who are supplying the stuff,' said Chris. 'There's more problems caused through drugs than anything else these days.'

'I agree,' said Raz. 'There's a big problem where I live in Vancouver with drugs too.'

'The trouble is, much of the drugs business is controlled by the "Mr. Bigs" of the world and they could be politicians or business men, but they conceal themselves behind masses of people underneath them so no-one knows who the king-pin is,' said Chris.

'We sound just like our fathers did, don't we?' Mike sniggered, remembering how his father, who was dead now, was always telling him about how life had been so good in the old days. 'Putting the world to rights, deriding the young and arguing about what's wrong in the country today. It's just looking back like our father's did and we belittled them at the time for being so dogmatic about everything'

'Well, none of us are exactly spring chickens any more, are we?' stated Mike, glancing around questioningly at the others. 'Maybe we just remember things as being better than they actually were. Let's face it, things have moved on a great deal since those days.'

'No, no,' said Chris adamantly. 'Let's face it, our years together at Mawson Road were brilliant, surely we all agree about that? How can you say they weren't Mike?' He felt flabbergasted that Mike could actually suggest that the period when they had all lived together had not been so good after all. He lit another cigarette and dragged hard. He still smoked forty cigarettes a day, although his American pals were long gone. These days he had to buy his cigarettes legitimately. He'd already noticed that none of the others appeared to smoke now, but he often felt an outcast when smoking these days. Mostly it was just young girls who seemed to smoke, probably because it was a trendy thing to be seen doing. Most of his friends had been warned off for health reasons.

'I agree we had a great time, but the world is very different now, Chris. Look at all the amazing advances over the past thirty years, things like computers, mobile 'phones, travel, videos, medical and scientific advances and all that stuff, surely that's made life much better? In my office we save so much time using all the new technology, it's quite unbelievable, it really is,' answered Mike.

'Yes, but are we happier? Does it give us any more free time?' asked Tony. 'I work harder than ever these days for some reason and I see far less of my family than I should.'

'Technology doesn't necessarily mean more free time,' replied Mike. 'But it give us greater efficiency and makes lots of things much easier. It's also made the world much smaller.'

'In my business, the internet revolution is going to be really big. I'm only sorry that I'm going to retire when it's probably only just starting,' said Raz, who had known for some time of the revolutionary advances that were on their way, ready to change the world forever.

'Yes, I know what you're both saying,' agreed Tony, 'but it seems to me that everyone's rushing around like lunatics, working incredible long hours, searching for things on the internet and working away at their computers. Nobody's got any time for anything else.'

'Bollocks, Tony!' cried Mike. 'Restaurants and pubs are chock-a-block and many of the cinemas are full much of the time, most major football, cricket and rugger games are fully booked - people have far more leisure time these days.'

'Yes, but then there's a lot of old fogies like us who are just about to retire,' laughed Raz. 'The world is full of old people milling around looking for something to do with their leisure time, getting in the way of people who are working.'

'And don't they bloody well get in the way all the time, clogging up the roads with their Metro's at thirty miles an hour,' agreed Chris sarcastically, taking a mouthful of his beer.

'Well, we're all getting there,' said Raz. 'It won't be long before you collect your bus-pass Chris. You seem to forget we're not young anymore. Just look at us all.' He opened his arms wide to embrace them all.

Chris sat there slightly stunned. He hated to think of himself as old, even though he was almost sixty, but he realised with a jolt that Raz was right, all four of them sitting around the table were almost of pensionable age. They would certainly be regarded by most young people as old, even though they all seemed to be fairly active in their own lives. It really was incredible he thought to himself, it seemed just like yesterday when they had been irresponsible and free, screwing around and drinking heavily and just having fun together. He recalled again the time when his father had taken him aside and advised him to sow his wild oats whilst he was young, and how quickly his life would pass; and now here he was in the year 2000, sitting with his buddies, a group of old men talking about the past with only their twilight years left. The sudden realisation of this made him break out into a sweat as he realised the full implications of Raz's statement. He caught the tail-end of Mike speaking.

'...not only that, but my own daughter said to me, you must be careful at your age Dad!' The others chortled with laughter at the story Chris had missed and chorused agreement. Chris wondered whether it had been such a good idea to bring them all together again, seeing how they had all changed so much. He did not feel completely at ease, he had begun to feel somewhat isolated from the lives of the other three as they chatted about their families together. They all had wives and children, dependants who needed them. He was alone without any children and with no wife to bother with. He enjoyed his life and most of his current friends were either single or couples without children, but sitting here listening to his old friends, he felt a feeling almost akin to jealousy that the others had so much to share about their lives which he felt excluded from. He abandoned these confused thoughts to listen to Mike talking, 'I think that kids have a great world to live in these days. There's loads of opportunity, good education, plenty of jobs and many exciting changes happening. The Western world in particular has never had it so good. There's a buoyant economy in much of the world these days. Look at our country, everyone has a car, a TV, lots of material goods and we can all earn good money. Admittedly there are still poor people and poor areas, even homeless people, but I think that things are turning around for the better. I personally think young people have a brilliant future ahead of them, especially with this new technology that they've been brought up with. After all, it's all second nature to them now.'

'But the poor bastards like me feel that we've been left behind,' said Chris. 'I hardly ever use a computer at work, the secretaries in the office do that. I don't know much about them at all.'

'Me too,' said Tony. 'The only person in my four salons that works the computers is our company secretary.'

'Well, you can both get some training. The government's sponsoring courses all the time, if you don't learn now you'll both get left behind. The technological revolution is going to get bigger and bigger, in ten years time you won't be able to survive without some knowledge of how to work all the gadgets. I've just bought a 'phone that will allow me to book tickets and shop and do a host of other things on the internet, but soon everyone will need one,' explained Mike, hoping that Chris and Tony would understand how important the new technology was going to be in their futures.

'Anyway, who's for another beer chaps?' asked Mike rising slowly to his feet hoping to change the conversation to something lighter.

'I won't have another beer, thanks, I'll just have an orange juice,' said Tony.

'An orange juice!' exclaimed Chris indignantly. 'Tony, don't say you've caught another dose of the clap after all these years?'

The others exploded with laughter at Chris's remark as each of them recalled the merciless piss-taking that Tony had suffered when confined to drinking orange juice after contracting gonorrhoea, whilst they had all continued shagging and drinking excessively during his short period of abstinence, making him feel even more miserable at the time.

'I just can't drink very much these days,' confided Tony. 'In fact I hardly drink anything between one Christmas Day and the next.'

'Good God, Tony,' said Chris. 'How can you survive and enjoy yourself without a drink or two occasionally?' He felt astonishment at Tony's remark, coupled with a slight feeling of contempt at the news that his old drinking partner now hardly drank at all. What had happened to the man?

Mike brought the beers and an orange juice over to the table. 'I personally couldn't exist without wine with my food,' he said, easing himself into his chair. 'It's one of the great pleasures of my life now, good wine. Do you all remember that bloody Bulls Blood we all used to guzzle in those days?'

'Oh yes, that shit, but we didn't know any better then did we?' said Chris. 'There was hardly any good wine around but, of course, now we're inundated with it. In those days we just drank the cheapest crap we could pour down our throats, trying to get legless as quickly as possible.'

'You mean trying to get the birds as legless as possible,' Mike reminded Chris.

'Let's face it, in those days our whole life was spent legless, it was really just a bloody great circus!' said Chris.

'And didn't we all enjoy the show,' added Tony.

'We thoroughly enjoyed it, but those bloody awful headaches in the mornings are what I remember most,' groaned Raz. 'I must say that I drink more whisky these days than anything, though in Canada we do get some great wines from California. I feel really bloated after all this beer today, I'm just not used to it any more. My blood pressure's quite high since my car accident, so I really have to watch what I drink these days, it's just a sign of getting old.'

The landlord appeared at the table with two large plates of assorted sandwiches. 'That'll help to soak up the alcohol Raz,' smiled Mike who had ordered and paid for the sandwiches when he went to the bar.

'That's good of you Mike,' said Tony, reaching for a cheese and tomato sarnie.

'Cheers Mike,' added Chris and Raz in unison, taking a sandwich each.

They munched together silently for a few seconds, deep in their own thoughts. Chris still felt a little uncomfortable, realising that the era when they had been so close had been such a long time ago and now it emerged that Tony hardly drank at all and Raz was under Doctor's Orders; but hadn't he expected something like this? How could they all possibly be the same people after over thirty years? It was just not feasible. He felt somewhat disillusioned by the convention of the lives of his old companions, all the old swash-buckling attitudes that he remembered about them all appeared to have been erased by time and responsibility. He began to wish that the meeting would end so that he could step outside and breathe some fresh air deep into his lungs. He felt a wave of sadness engulf him, like a cloak covering his head and shoulders. He lit another cigarette to calm himself down and to give his hands something to do to soothe

the feelings of despondency churning around his body, agitating him and putting him on edge.

'By the way Chris,' said Mike, leaning over to confide in him, 'I won't need that bed tonight, if that's OK? My wife's brother lives in Nottingham and I dropped her off there on the way down, so I'll go back and stay with them tonight. I hope you don't mind?'

'That's OK Mike, I understand,' said Chris, feeling a mixture of relief tempered by hurt. Even Mike had changed so much. He was, of course, well and truly married like the others and his family obviously came first now. Chris smiled at his old friend and noticed the small specks of dandruff resting around the collar of his jacket, and the tatty blonde hairs sprouting from his ears. Mike had always been untidy, Chris remembered his room: 'the tip' he'd always called it. He wondered if Mike was still as untidy as he'd been in the old days, now that he'd been married twice. His thoughts were interrupted by Raz's deep voice, the big man was proposing a toast. 'Well chaps, may I suggest that we thank Chris for making this reunion possible and for getting us all together again, it's been bloody marvellous to see everyone again.'

As they raised their glasses and he surveyed their grateful smiling faces, just for a second it seemed like yesterday, when they had been young and free and with their whole lives ahead of them. Chris suddenly felt glad that he had bought them all together again for, despite the dejection that had gradually built up inside him during their meeting, it had satisfied his curiosity and despite his reservations, it had been good to see them all again even though he now viewed them all in a different light.

Of course their lives had changed, they were different people now with new priorities in a new age. Looking back at their time together and recalling those memories so vividly, he had wanted to bring them all together again, but now he felt somewhat disillusioned for he realised that the intervening years had created a distance between them when he had expected that there would be more intimacy. He also realised that he had clung to his memories so vividly that he had secretly hoped that they would still be the same people, whereas, of course, life had moved forwards and their experiences of life had changed them all, for good or bad. Rather pathetically, he had wanted them to see him as the same young man, but Raz had put him straight. He was not a young man any more, he was almost ancient, the same as they all were. He smiled gratefully to acknowledge their thanks as his three old friends drank his health, knowing that when they had all gone away and he went to his bed that night, he would cry for the first time in thirty years.